MAUPRAT

MAUPRAT

GEORGE SAND

Translated by: **STANLEY YOUNG**

Serenity
Publishers, LLC

ROCKVILLE, MARYLAND

2010

ISBN: 978-1-60450-820-8

Published by Serenity Publishers
An Arc Manor Company
P. O. Box 10339
Rockville, MD 20849-0339
www.SerenityPublishers.com

Printed in the United States of America/United Kingdom

CONTENTS

GEORGE SAND   7

LIFE OF GEORGE SAND   13

PREFACE   17

MAUPRAT   21

GEORGE SAND

Napoleon in exile declared that were he again on the throne he should make a point of spending two hours a day in conversation with women, from whom there was much to be learnt. He had, no doubt, several types of women in mind, but it is more than probable that the banishment of Madame de Stael rose before him as one of the mistakes in his career. It was not that he showed lack of judgment merely by the persecution of a rare talent, but by failing to see that the rare talent was pointing out truths very valuable to his own safety. This is what happened in France when George Sand—the greatest woman writer the world has known, or is ever likely to know—was attacked by the orthodox critics of her time. They feared her warnings; they detested her sincerity—a sincerity displayed as much in her life as in her works (the hypocrite's Paradise was precisely her idea of Hell); they resented bitterly an independence of spirit which in a man would have been in the highest degree distinguished, which remained, under every test, untamable. With a kind of *bonhomie* which one can only compare with Fielding's, with a passion as great as Montaigne's for acknowledging the truths of experience, with an absence of self-consciousness truly amazing in the artistic temperament of either sex, she wrote exactly as she thought, saw and felt. Humour was not her strong point. She had an exultant joy in living, but laughter, whether genial or sardonic, is not in her work. Irony she seldom, if ever, employed; satire she never attempted. It was on the maternal, the sympathetic side that her femininity, and therefore her creative genius, was most strongly developed. She was masculine only in the deliberate libertinism of certain episodes in her own life. This was a characteristic—one on no account to be overlooked or denied or disguised, but it was not her character. The character was womanly, tender, exquisitely patient and good-natured. She would take cross humanity in her arms, and carry it out into the sunshine of the fields; she would show it flowers and birds, sing songs to it, tell it stories, recall its original beauty. Even in her moods of depression and revolt, one recognises the fatigue of the strong. It is never for a moment the lassitude of the feeble, the weary spite of a sick and ill-used soul. As she was free from personal vanity, she was also free from hysteria. On marriage—the one subject which drove her to a certain though always disciplined violence—she clearly felt more for others than they felt for themselves; and in observing certain households and life partnerships, she may have been afflicted with a dismay which the unreflecting sufferers did not share. No writer who was carried away by egoistic anger or disappointment could have told these stories of unhappiness, infidelity, and luckless love with such dispassionate lucidity.

With the artist's dislike of all that is positive and arbitrary, she was, nevertheless, subject rather to her intellect than her emotions. An insult to her intelligence was the one thing she found it hard to pardon, and she allowed no external interference to disturb her relations with her own reasoning faculty. She followed caprices, no doubt, but she was never under any apprehension with regard to their true nature, displaying in this respect a detachment which is usually considered exclusively virile. *Elle et Lui,* which, perhaps because it is short and associated with actual facts, is the most frequently discussed in general conversation on her work, remains probably the sanest account of a sentimental experiment which was ever written. How far it may have seemed accurate to De Musset is not to the point. Her version of her grievance is at least convincing. Without fear and without hope, she makes her statement, and it stands, therefore, unique of its kind among indictments. It has been said that her fault was an excess of emotionalism; that is to say, she attached too much importance to mere feeling and described it, in French of marvellous ease and beauty, with a good deal of something else which one can almost condemn as the high-flown. Not that the high-flown is of necessity unnatural, but it is misleading; it places the passing mood, the lyrical note, dependent on so many accidents, above the essential temperament and the dominant chord which depend on life only. Where she falls short of the very greatest masters is in this all but deliberate confusion of things which must change or can be changed with things which are unchangeable, incurable, and permanent. Shakespeare, it is true, makes all his villains talk poetry, but it is the poetry which a villain, were he a poet, would inevitably write. George Sand glorifies every mind with her own peculiar fire and tears. The fire is, fortunately, so much stronger than the tears that her passion never degenerates into the maudlin. All the

8

same, she makes too universal a use of her own strongest gifts, and this is why she cannot be said to excel as a portrait painter. One merit, however, is certain: if her earliest writings were dangerous, it was because of her wonderful power of idealization, not because she filled her pages with the revolting and epicene sensuality of the new Italian, French, and English schools. Intellectual viciousness was not her failing, and she never made the modern mistake of confusing indecency with vigour. She loved nature, air, and light too well and too truly to go very far wrong in her imaginations. It may indeed be impossible for many of us to accept all her social and political views; they have no bearing, fortunately, on the quality of her literary art; they have to be considered under a different aspect. In politics, her judgment, as displayed in the letters to Mazzini, was profound. Her correspondence with Flaubert shows us a capacity for stanch, unblemished friendship unequalled, probably, in the biographies, whether published or unpublished, of the remarkable.

With regard to her impiety—for such it should be called—it did not arise from arrogance, nor was it based in any way upon the higher learning of her period. Simply she did not possess the religious instinct. She understood it sympathetically—in *Spiridion*, for instance, she describes an ascetic nature as it has never been done in any other work of fiction. Newman himself has not written passages of deeper or purer mysticism, of more sincere spirituality. Balzac, in *Seraphita*, attempted something of the kind, but the result was never more than a *tour de force*. He could invent, he could describe, but George Sand felt; and as she felt, she composed, living with and loving with an understanding love all her creations. But it has to be remembered always that she repudiated all religious restraint, that she believed in the human heart, that she acknowledged no higher law than its own impulses, that she saw love where others see only a cruel struggle for existence, that she found beauty where ordinary visions can detect little besides a selfishness worse than brutal and a squalor more pitiful than death. Everywhere she insists upon the purifying influence of affection, no matter how degraded in its circumstances or how illegal in its manifestation. No writer—not excepting the Brontes—has shown a deeper sympathy with uncommon temperaments, misunderstood aims, consciences with flickering lights, the discontented, the abnormal, or the unhappy. The great modern specialist for nervous diseases has not improved on her analysis of the neuropathic and hysterical. There is scarcely a novel of hers in which some character does not appear who is, in the usual phrase, out of the common run. Yet, with this perfect understanding of the exceptional case, she never permits any science of cause and effect to obscure the rules and principles which in the main control life for the majority. It was, no doubt, this balance which made her a popular writer, even while she never ceased to keep in touch with the most acute minds of France.

She possessed, in addition to creative genius of an order especially individual and charming, a capacity for the invention of ideas. There are in many of her chapters more ideas, more suggestions than one would find in a whole volume of Flaubert. It is not possible that these surprising, admirable, and usually sound thoughts were the result of long hours of reflection. They belonged to her nature and a quality of judgment which, even in her most extravagant romances, is never for a moment swayed from that sane impartiality described by the unobservant as common sense.

Her fairness to women was not the least astounding of her gifts. She is kind to the beautiful, the yielding, above all to the very young, and in none of her stories has she introduced any violently disagreeable female characters. Her villains are mostly men, and even these she invests with a picturesque fatality which drives them to errors, crimes, and scoundrelism with a certain plaintive, if relentless, grace. The inconstant lover is invariably pursued by the furies of remorse; the brutal has always some mitigating influence in his career; the libertine retains through many vicissitudes a seraphic love for some faithful Solveig.

Humanity meant far more to her than art: she began her literary career by describing facts as she knew them: critics drove her to examine their causes, and so she gradually changed from the chronicler with strong sympathies to the interpreter with a reasoned philosophy. She discovered that a great deal of the suffering in this world is due not so much to original sin, but to a kind of original stupidity, an unimaginative, stubborn stupidity. People were dishonest because they believed, wrongly, that dishonesty was somehow successful. They were cruel because they supposed that repulsive exhibitions of power inspired a prolonged fear. They were treacherous because they had never been taught the greater strength of candour. George Sand tried to point out the advantage of plain dealing, and the natural goodness of mankind when uncorrupted by a false education. She loved the wayward and the desolate: pretentiousness in any disguise was the one thing she suspected and could not tolerate. It may be questioned whether she ever deceived herself; but it must be said, that on the whole she flattered weakness—and excused, by enchanting eloquence, much which cannot always be justified merely on the ground that it is explicable. But to explain was something—all but everything at the time of her appearance in literature. Every novel she wrote made for charity—for a better acquaintance with our neighbour's woes and our own egoism. Such an attitude of mind is only possible to an absolutely frank, even Arcadian, nature. She did what she wished to do: she said what she had to say, not because she wanted to provoke excitement or astonish the multitude, but because she had succeeded eminently in leading her own life according to her own lights. The terror of appearing inconsistent excited her scorn. Appearances never troubled that unashamed soul. This is the magic, the peculiar fascination of her books. We find ourselves in the presence of a freshness, a primeval vigour which produces actually the effect of seeing new scenes, of facing a fresh climate. Her love of the soil, of flowers, and the sky, for whatever was young and unspoilt, seems to animate every page—even in her passages of rhetorical sentiment we never suspect the burning pastille, the gauze tea-gown, or the depressed pink light. Rhetoric it may be, but it is the rhetoric of the sea and the wheat field. It can be spoken in the open air and read by the light of day.

George Sand never confined herself to any especial manner in her literary work. Her spontaneity of feeling and the actual fecundity, as it were, of her imaginative gift, could not be restrained, concentrated, and formally arranged as it was in the case of the two first masters of modern French novel-writing. Her work in this respect may be compared to a gold mine, while theirs is rather the goldsmith's craft. It must not be supposed, however, that she was a writer without very strong views with regard to the construction of a plot and the development of character. Her literary essays and reviews show a knowledge of technique which could be accepted at any time as a text-book for the critics and the criticised. She knew exactly how artistic effects were obtained, how and why certain things were done, why realism, so-called, could never be anything but caricature, and why over-elaboration of small matters can never be otherwise than disproportionate. Nothing could be more just than her saying about Balzac that he was such a logician that he invented things more truthful than the truth itself. No one knew better than she that the truth, as it is commonly understood, does not exist; that it cannot be logical because of its mystery; and that it is the knowledge of its contradictions which shows the real expert in psychology.

Three of her stories—*La Petite Fadette, La Mare au Diable,* and *Les Maitres Mosaistes*—are as neat in their workmanship as a Dutch painting. Her brilliant powers of analysis, the intellectual atmosphere with which she surrounds the more complex characters in her longer romances, are entirely put aside, and we are given instead a series of pictures and dialogues in what has been called the purely objective style; so pure in its objectivity and detachment that it would be hard for any one to decide from internal evidence that they were in reality her own composition.

To those who seek for proportion and form there is, without doubt, much that is unsymmetrical in her designs. Interesting she always is, but to the trained eye scenes of minor importance are, strictly speaking, too long: descriptions in musical language sometimes distract the reader from the progress of the story. But this arose from her own joy in writing: much as she valued proportion, she liked expressing her mind better, not out of conceit or self-importance, but as the birds, whom she loved so well, sing.

Good nature is what we need above all in reading George Sand. It is there—infectious enough in her own pages, and with it the courage which can come only from a heart at peace with itself. This is why neither fashion nor new nor old criticism can affect the title of George Sand among the greatest influences of the last century and the present one. Much that she has said still seems untried and unexpected. Writers so opposite as Ibsen and Anatole France have expanded her themes. She is quoted unconsciously to-day by hundreds who are ignorant of their real source of inspiration. No woman ever wrote with such force before, and no woman since has even approached her supreme accomplishments.

PEARL MARY-TERESA CRAIGIE.

LIFE OF GEORGE SAND

George Sand, in whose life nothing was commonplace, was born in Paris, "in the midst of roses, to the sound of music," at a dance which her mother had somewhat rashly attended, on the 5th of July, 1804. Her maiden name was Armentine Lucile Aurore Dupin, and her ancestry was of a romantic character. She was, in fact, of royal blood, being the great-grand-daughter of the Marshal Maurice du Saxe and a Mlle. Verriere; her grandfather was M. Dupin de Francueil, the charming friend of Rousseau and Mme. d'Epinay; her father, Maurice Dupin, was a gay and brilliant soldier, who married the pretty daughter of a bird-fancier, and died early. She was a child of the people on her mother's side, an aristocrat on her father's. In 1807 she was taken by her father, who was on Murat's staff, into Spain, from which she returned to the house of her grandmother, at Nohant in Berry. This old lady adopted Aurore at the death of her father, in 1808. Of her childhood George Sand has given a most picturesque account in her "Histoire de ma Vie." In 1817 the girl was sent to the Convent of the English Augustinians in Paris, where she passed through a state of religious mysticism. She returned to Nohant in 1820, and soon threw off her pietism in the outdoor exercises of a wholesome country life. Within a few months, Mme. Dupin de Francueil died at a great age, and Aurore was tempted to return to Paris. Her relatives, however, were anxious that she should not do this, and they introduced to her the natural son of a retired colonel, the Baron Dudevant, whom, in September, 1822, she married. She brought him to live with her at Nohant, and she bore him two sons, Maurice and Solange, and a daughter. She quickly perceived, as her own intellectual nature developed, that her boorish husband was unsuited to her, but their early years of married life were not absolutely intolerable. In 1831, however, she could endure

13

him no longer, and an amicable separation was agreed upon. She left M. Dudevant at Nohant, resigning her fortune, and proceeded to Paris, where she was hard pressed to find a living. She endeavoured, without success, to paint the lids of cigar-boxes, and in final desperation, under the influence of Jules Sandeau—who became her lover, and who invented the pseudonym of George Sand for her—she turned her attention to literature. Her earliest work was to help Sandeau in the composition of his novel, "Rose et Blanche" Her first independent novel, "Indiana," appeared at the close of 1831, and her second, "Valentine," two months later. These books produced a great and immediate sensation, and she felt that she had found her vocation. In 1833 she produced "Lebia"; in 1834 the "Lettres d'un Voyageur" and "Jacques"; in 1835 "Andre" and "Leone Leoni." After this her works become too numerous and were produced with too monotonous a regularity to be chronicled here. But it should be said that "Mauprat" was written in 1836 at Nohant, while she was pleading for a legal separation from her husband, which was given her by the tribunal of Bourges, with full authority over the education of her children. These early novels all reflect in measure the personal sorrows of the author, although George Sand never ceased to protest against too strict a biographical interpretation of their incidents. "Spiridion" (1839), composed under the influence of Lamennais, deals with questions of free thought in religion. But the novels of the first period of her literary activity, which came to a close in 1840, are mainly occupied with a lyrical individualism, and are inspired by the wrongs and disillusions of the author's personal adventures.

The years 1833 and 1834 were marked by her too-celebrated relations with Alfred de Musset, with whom she lived in Paris and at Venice, and with whom she quarrelled at last in circumstances deplorably infelicitous. Neither of these great creatures had the reticence to exclude the world from a narrative of their misfortunes and adventures; of the two it was fairly certainly the woman who came the less injured out of the furnace. In "Elle et Lui" (1859) she gave long afterward her version of the unhappy and undignified story. Her stay in Venice appears to have impressed her genius more deeply than any other section of her numerous foreign sojournings.

The writings of George Sand's second period, which extended from 1840 to 1848, are of a more general character, and are tinged with a generous but not very enlightened ardour for social emancipation. Of these novels, the earliest is "Le Compagnon du Tour de France" (1840), which is scarcely a masterpiece. In the pursuit of foreign modes of thought, and impelled by experiences of travel, George Sand rose to far greater heights in "Jeanne" (1842), in "Consuelo" (1842-'43), and in "La Comtesse de Rudolstade" (1844). All these books were composed in her retirement at No-hant, where she definitely settled in 1839, after having travelled for several months in Switzerland with Liszt and Mme. d'Agoult, and having lived in the island of Majorca for some time with the dying Chopin, an episode which is enshrined in her "Lucrezia Floriani" (1847).

The Revolution of 1848 appeared to George Sand a realization of her Utopian dreams, and plunged her thoughts into a painful disorder. She soon, however, became dissatisfied with the result of her republican theo-ries, and she turned to two new sources of success, the country story and the stage. Her delicious romance of "Francois le Champi" (1850) attracted a new and enthusiastic audience to her, and her entire emancipation from "problems" was marked in the pages of "La Petite Fadette" and of "La Mare au Diable." To the same period belong "Les Visions de la Nuit des les Campagnes," "Les Maitres Sonneurs," and "Cosina." From 1850 to 1864 she gave a great deal of attention to the theatre, and of her numerous pieces several enjoyed a wide and considerable success, although it cannot be said that any of her plays have possessed the vitality of her best nov-els. The most solid of the former was her dramatization of her story, "Le Marquis de Villemer" (1864), which was one of the latest, and next to it "Le Mariage de Victorine" (1851), which was one of the earliest. Her suc-cesses on the stage, such as they are, appear mainly due to collaboration with others.

In her latest period, from 1860 to 1876, George Sand returned to her first lyrical manner, although with more reticence and a wider experi-ence of life. Of the very abundant fruitage of these last years, not many rank with the masterpieces of her earlier periods, although such novels as "Tamaris" (1862), "La Confession d'une Jeune Fille" (1865), and "Cadio," seemed to her admirers to show no decline of force or fire. Still finer, per-haps, were "Le Marquis de Villemer" (1861) and "Jean de la Roche" (1860). Her latest production, which appeared after her death, was the "Contes d'une Grand'mere," a collection full of humanity and beauty. George Sand died at Nohant on the 8th of June, 1876. She had great qualities of soul, and in spite of the naive irregularities of her conduct in early middle life, she cannot be regarded otherwise than as an excellent woman. She was brave, courageous, heroically industrious, a loyal friend, a tender and wise mother. Her principle fault has been wittily defined by Mr. Henry James, who has remarked that in affairs of the heart George Sand never "behaved like a gentleman."

E. G.

PREFACE

When I wrote my novel *Mauprat* at Nohant—in 1846, if I remember rightly—I had just been suing for a separation. Hitherto I had written much against the abuses of marriage, and perhaps, though insufficiently explaining my views, had induced a belief that I failed to appreciate its essence; but it was at this time that marriage itself stood before me in all the moral beauty of its principle.

Misfortune is not without its uses to the thoughtful mind. The more clearly I had realized the pain and pity of having to break a sacred bond, the more profoundly I felt that where marriage is wanting, is in certain elements of happiness and justice of too lofty a nature to appeal to our actual society. Nay, more; society strives to take from the sanctity of the institution by treating it as a contract of material interests, attacking it on all sides at once, by the spirit of its manners, by its prejudices, by its hypocritical incredulity.

While writing a novel as an occupation and distraction for my mind, I conceived the idea of portraying an exclusive and undying love, before, during, and after marriage. Thus I drew the hero of my book proclaiming, at the age of eighty, his fidelity to the one woman he had ever loved.

The ideal of love is assuredly eternal fidelity. Moral and religious laws have aimed at consecrating this ideal. Material facts obscure it. Civil laws are so framed as to make it impossible or illusory. Here, however, is not the place to prove this. Nor has *Mauprat* been burdened with a proof of the theory; only, the sentiment by which I was specially penetrated at the time of writing it is embodied in the words of *Mauprat* towards the end of the book: "She was the only woman I loved in all my life; none other ever won a glance from me, or knew the pressure of my hand."

GEORGE SAND.
June 5, 1857.

TO

GUSTAVE PAPET

Though fashion may proscribe the patriarchal fashion of dedications, I would ask you, brother and friend, to accept this of a tale which is not new to you. I have drawn my materials in part from the cottages of our Noire valley. May we live and die there, repeating every evening our beloved invocation:

SANCTA SIMPLICITAS!

George Sand.

MAUPRAT

On the borders of La Marche and Berry, in the district known as Varenne, which is naught but a vast moor studded with forests of oak and chestnut, and in the most thickly wooded and wildest part of the country, may be found, crouching within a ravine, a little ruined chateau. The dilapidated turrets would not catch your eye until you were about a hundred yards from the principal portcullis. The venerable trees around and the scattered rocks above, bury it in everlasting obscurity; and you would experience the greatest difficulty, even in broad daylight, in crossing the deserted path leading to it, without stumbling against the gnarled trunks and rubbish that bar every step. The name given to this dark ravine and gloomy castle is Roche-Mauprat.

It was not so long ago that the last of the Mauprats, the heir to this property, had the roofing taken away and all the woodwork sold. Then, as if to give a kick to the memory of his ancestors, he ordered the entrance gate to be thrown down, the north tower to be gutted, and a breach to be made in the surrounding wall. This done, he departed with his workmen, shaking the dust from off his feet, and abandoning his domain to foxes, and cormorants, and vipers. Since then, whenever the wood-cutters and charcoal-burners from the huts in the neighbourhood pass along the top of the Roche-Mauprat ravine, if it is in daytime they whistle with a defiant air or hurl a hearty curse at the ruins; but when day falls and the goat-sucker begins to screech from the top of the loopholes, wood-cutter and charcoal-burner pass by silently, with quickened step, and cross themselves from time to time to ward off the evil spirits that hold sway among the ruins.

For myself, I own that I have never skirted the ravine at night without feeling a certain uneasiness; and I would not like to swear that on some stormy nights I have not given my horse a touch of the spur, in order to escape the more quickly from the disagreeable impression this neighbourhood made on me.

The reason is that in childhood I classed the name of Mauprat with those of Cartouche and Bluebeard; and in the course of horrible dreams I often used to mix up the ancient legends of the Ogre and the Bogey with the quite recent events which in our province had given such a sinister lustre to this Mauprat family.

Frequently, out shooting, when my companions and I have left our posts to go and warm ourselves at the charcoal fires which the workmen keep up all night, I have heard this name dying away on their lips at our approach. But when they had recognised us and thoroughly satisfied themselves that the ghosts of none of these robbers were hiding in our midst, they would tell us in a whisper such stories as might make one's hair stand on end, stories which I shall take good care not to pass on to you, grieved as I am that they should ever have darkened and pained my own memory.

Not that the story I am about to tell is altogether pleasant and cheerful. On the contrary, I must ask your pardon for unfolding so sombre a tale. Yet, in the impression which it has made on myself there is something so consoling and, if I may venture the phrase, so healthful to the soul, that you will excuse me, I hope, for the sake of the result. Besides this is a story which has just been told to me. And now you ask me for one. The opportunity is too good to be missed for one of my laziness or lack of invention.

It was only last week that I met Bernard Mauprat, the last of the line, the man who, having long before severed himself from his infamous connections, determined to demolish his manor as a sign of the horror aroused in him by the recollections of childhood. This Bernard is one of the most respected men in the province. He lives in a pretty house near Chateauroux, in a flat country. Finding myself in the neighbourhood, with a friend of mine who knows him, I expressed a wish to be introduced; and my friend, promising me a hearty welcome, took me to his house then and there.

I already knew in outline the remarkable history of this old man; but I had always felt a keen desire to fill in the details, and above all to receive them from himself. For me, the strange destiny of the man was a philosophical problem to be solved. I therefore noticed his features, his manners, and his home with peculiar interest.

Bernard Mauprat must be fully eighty-four, though his robust health, his upright figure, his firm step, and the absence of any infirmity might indicate some fifteen or twenty years less. His face would have appeared to me extremely handsome, had not a certain harshness of expression brought before my eyes, in spite of myself, the shades of his fathers. I very much fear that, externally at all events, he must resemble them. This he alone could have told us; for neither my friend nor myself had known any other Mauprat. Naturally, however, we were very careful not to inquire.

It struck us that his servants waited on him with a promptitude and punctuality quite marvellous in Berrichon domestics. Nevertheless, at the least semblance of delay he raised his voice, knitted his eyebrows (which still showed very black under his white hair), and muttered a few expressions of impatience which lent wings even to the slowest. At first I was somewhat shocked at this habit; it appeared to savour rather too strongly of the Mauprats. But the kindly and almost paternal manner in which he spoke to them a moment later, and their zeal, which seemed so distinct from fear, soon reconciled me to him. Towards us, moreover, he showed an exquisite politeness, and expressed himself in the choicest terms. Unfortunately, at the end of dinner, a door which had been left open and through which a cold air found its way to his venerable skull, drew from him such a frightful oath that my friend and I exchanged a look of surprise. He noticed it.

"I beg your pardon, gentlemen," he said. "I am afraid you find me an odd mixture. Ah, you see but a short distance. I am an old branch, happily torn from a vile trunk and transplanted into good soil, but still knotted and rough like the wild holly of the original stock. I have, believe me, had no little trouble in reaching the state of comparative gentleness and calm in which you behold me. Alas! if I dared, I should reproach Providence with a great injustice—that of having allotted me a life as short as other men's. When one has to struggle for forty or fifty years to transform one's self from a wolf into a man, one ought to live a hundred years longer to enjoy one's victory. Yet what good would that do me?" he added in a tone of sadness. "The kind fairy who transformed me is here no more to take pleasure in her work. Bah! it is quite time to have done with it all."

Then he turned towards me, and, looking at me with big dark eyes, still strangely animated, said:

"Come, my dear young man; I know what brings you to see me; you are curious to hear my history. Draw nearer the fire, then. Mauprat though I am, I will not make you do duty for a log. In listening you are giving me the greatest pleasure you could give. Your friend will tell you, however, that I do not willingly talk of myself. I am generally afraid of having to deal with blockheads, but you I have already heard of; I know your character and your profession; you are an observer and narrator—in other words, pardon me, inquisitive and a chatterbox."

He began to laugh, and I made an effort to laugh too, though with a rising suspicion that he was making game of us. Nor could I help thinking of the nasty tricks that his grandfather took a delight in playing on the imprudent busybodies who called upon him. But he put his arm through mine in a friendly way, and making me sit down in front of a good fire, near a table covered with cups—

"Don't be annoyed," he said. "At my age I cannot get rid of hereditary sarcasm; but there is nothing spiteful in mine. To speak seriously, I am delighted to see you and to confide in you the story of my life. A man as unfortunate as I have been deserves to find a faithful biographer to clear his memory from all stain. Listen, then, and take some coffee."

I offered him a cup in silence. He refused it with a wave of the arm and a smile which seemed to say, "That is rather for your effeminate generation."

Then he began his narrative in these words:

I

You live not very far from Roche-Mauprat, and must have often passed by the ruins. Thus there is no need for me to describe them. All I can tell you is that the place has never been so attractive as it is now. On the day that I had the roof taken off, the sun for the first time brightened the damp walls within which my childhood was passed; and the lizards to which I have left them are much better housed there than I once was. They can at least behold the light of day and warm their cold limbs in the rays of the sun at noon.

There used to be an elder and a younger branch of the Mauprats. I belong to the elder. My grandfather was that old Tristan de Mauprat who ran through his fortune, dishonoured his name, and was such a blackguard that his memory is already surrounded by a halo of the marvelous. The peasants still believe that his ghost appears, either in the body of a wizard who shows malefactors the way to the dwellings of Varenne, or in that of an old white hare which reveals itself to people meditating some evil deed. When I came into the world the only living member of the younger branch was Monsieur Hubert de Mauprat, known as the chevalier, because he belonged to the Order of the Knights of Malta; a man just as good as his cousin was bad. Being the youngest son of his family, he had taken the vow of celibacy; but, when he found himself the sole survivor of several brothers and sisters, he obtained release from his vow, and took a wife the year before I was born. Rumour says that before changing his existence in this way he made strenuous efforts to find some descendant of the elder branch worthy to restore the tarnished family name, and preserve the fortune which had accumulated in the hands of the younger branch. He had endeavoured to put his cousin Tristan's affairs in order, and had frequently paid off the latter's creditors. Seeing, however, that the only effect of his kindness was to encourage the vices of the family, and that, instead of respect and gratitude, he received nothing but secret hatred and churlish jealousy, he abandoned all attempts at friendship, broke with his cousins, and in spite of his advanced age (he was over sixty), took a wife in order to have heirs of his own. He had one daughter, and there his hopes of posterity ended; for soon afterward his wife died of a violent illness which the doctors called iliac passion. He then left that part of the country and returned but rarely to his estates. These were situated about six leagues from Roche-Mauprat, on the borders of the Varenne du Fromental. He was a prudent man and a just, because he was cultured, because his father had moved with the spirit of his century, and had had him educated. None the less he had preserved a firm character and an enterprising mind, and, like his ancestors, he was proud of hearing as a sort of surname the knightly title of Headbreaker, hereditary in the original Mauprat stock. As for the elder branch, it had turned out so badly, or rather had preserved from the old feudal days such terrible habits of brigandage, that it had won for itself the distinctive title of Hamstringer.[1] Of the sons of Tristan, my father, the eldest, was the only one who married. I was his only child. Here it is necessary to mention a fact of which I was long ignorant. Hubert de Mauprat, on hearing of my birth, begged me of my parents, undertaking to make me his heir if he were allowed absolute control over my education. At a shooting-party about this time my father was killed by an accidental shot, and my grandfather refused the chevalier's offer, declaring that his children were the sole legitimate heirs of the younger branch, and that consequently he would resist with all his might any substitution in my favour. It was then that Hubert's daughter was born. But when, seven years later, his wife died leaving him this one child, the desire, so strong in the nobles of that time, to perpetuate their name, urged him to renew his request to my mother. What her answer was I do not know; she fell ill and died. The country doctors again brought in a verdict of iliac passion. My grandfather had spent the last two days she passed in this world with her.

---

1   I hazard "Headbreaker" and "Hamstringer" as poor equivalents for the "Casse-Tete" and "Coupe-Jarret" of the French.—TR.

Pour me out a glass of Spanish wine; for I feel a cold shiver running through my body. It is nothing serious—merely the effect that these early recollections have on me when I begin to narrate them. It will soon pass off.

He swallowed a large glass of wine, and we did the same; for a sensation of cold came upon us too as we gazed at his stern face and listened to his brief, abrupt sentences. He continued:

Thus at the age of seven I found myself an orphan. My grandfather searched my mother's house and seized all the money and valuables he could carry away. Then, leaving the rest, and declaring he would have nothing to do with lawyers, he did not even wait for the funeral, but took me by the collar and flung me on to the crupper of his horse, saying: "Now, my young ward, come home with me; and try to stop that crying soon, for I haven't much patience with brats." In fact, after a few seconds he gave me such hard cuts with his whip that I stopped crying, and, withdrawing myself like a tortoise into my shell, completed the journey without daring to breathe.

He was a tall old man, bony and cross-eyed. I fancy I see him now as he was then. The impression that evening made on me can never be effaced. It was a sudden realization of all the horrors which my mother had foreshadowed when speaking of her execrable father-in-law and his brigands of sons. The moon, I remember, was shining here and there through the dense foliage of the forest. My grandfather's horse was lean, hardy, and bad-tempered like himself. It kicked at every cut of the whip, and its master gave it plenty. Swift as an arrow it jumped the ravines and little torrents which everywhere intersect Varenne in all directions. At each jump I lost my balance, and clung in terror to the saddle or my grandfather's coat. As for him, he was so little concerned about me that, had I fallen, I doubt whether he would have taken the trouble to pick me up. Sometimes, noticing my terror, he would jeer at me, and, to make me still more afraid, set his horse plunging again. Twenty times, in a frenzy of despair, I was on the point of throwing myself off; but the instinctive love of life prevented me from giving way to the impulse. At last, about midnight, we suddenly stopped before a small pointed gate, and the drawbridge was soon lifted behind us. My grandfather took me, bathed in a cold sweat as I was, and threw me over to a great fellow, lame and horribly ugly, who carried me into the house. This was my Uncle John, and I was at Roche-Mauprat.

At that time my grandfather, along with his eight sons, formed the last relic in our province of that race of petty feudal tyrants by which France had been overrun and harassed for so many centuries. Civilization, already advancing rapidly towards the great convulsion of the Revolution, was gradually stamping out the systematic extortions of these robbers. The light of education, a species of good taste reflected, however dimly, from a polished court, and perhaps a presentiment of the impending terrible awakening of the people, were spreading through the castles and even through the half-rustic manors of the lordlings. Ever in our midland provinces, the most backward by reason of their situation, the sentiment of social equality was already driving out the customs of a barbarous age. More than one vile scapegrace had been forced to reform, in spite of his privileges; and in certain places where the peasants, driven to desperation, had rid themselves of their overlord, the law had not dreamt of interfering, nor had the relatives dared to demand redress.

In spite of the prevailing tone of mind, my grandfather had long maintained his position in the country without experiencing any opposition. But, having had a large family, endowed like himself with a goodly number of vices, he finally found himself pestered and besieged by creditors who, instead of being frightened by his threats, as of old, were themselves threatening to make him suffer. He was obliged to devise some means of avoiding the bailiffs on the one hand, and, on the other, the fights which were continually taking place. In these fights the Mauprats no longer shone, despite their numbers, their complete union, and their herculean strength; since the whole population of the district sided with their opponents and took upon itself the duty of stoning them. So, rallying his progeny around him, as the wild boar gathers together its young after a hunt, Tristan withdrew into his castle and ordered the drawbridge to be raised. Shut up with him were ten or twelve peasants, his servants, all of them poachers or refugees, who like himself had some interest in "retiring from the world" (his own expression), and in finding a place of safety behind good stout walls. An enormous pile of hunting weapons, duck-guns, carbines, blunderbusses, spears, and cutlasses, were raised on the platform, and the porter received orders never to let more than two persons at a time approach within range of his gun.

From that day Mauprat and his sons broke with all civil laws as they had already broken with all moral laws. They formed themselves into a band of adventurers. While their well-beloved and trusty poachers supplied the house with game, they levied illegal taxes on the small farms in the neighbourhood. Now, without being cowards (and they are far from that), the peasants of our province, as you know, are meek and timid, partly from listlessness, partly from distrust of the law, which they have never understood, and of which even to this day they have but a scanty knowledge. No province of France has preserved more old traditions or longer endured the abuses of feudalism. Nowhere else, perhaps, has the title of the lord of the manor been handed down, as hitherto with us, to the owners of certain estates; and nowhere is it so easy to frighten the people with reports of some absurd and impossible political event. At the time of which I speak the Mauprats, being the only powerful family in a district remote from towns and cut off from communication with the outside world, had little difficulty in persuading their vassals that serfdom was about to be re-established, and that it would go hard with all who resisted. The peasants hesitated, listened timorously to the few among themselves who preached independence, then thought the matter over and decided to submit. The Mauprats were clever enough not to demand money of them, for money is what the peasant in such a district obtains with the greatest difficulty, and parts from with the greatest reluctance. "Money is dear," is one of his proverbs, because in his eyes money stands for something different from manual labour. It means traffic with men and things outside his world, an effort of foresight or circumspection, a bargain, a sort of intellectual struggle, which lifts him out of his ordinary heedless habits; it means, in a word, mental labour, and this for him is the most painful and the most wearing.

The Mauprats, knowing how the ground lay, and having no particular need of money any longer, since they had repudiated their debts, demanded payments in kind only. They ruled that one man should contribute capons, another calves, a third corn, a fourth fodder, and so on. They were careful, too, to tax judiciously, to demand from each the commodity he could provide with least inconvenience to himself. In return they promised help and protection to all; and up to a certain point they kept their word. They cleared the land of wolves and foxes, gave a welcome and a hiding-place to all deserters, and helped to defraud the state by intimidating the excise officers and tax-collectors.

They took advantage of their power to give the poor man a false notion of his real interests, and to corrupt the simple folk by undermining all sense of their dignity and natural liberty. They made the whole district combine in a sort of secession from the law, and they so frightened the functionaries appointed to enforce respect for it, that after a few years it fell into a veritable desuetude. Thus it happened that, while France at a short distance from this region was advancing with rapid strides towards the enfranchisement of the poorer classes, Varenne was executing a retrograde march and returning at full speed to the ancient tyranny of the country squires. It was easy enough for the Mauprats to pervert these poor folk; they feigned a friendly interest in them to mark their difference from the other nobles in the province whose manners still retained some of the haughtiness of their ancient power. Above all, my grandfather lost no opportunity of making the peasants share his own hatred of his own cousin, Hubert de Mauprat. The latter, whenever he interviewed his vassals, would remain seated in his arm-chair, while they stood before him bareheaded; whereas Tristan de Mauprat would make them sit down at his table, and drink some of the wine they had brought him as a sign of voluntary hom- age. He would then have them led home by his men in the middle of the night, all dead drunk, torches in hand, and making the forest resound with ribald songs. Libertinism completed the demoralization of the peasantry. In every family the Mauprats soon had their mistresses. This was toler- ated, partly because it was profitable, and partly (alas! that it should have to be said) because it gratified vanity. The very isolation of the houses was favourable to the evil. No scandal, no denunciation were to be feared. The tiniest village would have been sufficient for the creation and maintenance of a public opinion. There, however, there were only scattered cottages and isolated farms; wastes and woods so separated the families from one another that the exercise of any mutual control was impossible. Shame is stronger than conscience. I need not tell you of all the bonds of infamy that united masters and slaves. Debauchery, extortion, and fraud were both precept and example for my youth, and life went on merrily. All notions of justice were scoffed at; creditors were defrauded of both interest and capital; any law officer who ventured to serve a summons received a sound thrashing, and the mounted police were fired on if they approached too near the turrets. A plague on parliament; starvation to all imbued with the new philosophy; and death to the younger branch of the Mauprats—such were the watchwords of these men who, to crown all, gave themselves the airs of knights-errant of the twelfth century. My grandfather talked of nothing but his pedigree and the prowess of his ancestors. He regretted the good old days when every lordling had instruments of torture in his manor, and dungeons, and, best, of all cannon. In ours we only had pitch- forks and sticks, and a second-rate culverin which my Uncle John used to point—and point very well, in fact—and which was sufficient to keep at a respectful distance the military force of the district.

II

Old Mauprat was a treacherous animal of the carnivorous order, a cross between a lynx and a fox. Along with a copious and easy flow of lan- guage, he had a veneer of education which helped his cunning. He made a point of excessive politeness, and had great powers of persuasion, even with the objects of his vengeance. He knew how to entice them to his castle, where he would make them undergo frightful ill-treatment, for which, however, having no witnesses, they were unable to obtain redress by law. All his villainies bore the stamp of such consummate skill that the country came to view them with a sort of awe akin to respect. No one could ever catch him out of his den, though he issued forth often enough, and apparently without taking many precautions. In truth, he was a man with a genius for evil; and his sons, bound to him by no ties of affection, of which, indeed, they were incapable, yet acknowledged the sway of this superior evil genius, and gave him a uniform and ready obedience, in which there was something almost fanatic. He was their deliverer in all desperate cases; and when the weariness of confinement under our chilly vaults began to fill them with *ennui*, his mind, brutal even in jest, would cure them by arranging for their pleasure shows worthy of a den of thieves. Sometimes poor mendicant monks collecting alms would be terrified or tortured for their benefit; their beards would be burned off, or they would be lowered into a well and kept hanging between life and death until they had sung some foul song or uttered some blasphemy. Everybody knows the story of the notary who was allowed to enter in company with his four clerks, and whom they received with all the assiduity of pompous hospitality. My grandfather pretended to agree with a good grace to the execution of their warrant, and politely helped them to make an inventory of his furniture, of which the sale had been decreed. After this, when dinner was served and the king's men had taken their places at table, he said to the notary:

"Ah, mon Dieu! I was forgetting a poor hack of mine in the stable. It's a small matter. Still, you might be reprimanded for omitting it; and as I see that you are a worthy fellow I should be sorry to mislead you. Come with me and see it; it won't take us a moment."

The notary followed Mauprat unsuspectingly. Just as they were about to enter the stable together, Mauprat, who was leading the way, told him to put in his head only. The notary, anxious to show great consideration in the performance of his duties, and not to pry into things too closely, did as he was told. Then Mauprat suddenly pushed the door to and squeezed his neck so violently between it and the wall that the wretched man could not breathe. Deeming him sufficiently punished, Tristan opened the door again, and, asking pardon for his carelessness, with great civility offered the man his arm to take him back to dinner. This the notary did not consider it wise to refuse; but as soon as he re-entered the room where his colleagues were, he threw himself into a chair, and pointing to his livid face and mangled neck, demanded justice for the trap into which he had just been led. It was then that my grandfather, revelling in his rascally wit, went through a comedy scene of sublime audacity. He gravely reproached the notary with accusing him unjustly, and always addressing him kindly and with studied politeness, called the others to bear witness to his conduct, begging them to make allowances if his precarious position had forced him to give them such a poor reception, all the while doing the honours of the table in splendid style. The poor notary did not dare to press the matter and was compelled to dine, although half dead. His companions were so completely duped by Mauprat's assurance that they ate and drank merrily, treating the notary as a lunatic and a boor. They left Roche-Mauprat all drunk, singing the praises of their host, and laughing at the notary, who fell down dead upon the threshold of his house on dismounting from his horse.

The eight sons, the pride and strength of old Mauprat, all resembled him in physical vigour, brutality of manners, and, to some extent, in craftiness and jesting ill-nature. The truth is they were veritable brutes, capable of any evil, and completely dead to any noble thought or generous sentiment. Nevertheless, they were endowed with a sort of reckless, dashing courage which now and then seemed to have in it an element of grandeur. But it is time that I told you about myself, and gave you some idea of the development of my character in the thick of this filthy mire into which it had pleased God to plunge me, on leaving my cradle.

I should be wrong if, in order to gain your sympathy in these early years of my life, I asserted that I was born with a noble nature, a pure and incorruptible soul. As to this, I know nothing. Maybe there are no incorruptible souls. Maybe there are. That is what neither you nor any one will ever know. The great questions awaiting an answer are these: "Are our innate tendencies invincible? If not, can they be modified merely or wholly destroyed by education?" For myself, I would not dare to affirm. I am neither a metaphysician, nor a psychologist, nor a philosopher; but I have had a terrible life, gentlemen, and if I were a legislator, I would order that man to have his tongue torn out, or his head cut off, who dared to preach or write that the nature of individuals is unchangeable, and that it is no more possible to reform the character of a man than the appetite of a tiger. God has preserved me from believing this.

All I can tell you is that my mother instilled into me good principles, though, perhaps, I was not endowed by nature with her good qualities. Even with her I was of a violent disposition, but my violence was sullen and suppressed. I was blind and brutal in anger, nervous even to cowardice at the approach of danger, daring almost to foolhardiness when hand to hand with it—that is to say, at once timid and brave from my love of life.

My obstinacy was revolting; yet my mother alone could conquer me; and without attempting to reason, for my mind developed very slowly, I used to obey her as if by a sort of magnetic necessity. This one guiding hand which I remember, and another woman's which I felt later, were and have been sufficient to lead me towards good. But I lost my mother before she had been able to teach me anything seriously; and when I was transplanted to Roche-Mauprat, my feeling for the evil done there was merely an instinctive aversion, feeble enough, perhaps, if fear had not been mingled with it.

But I thank Heaven from the bottom of my heart for the cruelties heaped upon me there, and above all for the hatred which my Uncle John conceived for me. My ill-fortune preserved me from indifference in the presence of evil, and my sufferings helped me to detest those who wrought it.

This John was certainly the most detestable of his race. Ever since a fall from his horse had maimed him, his evil temper had developed in proportion to his inability to do as much harm as his companions. Compelled to remain at home when the others set out on their expeditions, for he could not bestride a horse, he found his only chance of pleasure in those fruitless little attacks which the mounted police sometimes made on the castle, as if to ease their conscience. Then, intrenched behind a rampart of freestone which he had had built to suit himself, John, calmly seated near his culverin, would pick off a gentleman from time to time, and at once regain, as he said, his sleeping and eating power, which want of exercise had taken from him. And he would even climb up to his beloved platform without waiting for the excuse of an attack, and there, crouching down like a cat ready to spring, as soon as he saw any one appear in the distance without giving the signal, he would try his skill upon the target, and make the man retrace his steps. This he called sweeping the path clean.

As I was too young to accompany my uncles on their hunting and plundering expeditions, John naturally became my guardian and tutor— that is to say, my jailor and tormentor. I will not give you all the details of that infernal existence. For nearly ten years I endured cold, hunger, insults, the dungeon, and blows, according to the more or less savage caprices of this monster. His fierce hatred of me arose from the fact that he could not succeed in depraving me; my rugged, headstrong, and unsociable nature preserved me from his vile seductions. It is possible that I had not any strong tendencies to virtue; to hatred I luckily had. Rather than do the bidding of my tyrant I would have suffered a thousand deaths. And so I grew up without conceiving any affection for vice. However, my notions about society were so strange that my uncles' mode of life did not in itself cause me any repugnance. Seeing that I was brought up behind the walls of Roche-Mauprat, and that I lived in a state of perpetual siege, you will understand that I had precisely such ideas as any armed retainer in the barbarous ages of feudalism might have had. What, outside our den, was termed by other men assassinating, plundering, and torturing, I was taught to call fighting, conquering, and subduing. My sole knowledge of history consisted of an acquaintance with certain legends and ballads of chivalry which my grandfather used to repeat to me of an evening, when he had time to think of what he was pleased to call my education. Whenever I asked him any question about the present time, he used to answer that times had sadly changed, that all Frenchmen had become traitors and felons, that they had frightened their kings, and that these, like cravens, had deserted the nobles, who in their turn had been cowardly enough to renounce their privileges and let laws be made for them by clodhoppers. I listened with surprise, almost with indignation, to this account of the age in which I lived, for me an age of shadows and mysteries. My grandfather had but vague ideas of chronology; not a book of any kind was to be found at Roche-Mauprat, except, I should say, the History of the Sons of Aymon, and a few chronicles of the same class brought by our servants from country fairs. Three names, and only three, stood clear in the chaos of my ignorance—Charlemagne, Louis XI, and Louis XIV; because my grandfather would frequently introduce these into dissertations on the unrecognised rights of the nobles. In truth, I was so ignorant that I scarcely knew the difference between a reign and a race; and I was by no means sure that my grandfather had not seen Charlemagne, for he spoke of him more frequently and more gladly than of any other man.

But, while my native energy led me to admire the exploits of my uncles, and filled me with a longing to share in them, the cold-blooded cruelty they perpetrated on returning from their expeditions, and the perfidious artifices by which they lured their dupes to the castle, in order to torture them to extort ransom, roused in me strange and painful emotions, which, now that I am speaking in all sincerity, it would be difficult for me to account for exactly. In the absence of all ordinary moral principles it might have been natural for me to accept the theory which I daily saw carried into practice, that makes it right; but the humiliation and suffering which my Uncle John inflicted on me in virtue of this theory, taught me to be dissatisfied with it. I could appreciate the right of the bravest, and I genuinely despised those who, with death in their power, yet chose life at the price of such ignominy as they had to bear at Roche-Mauprat. But I could only explain these insults and horrors heaped on prisoners, some of them women and mere children, as manifestations of bloodthirsty appetites. I do not know if I was sufficiently susceptible of a noble sentiment to be inspired with pity for the victim; but certain it is that I experienced that feeling of selfish commiseration which is common to all natures, and which, purified and ennobled, has become charity among civilized peoples. Under my coarse exterior my heart no doubt merely felt passing shocks of fear and disgust at the sight of punishments which I myself might have to endure any day at the caprice of my oppressors; especially as John, when he saw me turn pale at these frightful spectacles, had a habit of saying, in a mocking tone:

"That's what I'll do to you when you are disobedient."

All I know is that in presence of such iniquitous acts I experienced a horrible uneasiness; my blood curdled in my veins, my throat began to close, and I had to rush away, so as not to repeat the cries which pierced my ears. In time, however, I became somewhat hardened to these terrible impressions. The fibres of feeling grew tougher, and habit gave me power to hide what they termed my cowardice. I even felt ashamed of the signs of weakness I showed, and forced my face into the hyena smile which I saw on the faces of my kinsmen. But I could never prevent convulsive shudders from running through my limbs, and the coldness as of death from falling on my heart, at the recollection of these scenes of agony. The women, dragged half-willingly, half by force, under the roof of Roche-Mauprat, caused me inconceivable agitation. I began to feel the fires of youth kindling within me, and even to look with envy on this part of my uncles' spoil; but with these new-born desires were mingled inexpressible pangs. To all around me women were merely objects of contempt, and vainly did I try to separate this idea from that of the pleasure which was luring me. My mind was bewildered, and my irritated nerves imparted a violent and sickly strain to all my temptations. In other matters, I had as vile a disposition as my companions; if my heart was better than theirs, my manners were no less arrogant, and my jokes in no better taste. And here it may be well to give you an illustration of my youthful malice, especially as the results of these events have had an influence on the rest of my life.

III

Some three leagues from Roche-Mauprat, on your way to Fromental, you must have noticed an old tower standing by itself in the middle of the woods. It is famous for the tragic death of a prisoner about a century ago. The executioner, on his rounds, thought good to hang him without any further formality, merely to gratify an old Mauprat, his overlord.

At the time of which I am speaking Gazeau Tower was already deserted and falling into ruins. It was state property, and, more from negligence than kindness, the authorities had allowed a poor old fellow to take up his abode there. He was quite a character, used to live completely alone, and was known in the district as Gaffer Patience.

"Yes," I interrupted; "I have heard my nurse's grandmother speak of him; she believed he was a sorcerer."

Exactly so; and while we are at this point let me tell you what sort of a man this Patience really was, for I shall have to speak of him more than once in the course of my story. I had opportunities of studying him thoroughly.

Patience, then, was a rustic philosopher. Heaven had endowed him with a keen intellect, but he had had little education. By a sort of strange fatality, his brain had doggedly resisted the little instruction he might have received. For instance, he had been to the Carmelite's school at—, and instead of showing any aptitude for work, he had played truant with a keener delight than any of his school-fellows. His was an eminently contemplative nature, kindly and indolent, but proud and almost savage in its love of independence; religious, yet opposed to all authority; somewhat captious, very suspicious, and inexorable with hypocrites. The observances of the cloister inspired him with but little awe; and as a result of once or twice speaking his mind too freely to the monks he was expelled from the school. From that time forth he was the sworn foe of what he called monkism, and declared openly for the cure of the Briantes, who was accused of being a Jansenist. In the instruction of Patience, however, the cure succeeded no better than the monks. The young peasant, endowed though he was with herculean strength and a great desire for knowledge, displayed an unconquerable aversion for every kind of work, whether physical or mental. He professed a sort of artless philosophy which the cure found it very difficult to argue against. There was, he said, no need for a man to work as long as he did not want money; and he was in no need of money as long as his wants were moderate. Patience practised what he preached: during the years when passions are so powerful he lived a life of austerity, drank nothing but water, never entered a tavern, and never joined in a dance. He was always very awkward and shy with women, who, it must be owned, found little to please in his eccentric character, stern face, and somewhat sarcastic wit. As if to avenge himself for this by showing his contempt, or to console himself by displaying his wisdom, he took a pleasure, like Diogenes of old, in decrying the vain pleasures of others; and if at times he was to be seen passing under the branches in the middle of the fetes, it was merely to throw out some shaft of scorn, a flash from his inexorable good sense. Sometimes, too, his uncompromising morality found expression in biting words, which left clouds of sadness or fear hanging over agitated consciences. This naturally gained him violent enemies; and the efforts of impotent hatred, helped by the feeling of awe which his eccentric behaviour produced, fastened upon him the reputation of a sorcerer.

When I said that Patience was lacking in education, I expressed myself badly. Longing for a knowledge of the sublime mysteries of Nature, his mind wished to soar to heaven on its first flight. From the very beginning, the Jansenist vicar was so perplexed and startled by the audacity of his pupil, he had to say so much to calm him into submission, he was obliged to sustain such assaults of bold questions and proud objections, that he had no leisure to teach him the alphabet; and at the end of ten years of studies, broken off and taken up at the bidding of a whim or on compulsion, Patience could not even read. It was only with great difficulty, after poring over a book for some two hours, that he deciphered a single page, and even then he did not grasp the meaning of most of the words expressing abstract ideas. Yet these abstract ideas were undoubtedly in him; you felt their presence while watching and listening to him; and the way in which he managed to embody them in homely phrase enlivened with a rude poetry was so marvellous, that one scarcely knew whether to feel astounded or amused.

Always serious, always positive himself, he scorned dalliance with any dialectic. A Stoic by nature and on principle, enthusiastic in the propagation of his doctrine of severance from false ideas, but resolute in the practice of resignation, he made many a breach in the poor cure's defences; and it was in these discussions, as he often told me in his last years, that he acquired his knowledge of philosophy. In order to make a stand against the battering-ram of natural logic, the worthy Jansenist was obliged to invoke the testimony of all the Fathers of the Church, and to oppose these, often even to corroborate them, with the teaching of all the sages and scholars of antiquity. Then Patience, his round eyes starting from his head (this was his own expression), lapsed into silence, and, delighted to learn without having the bother of studying, would ask for long explanations of the doctrines of these men, and for an account of their lives. Noticing this attention and this silence, his adversary would exult; but just as he thought he had convinced this rebellious soul, Patience, hearing the village clock strike midnight, would rise, take an affectionate leave of his host, and on the very threshold of the vicarage, would dismay the good man with some laconic and cutting comment that confounded Saint Jerome and Plato alike, Eusebius equally with Seneca, Tertullian no less than Aristotle.

The cure was not too ready to acknowledge the superiority of this untutored intellect. Still, he was quite astonished at passing so many winter evenings by his fireside with this peasant without feeling either bored or tired; and he would wonder how it was that the village schoolmaster, and even the prior of the convent, in spite of their Greek and Latin, appeared to him, the one a bore, the other a sophist, in all their discussions. Knowing the perfect purity of the peasant's life, he attributed the ascendency of his mind to the power of virtue and the charm it spreads over all things. Then, each evening, he would humbly accuse himself before God of not having disputed with his pupil from a sufficiently Christian point of view; he would confess to his guardian angel that pride in his own learning and joy at being listened to so devoutly had carried him somewhat beyond the bounds of religious instruction; that he had quoted profane writers too complacently; that he had even experienced a dangerous pleasure in roaming with his disciple through the fields of the past, plucking pagan flowers unsprinkled by the waters of baptism, flowers in whose fragrance a priest should not have found such delight.

On his side, Patience loved the cure dearly. He was his only friend, his only bond of union with society, his only bond of union, through the light of knowledge, with God. The peasant largely over-estimated his pastor's learning. He did not know that even the most enlightened men often draw wrong conclusions, or no conclusions at all, from the course of progress. Patience would have been spared great distress of mind if he could have seen for certain that his master was frequently mistaken and that it was the man, not the truth, that was at fault. Not knowing this, and finding the experience of the ages at variance with his innate sense of justice, he was continually a prey to agonizing reveries; and, living by himself, and wandering through the country at all hours of the day and night, wrapped in thoughts undreamed of by his fellows, he gave more and more credit to the tales of sorcery reported against him.

The convent did not like the pastor. A few monks whom Patience had unmasked hated Patience. Hence, both pastor and pupil were persecuted. The ignorant monks did not scruple to accuse the cure to his bishop of devoting himself to the occult sciences in concert with the magician Patience. A sort of religious war broke out in the village and neighbourhood. All who were not for the convent were for the cure, and *vice versa*. Patience scorned to take part in this struggle. One morning he went to see his friend, with tears in his eyes, and said to him:

"You are the one man in all the world that I love, and I will not have you persecuted on my account. Since, after you, I neither know nor care for a soul, I am going off to live in the woods, like the men of primitive times. I have inherited a field which brings me in fifty francs a year. It is the only land I have ever stirred with these hands, and half its wretched rent has gone to pay the tithe of labour I owe the seignior. I trust to die without ever doing duty as a beast of burden for others. And yet, should they remove you from your office, or rob you of your income, if you have a field that needs ploughing, only send me word, and you will see that these arms have not grown altogether stiff in their idleness."

It was in vain that the pastor opposed this resolve. Patience departed, carrying with him as his only belonging the coat he had on his back, and an abridgment of the teachings of Epictetus. For this book he had a great affection, and, thanks to much study of it, could read as many as three of its pages a day without unduly tiring himself. The rustic anchorite went into the desert to live. At first he built himself a hut of branches in a wood. Then, as wolves attacked him, he took refuge in one of the lower halls of Gazeau Tower, which he furnished luxuriously with a bed of moss, and some stumps of trees; wild roots, wild fruit, and goat's milk constituted a daily fare very little inferior to what he had had in the village. This is no exaggeration. You have to see the peasants in certain parts of Varenne to form an idea of the frugal diet on which a man can live and keep in good health. In the midst of these men of stoical habits all round him, Patience was still exceptional. Never had wine reddened his lips, and bread had seemed to him a superfluity. Besides, the doctrine of Pythagoras was not wholly displeasing to him; and in the rare interviews which he henceforth had with his friend he would declare that, without exactly believing in metempsychosis, and without making it a rule to eat vegetables only, he felt a secret joy at being able to live thus, and at having no further occasion to see death dealt out every day to innocent animals.

Patience had formed this curious resolution at the age of forty. He was sixty when I saw him for the first time, and he was then possessed of extraordinary physical vigour. In truth, he was in the habit of roaming about the country every year. However, in proportion as I tell you about my own life, I shall give you details of the hermit life of Patience.

At the time of which I am about to speak, the forest rangers, more from fear of his casting a spell over them than out of compassion, had finally ceased their persecutions, and given him full permission to live in Gazeau Tower, not, however, without warning him that it would probably fall about his head during the first gale of wind. To this Patience had replied philosophically that if he was destined to be crushed to death, the first tree in the forest would do the work quite as well as the walls of Gazeau Tower.

Before putting my actor Patience on the stage, and with many apologies for inflicting on you such a long preliminary biography, I have still to mention that during the twenty years of which I have spoken the cure's mind had bowed to a new power. He loved philosophy, and in spite of himself, dear man, could not prevent this love from embracing the philosophers too, even the least orthodox. The works of Jean Jacques Rousseau carried him away into new regions, in spite of all his efforts at resistance; and when one morning, when returning from a visit to some sick folk, he came across Patience gathering his dinner of herbs from the rocks of Crevant, he sat down near him on one of the druidical stones and made, without knowing it, the profession of faith of the Savoyard vicar. Patience drank more willingly of this poetic religion than of the ancient orthodoxy. The pleasure with which he listened to a summary of the new doctrines led the cure to arrange secret meetings with him in isolated parts of Varenne, where they agreed to come upon each other as if by chance. At these mysterious interviews the imagination of Patience, fresh and ardent from long solitude, was fired with all the magic of the thoughts and hopes which were then fermenting in France, from the court of Versailles to the most uninhabitable heath. He became enamoured of Jean Jacques, and made the cure read as much of him as he possibly could without neglecting his duties. Then he begged a copy of the *Contrat Social,* and hastened to Gazeau Tower to spell his way through it feverishly. At first the cure had given him of this manna only with a sparing hand, and while making him admire the lofty thoughts and noble sentiments of the philosopher, had thought to put him on his guard against the poison of anarchy. But all the old learning, all the happy texts of bygone days—in a word, all the theology of the worthy priest—was swept away like a fragile bridge by the torrent of wild eloquence and ungovernable enthusiasm which Patience had accumulated in his desert. The vicar had to give way and fall back terrified upon himself. There he discovered that the shrine of his own science was everywhere cracking and crumbling to ruin. The new sun which was rising on the political horizon and making havoc in so many minds, melted his own like a light snow under the first breath of spring. The sublime enthusiasm of Patience; the strange poetic life of the man which seemed to reveal him as one inspired; the romantic turn which their mysterious relations were taking (the ignoble persecutions of the convent making it noble to revolt)—all this so worked upon the priest that by 1770 he had already travelled far from Jansenism, and was vainly searching all the religious heresies for some spot on which he might rest before falling into the abyss of philosophy so often opened at his feet by Patience, so often hidden in vain by the exorcisms of Roman theology.

IV

After this account of the philosophical life of Patience, set forth by me now in manhood (continued Bernard, after a pause), it is not altogether easy to return to the very different impressions I received in boyhood on meeting the wizard of Gazeau Tower. I will make an effort, however, to reproduce my recollections faithfully.

It was one summer evening, as I was returning from bird-snaring with several peasant-boys, that I passed Gazeau Tower for the first time. My age was about thirteen, and I was bigger and stronger than any of my comrades; besides, I exercised over them, sternly enough, the authority I drew from my noble birth. In fact, the mixture of familiarity and etiquette in our intercourse was rather fantastic. Sometimes, when the excitement of sport or the fatigue of the day had greater powers over them than I, they used to have their own way; and I already knew how to yield at the right moment, as tyrants do, so as always to avoid the appearance of being compelled. However, I generally found a chance for revenge, and soon saw them trembling before the hated name of my family.

Well, night was coming on, and we were walking along gaily, whistling, knocking down crab-apples with stones, imitating the notes of birds, when the boy who was ahead suddenly stopped, and, coming back to us, declared that he was not going by the Gazeau Tower path, but would rather cut across the wood. This idea was favoured by two others. A third objected that we ran the risk of losing ourselves if we left the path, that night was near, and that there were plenty of wolves about.

"Come on, you funks!" I cried in a princely tone, pushing forward the guide; "follow the path, and have done with this nonsense."

"Not me," said the youngster. "I've just seen the sorcerer at his door saying magic words, and I don't want to have a fever all the year."

"Bah!" said another; "he doesn't do harm to everybody. He never hurts children; and, besides, we have only to pass by very quietly without saying anything to him. What do you suppose he'll do to us?"

"Oh, it would be all right if we were alone," answered the first; "but M. Bernard is here; we're sure to have a spell cast on us."

"What do you say, you fool?" I cried, doubling my fist.

"It's not my fault, my lord," replied the boy. "That old wretch doesn't like the gentry, and he has said he would be glad to see M. Tristan and all his sons hanging from the same bough."

"He said that, did he? Good!" I answered. "Come on, and you shall see. All who are my friends will follow; any one that leaves me is a coward."

Two of my companions, out of vanity, let themselves be drawn on. The others pretended to imitate them; but, after a few steps, they had all taken flight and disappeared into the copse. However, I went on proudly, escorted by my two acolytes. Little Sylvain, who was in front, took off his hat as soon as he saw Patience in the distance; and when we arrived opposite him, though the man was looking on the ground without appearing to notice us, he was seized with terror, and said, in a trembling voice:

"Good evening, Master Patience; a good night's rest to you."

The sorcerer, roused out of his reverie, started like a man waked from sleep; and I saw, not without a certain emotion, his weather-beaten face half covered with a thick gray beard. His big head was quite bald, and the bareness of his forehead only served to make his bushy eyebrows more prominent. Behind these his round deepset eyes seemed to flash like lightning at the end of summer behind the fading foliage. He was of small stature, but very broad-shouldered; in fact, built like a gladiator. The rags in which he was clad were defiantly filthy. His face was short and of a vulgar type, like that of Socrates; and if the fire of genius glowed in his strongly marked features, I certainly could not perceive it. He appeared to me a wild beast, an unclean animal. Filled with a sense of loathing, and determined to avenge the insult he had offered to my name, I put a stone in my sling, and without further ado hurled it at him with all my might.

At the moment the stone flew out, Patience was in the act of replying to the boy's greeting.

"Good evening, lads; God be with you!" he was saying when the stone whistled past his ear and struck a tame owl of which Patience had made a pet, and which at the approach of night was beginning to rouse itself in the ivy above the door.

The owl gave a piercing cry and fell bleeding at the feet of its master, who answered it with a roar of anger. For a few seconds he stood motionless with surprise and fury. Then suddenly, taking the palpitating victim by the feet, he lifted it up, and, coming towards us, cried in a voice of thunder:

"Which of you wretches threw that stone?"

The boy who had been walking behind, flew with the swiftness of the wind; but Sylvain, seized by the great hand of the sorcerer, fell upon his knees, swearing by the Holy Virgin and by Saint Solange, the patroness of Berry, that he was innocent of the death of the bird. I felt, I confess, a strong inclination to let him get out of the scrape as best he could, and make my escape into the thicket. I had expected to see a decrepit old juggler, not to fall into the hands of a robust enemy; but pride held me back.

"If you did this," said Patience to my trembling comrade, "I pity you; for you are a wicked child, and you will grow into a dishonest man. You have done a bad deed; you have made it your pleasure to cause pain to an old man who never did you any harm; and you have done this treacherously, like a coward, while feigning politeness and bidding him good-evening. You are a liar, a miscreant; you have robbed me of my only society, my only riches; you have taken delight in evil. God preserve you from living if you are going on in this way."

"Oh, Monsieur Patience!" cried the boy, clasping his hands; "do not curse me; do not bewitch me; do not give me any illness; it wasn't I! May God strike me dead if it was!"

"If it wasn't you, it was this one, then!" said Patience, seizing me by the coat-collar and shaking me like a young tree to be uprooted.

"Yes, I did it," I replied, haughtily; "and if you wish to know my name, learn that I am called Bernard Mauprat, and that a peasant who lays a hand on a nobleman deserves death."

"Death! You! You would put me to death, Mauprat!" cried the old man, petrified with surprise and indignation. "And what would God be, then, if a brat like you had a right to threaten a man of my age? Death! Ah, you are a genuine Mauprat, and you bite like your breed, cursed whelp! Such things as they talk of putting to death the very moment they are born! Death, my wolf-cub! Do you know it is yourself who deserves death, not for what you have just done, but for being the son of your father, and the nephew of your uncles? Ah! I am glad to hold a Mauprat in the hollow of my hand, and see whether a cur of a nobleman weighs as much as a Christian."

As he spoke he lifted me from the ground as he would have lifted a hare.

"Little one," he said to my comrade, "you can run home; you needn't be afraid. Patience rarely gets angry with his equals; and he always pardons his brothers, because his brothers are ignorant like himself, and know not what they do; but a Mauprat, look you, is a thing that knows how to read and write, and is only the viler for it all. Run away, then. But no; stay; I should like you once in your life to see a nobleman receive a thrashing from the hand of a peasant. And that is what you are going to see; and I ask you not to forget it, little one, and to tell your parents about it."

Livid, and gnashing my teeth with rage, I made desperate efforts to resist. Patience, with hideous calmness, bound me to a tree with an osier shoot. At the touch of his great horny hand I bent like a reed; and yet I was remarkably strong for my age. He fixed the owl to a branch above my head, and the bird's blood, as it fell on me drop by drop, caused me unspeakable horror; for though this was only the correction we administer to sporting dogs that worry game, my brain, bewildered by rage, despair, and my comrades' cries, began to imagine some frightful witchcraft. However, I really think I would rather have been metamorphosed into an owl at once than undergo the punishment he inflicted on me. In vain did I fling threats at him; in vain did I take terrible vows of vengeance; in vain did the peasant child throw himself on his knees again and supplicate:

"Monsieur Patience, for God's sake, for your own sake, don't harm him; the Mauprats will kill you."

He laughed, and shrugged his shoulders. Then, taking a handful of holly twigs, he flogged me in a manner, I must own, more humiliating than cruel; for no sooner did he see a few drops of my blood appear, than he stopped and threw down the rod. I even noticed a sudden softening of his features and voice, as if he were sorry for his severity.

"Mauprat," he said, crossing his arms on his breast and looking at me fixedly, "you have now been punished; you have now been insulted, my fine gentleman; that is enough for me. As you see, I might easily prevent you from ever harming me by stopping your breath with a touch of my finger, and burying you under the stone at my door. Who would think of coming to Gaffer Patience to look for this fine child of noble blood? But, as you may also see, I am not fond of vengeance; at the first cry of pain that escaped you, I stopped. No; I don't like to cause suffering; I'm not a Mauprat. Still, it was well for you to learn by experience what is to be a victim. May this disgust you of the hangman's trade, which had been handed down from father to son in your family. Good-evening! You can go now; I no longer bear you malice; the justice of God is satisfied. You can tell your uncles to put me on their gridiron; they will have a tough morsel to eat; and they will swallow flesh that will come to life again in their gullets and choke them."

Then he picked up the dead owl, and looking at it sadly:

"A peasant's child would not have done this," he said. "This is sport for gentle blood."

As he retired to his door he gave utterance to an exclamation which escaped him only on solemn occasions, and from which he derived his curious surname:

"Patience, patience!" he cried.

This, according to the gossips, was a cabalistic formula of his; and whenever he had been heard to pronounce it, some misfortune had happened to the individual who had offended him. Sylvain crossed himself to ward off the evil spirit. The terrible words resounded through the tower into which Patience had just withdrawn, then the door closed behind him with a bang.

My comrade was so eager to be off that he was within an ace of leaving me there bound to the tree. As soon as he had released me, he exclaimed:

"A sign of the cross! For God's sake, a sign of the cross! If you don't cross yourself you are bewitched; we shall be devoured by wolves as we go, or else we shall meet the great monster."

"Idiot!" I said; "I have something else to think about. Listen; if you are ever unlucky enough to tell a single soul of what has happened, I will strangle you."

"Alas! sir, what am I to do?" he replied with a mixture of innocence and malice. "The sorcerer said I was to tell my parents."

I raised my fist to strike him, but my strength failed. Choking with rage at the treatment I had just undergone, I fell down almost in a faint, and Sylvain seized the opportunity for flight.

When I came to I found myself alone. I did not know this part of Varenne; I had never been here before, and it was horribly wild. All through the day I had seen tracks of wolves and wild boars in the sand. And now night had come and I was still two leagues from Roche-Mauprat. The gate would be shut, the drawbridge up; and I should get a bullet through me if I tried to enter after nine o'clock. As I did not know the way, it was a hundred to one against my doing the two leagues in an hour. However, I would have preferred to die a thousand deaths rather than ask shelter of the man in Gazeau Tower, even had he granted it gracefully. My pride was bleeding more than my flesh.

I started off at a run, heedless of all risks. The path made a thousand turns; a thousand other paths kept crossing it. When I reached the plain I found myself in a pasture surrounded by hedges. There every trace of the path disappeared. I jumped the hedge at a venture, and fell into a field. The night was pitch-dark; even had it been day it would have been impossible to ascertain my way in the midst of little properties buried between high banks bristling with thorns. Finally I reached a heath, then some woods; and my fears, which had been somewhat subdued, now grew intense. Yes, I own I was a prey to mortal terrors. Trained to bravery, as a dog is to sport, I bore myself well enough before others. Spurred by vanity, indeed, I was foolishly bold when I had spectators; but left to myself, in the middle of the night, exhausted by toil and hunger, though with no longing for food, unhinged by the emotions I had just experienced, certain that my uncles would beat me when I returned, yet as anxious to return as if I were going to find paradise on earth at Roche-Mauprat, I wandered about until daybreak, suffering indescribable agonies. The howls of wolves, happily far off, more than once reached my ears and froze the blood in my veins; and, as if my position had not been perilous enough in reality, my overwrought imagination must needs add to it a thousand extravagant fantasies. Patience had the reputation of being a wolf-rearer. This, as you know, is a cabalistic speciality accredited in all countries. I kept on fancying, therefore, that I saw this devilish little gray-beard, escorted by his ravening pack, and himself in the form of a demi-wolf, pursing me through the woods. Several times when rabbits got up at my feet I almost fell backwards from the shock. And now, as I was certain that nobody could see, I made many a sign of the cross; for, while affecting incredulity, I was, of course, at heart filled with all the superstitions born of fear.

At last, at daybreak, I reached Roche-Mauprat. I waited in a moat until the gates were opened, and then slipped up to my room without being seen by anybody. As it was not altogether an unfailing tenderness that watched over me at Roche-Mauprat, my absence had not been noticed during the night. Meeting my Uncle John on the stairs, I led him to believe that I had just got up; and, as the artifice proved successful, I went off to the hayloft and slept for the rest of the day.

V

As I had nothing further to fear for myself, it would have been easy to take vengeance on my enemy. Everything was favourable. The words he had uttered against my family would have been sufficient without any mention of the outrage done to my own person, which, in truth, I hardly cared to make known. I had only to say a word, and in a quarter of an hour seven Mauprats would have been in the saddle, delighted at the opportunity of making an example of a man who paid them no dues. Such a man would have seemed to them good for nothing but hanging as a warning to others.

But even if things had not been likely to reach this pitch, I somehow felt an unconquerable aversion to asking eight men to avenge me on a single one. Just as I was about to ask them (for, in my anger, I had firmly resolved to do so), I was held back by some instinct for fair dealing to which I had hitherto been a stranger, and whose presence in myself I could hardly explain. Perhaps, too, the words of Patience had, unknown to myself, aroused in me a healthy sense of shame. Perhaps his righteous maledictions on the nobles had given me glimpses of the idea of justice. Perhaps, in short, what I had hitherto despised in myself as impulses of weakness and compassion, henceforth began dimly to take a more solemn and less contemptible shape.

Be that as it may, I kept silent. I contented myself with thrashing Sylvain as a punishment for having deserted me, and to impress upon him that he was not to breathe a word about my unfortunate adventure. The bitterness of the recollection was intensified by an incident which happened toward the end of autumn when I was out with him beating the woods for game. The poor boy was genuinely attached to me; for, my brutality notwithstanding, he always used to be at my heels the instant I was outside the castle. When any of his companions spoke ill of me, he would take up my cause, and declare that I was merely somewhat hasty and not really bad at heart. Ah, it is the gentle, resigned souls of the humble that keep up the pride and roughness of the great. Well, we were trying to trap larks when my sabot-shot page, who always hunted about ahead of me, came back, saying in his rude dialect:

"I can see the wolf-driver with the mole-catcher."

This announcement sent a shudder through all my limbs. However, the longing for revenge produced a reaction, and I marched straight on to meet the sorcerer. Perhaps, too, I felt somewhat reassured by the presence of his companion, who was a frequenter of Roche-Mauprat, and would be likely to show me respect and afford me assistance.

Marcasse, the mole-catcher, as he was called, professed to rid the dwellings and fields of the district of polecats, weasels, rats and other vermin. Nor did he confine his good offices to Berry; every year he went the round of La Marche, Nivernais, Limousin, and Saintonge, visiting, alone and on foot, all the places that had the good sense to appreciate his talents. He was well received everywhere, in the castle no less than in the cottage; for his was a trade that had been carried on successfully and honestly in his family for generations (indeed, his descendants still carry it on). Thus he had work and a home awaiting him for every day in the year. As regular in his round as the earth in her rotation, he would reappear on a given day at the very place where he had appeared the year before, and always with the same dog and with the same long sword.

This personage was as curious as the sorcerer Patience; perhaps more comic in his way than the sorcerer. He was a bilious, melancholy man, tall, lean, angular, full of languor, dignity, and deliberation in speech and action. So little did he like talking that he answered all questions in monosyllables; and yet he never failed to obey the laws of the most scrupulous politeness, and rarely said a word without raising his hand to the corner of his hat as a sign of respect and civility. Was he thus by nature, or, in his itinerant trade, had this wise reserve arisen from a fear of alienating some of his numerous clients by incautious chatter? No one knew. In all houses he was allowed a free hand; during the day he had the key of every granary; in the evening, a place at the fireside of every kitchen. He knew everything that happened; for his dreamy, absorbed air led people to talk freely in his presence; yet he had never been known to inform any household of the doings of another.

If you wish to know how I had become struck by this strange character, I may tell you that I had been a witness of my uncle's and grandfather's efforts to make him talk. They hoped to draw from him some information about the chateau of Saint-Severe, the home of a man they hated and envied, M. Hubert de Mauprat. Although Don Marcasse (they called him Don because he seemed to have the bearing and pride of a ruined hidalgo), although Don Marcasse, I say, had shown himself as incompressible here as elsewhere, the Coupe-Jarret Mauprats never failed to squeeze him a little more in the hope of extracting some details about the Casse-Tete Mauprats.

Nobody, then, could discover Marcasse's opinions about anything; it would have been simplest to suppose that he did not take the trouble to have any. Yet the attraction which Patience seemed to feel towards him— so great that he would accompany him on his travels for several weeks altogether—led one to believe that there was some witchery in the man's mysterious air, and that it was not solely the length of his sword and the skill of his dog which played such wonderful havoc with the moles and weasels. There were whispered rumours of the enchanted herbs that he employed to lure these suspicious animals from their holes into his nets. However, as people found themselves better off for his magic, no one dreamt of denouncing it as criminal.

I do not know if you have ever seen one of the rat-hunts. It is a curious sight, especially in a fodder-loft. The man and dog climbing up ladders and running along beams with marvellous assurance and agility, the dog sniffing every hole in the wall, playing the cat, crouching down and lying in wait until the game comes out for his master's rapier; the man thrusting through bundles of straw and putting the enemy to the sword—all this, when arranged and carried out with gravity and dignity by Don Marcasse, was, I assure you, a most singular and interesting performance.

When I saw this trusty fellow I felt equal to braving the sorcerer, and advanced boldly. Sylvain stared at me in admiration, and I noticed that Patience himself was not prepared for such audacity. I pretended to go up to Marcasse and speak to him, as though quite unconcerned about the presence of my enemy. Seeing this he gently thrust aside the mole-catcher, and, laying his heavy hand on my head, said very quietly:

"You have grown of late, my fine gentleman!"

The blood rushed to my face, and, drawing back scornfully, I answered:

"Take care what you are doing, clodhopper; you should remember that if you still have your two ears, it is to my kindness that you owe them."

"My two ears!" said Patience, with a bitter laugh.

Then making an allusion to the nickname of my family, he added:

"Perhaps you mean my two hamstrings? Patience, patience! The time, maybe, is not far distant when clodhoppers will rid the nobles of neither ears nor hamstrings, but of their heads and their purses."

"Silence, Master Patience!" said the mole-catcher solemnly; "these are not the words of a philosopher."

"You are quite right, quite right," replied the sorcerer; "and in truth, I don't know why I allow myself to argue with this lad. He might have had me made into pap by his uncles. I whipped him in the summer for playing me a stupid trick; and I don't know what happened to the family, but the Mauprats lost a fine chance of injuring a neighbour."

"Learn, peasant," I said, "that a nobleman always takes vengeance nobly. I did not want my wrongs avenged by people more powerful than yourself; but wait a couple of years; I promise I will hang you with my own hand on a certain tree that I shall easily recognise, not very far from the door of Gazeau Tower. If I don't I will renounce my birthright; if I spare you I will take the title of wolf-driver."

Patience smiled; then, suddenly becoming serious, he fixed on me that searching look which rendered his physiognomy so striking. Then turning to the weasel-hunter:

"It is strange," he said; "there must be something in blood. Take the vilest noble, and you will find that in certain things he has more spirit than the bravest of us. Ah! it is simple enough," he added, speaking to himself; "they are brought up like that, whilst we—we, they tell us, are born to obey. Patience!"

He was silent for an instant; then, rousing himself from his reverie, he said to me in a kindly though somewhat mocking tone:

"And so you want to hang me, Monseigneur Straw-Stalk? You will have to eat a lot of beef, then, for you are not yet tall enough to reach the branch which is to bear me; and before then . . . perhaps many things will happen that are not dreamt of in your little philosophy."

"Nonsense! Why talk nonsense?" said the mole-catcher, with a serious air; "come, make peace. Monseigneur Bernard, I ask pardon for Patience; he is an old man, a fool."

"No, no," said Patience; "I want him to hang me; he is right; this is merely my due; and, in fact, it may come more quickly than all the rest. You must not make too much haste to grow, monsieur; for I—well, I am making more haste to grow old than I would wish; and you who are so brave, you would not attack a man no longer able to defend himself."

"You didn't hesitate to use your strength against me!" I cried. "Confess, now; didn't you treat me brutally? Wasn't it a coward's work, that?"

"Oh, children, children!" he said. "See how the thing reasons! Out of the mouths of children cometh truth."

And he moved away dreamily, and muttering to himself as was his wont. Marcasse took off his hat to me and said in an impassive tone:

"He is wrong . . . live at peace . . . pardon . . . peace . . . farewell!"

They disappeared; and there ended my relations with Patience. I did not come in contact with him again until long afterward.

VI

I was fifteen when my grandfather died. At Roche-Mauprat his death caused no sorrow, but infinite consternation. He was the soul of every vice that reigned therein, and it is certain that he was more cruel, though less vile, than his sons. On his death the sort of glory which his audacity had won for us grew dim. His sons, hitherto held under firm control, became more and more drunken and debauched. Moreover, each day added some new peril to their expeditions.

Except for the few trusty vassals whom we treated well, and who were all devoted to us, we were becoming more and more isolated and resourceless. People had left the neighbouring country in consequence of our violent depredations. The terror that we inspired pushed back daily the bounds of the desert around us. In making our ventures we had to go farther afield, even to the borders of the plain. There we had not the upper hand; and my Uncle Laurence, the boldest of us all, was dangerously wounded in a skirmish. Other schemes had to be devised. John suggested them. One was that we should slip into the fairs under various disguises, and exercise our skill in thieving. From brigands we became pick-pockets, and our detested name sank lower and lower in infamy. We formed a fellowship with the most noisome characters our province concealed, and, by an exchange of rascally services, once again managed to avoid destitution.

I say we, for I was beginning to take a place in this band of cutthroats when my grandfather died. He had yielded to my entreaties and allowed me to join in some of the last expeditions he attempted. I shall make no apologies; but here, gentlemen, you behold a man who has followed the profession of a bandit. I feel no remorse at the recollection, no more than a soldier would feel at having served a campaign under orders from his general. I thought that I was still living in the middle ages. The laws of the land, with all their strength and wisdom, were to me words devoid of meaning. I felt brave and full of vigour; fighting was a joy. Truly, the results of our victories often made me blush; but, as they in no way profited myself, I washed my hands of them. Nay, I remember with pleasure that I helped more than one victim who had been knocked down to get up and escape.

This existence, with its movement, its dangers, and its fatigues, had a numbing effect on me. It took me away from any painful reflections which might have arisen in my mind. Besides, it freed me from the immediate tyranny of John. However, after the death of my grandfather, when our band degraded itself to exploits of a different nature, I fell back under his odious sway. I was by no means fitted for lying and fraud. I displayed not only aversion but also incapacity for this new industry. Consequently my uncle looked upon me as useless, and began to maltreat me again. They would have driven me away had they not been afraid that I might make my peace with society, and become a dangerous enemy to themselves. While they were in doubt as to whether it was wiser to feed me or to live in fear of me, they often thought (as I have since learned) of picking a quarrel with me, and forcing a fight in which I might be got rid of. This was John's suggestion. Antony, however, who retained more of Tristan's energy and love of fair play at home than any of his brothers, proved clearly that I did more good than harm. I was, he declared, a brave fighter, and there was no knowing when they might need an extra hand. I might also be shaped into a swindler. I was very young and very ignorant; but John, perhaps, would endeavour to win me over by kindness, and make my lot less wretched. Above all, he might enlighten me as to my true position, by explaining that I was an outcast from society, and could not return to it without being hanged immediately. Then, perhaps, my obstinacy and pride would give way, out of regard to my own well-being on the one hand, and from necessity on the other. At all events, they should try this before getting rid of me.

"For," said Antony to round off his homily, "we were ten Mauprats last year; our father is dead, and, if we kill Bernard, we shall only be eight."

This argument gained the day. They brought me forth from the species of dungeon in which I had languished for several months; they gave me new clothes; they exchanged my old gun for a beautiful carbine that I had always coveted; they explained to me my position in the world; they honoured me with the best wine at meals. I promised to reflect, and meanwhile, became rather more brutalized by inaction and drunkenness than I had been by brigandage.

However, my captivity had made such a terrible impression on me that I took a secret oath to dare any dangers that might assail me on the territories of the King of France, rather than endure a repetition of that hideous experience. Nothing but a miserable point of honour now kept me at Roche-Mauprat. It was evident that a storm was gathering over our heads. The peasants were discontented, in spite of all our efforts to attach them to us; doctrines of independence were secretly insinuating themselves into their midst; our most faithful retainers were growing tired of merely having their fill of bread and meat; they were demanding money, and we had none. We had received more than one serious summons to pay our fiscal dues to the state, and as our private creditors had joined hands with the crown officers and the recalcitrant peasants, everything was threatening us with a catastrophe like that which had just overtaken the Seigneur de Pleumartin in our province.[2]

My uncles had long thought of making common cause with this country squire in his marauding expeditions and his resistance to authority. However, just as Pleumartin, about to fall into the hands of his enemies, had given his word of honour that he would welcome us as friends and allies if we went to his assistance, we had heard of his defeat and tragic end. Thus we ourselves were now on our guard night and day. It was a question of either fleeing the country or bracing ourselves for a decisive struggle. Some counselled the former alternative; the others declared their resolve to follow the advice of their dying father and to find a grave under the ruins of the keep. Any suggestion of flight or compromise they denounced as contemptible cowardice. The fear, then, of incurring such a reproach, and perhaps in some measure an instinctive love of danger, still kept me back. However, my aversion to this odious existence was only lying dormant, ready to break out violently at any moment.

One evening, after a heavy supper, we remained at table, drinking and conversing—God knows in what words and on what subject! It was

2   The reputation which the Seigneur de Pleumartin has left behind him in the province will preserve the story of Mauprat from the reproach of exaggeration. Pen would refuse to trace the savage obscenities and refinements of cruelty which marked the life of this madman, and which perpetuated the traditions of feudal brigandage in Berry down to the last days of the ancient monarchy. His chateau was besieged, and after a stubborn resistance he was taken and hanged. There are many people still living, nor yet very advanced in years, who knew the man.

frightful weather. The rain, driven through the broken windows, was running in streams across the stone floor of the hall; and the old walls were trembling in the storm. The night wind was whistling through chinks in the roof and making the flames of our resin torches flicker weirdly. During the meal my uncles had rallied me very much on what they called my virtue; they had treated my shyness in the presence of women as a sign of continence; and it was especially in this matter that they urged me to evil by ridiculing my modesty. While parrying these coarse gibes and making thrusts in the same strain, I had been drinking enormously. Consequently, my wild imagination had become inflamed, and I boasted that I would be bolder and more successful with the first woman brought to Roche-Mauprat than any of my uncles. The challenge was accepted amid roars of laughter. Peals of thunder sent back an answer to the infernal merriment.

All at once the horn was heard at the portcullis. Everybody stopped talking. The blast just blown was the signal used by the Mauprats to summon each other or make themselves known. It was my Uncle Laurence, who had been absent all day and who was now asking to be let in. We had so little confidence in others that we acted as our own turnkeys in the fortress. John rose and took down the keys, but he stopped immediately on hearing a second blast of the horn. This meant that Laurence was bringing in a prize, and that we were to go and meet him. In the twinkling of an eye all the Mauprats were at the portcullis, torch in hand—except myself, whose indifference at this moment was profound, and whose legs were seriously conscious of wine.

"If it is a woman," cried Antony as he went out, "I swear by the soul of my father that she shall be handed over to you, my valiant young man, and we'll see if your courage comes up to your conceit."

I remained with my elbows on the table, sunk in an uncomfortable stupor.

When the door opened again I saw a woman in a strange costume entering with a confident step. It required an effort to keep my mind from wandering, and to grasp what one of the Mauprats came and whispered to me. In the middle of a wolf-hunt, at which several of the nobles in the neighbourhood had been present with their wives, this young lady's horse had taken fright and bolted away from the rest of the field. When it had pulled up after a gallop of about a league, she had tried to find her way back; but, not knowing the Varenne district, where all the landmarks are so much alike, she had gone farther and farther astray. The storm and the advent of night had completed her perplexity. Laurence, happening to meet her, had offered to escort her to the chateau of Rochemaure, which, as a fact, was more than six leagues distant; but he had declared that it was quite near, and had pretended to be the gamekeeper there. She did not actually know the lady of Rochemaure, but being a distant connection of hers, she counted upon a welcome. Never having seen the face of a single Mauprat, and little dreaming that she was so near their haunt, she had followed her guide confidingly; and as she had never in her life caught a glimpse of Roche-Mauprat, whether in the distance or close at hand, she was led upon the scene of our orgies without having the least suspicion of the trap into which she had fallen.

When I rubbed my heavy eyes and beheld this woman, so young and so beautiful, with her expression of calm sincerity and of goodness, the like of which I had never seen on the brow of any other (for all those who had passed the portcullis of our abode were either insolent prostitutes or stupid victims), I could not but think I was dreaming.

Remembering how prominently fairies figured in my legends of chivalry, I almost fancied that Morgana or Urganda had come among us to administer justice; and, for the moment, I felt an inclination to throw myself on my knees and protest against any judgment which should confound me with my uncles. Antony, to whom Laurence had quickly given the cue, approached her with as much politeness as he had in his composition, and begged her to excuse his hunting costume, likewise that of his friends. They were all nephews or cousins of the lady of Rochemaure, whom they were now awaiting before sitting down to table. Being very religious, she was at present in the chapel, in pious conference with the chaplain. The air of simple confidence with which the stranger listened to these absurd lies went to my heart, but I had not a very clear idea of what I felt.

"Please," she said to my Uncle John, who was dancing attendance on her with the leer of a satyr, "please do not let me disturb this lady. I am so troubled about the anxiety I must be causing my father and my friends at the present moment, that I could not really stop here. All I ask is that she will be kind enough to lend me a fresh horse and a guide, so that I may return to the place where I presume my people may have gone to wait for me."

"Madame," replied John, with assurance, "it is impossible for you to start again in such weather as this; besides, if you did, that would only serve to delay the hour of rejoining those who are looking for you. Ten of our men, well mounted and provided with torches, shall set out this very moment in ten different directions and scour every corner of Varenne. Thus, in two hours at the most, your relatives will be certain to have news of you, and you will soon see them arriving here, where we will entertain them as best we can. Please, then, set your mind at rest, and take some cordial to restore you; for you must be wet through and quite exhausted."

"Were it not for the anxiety I feel," she answered with a smile, "I should be famished. I will try to eat something; but do not put yourselves to any inconvenience on my account. You have been far too good already."

Approaching the table, where I was still resting on my elbows, she took some fruit that was by my side without noticing me. I turned and stared at her insolently with a besotted expression. She returned my gaze haughtily—at least, so it appeared to me then. I have since learned that she did not even see me; for, while making a great effort to appear calm and to reply with an air of confidence to the offers of hospitality, she was at heart very much disturbed by the unexpected presence of so many strange men with their forbidding mien and rough garb. However, she did not suspect anything. I overheard one of the Mauprats near me saying to John:

"Good! It's all right; she is falling into the trap. Let us make her drink; then she will begin to talk."

"One moment," replied John; "watch her carefully; this is a serious matter; there is something better to be had out of this than a little passing pleasure. I am going to talk it over with the others; you will be sent for to give your opinion. Meanwhile keep an eye on Bernard."

"What is the matter?" I said abruptly, as I faced him. "Does not this girl belong to me? Did not Antony swear it by the soul of my grandfather?"

"Yes, confound it, that's true," said Antony, approaching our group, whilst the other Mauprats surrounded the lady. "Listen, Bernard; I will keep my word on one condition."

"What is that?"

"It is quite simple: that you won't within the next ten minutes tell this wench that she is not at old Rochemaure's."

"What do you take me for?" I answered, pulling my hat over my eyes. "Do you think that I am an idiot? Wait a minute; would you like me to go and get my grandmother's dress which is upstairs and pass myself off for this same lady of Rochemaure?"

"A splendid idea!" replied Laurence.

"But before anything is done," said John, "I want to speak to you all."

And making signs to the others, he drew them out of the hall. Just as they were going out I thought I noticed that John was trying to persuade Antony to keep watch over me. But Antony, with a firmness which I could not understand, insisted on following the rest. I was left alone with the stranger.

For a moment I remained bewildered, almost stupefied, and more embarrassed than pleased at the *tete-a-tete*. Then I endeavoured to think of some explanation of these mysterious things that were happening around me, and succeeded, as far as the fumes of the wine would allow me, in imagining something fairly probable, though, indeed, remote enough from the actual truth.

I thought I could account for everything I had just seen and heard by supposing, first, that the lady, quiet and richly dressed though she was, was one of those daughters of Bohemia that I had sometimes seen at fairs; secondly, that Laurence, having met her in the country, had brought her here to amuse the company; and, thirdly, that they had told her of my condition of swaggering drunkenness, and had prevailed on her to put my gallantry to the proof, whilst they were to watch me through the keyhole. My first movement, as soon as these ideas had taken possession of me, was to rise and go straight to the door. This I locked with a double turn and then bolted. When I had done this I returned to the lady, determined that I would not, at all events, give her cause to laugh at my bashfulness.

She was sitting close to the fire, and as she was occupied in drying her wet garments, leaning forward over the hearth, she had not taken any notice of what I was doing; but when I approached her the strange expression on my face caused her to start. I had made up my mind to kiss her, as a beginning; but, I know not by what miracle, as soon as she raised her eyes to mine, this familiarity became impossible. I only had sufficient courage to say:

"Upon my word, mademoiselle, you are a charming creature, and I love you—as true as my name is Bernard Mauprat."

"Bernard Mauprat!" she cried, springing up; "you are Bernard Mauprat, you? In that case, change your manner and learn to whom you are talking. Have they not told you?"

"No one has told me, but I can guess," I replied with a grin, while trying hard to trample down the feeling of respect with which her sudden pallor and imperious attitude inspired me.

"If you can guess," she said, "how is it possible that you allow yourself to speak to me in this way? But they were right when they said you were ill-mannered; and yet I always had a wish to meet you."

"Really!" I said, with the same hideous grin. "You! A princess of the king's highway, who have known so many men in your life? But let my lips meet your own, my sweet, and you shall see if I am not as nicely mannered as those uncles of mine whom you were listening to so willingly just now."

"Your uncles!" she cried, suddenly seizing her chair and placing it between us as if from some instinct of self-defence. "Oh, mon Dieu! mon Dieu! Then I am not at Madame de Rochemaure's?"

"Our name certainly begins in the same way, and we come of as good a rock as anybody."

"Roche-Mauprat!" she muttered, trembling from head to foot, like a hind when it hears the howl of wolves.

And her lips grew quite white. Her agony was manifest in every gesture. From an involuntary feeling of sympathy I shuddered myself, and I was on the point of changing my manner and language forthwith.

"What can there be in this to astound her so?" I asked myself. "Is she not merely acting a part? And even if the Mauprats are not hidden behind some wainscot listening to us, is she not sure to give them an account of everything that takes place? And yet she is trembling like an aspen leaf. But what if she is acting? I once saw an actress play Genevieve de Brabant, and she wept so that one might have been deceived."

I was in a state of great perplexity, and I cast harassed glances now at her, now at the doors, which I fancied every moment would be thrown wide open amid roars of laughter from my uncles.

This woman was beautiful as the day. I do not believe there has ever lived a woman as lovely as she. It is not I alone who say so; she has left a reputation for beauty which has not yet died out in her province. She was rather tall, slender, and remarkable for the easy grace of her movements. Her complexion was very fair, while her eyes were dark and her hair like ebony. Her glance and her smile showed a union of goodness and acuteness which it was almost impossible to conceive; it was as if Heaven had given her two souls, one wholly of intellect, the other wholly of feeling. She was naturally cheerful and brave—an angel, indeed, whom the sorrows of humanity had not yet dared to touch. She knew not what it was to suffer; she knew not what it was to distrust and dread. This, indeed, was the first trial of her life, and it was I, brute that I was, who made her undergo it. I took her for a gipsy, and she was an angel of purity.

She was my young cousin (or aunt, after the Breton fashion), Edmee de Mauprat, the daughter of M. Hubert, my great-uncle (again in the Breton fashion), known as the Chevalier—he who had sought release from the Order of Malta that he might marry, though already somewhat advanced in years. My cousin was the same age as myself; at least, there was a difference of only a few months between us. Both of us were now seventeen, and this was our first interview. She whom I ought to have protected at the peril of my life against the world was now standing before me trembling and terror-stricken, like a victim before the executioner.

She made a great effort, and approaching me as I walked about the hall deep in thought, she explained who she was, adding:

"It is impossible that you can be an infamous creature like all these brigands whom I have just seen, and of whose hideous life I have often heard. You are young; your mother was good and wise. My father wanted to adopt you and bring you up as his son. Even to-day he is still full of grief at not being able to draw you out of the abyss in which you lie. Have you not often received messages from him? Bernard, you and I are of the same family; think of the ties of blood; why would you insult me? Do they intend to assassinate me here or torture me? Why did they deceive me by saying that I was at Rochemaure? Why did they withdraw in this mysterious way? What are they preparing? What is going to happen?"

Her words were cut short by the report of a gun outside. A shot from the culverin replied to it, and the alarm trumpet shook the gloomy walls of the keep with its dismal note. Mademoiselle de Mauprat fell back into her chair. I remained where I was, wondering whether this was some new scene in the comedy they were enjoying at my expense. However, I resolved not to let the alarm cause me any uneasiness until I had certain proof that it was not a trick.

"Come, now," I said, going up to her again, "own that all this is a joke. You are not Mademoiselle de Mauprat at all; and you merely want to discover if I am an apprentice capable of making love."

"I swear by Christ," she answered, taking my hands in her own, which were cold as death, "that I am Edmee, your cousin, your prisoner—yes, and your friend; for I have always felt an interest in you; I have always implored my father not to cease his efforts for you. But listen, Bernard; they are fighting, and fighting with guns! It must be my father who has come to look for me, and they are going to kill him. Ah!" she cried, falling on her knees before me, "go and prevent that, Bernard! Tell your uncles to respect my father, the best of men, if you but knew! Tell them that, if they hate our family, if they must have blood, they may kill me! Let them tear my heart out; but let them respect my father . . ."

Some one outside called me in a violent voice.

"Where is the coward? Where is that wretched boy?" shouted my Uncle Laurence.

Then he shook the door; but I had fastened it so securely that it resisted all his furious blows.

"That miserable cur is amusing himself by making love while our throats are being cut! Bernard, the mounted police are attacking us! Your Uncle Louis had just been killed! Come and help us! For God's sake, come, Bernard!"

"May the devil take the lot of you," I cried, "and may you be killed yourself, if I believe a single word of all this. I am not such a fool as you imagine; the only cowards here are those who lie. Didn't I swear that the woman should be mine? I'm not going to give her up until I choose."

"To hell with you!" replied Laurence; "you are pretending . . ."

The shots rang out faster. Frightful cries were heard. Laurence left the door and ran in the direction of the noise. His eagerness proved him so much in earnest that I could no longer refuse to believe him. The thought that they would accuse me of cowardice overcame me. I advanced towards the door.

"O Bernard! O Monsieur de Mauprat!" cried Edmee, staggering after me; "let me go with you. I will throw myself at your uncles' feet; I will make them stop the fight; I will give them all I possess, my life, if they wish . . . if only they will spare my father."

"Wait a moment," I said, turning towards her; "I am by no means certain that this is not a joke at my expense. I have a suspicion that my uncles are there, behind that door, and that, while our whippers-in are firing off guns in the courtyard, they are waiting with a blanket to toss me. Now, either you are my cousin, or you are a . . . You must make me a solemn promise, and I will make you one in return. If you are one of these wandering charmers and I quit this room the dupe of your pretty acting, you must swear to be my mistress, and to allow none other near you until I have had my rights; otherwise, for my part, I swear that you shall be chastised, even as my spotted dog Flora was chastised this morning. If, on the other hand, you are Edmee, and I swear to intervene between your father and those who would kill him, what promise will you make me, what will you swear?"

"If you save my father," she cried, "I swear to you that I will marry you, I swear it."

"Ho! ho! indeed!" I said, emboldened by her enthusiasm, the sublimity of which I did not understand. "Give me a pledge, then, so that in any case I do not go out from here like a fool."

I took her in my arms and kissed her. She did not attempt to resist. Her cheeks were like ice. Mechanically she began to follow me as I moved to the door. I was obliged to push her back. I did so without roughness; but she fell as one in a faint. I began to grasp the gravity of my position; for there was nobody in the corridor and the tumult outside was becoming more and more alarming. I was about to run and get my weapons, when a last feeling of distrust, or it may have been another sentiment, prompted me to go back and double-lock the door of the hall where I was leaving Edmee. I put the key into my belt and hastened to the ramparts, armed with a gun, which I loaded as I ran.

It was simply an attack made by the mounted police, and had nothing whatever to do with Mademoiselle de Mauprat. A little while before our creditors had obtained a writ of arrest against us. The law officers, beaten and otherwise severely handled, had demanded of the King's advocate at the provincial court of Bourges another warrant of arrest. This the armed police were now doing their best to execute. They had hoped to effect an easy capture by means of a night surprise. But we were in a better state of defence than they had anticipated. Our men were brave and well armed; and then we were fighting for our very existence; we had the courage of despair, and this was an immense advantage. Our band amounted to twenty-four all told; theirs to more than fifty soldiers, in addition to a score or more of peasants, who were slinging stones from the flanks. These, however, did more harm to their allies than they did to us.

For half an hour the fighting was most desperate. At the end of this time the enemy had become so dismayed by our resistance that they fell back, and hostilities were suspended. However, they soon returned to the attack, and again were repulsed with loss. Hostilities were once more suspended. They then, for the third time, called upon us to surrender, promising that our lives should be spared. Antony Mauprat replied with an obscene jest. They remained undecided, but did not withdraw.

I had fought bravely; I had done what I called my duty. There was a long lull. It was impossible to judge the distance of the enemy, and we dared not fire at random into the darkness, for our ammunition was too precious. All my uncles remained riveted on the ramparts, in case of fresh attack. My Uncle Louis was dangerously wounded. Thoughts of my prisoner returned to my mind. At the beginning of the fight I had heard John Mauprat saying, that if our defeat seemed imminent, we must offer to hand her over to the enemy, on condition that they should raise the seige; that if they refused, we must hang her before their eyes. I had no longer any doubts about the truth of what she had told me. When victory appeared to declare for us they forgot the captive. But I noticed the crafty John quitting the culverin which he so loved to fire, and creeping away like a cat into the darkness. A feeling of ungovernable jealousy seized me. I threw down my gun and dashed after him, knife in hand, resolved, I believe, to stab him if he attempted to touch what I considered my booty. I saw him approach the door, try to open it, peer attentively through the keyhole, to assure himself that his prey had not escaped him. Suddenly shots were heard again. He sprang to his maimed feet with that marvellous agility of his, and limped off to the ramparts. For myself, hidden as I was by the darkness, I let him pass and did not follow. A passion other than the love of slaughter had just taken possession of me. A flash of jealousy had fired my senses. The smell of powder, the sight of blood, the noise, the danger, and the many bumpers of brandy we had passed round to keep up our strength had strangely heated my brain. I took the key from my belt and opened the door noisily. And now, as I stood before my captive again, I was no longer the suspicious and clumsy novice she had so easily moved to pity: I was the wild outlaw of Roche-Mauprat, a hundred times more dangerous than at first. She rushed towards me eagerly. I opened my arms to catch her; instead of being frightened she threw herself into them, exclaiming:

"Well! and my father?"

"Your father," I said, kissing her, "is not there. At the present moment there is no question either of him or of you. We have brought down a dozen gendarmes, that is all. Victory, as usual, is declaring for us. So, don't trouble yourself any more about your father; and I, I won't trouble myself further about the King's men. Let us live in peace and rejoice in love."

With these words I raised to my lips a goblet of wine which had been left on the table. But she took it out of my hands with an air of authority that made me all the bolder.

"Don't drink any more," she said; "think seriously of what you are saying. Is what you tell me true? Will you answer for it on your honour, on the soul of your mother?"

"Every word is true; I swear it by your pretty rosy lips," I replied, trying to kiss her again.

But she drew back in terror.

"Oh, mon Dieu!" she exclaimed, "he is drunk! Bernard! Bernard! remember what you promised; do not break your word. You have not forgotten, have you, that I am your kinswoman, your sister?"

"You are my mistress or my wife," I answered, still pursuing her.

"You are a contemptible creature!" she rejoined, repulsing me with her riding whip. "What have you done that I should be aught to you? Have you helped my father?"

"I swore to help him; and I would have helped him if he had been there; it is just the same, therefore, as if I really had. But, had he been there, and had I tried to save him and failed, do you know that for this treachery Roche-Mauprat could not have provided any instrument of torture cruel enough and slow enough to drag the life out of me inch by inch? For all I know, they may actually have heard my vow; I proclaimed it loudly enough. But what do I care? I set little store by a couple of days more or less of life. But I do set some store by your favour, my beauty. I don't want to be the languishing knight that every one laughs at. Come, now, love me at once; or, my word, I will return to the fight, and if I am killed, so much the worse for you. You will no longer have a knight to help you, and you will still have seven Mauprats to keep at bay. I'm afraid you are not strong enough for that rough work, my pretty little love-bird."

These words, which I threw out at random, merely to distract her attention so that I might seize her hands or her waist, made a deep impression on her. She fled to the other end of the hall, and tried to force open the window; but her little hands could not even move the heavy leaden sash in the rusty ironwork. Her efforts made me laugh. She clasped her hands in terror, and remained motionless. Then all at once the expression of her face changed. She seemed to have resolved how to act, and came toward me smiling and with outstretched hand. So beautiful was she thus that a mist came over my eyes and for a moment I saw her not.

Ah, gentlemen, forgive my childishness. I must tell you how she was dressed. After that weird night she never wore that costume again, and yet I can remember it so exactly. It is a long, long time ago. But were I to live as long as I have already lived again, I should not forget a single detail, so much was I struck by it amid the tumult that was raging within me and without; amid the din of shots striking the ramparts, the lightning flashes ripping the sky, and the violent palpitations which sent my blood surging from my heart to my brain, and from my head to my breast.

Oh, how lovely she was! It seems as if her shade were even now passing before my eyes. Yes; I fancy I see her in the same dress, the riding-habit which used to be worn in those days. The skirt of it was of cloth and very full; round the waist was a red sash, while a waistcoat of pearl-gray satin, fastened with buttons, fitted closely to the figure; over this was a hunting-jacket, trimmed with lace, short and open in front; the hat, of gray felt, with a broad brim turned up in front, was crowned with half a dozen red feathers. The hair, which was not powdered, was drawn back from the face and fell down in two long plaits, like those of the Bernese women. Edmee's were so long that they almost reached the ground.

Her garb, to me so strangely fascinating, her youth and beauty, and the favour with which she now seemed to regard my pretensions, combined to make me mad with love and joy. I could imagine nothing more beautiful than a lovely woman yielding without coarse words, and without tears of shame. My first impulse was to take her in my arms; but, as if overcome by that irresistible longing to worship which characterizes a first love, even with the grossest of beings, I fell down before her and pressed her knees to my breast; and yet, on my own supposition, it was to a shameless wanton that this homage was paid. I was none the less nigh to swooning from bliss.

She took my head between her two beautiful hands, and exclaimed:

"Ah, I was right! I knew quite well that you were not one of those reprobates. You are going to save me, aren't you? Thank God! How I thank you, O God! Must we jump from the window? Oh, I am not afraid; come—come!"

I seemed as if awakened from a dream, and, I confess, the awakening was not a little painful.

"What does this mean?" I asked, as I rose to my feet. "Are you still jesting with me? Do you not know where you are? Do you think that I am a child?"

"I know that I am at Roche-Mauprat," she replied, turning pale again, "and that I shall be outraged and assassinated in a couple of hours, if meanwhile I do not succeed in inspiring you with some pity. But I shall succeed," she cried, falling at my feet in her turn; "you are not one of those men. You are too young to be a monster like them. I could see from your eyes that you pitied me. You will help me to escape, won't you, won't you, my dear heart?"

She took my hands and kissed them frenziedly, in the hope of moving me. I listened and looked at her with a sullen stupidity scarcely calculated to reassure her. My heart was naturally but little accessible to feelings of generosity and compassion, and at this moment a passion stronger than all the rest was keeping down the impulse she had striven to arouse. I devoured her with my eyes, and made no effort to understand her words. I only wished to discover whether I was pleasing to her, or whether she was trying to make use of me to effect her escape.

"I see that you are afraid," I said. "You are wrong to be afraid of me. I shall certainly not do you any harm. You are too pretty for me to think of anything but of caressing you."

"Yes; but your uncles will kill me," she cried; "you know they will. Surely you would not have me killed? Since you love me, save me; I will love you afterwards."

"Oh, yes; afterwards, afterwards," I answered, laughing with a silly, un-believing air; "after you have had me hanged by those gendarmes to whom I have just given such a drubbing. Come, now; prove that you love me at once; I will save you afterwards. You see, I can talk about 'afterwards' too."

I pursued her round the room. Though she fled from me, she gave no signs of anger, and still appealed to me with soft words. In me the poor girl was husbanding her one hope, and was fearful of losing it. Ah, if I had only been able to realize what such a woman as she was, and what my own position meant! But I was unable then. I had but one fixed idea—the idea which a wolf may have on a like occasion.

At last, as my only answer to all her entreaties was, "Do you love me, or are you fooling me?" she saw what a brute she had to deal with, and, making up her mind accordingly, she came towards me, threw her arms round my neck, hid her face in my bosom, and let me kiss her hair. Then she put me gently from her, saying:

"Ah, mon Dieu! don't you see how I love you—how I could not help loving you from the very first moment I saw you? But don't you understand that I hate your uncles, and that I would be yours alone?"

"Yes," I replied, obstinately, "because you say to yourself: 'This is a booby whom I shall persuade to do anything I wish, by telling him that I love him; he will believe it, and I will take him away to be hanged.' Come; there is only one word which will serve if you love me."

She looked at me with an agonized air. I sought to press my lips to hers whenever her head was not turned away. I held her hands in mine. She was powerless now to do more than delay the hour of her defeat. Suddenly the colour rushed back to the pale face; she began to smile; and with an expression of angelic coquetry, she asked:

"And you—do you love me?"

From this moment the victory was hers. I no longer had power to will what I wished. The lynx in me was subdued; the man rose in its place; and I believe that my voice had a human ring, as I cried for the first time in my life:

"Yes, I love you! Yes, I love you!"

"Well, then," she said, distractedly, and in a caressing tone, "let us love each other and escape together."

"Yes, let us escape," I answered. "I loathe this house, and I loathe my uncles. I have long wanted to escape. And yet I shall only be hanged, you know."

"They won't hang you," she rejoined with a laugh; "my betrothed is a lieutenant-general."

"Your betrothed!" I cried, in a fresh fit of jealousy more violent than the first. "You are going to be married?"

"And why not?" she replied, watching me attentively.

I turned pale and clinched my teeth.

"In that case, . . ." I said, trying to carry her off in my arms.

"In that case," she answered, giving me a little tap on the cheek, "I see that you are jealous; but his must be a particular jealousy who at ten o'clock yearns for his mistress, only to hand her over at midnight to eight drunken men who will return her to him on the morrow as foul as the mud on the roads."

"Ah, you are right!" I exclaimed. "Go, then; go. I would defend you to the last drop of my blood; but I should be vanquished by numbers, and I should die with the knowledge that you were left to them. How horrible! I shudder to think of it. Come—you must go."

"Yes! yes, my angel!" she cried, kissing me passionately on the cheek.

These caresses, the first a woman had given me since my childhood, recalled, I know not how or why, my mother's last kiss, and, instead of pleasure, caused me profound sadness. I felt my eyes filling with tears. Noticing this, she kissed my tears, repeating the while:

"Save me! Save me!"

"And your marriage?" I asked. "Oh! listen. Swear that you will not marry before I die. You will not have to wait long; for my uncles administer sound justice and swift, as they say."

"You are not going to follow me, then?" she asked.

"Follow you? No; it is as well to be hanged here for helping you to escape as to be hanged yonder for being a bandit. Here, at least, I avoid a twofold shame: I shall not be accounted an informer, and shall not be hanged in a public place."

"I will not leave you here," she cried, "though I die myself. Fly with me. You run no risk, believe me. Before God, I declare you are safe. Kill me, if I lie. But let us start—quickly. O God! I hear them singing. They are coming this way. Ah, if you will not defend me, kill me at once!"

She threw herself into my arms. Love and jealousy were gradually overpowering me. Indeed, I even thought seriously of killing her; and I kept my hand on my hunting-knife as long as I heard any noise or voices near the hall. They were exulting in their victory. I cursed Heaven for not giving it to our foes. I clasped Edmee to my breast, and we remained motionless in each other's arms, until a fresh report announced that the fight was beginning again. Then I pressed her passionately to my heart.

"You remind me," I said, "of a poor little dove which one day flew into my jacket to escape from a kite, and tried to hide itself in my bosom."

"And you did not give it up to the kite, did you?" asked Edmee.

"No, by all the devils! not any more than I shall give you up, you, the prettiest of all the birds in the woods, to these vile night-birds that are threatening you."

"But how shall we escape?" she cried, terror-stricken by the volleys they were firing.

"Easily," I said. "Follow me."

I seized a torch, and lifting a trap-door, I made her descend with me to the cellar. Thence we passed into a subterranean passage hollowed out of the rock. This, in bygone days had enabled the garrison, then more numerous, to venture upon an important move in case of an attack; some of the besieged would emerge into the open country on the side opposite the portcullis and fall on the rear of the besiegers, who were thus caught between two fires. But many years had passed since the garrison of Roche-Mauprat was large enough to be divided into two bodies; and besides, during the night it would have been folly to venture beyond the walls. We arrived, therefore, at the exit of the passage without meeting with any obstacle. But at the last moment I was seized with a fit of madness. I threw down my torch, and leaned against the door.

"You shall not go out from here," I said to the trembling Edmee, "without promising to be mine."

We were in darkness; the noise of the fight no longer reached us. Before any one could surprise us here we had ample time to escape. Everything was in my favour. Edmee was now at the mercy of my caprice. When she saw that the seductions of her beauty could no longer rouse me to ecstasy, she ceased to implore, and drew backward a few steps.

"Open the door," she said, "and go out first, or I will kill myself. See, I have your hunting-knife. You left it by the side of the trap-door. To return to your uncles you will have to walk through my blood."

Her resolute manner frightened me.

"Give me that knife," I said, "or, be the consequences what they may, I will take it from you by force."

"Do you think I am afraid to die?" she said calmly. "If this knife had only been in my hand yonder in the chateau, I should not have humbled myself before you."

"Confound it!" I cried, "you have deceived me. Your love is a sham. Begone! I despise you. I will not follow such as you."

At the same time I opened the door.

"I would not go without you," she cried; "and you—you would not have me go without dishonour. Which of us is the more generous?"

"You are mad," I said. "You have lied to me; and you do not know what to do to make a fool of me. However, you shall not go out from here without swearing that your marriage with the lieutenant-general or any other man shall not take place before you have been my mistress."

"Your mistress!" she said. "Are you dreaming? Could you not at least soften the insult by saying your wife?"

"That is what any one of my uncles would say in my place; because they would care only about your dowry. But I—I yearn for nothing but your beauty. Swear, then, that you will be mine first; afterwards you shall be free, on my honour. And if my jealousy prove so fierce that it may not be borne, well, since a man may not go from his word, I will blow my brains out."

"I swear," said Edmee, "to be no man's before being yours."

"That is not it. Swear to be mine before being any other's."

"It is the same thing," she answered. "Yes; I swear it."

"On the gospel? On the name of Christ? By the salvation of your soul? By the memory of your mother?"

"On the gospel; in the name of Christ; by the salvation of my soul; by the memory of my mother."

"Good."

"One moment," she rejoined; "I want you to swear that my promise and its fulfilment shall remain a secret; that my father shall never know it, or any person who might tell him."

"No one in the world shall hear it from me. Why should I want others to know, provided only that you keep your word?"

She made me repeat the formula of an oath. Then we hurried forth into the open, holding each other's hands as a sign of mutual trust.

But now our flight became dangerous. Edmee feared the besiegers almost as much as the besieged. We were fortunate enough not to meet any. Still, it was by no means easy to move quickly. The night was so dark that we were continually running against trees, and the ground was so slippery that we were unable to avoid falls. A sudden noise made us start; but, from the rattle of the chain fixed on its foot, I immediately recognised my grandfather's horse, an animal of an extraordinary age, but still strong and spirited. It was the very horse that had brought me to Roche-Mauprat ten years before. At present the only thing that would serve as a bridle was the rope round its neck. I passed this through its mouth, and I threw my jacket over the crupper and helped my companion to mount; I undid the chain, sprang on the animal's back, and urging it on desperately, made it set off at a gallop, happen what might. Luckily for us, it knew the paths better than I, and, as if by instinct, followed their windings without knocking against any trees. However, it frequently slipped, and in recovering itself, gave us such jolts that we should have lost our seats a thousand times (equipped as we were) had we not been hanging between life and death. In such a strait desperate ventures are best, and God protects those whom man pursues. We were congratulating ourselves on being out of danger, when all at once the horse struck against a stump, and catching his hoof in a root on the ground, fell down. Before we were up he had made off into the darkness, and I could hear him galloping farther and farther away. As we fell I had caught Edmee in my arms. She was unhurt. My own ankle, however, was sprained so severely that it was impossible for me to move a step. Edmee thought that my leg had been broken. I was inclined to think so myself, so great was the pain; but soon I thought no further either of my agony or my anxiety. Edmee's tender solicitude made me forget everything. It was in vain that I urged her to continue her flight without me. I pointed out that she could now escape alone; that we were some distance from the chateau; that day would soon be breaking; that she would be certain to find some house, and that everywhere the people would protect her against the Mauprats.

"I will not leave you," she persisted in answering. "You have devoted yourself to me; I will show the same devotion to you. We will both escape, or we will die together."

"I am not mistaken," I cried; "it is a light that I see between the branches. Edmee, there is a house yonder; go and knock at the door. You need not feel anxious about leaving me here; and you will find a guide to take you home."

"Whatever happens," she said, "I will not leave you; but I will try to find some one to help you."

"Yet, no," I said, "I will not let you knock at that door alone. That light, in the middle of the night, in a house situated in the heart of the woods, may be a lure."

I dragged myself as far as the door. It felt cold, as if of metal. The walls were covered with ivy.

"Who is there?" cried some one within, before we had knocked.

"We are saved!" cried Edmee; "it is Patience's voice."

"We are lost!" I said; "he and I are mortal enemies."

"Fear nothing," she said; "follow me. It was God that led us here."

"Yes, it was God that led you here, daughter of Heaven, morning star!" said Patience, opening the door; "and whoever is with you is welcome too at Gazeau Tower."

We entered under a surbased vault, in the middle of which hung an iron lamp. By the light of this dismal luminary and of a handful of brushwood which was blazing on the hearth we saw, not without surprise, that Gazeau Tower was exceptionally honoured with visitors. On one side the light fell upon the pale and serious face of a man in clerical garb. On the other, a broad-brimmed hat overshadowed a sort of olive-green cone terminating in a scanty beard; and on the wall could be seen the shadow of a nose so distinctly tapered that nothing in the world might compare with it except, perhaps, a long rapier lying across the knees of the personage in question, and a little dog's face which, from its pointed shape, might have been mistaken for that of a gigantic rat. In fact, it seemed as if a mysterious harmony reigned between these three salient points—the nose of Don Marcasse, his dog's snout, and the blade of his sword. He got up slowly and raised his hand to his hat. The Jansenist cure did the same. The dog thrust its head forward between its master's legs, and, silent like him, showed its teeth and put back its ears without barking.

"Quiet, Blaireau!" said Marcasse to it.

VII

No sooner had the cure recognised Edmee than he started back with an exclamation of surprise. But this was nothing to the stupefaction of Patience when he had examined my features by the light of the burning brand that served him as torch.

"The lamb in the company of the wolf!" he cried. "What has happened, then?"

"My friend," replied Edmee, putting, to my infinite astonishment, her little white hand into the sorcerer's big rough palm, "welcome him as you welcome me. I was a prisoner at Roche-Mauprat, and it was he who rescued me."

"May the sins of his fathers be forgiven him for this act!" said the cure.

Patience took me by the arm, without saying anything, and led me nearer the fire. They seated me on the only chair in the house, and the cure took upon himself the task of attending to my leg, while Edmee gave an account, up to a certain point, of our adventure. Then she asked for information about the hunt and about her father. Patience, however, could give her no news. He had heard the horn in the woods, and the firing at the wolves had disturbed his tranquility several times during the day. But since the storm broke over them the noise of the wind had drowned all other sounds, and he knew nothing of what was taking place in Varenne. Marcasse, meanwhile, had very nimbly climbed a ladder which served as an approach to the upper stories of the house, now that the staircase was broken. His dog followed him with marvellous skill. Soon they came down again, and we learned that a red light could be distinguished on the horizon in the direction of Roche-Mauprat. In spite of the loathing I had for this place and its owners, I could not repress a feeling very much like consternation on hearing that the hereditary manor which bore my own name had apparently been taken and set on fire. It meant disgrace, defeat; and this fire was as a seal of vassalage affixed to my arms by those I called clodhoppers and serfs. I sprang up from my chair, and had I not been held back by the violent pain in my foot, I believe I should have rushed out.

"What is the matter?" said Edmee, who was by my side at the time.

"The matter is," I answered abruptly, "that I must return yonder; for it is my duty to get killed rather than let my uncles parley with the rabble."

"The rabble!" cried Patience, addressing me for the first time since I arrived. "Who dares to talk of rabble here? I myself am of the rabble. It is my title, and I shall know how to make it respected."

"By Jove! Not by me," I said, pushing away the cure, who had made me sit down again.

"And yet it would not be for the first time," replied Patience, with a contemptuous smile.

"You remind me," I answered, "that we two have some old accounts to settle."

And heedless of the frightful agony caused by my sprain, I rose again, and with a backhander I sent Don Marcasse, who was endeavouring the play the cure's part of peacemaker, head over heels into the middle of the ashes. I did not mean him any harm, but my movements were somewhat rough, and the poor man was so frail that to my hand he was but as a weasel would have been to his own. Patience was standing before me with his arms crossed, in the attitude of a stoic philosopher, but the fire was flashing in his eyes. Conscious of his position as my host, he was evidently waiting until I struck the first blow before attempting to crush me. I should not have kept him waiting long, had not Edmee, scorning the danger of interfering with a madman, seized my arm and said, in an authoritative tone:

"Sit down again, and be quiet; I command you."

So much boldness and confidence surprised and pleased me at the same time. The rights which she arrogated to herself over me were, in some measure, a sanction of those I claimed to have over her.

"You are right," I answered, sitting down.

And I added, with a glance at Patience:

"Some other time."

"Amen," he answered, shrugging his shoulders.

Marcasse had picked himself up with much composure, and shaking off the ashes with which he was covered, instead of finding fault with me, he tried, after his fashion to lecture Patience. This was in reality by no means easy to do; yet nothing could have been less irritating than that monosyllabic censure throwing out its little note in the thick of a quarrel like an echo in a storm.

"At your age," he said to his host; "not patient at all. Wholly to blame—yes—wrong—you!"

"How naughty you are!" Edmee said to me, putting her hand on my shoulder; "do not begin again, or I shall go away and leave you."

I willingly let myself be scolded by her; nor did I realize that during the last minutes we had exchanged parts. The moment we crossed the threshold of Gazeau Tower she had given evidence of that superiority over me which was really hers. This wild place, too, these strange witnesses, this fierce host, had already furnished a taste of the society into which I had entered, and whose fetters I was soon to feel.

"Come," she said, turning to Patience, "we do not understand each other here; and, for my part, I am devoured by anxiety about my poor father, who is no doubt searching for me, and wringing his hands at this very moment. My good Patience, do find me some means of rejoining him with this unfortunate boy, whom I dare not leave to your care, since you have not sufficient love for me to be patient and compassionate with him."

"What do you say?" said Patience, putting his hand to his brow as if waking from a dream. "Yes, you are right; I am an old brute, an old fool. Daughter of God, tell this boy, this nobleman, that I ask his pardon for the past, and that, for the present, my poor cell is at his disposal. Is that well said?"

"Yes, Patience," answered the cure. "Besides, everything may be managed. My horse is quiet and steady, and Mademoiselle de Mauprat can ride it, while you and Marcasse lead it by the bridle. For myself, I will remain here with our invalid. I promise to take good care of him and not to annoy him in any way. That will do, won't it, Monsieur Bernard? You don't bear me any ill-will, and you may be very sure that I am not your enemy."

"I know nothing about it," I answered; "it is as you please. Look after my cousin; take her home safely. For my own part, I need nothing and care for no one. A bundle of straw and a glass of wine, that is all I should like, if it were possible to have them."

"You shall have both," said Marcasse, handing me his flask, "but first of all here is something to cheer you up. I am going to the stable to get the horse ready."

"No, I will go myself," said Patience; "you see to the wants of this young man."

And he passed into another lower hall, which served as a stable for the cure's horse during the visits which the good priest paid him. They brought the animal through the room where we were; and Patience, after arranging the cure's cloak on the saddle, with fatherly care helped Edmee to mount.

"One moment," she said, before letting them lead her out. "Monsieur le Cure, will you promise me on the salvation of your soul not to leave my cousin before I return with my father to fetch him?"

"I promise solemnly," replied the cure.

"And you, Bernard," said Edmee, "will you give me your word of honour to wait for me here?"

"I can't say," I answered; "that will depend on the length of your absence and on my patience; but you know quite well, cousin, that we shall meet again, even if it be in hell; and for my part, the sooner the better."

By the light of the brand which Patience was holding to examine the horse's harness, I saw her beautiful face flush and then turn pale. Then she raised her eyes which had been lowered in sorrow, and looked at me fixedly with a strange expression.

"Are we ready to start?" said Marcasse, opening the door.

"Yes, forward," said Patience, taking the bridle. "Edmee, my child, take care to bend down while passing under the door."

"What is the matter, Blaireau?" said Marcasse, stopping on the threshold and thrusting out the point of his sword, gloriously rusted by the blood of the rodent tribe.

Blaireau did not stir, and if he had not been born dumb, as his master said, he would have barked. But he gave warning as usual by a sort of dry cough. This was his most emphatic sign of anger and uneasiness.

"There must be something down there," said Marcasse; and he boldly advanced into the darkness, after making a sign to the rider not to follow. The report of firearms made us all start. Edmee jumped down lightly from her horse, and I did not fail to notice that some impulse at once prompted her to come and stand behind my chair. Patience rushed out of the tower. The cure ran to the frightened horse, which was rearing and backing toward us. Blaireau managed to bark. I forgot my sprain, and in a single bound I was outside.

A man covered with wounds, and with the blood streaming from him, was lying across the doorway. It was my Uncle Laurence. He had been mortally wounded at the siege of Roche-Mauprat, and had come to die under our eyes. With him was his brother Leonard, who had just fired his last pistol shot at random, luckily without hitting any one. Patience's first impulse was to prepare to defend himself. On recognising Marcasse, however, the fugitives, far from showing themselves hostile, asked for shelter and help. As their situation was so desperate no one thought that assistance should be refused. The police were pursuing them. Roche-Mauprat was in flames; Louis and Peter had died fighting; Antony, John, and Walter had fled in another direction, and, perhaps, were already prisoners. No words would paint the horror of Laurence's last moments. His agony was brief but terrible. His blasphemy made the cure turn pale. Scarce had the door been shut and the dying man laid on the floor than the horrible death-rattle was heard. Leonard, who knew of no remedy but brandy, snatched Marcasse's flask out of my hand (not without swearing and scornfully reproaching me for my flight), forced open his brother's clinched teeth with the blade of his hunting-knife, and, in spite of our warning, poured half the flask down his throat. The wretched man bounded into the air, brandished his arms in desperate convulsions, drew himself up to his full height, and fell back stone dead upon the blood-stained floor. There was no time to offer up a prayer over the body, for the door resounded under the furious blows of our assailants.

"Open in the King's name!" cried several voices; "open to the police!"

"Help! help!" cried Leonard, seizing his knife and rushing towards the door. "Peasants, prove yourselves nobles! And you, Bernard, atone for your fault; wash out your shame; do not let a Mauprat fall into the hands of the gendarmes alive!"

Urged on by native courage and by pride, I was about to follow his example, when Patience rushed at him, and exerting his herculean strength, threw him to the ground. Putting one knee on his chest, he called to Marcasse to open the door. This was done before I could take my uncle's part against his terrible assailant. Six gendarmes at once rushed into the tower and, with their guns pointed, bade us move at our peril.

"Stay, gentlemen," said Patience, "don't harm any one. This is your prisoner. Had I been alone with him, I should either have defended him or helped him to escape; but there are honest people here who ought not to suffer for a knave; and I did not wish to expose them to a fight. Here is the Mauprat. Your duty, as you know, is to deliver him safe and sound into the hands of justice. This other is dead."

"Monsieur, surrender!" said the sergeant of the gendarmes, laying his hand on Leonard.

"Never shall a Mauprat drag his name into the dock of a police court," replied Leonard, with a sullen expression. "I surrender, but you will get nothing but my skin."

And he allowed himself to be placed in a chair without making any resistance.

But while they were preparing to bind him he said to the cure:

"Do me one last kindness, Father. Give me what is left in the flask; I am dying of thirst and exhaustion."

The good cure handed him the flask, which he emptied at a draught. His distorted face took on an expression of awful calm. He seemed absorbed, stunned, incapable of resistance. But as soon as they were engaged in binding his feet, he snatched a pistol from the belt of one of the gendarmes and blew his brains out.

This frightful spectacle completely unnerved me. Sunk in a dull stupor, no longer conscious of what was happening around me, I stood there as if turned to stone, and it was only after some minutes that I realized that I was the subject of a serious discussion between the police and my hosts. One of the gendarmes declared that he recognised me as a Hamstringer Mauprat. Patience declared that I was nothing but M. Hubert de Mauprat's gamekeeper, in charge of his daughter. Annoyed at the discussion, I was about to make myself known when I saw a ghost rise by my side. It was Edmee. She had taken refuge between the wall and the cure's poor frightened horse, which, with outstretched legs and eyes of fire, made her a sort of rampart with its body. She was as pale as death, and her lips were so compressed with horror that at first, in spite of desperate efforts to speak, she was unable to express herself otherwise than by signs. The sergeant, moved by her youth and her painful situation, waited with deference until she could manage to make herself understood. At last she persuaded them not to treat me as a prisoner, but to take me with her to her father's chateau, where she gave her word of honour that satisfactory explanations and guarantees would be furnished on my account. The cure and the other witnesses, having pledged their words to this, we set out all together, Edmee on the sergeant's horse, he on an animal belonging to one of his men, myself on the cure's, Patience and the cure afoot between us, the police on either side, and Marcasse in front, still impassive amid the general terror and consternation. Two of the gendarmes remained behind to guard the bodies and prepare a report.

VIII

We had travelled about a league through the woods. Wherever other paths had crossed our own, we had stopped to call aloud; for Edmee, convinced that her father would not return home without finding her, had implored her companions to help her to rejoin him. To this shouting the gendarmes had been very averse, as they were afraid of being discovered and attacked by bodies of the fugitives from Roche-Mauprat. On our way they informed us that this den had been captured at the third assault. Until then the assailants had husbanded their forces. The officer in command of the gendarmes was anxious to get possession of the keep without destroying it; and, above all, to take the defenders alive. This, however, was impossible on account of the desperate resistance they made. The besiegers suffered so severely in their second attempt that they found themselves compelled to adopt extreme measures or to retreat. They therefore set the outer buildings on fire, and in the ensuing assault put forth all their strength. Two Mauprats were killed while fighting on the ruins of their bastion; the other five disappeared. Six men were dispatched in pursuit of them in one direction, six in another. Traces of the fugitives had been discovered immediately, and the men who gave us these details had followed Laurence and Leonard so closely that several of their shots had hit the former only a short distance from Gazeau Tower. They had heard him cry that he was done for; and, as far as they could see, Leonard had carried him to the sorcerer's door. This Leonard was the only one of my uncles who deserved any pity, for he was the only one who might, perhaps, have been encouraged to a better kind of life. At times there was a touch of chivalry in his brigandage, and his savage heart was capable of affection. I was deeply moved, therefore, by his tragic death, and let myself be carried along mechanically, plunged in gloomy thoughts, and determined to end my days in the same manner should I ever be condemned to the disgrace he had scorned to endure.

All at once the sound of horns and the baying of hounds announced the approach of a party of huntsmen. While we, on our side, were answering with shouts, Patience ran to meet them. Edmee, longing to see her father again, and forgetting all the horrors of this bloody night, whipped up her horse and reached the hunters first. As soon as we came up with them, I saw Edmee in the arms of a tall man with a venerable face. He was richly dressed; his hunting-coat, with gold lace over all the seams, and the magnificent Norman horse, which a groom was holding behind him, so struck me that I thought I was in the presence of a prince. The signs of love which he was showing his daughter were so new to me that I was inclined to deem them exaggerated and unworthy of the dignity of a man. At the same time they filled me with a sort of brute jealousy; for it did not occur to my mind that a man so splendidly dressed could be my uncle. Edmee was speaking to him in a low voice, but with great animation. Their conversation lasted a few moments. At the end of it the old man came and embraced me cordially. Everything about these manners seemed so new to me, that I responded neither by word nor gesture to the protestations and caresses of which I was the object. A tall young man, with a handsome face, as elegantly dressed as M. Hubert, also came and shook my hand and proffered thanks; why, I could not understand. He next entered into a discussion with the gendarmes, and I gathered that he was the lieutenant-general of the province, and that he was ordering them to set me at liberty for the present, that I might accompany my uncle to his chateau, where he undertook to be responsible for me. The gendarmes then left us, for the chevalier and the lieutenant-general were sufficiently well escorted by their own men not to fear attack from any one. A fresh cause of astonishment for me was to see the chevalier bestowing marks of warm friendship on Patience and Marcasse. As for the cure, he was upon a footing of equality with these seigneurs. For some months he had been

chaplain at the chateau of Saint-Severe, having previously been compelled
to give up his living by the persecutions of the diocesan clergy.

All this tenderness of which Edmee was the object, this family affection so completely new to me, the genuinely cordial relations existing between respectful plebeians and kindly patricians—everything that I now
saw and heard seemed like a dream. I looked on with a sensation that
it was all unintelligible to me. However, soon after our caravan started
my brain began to work; for I then saw the lieutenant-general (M. de la
Marche) thrust his horse between Edmee's and my own, as if he had a
right to be next to her. I remembered her telling me at Roche-Mauprat
that he was her betrothed. Hatred and anger at once surged up within me,
and I know not what absurdity I should have committed, had not Edmee,
apparently divining the workings of my unruly soul, told him that she
wanted to speak to me, and thus restored me to my place by her side.

"What have you to say to me?" I asked with more eagerness than
politeness.

"Nothing," she answered in an undertone. "I shall have much to say
later. Until then will you do everything I ask of you?"

"And why the devil should I do everything you ask of me, cousin?"

For a moment she hesitated to reply; then, making an effort, she said:

"Because it is thus that a man proves to a woman that he loves her."

"Do you believe that I don't love you?" I replied abruptly.

"How should I know?" she said.

This doubt astonished me very much, and I tried to combat it after
my fashion.

"Are you not beautiful?" I said; "and am not I a young man? Perhaps
you think I am too much of a boy to notice a woman's beauty; but now that
my head is calm, and I am sad and quite serious, I can assure you that I
am even more deeply in love with you than I thought. The more I look at
you the more beautiful you seem. I did not think that a woman could be
so lovely. I tell you I shall not sleep till . . ."

"Hold your tongue," she said sharply.

"Oh, I suppose you are afraid that man will hear me," I answered,
pointing to M. de la Marche. "Have no fear; I know how to keep my
word; and, as you are the daughter of a noble house, I hope you know how
to keep yours."

She did not reply. We had reached a part of the road where it was
only possible for two to walk abreast. The darkness was profound, and
although the chevalier and the lieutenant-general were at our heels, I was
going to make bold to put my arm round her waist, when she said to me,
in a sad and weary voice:

"Cousin, forgive me for not talking to you. I'm afraid I did not quite understand what you said. I am so exhausted that I feel as if I were going to die. Luckily, we have reached home now. Promise me that you will love my father, that you will yield to all his wishes, that you will decide nothing without consulting me. Promise me this if you would have me believe in your friendship."

"Oh, my friendship? you are welcome not to believe in that," I answered; "but you must believe in my love. I promise everything you wish. And you, will you not promise me anything? Do, now, with a good grace."

"What can I promise that is not yours?" she said in a serious tone. "You saved my honour; my life belongs to you."

The first glimmerings of dawn were now beginning to light the horizon. We had reached the village of Saint-Severe, and soon afterward we entered the courtyard of the chateau. On dismounting from her horse Edmee fell into her father's arms; she was as pale as death. M. de la Marche uttered a cry, and helped to carry her away. She had fainted. The cure took charge of me. I was very uneasy about my fate. The natural distrust of the brigand sprang up again as soon as I ceased to be under the spell of her who had managed to lure me from my den. I was like a wounded wolf; I cast sullen glances about me, ready to rush at the first being who should stir my suspicions by a doubtful word or deed. I was taken into a splendid room, and a meal, prepared with a luxury far beyond anything I could have conceived, was immediately served. The cure displayed the kindest interest in me; and, having succeeded in reassuring me a little, he went to attend to his friend Patience. The disturbed state of my mind and my remnant of uneasiness were not proof against the generous appetite of youth. Had it not been for the respectful assiduity of a valet much better dressed than myself, who stood behind my chair, and whose politeness I could not help returning whenever he hastened to anticipate my wants, I should have made a terrific breakfast; as it was, the green coat and silk breeches embarrassed me considerably. It was much worse when, going down on his knees, he set about taking off my boots preparatory to putting me to bed. For the moment I thought he was playing a trick upon me, and came very near giving him a good blow on the head; but his manner was so serious as he went through this task that I sat and stared at him in amazement.

At first, at finding myself in bed without arms, and with people entering and leaving my room always on tip-toe, I again began to feel suspicious. I took advantage of a moment when I was alone to get out of bed and take from the table, which was only half cleared, the longest knife I could find. Feeling easier in my mind, I returned to bed and fell into a sound sleep, with the knife firmly clasped in my hand.

When I awoke again the rays of the setting sun, softened by my red damask curtains, were falling on my beautifully fine sheets and lighting up the golden pomegranates that adorned the corners of the bed. This bed was so handsome and soft that I felt inclined to make it my apologies for having slept in it. As I was about to get up I saw a kindly, venerable face looking through the half-drawn curtains and smiling. It was the Chevalier Hubert de Mauprat. He inquired anxiously about the state of my health. I endeavoured to be polite and to express my gratitude; but the language I used seemed so different from his that I was disconcerted and pained at my awkwardness without being able to realize why. To crown my misery, a movement that I made caused the knife which I had taken as bedfellow to fall at M. de Mauprat's feet. He picked it up, looked at it, and then at myself with extreme surprise. I turned as red as fire and stammered out I know not what. I expected he would reprove me for this insult to his hospitality. However, he was too polite to insist upon a more complete ex-planation. He quietly placed the knife on the mantel-piece and, returning to me, spoke as follows:

"Bernard, I now know that I owe to you the life that I hold dearest in the world. All my own life shall be devoted to giving you proofs of my gratitude and esteem. My daughter also is sacredly indebted to you. You need, then, have no anxiety about your future. I know what persecution and vengeance you exposed yourself to in coming to us; but I know, too, from what a frightful existence my friendship and devotion will be able to deliver you. You are an orphan, and I have no son. Will you have me for your father?"

I stared at the chevalier with wild eyes. I could not believe my ears. All feeling within me seemed paralyzed by astonishment and timidity. I was unable to answer a word. The chevalier himself evidently felt some aston-ishment; he had not expected to find a nature so brutishly ill-conditioned.

"Come," he said; "I hope that you will grow accustomed to us. At all events, shake hands, to show that you trust me. I will send up your servant; give him your orders; he is at your disposal. I have only one promise to ex-act from you, and that is that you will not go beyond the walls of the park until I have taken steps to make you safe from the pursuit of justice. At present it is possible that the charges which have been hanging over your uncles' heads might be made to fall on your own."

"My uncles!" I exclaimed, putting my hand to my brow. "Is this all a hideous dream? Where are they? What has become of Roche-Mauprat?"

"Roche-Mauprat," he answered, "has been saved from the flames. Only a few of the outer buildings have been destroyed; but I undertake to repair the house and to redeem your fief from the creditors who claim it. As to your uncles . . . you are probably the sole heir of a name that it behoves you to rehabilitate."

"The sole heir?" I cried. "Four Mauprats fell last night; but the other three . . ."

"The fifth, Walter, perished in his attempt to escape. His body was discovered this morning in the pond of Les Froids. Neither John nor Antony has been caught, but the horse belonging to one and a cloak of the other's, found near the spot where Walter's body was lying, seem to hint darkly that their fate was as his. Even if one of them manages to escape, he will never dare make himself known again, for there would be no hope for him. And since they have drawn down upon their heads the inevitable storm, it is best, both for themselves and for us, who unfortunately bear the same name, that they should have come to this tragic end—better to have fallen weapon in hand, than to have suffered an infamous death upon the gallows. Let us bow to what God has ordained for them. It is a stern judgment; seven men in the pride of youth and strength summoned in a single night to their terrible reckoning! . . . We must pray for them, Bernard, and by dint of good works try to make good the evil they have done, and remove the stains they have left on our escutcheon."

These concluding words summed up the chevalier's whole character. He was pious, just, and full of charity; but, with him, as with most nobles, the precepts of Christian humility were wont to fall before the pride of rank. He would gladly have had a poor man at his table, and on Good Friday, indeed, he used to wash the feet of twelve beggars; but he was none the less attached to all the prejudices of our caste. In trampling under foot the dignity of man, my cousins, he considered, had, as noblemen, been much more culpable than they would have been as plebeians. On the latter hypothesis, according to him, their crimes would not have been half so grave. For a long time I shared the conviction myself; it was in my blood, if I may use the expression. I lost it only in the stern lessons of my destiny.

He then confirmed what his daughter had told me. From my birth he had earnestly desired to undertake my education. But his brother Tristan had always stubbornly opposed this desire. There the chevalier's brow darkened.

"You do not know," he said, "how baneful have been the consequences of that simple wish of mine—baneful for me, and for you too. But that must remain wrapped in mystery—a hideous mystery, the blood of the Atridae. . . ."

He took my hand, and added, in a broken voice:

"Bernard, we are both of us victims of a vicious family. This is not the moment to pile up charges against those who in this very hour are standing before the terrible tribunal of God; but they have done me an irreparable wrong—they have broken my heart. The wrong they have done you shall be repaired—I swear it by the memory of your mother. They have deprived you of education; they have made you a partner in their brigandage; yet your soul has remained great and pure as was the soul of the angel who gave you birth. You will correct the mistakes which others made in your childhood; you will receive an education suitable to your rank. And then, Bernard, you will restore the honour of your family. You will, won't you? Promise me this, Bernard. It is the one thing I long for. I will throw myself at your knees if so I may win your confidence; and I shall win it, for Providence has destined you to be my son. Ah, once it was my dream that you should be more completely mine. If, when I made my second petition, they had granted you to my loving care, you would have been brought up with my daughter and you would certainly have become her husband. But God would not have it so. You have now to begin your education, whereas hers is almost finished. She is of an age to marry; and, besides, her choice is already made. She loves M. de la Marche; in fact, their marriage is soon to take place. Probably she had told you."

I stammered out a few confused words. The affection and generous ideas of this noble man had moved me profoundly, and I was conscious of a new nature, as it were, awakening within me. But when he pronounced the name of his future son-in-law, all my savage instincts rose up again, and I felt that no principle of social loyalty would make me renounce my claim to her whom I regarded as my fairly won prize. I grew pale; I grew red; I gasped for breath. Luckily, we were interrupted by the Abbe Aubert (the Jansenist cure), who came to inquire how I was after my fall. Then for the first time the chevalier heard of my accident; an incident that had escaped him amid the press of so many more serious matters. He sent for his doctor at once, and I was overwhelmed with kind attentions, which seemed to me rather childish, but to which I submitted from a sense of gratitude.

I had not dared to ask the chevalier for any news of his daughter. With the abbe, however, I was bolder. He informed me that the length and uneasiness of her sleep were causing some anxiety; and the doctor, when he returned in the evening to dress my ankle, told me that she was very feverish, and that he was afraid she was going to have some serious illness.

For a few days, indeed, she was ill enough to cause anxiety. In the terrible experience she had gone through she had displayed great energy; but the reaction was correspondingly violent. For myself, I was also kept to my bed. I could not take a step without feeling considerable pain, and the doctor threatened that I should be laid up for several months if I did not submit to inaction for a few days. As I was otherwise in vigorous health, and had never been ill in my life, the change from any active habits to this sluggish captivity caused me indescribable *ennui*. Only those who have lived in the depths of woods, and experienced all the hardships of a rough life, can understand the kind of horror and despair I felt on finding myself shut up for more than a week between four silk curtains. The luxuriousness of my room, the gilding of my bed, the minute attentions of the lackeys, everything, even to the excellence of the food—trifles which I had somewhat appreciated the first day—became odious to me at the end of twenty-four hours. The chevalier paid me affectionate but short visits; for he was absorbed by the illness of his darling daughter. The abbe was all kindness. To neither did I dare confess how wretched I felt; but when I was alone I felt inclined to roar like a caged lion; and at night I had dreams in which the moss in the woods, the curtain of forest trees, and even the gloomy battlements of Roche-Mauprat, appeared to me like an earthly paradise. At other times, the tragic scenes that had accompanied and followed my escape were reproduced so vividly by my memory that, even when awake, I was a prey to a sort of delirium.

A visit from M. de la Marche stirred my ideas to still wilder disorder. He displayed the deepest interest in me, shook me by the hand again and again, and implored my friendship, vowed a dozen times that he would lay down his life for me, and made I don't know how many other protestations which I scarcely heard, for his voice was like a raging torrent in my ears, and if I had had my hunting-knife I believe I should have thrown myself upon him. My rough manners and sullen looks astonished him very much; but, the abbe having explained that my mind was disturbed by the terrible events which had happened in my family, he renewed his protestations, and took leave of me in the most affectionate and courteous manner.

This politeness which I found common to everybody, from the master of the house to the meanest of his servants, though it struck me with admiration, yet made me feel strangely ill at ease; for, even if it had not been inspired by good-will towards me, I could never have brought myself to understand that it might be something very different from real goodness. It bore so little resemblance to the facetious braggadocio of the Mauprats, that it seemed to me like an entirely new language, which I understood but could not speak.

However, I recovered the power of speech when the abbe announced that he was to have charge of my education, and began questioning me about my attainments. My ignorance was so far beyond anything he could have imagined that I was getting ashamed to lay it all bare; and, my savage pride getting the upper hand, I declared that I was a gentleman, and had no desire to become a clerk. His only answer was a burst of laughter, which offended me greatly. He tapped me quickly on the shoulder, with a good-natured smile, saying that I should change my mind in time, but that I was certainly a funny fellow. I was purple with rage when the chevalier entered. The abbe told him of our conversation and of my little speech. M. Hubert suppressed a smile.

"My boy," he said, in a kind tone, "I trust I may never do anything to annoy you, even from affection. Let us talk no more about work to-day. Before conceiving a taste for it you must first realize its necessity. Since you have a noble heart you can not but have a sound mind; the desire for knowledge will come to you of itself. And now to supper. I expect you are hungry. Do you like wine?"

"Much better than Latin," I replied.

"Come, abbe," he continued laughingly, "as a punishment for having played the pedant you must drink with us. Edmee is now quite out of danger. The doctor has said that Bernard can get up and walk a few steps. We will have supper served in this room."

The supper and wine were so good, indeed, that I was not long in getting tipsy, according to the Roche-Mauprat custom. I even saw they aided and abetted, in order to make me talk, and show at once what species of boor they had to deal with. My lack of education surpassed anything they had anticipated; but I suppose they augured well from my native powers; for, instead of giving me up, they laboured at the rough block with a zeal which showed at least that they were not without hope. As soon as I was able to leave my room I lost the feeling of *ennui*. The abbe was my inseparable companion through the whole first day. The length of the second was diminished by the hope they gave me of seeing Edmee on the morrow, and by the kindness I experienced from every one. I began to feel the charm of these gentle manners in proportion as I ceased to be astonished at them. The never-failing goodness of the chevalier could not but overcome my boorishness; nay, more, it rapidly won my heart. This was the first affection of my life. It took up its abode in me side by side with a violent love for his daughter, nor did I even dream of pitting one of these feelings against the other. I was all yearning, all instinct, all desire. I had the passions of a man in the soul of a child.

IX

At last, one morning after breakfast, Mr. Hubert took me to see his daughter. When the door of her room was opened I felt almost suffocated by the warm-scented air which met me. The room itself was charming in its simplicity; the curtains and coverings of chintz, with a white ground. Large china vases filled with flowers exhaled a delicate perfume. African birds were sporting in a gilded cage, and singing their sweet little love songs. The carpet was softer to the feet than is the moss of the woods in the month of March. I was in such a state of agitation that my eyes grew more and more dim every moment. My feet caught in one another most awkwardly, and I kept stumbling against the furniture without being able to advance. Edmee was lying on a long white chair, carelessly fingering a mother-of-pearl fan. She seemed to me even more beautiful than before, yet so changed that a feeling of apprehension chilled me in the middle of my ecstasy. She held out her hand to me; I did not like to kiss it in the presence of her father. I could not hear what she was saying to me—I believe her words were full of affection. Then, as if overcome with fatigue, she let her head fall back on the pillow and closed her eyes.

"I have some work to do," said the chevalier to me. "Stay here with her; but do not make her talk too much, for she is still very weak."

This recommendation really seemed a sarcasm. Edmee was pretending to be sleepy, perhaps to conceal some of the embarrassment that weighed on her heart; and, as for myself, I felt so incapable of overcoming her reserve that it was in reality a kindness to counsel silence.

The chevalier opened a door at one end of the room and closed it after him; but, as I could hear him cough from time to time, I gathered that his study was separated from his daughter's room only by a wooden partition. Still, it was bliss to be alone with her for a few moments, as long as she appeared to be asleep. She did not see me, and I could gaze on her at will. So pale was she that she seemed as white as her muslin dressing-gown, or as her satin slippers with their trimming of swan's down. Her delicate, transparent hand was to my eyes like some unknown jewel. Never before had I realized what a woman was; beauty for me had hitherto meant youth and health, together with a sort of manly hardihood. Edmee, in her riding-habit, as I first beheld her, had in a measure displayed such beauty, and I had understood her better then. Now, as I studied her afresh, my very ideas, which were beginning to get a little light from without, all helped to make this second *tete-a-tete* very different from the first.

But the strange, uneasy pleasure I experienced in gazing on her was disturbed by the arrival of a duenna, a certain Mademoiselle Leblanc, who performed the duties of lady's maid in Edmee's private apartments, and filled the post of companion in the drawing-room. Perhaps she had received orders from her mistress not to leave us. Certain it is that she took her place by the side of the invalid's chair in such a way as to present to my disappointed gaze her own long, meagre back, instead of Edmee's beautiful face. Then she took some work out of her pocket, and quietly began to knit. Meanwhile the birds continued to warble, the chevalier to cough, Edmee to sleep or to pretend to sleep, while I remained at the other end of the room with my head bent over the prints in a book that I was holding upside down.

After some time I became aware that Edmee was not asleep, and that she was talking to her attendant in a low voice. I fancied I noticed the latter glancing at me from time to time out of the corner of her eye in a somewhat stealthy manner. To escape the ordeal of such an examination, and also from an impulse of cunning, which was by no means foreign to my nature, I let my head fall on the book, and the book on the pier-table, and in this posture I remained as if buried in sleep or thought. Then, little by little, their voices grew louder, until I could hear what they were saying about me.

"It's all the same; you have certainly have chosen a funny sort of page, mademoiselle."

"A page, Leblanc! Why do you talk such nonsense? As if one had pages nowadays! You are always imagining we are still in my grandmother's time. I tell you he is my father's adopted son."

"M. le Chevalier is undoubtedly quite right to adopt a son; but where on earth did he fish up such a creature as that?"

I gave a side glance at them and saw that Edmee was laughing behind her fan. She was enjoying the chatter of this old maid, who was supposed to be a wag and allowed perfect freedom of speech. I was very much hurt to see my cousin was making fun of me.

"He looks like a bear, a badger, a wolf, a kite, anything rather than a man," continued Leblanc. "What hands! what legs! And now he has been cleaned up a little, he is nothing to what he was! You ought to have seen him the day he arrived with his smock and his leather gaiters; it was enough to take away one's breath."

"Do you think so?" answered Edmee. "For my part, I preferred him in his poacher's garb. It suited his face and figure better."

"He looked like a bandit. You could not have looked at him properly, mademoiselle."

"Oh! yes, I did."

The tone in which she pronounced these words, "Yes, I did," made me shudder; and somehow I again felt upon my lips the impress of the kiss she had given me at Roche-Mauprat.

"It would not be so bad if his hair were dressed properly," continued the duenna; "but, so far, no one had been able to persuade him to have it powdered. Saint-Jean told me that just as he was about to put the powder puff to his head he got up in a rage and said, 'Anything you like except that confounded flour. I want to be able to move my head about without coughing and sneezing.' Heavens, what a savage!"

"Yet, in reality, he is quite right. If fashion did not sanction the absurdity, everybody would perceive that it is both ugly and inconvenient. Look and see if it is not more becoming to have long black hair like his?"

"Long hair like that? What a mane. It is enough to frighten one."

"Besides, boys do not have their hair powdered, and he is still a boy."

"A boy? My stars! what a brat Boys? Why he would eat them for his breakfast; he's a regular ogre. But where does the hulking dog spring from? I suppose M. le Chevalier brought him here from behind some plough. What is his name again? . . . You did tell me his name, didn't you?"

"Yes, inquisitive; I told you he is called Bernard."

"Bernard! And nothing else?"

"Nothing, for the present. What are you looking at?"

"He is sleeping like a dormouse. Look at the booby. I was wondering whether he resembled M. le Chevalier. Perhaps it was a momentary error—a fit of forgetfulness with some milk-maid."

"Come, come, Leblanc; you are going too far . . ."

"Goodness gracious, mademoiselle, has not M. le Chevalier been young like any other man? And that does not prevent virtue coming on with years, does it?"

"Doubtless your own experience has shown you that this is possible. But listen: don't take upon yourself to make fun of this young man. It is possible that you have guessed right; but my father requires him to be treated as one of the family."

"Well, well; that must be pleasant for you, mademoiselle. As for myself, what does it matter to me? I have nothing to do with the gentleman."

"Ah, if you were thirty years younger."

"But did your father consult you, mademoiselle, before planting yon great brigand in your room?"

"Why ask such a question? Is there anywhere in the world a better father than mine?"

"But you are very good also. . . . There are many young ladies who would have been by no means pleased."

"And why, I should like to know? There is nothing disagreeable about the fellow. When he has been polished a little . . ."

"He will always be perfectly ugly."

"My dear Leblanc, he is far from ugly. You are too old; you are no longer a judge of young men."

Their conversation was interrupted by the chevalier, who came in to look for a book.

"Mademoiselle Leblanc is here, is she?" he said in a very quiet tone. "I thought you were alone with my son. Well, Edmee, have you had a talk with him? Did you tell him that you would be his sister? Are you pleased with her, Bernard?"

Such answers as I gave could compromise no one. As a rule, they consisted of four or five incoherent words crippled by shame. M. de Mauprat returned to his study, and I had sat down again, hoping that my cousin was going to send away her duenna and talk to me. But they exchanged a few words in a whisper; the duenna remained, and two mortal hours passed without my daring to stir from my chair. I believe Edmee really was asleep this time. When the bell rang for dinner her father came in again to fetch me, and before leaving her room he said to her again:

"Well, have you had a chat?"

"Yes, father, dear," she replied, with an assurance that astounded me.

My cousin's behaviour seemed to me to prove beyond doubt that she had merely been trifling with me, and that she was not afraid of my reproaches. And yet hope sprang up again when I remembered the strain in which she had spoken of me to Mademoiselle Leblanc. I even succeeded in persuading myself that she feared arousing her father's suspicions, and that she was now feigning complete indifference only to draw me the more surely to her arms as soon as the favourable moment had arrived. As it was impossible to ascertain the truth, I resigned myself to waiting. But days and nights passed without any explanation being sent, or any secret message bidding me be patient. She used to come down to the drawing-room for an hour in the morning; in the evening she was present at dinner, and then would play piquet or chess with her father. During all this time she was so well watched that I could not exchange a glance with her. For the rest of the day she remained in her own room—inaccessible. Noticing that I was chafing at the species of captivity in which I was compelled to live, the chevalier frequently said to me:

"Go and have a chat with Edmee. You can go to her room and tell her that I sent you."

But it was in vain that I knocked. No doubt they had heard me coming and had recognised me by my heavy shuffling step. The door was never opened to me. I grew desperate, furious.

Here I must interrupt the account of my personal impressions to tell you what was happening at this time in the luckless Mauprat family. John and Antony had really managed to escape, and though a very close search had been made for them, they had not as yet been captured. All their property was seized, and an order issued by the courts for the sale of the Roche-Mauprat fief. As it proved, however, a sale was unnecessary. M. Hubert de Mauprat put an end to the proceedings by coming forward as purchaser. The creditors were paid off, and the title-deeds of Roche-Mauprat passed into his hands.

The little garrison kept by the Mauprats, made up of adventurers of the lowest type, had met the same fate as their masters. As I have already said, the garrison had long been reduced to a few individuals. Two or three of these were killed, others took to flight; one only was captured. This man was tried and made to suffer for all. A serious question arose as to whether judgment should not also be given against John and Antony de Mauprat by default. There was apparently no doubt that they had fled; the pond in which Walter's body was found floating had been drained, yet no traces of the bodies had been discovered. The chevalier, however, for the sake of the name he bore, strove to prevent the disgrace of an ignomini-ous sentence; as if such a sentence could have added aught to the horror of the name of Mauprat. He brought to bear all M. de la Marche's influence and his own (which was very real in the province, especially on account of his high moral character), to hush up the affair, and he succeeded. As for myself, though I had certainly had a hand in more than one of my uncles' robberies, there was no thought of discussing me even at the bar of public opinion. In the storm of anger that my uncles had aroused people were pleased to consider me simply as a young captive, a victim of their cruelty, and thoroughly well disposed towards everybody. Certainly, in his gener-ous good nature and desire to rehabilitate the family, the chevalier greatly exaggerated my merits, and spread a report everywhere that I was an angel of sweetness and intelligence.

On the day that M. Hubert became purchaser of the estate he entered my room early in the morning accompanied by his daughter and the abbe. Showing me the documents which bore witness to his sacrifice (Roche-Mauprat was valued at about two hundred thousand francs), he declared that I was forthwith going to be put in possession not only of my share in the inheritance, which was by no means considerable, but also of half the revenue of the property. At the same time, he said, the whole estate, lands

MAUPRAT

and produce, should be secured to me by his will on one condition, namely, that I would consent to receive an education suitable to my position.

The chevalier had made all these arrangements in the kindness of his heart and without ostentation, partly out of gratitude for the service he knew I had rendered Edmee, and partly from family pride; but he had not expected that I should prove so stubborn on the question of education. I cannot tell you the irritation I felt at this word "condition"; especially as I thought I detected in it signs of some plan that Edmee had formed to free herself from her promise to me.

"Uncle," I answered, after listening to all his magnificent offers in absolute silence, "I thank you for all you wish to do for me; but it is not right that I should avail myself of your kindness. I have no need of a fortune. A man like myself wants nothing but a little bread, a gun, a hound, and the first inn he comes to on the edge of the wood. Since you are good enough to act as my guardian pay me the income on my eighth of the fief and do not ask me to learn that Latin bosh. A man of birth is sufficiently well educated when he knows how to bring down a snipe and sign his name. I have no desire to be seigneur of Roche-Mauprat; it is enough to have been a slave there. You are most kind, and on my honour I love you; but I have very little love for conditions. I have never done anything from interested motives. I would rather remain an ignoramus than develop a pretty wit for another's dole. Moreover, I could never consent to make such a hole in my cousin's fortune; though I know perfectly well that she would willingly sacrifice a part of her dowry to obtain release from . . ."

Edmee, who until now had remained very pale and apparently heedless of my words, all at once cast a lightning glance at me and said with an air of unconcern:

"To obtain a release from what, may I ask, Bernard?"

I saw that, in spite of this show of courage, she was very much perturbed; for she broke her fan while shutting it. I answered her with a look in which the artless malice of the rustic must have been apparent:

"To obtain release, cousin, from a certain promise you made me at Roche-Mauprat."

She grew paler than ever, and on her face I could see an expression of terror, but ill-disguised by a smile of contempt.

"What was the promise you made him, Edmee?" asked the chevalier, turning towards her ingenuously.

At the same time the abbe pressed my arm furtively, and I understood that my cousin's confessor was in possession of the secret.

I shrugged my shoulders; their fears did me an injustice, though they roused my pity.

"She promised me," I replied, with a smile, "that she would always look upon me as a brother and a friend. Were not those your words, Edmee, and do you think it is possible to make them good by mere money?"

She rose as if filled with new life, and, holding out her hand to me, said in a voice full of emotion:

"You are right, Bernard; yours is a noble heart, and I should never forgive myself if I doubted it for a moment."

I caught sight of a tear on the edge of her eye-lid, and I pressed her hand somewhat too roughly, no doubt, for she could not restrain a little cry, followed, however, by a charming smile. The chevalier clasped me to his breast, and the abbe rocked about in his chair and exclaimed repeatedly:

"How beautiful! How noble! How very beautiful! Ah," he added, "that is something that cannot be learnt from books," turning to the chevalier. "God writes his words and breathes forth his spirit upon the hearts of the young."

"You will see," said the chevalier, deeply moved, "that this Mauprat will yet build up the honour of the family again. And now, my dear Bernard, I will say no more about business. I know how I ought to act, and you cannot prevent me from taking such steps as I shall think fit to insure the rehabilitation of my name by yourself. The only true rehabilitation is guaranteed by your noble sentiments; but there is still another which I know you will not refuse to attempt—the way to this lies through your talents and intelligence. You will make the effort out of love for us, I hope. However, we need not talk of this at present. I respect your proud spirit, and I gladly renew my offers without conditions. And now, abbe, I shall be glad if you will accompany me to the town to see my lawyer. The carriage is waiting. As for you, children, you can have lunch together. Come, Bernard, offer your arm to your cousin, or rather, to your sister. You must acquire some courtesy of manner, since in her case it will be but the expression of your heart."

"That is true, uncle," I answered, taking hold of Edmee's arm somewhat roughly to lead her downstairs.

I could feel her trembling; but the pink had returned to her cheeks, and a smile of affection was playing about her lips.

As soon as we were seated opposite each other at table our happy harmony was chilled in a very few moments. We both returned to our former state of embarrassment. Had we been alone I should have got out of the difficulty by one of those abrupt sallies which I knew how to force from myself when I grew too much ashamed of my bashfulness; but the presence of Saint-Jean, who was waiting upon us, condemned me to silence on the subject next to my heart. I decided, therefore, to talk about Patience. I asked her how it came to pass that she was on such good terms with him, and in what light I ought to look upon the pretended sorcerer. She gave me the main points in the history of the rustic philosopher, and explained that it was the Abbe Aubert who had taken her to Gazeau Tower. She had been much struck by the intelligence and wisdom of the stoic hermit, and used to derive great pleasure from conversation with him. On his side, Patience had conceived such a friendship for her that for some time he had relaxed his strict habits, and would frequently pay her a visit when he came to see the abbe.

As you may imagine, she had no little difficulty in making these explanations intelligible to me. I was very much surprised at the praise she bestowed on Patience, and at the sympathy she showed for his revolutionary ideas. This was the first time I had heard a peasant spoken of as a man. Besides, I had hitherto looked upon the sorcerer of Gazeau Tower as very much below the ordinary peasant, and here was Edmee praising him above most of the men she knew, and even siding with him against the nobles. From this I drew the comfortable conclusion that education was not so essential as the chevalier and the abbe would have me believe.

"I can scarcely read any better than Patience," I added, "and I only wish you found as much pleasure in my society as in his; but it hardly appears so, cousin, for since I came here . . ."

We were then leaving the table, and I was rejoicing at the prospect of being alone with her at last, so that I might talk more freely, when on going into the drawing-room we found M. de la Marche there. He had just arrived, and was in the act of entering by the opposite door. In my heart I wished him at the devil.

M. de la March was one of the fashionable young nobles of the day. Smitten with the new philosophy, devoted to Voltaire, a great admirer of Franklin, more well-meaning than intelligent, understanding the oracles less than he desired or pretended to understand them; a pretty poor logician, since he found his ideas much less excellent and his political hopes much less sweet on the day that the French nation took it into its head to realize them; for the rest, full of fine sentiments, believing himself much more sanguine and romantic than he was in reality; rather more faithful to the prejudices of caste and considerably more sensitive to the opinion of the world than he flattered and prided himself on being—such was the man. His face was certainly handsome, but I found it excessively dull; for I had conceived the most ridiculous animosity for him. His polished manners seemed to me abjectly servile with Edmee. I should have blushed to imitate them, and yet my sole aim was to surpass him in the little services he rendered her. We went out into the park. This was very large, and through it ran the Indre, here merely a pretty stream. During our walk he made himself agreeable in a thousand ways; not a violet did he see but he must pluck it to offer to my cousin. But, when we arrived at the banks of the stream, we found that the plank which usually enabled one to cross at this particular spot had been broken and washed away by the storms of a few days before. Without asking permission, I immediately took Edmee in my arms, and quietly walked through the stream. The water came up to my waist, but I carried my cousin at arm's length so securely and skilfully that she did not wet a single ribbon. M. de la Marche, unwilling to appear more delicate than myself, did not hesitate to wet his fine clothes and follow me, though with some rather poor efforts the while to force a laugh. However, though he had not any burden to carry, he several times stumbled over the stones which covered the bed of the river, and rejoined us only with great difficulty. Edmee was far from laughing. I believe that this proof of my strength and daring, forced on her in spite of herself, terrified her as an evidence of the love she had stirred in me. She even appeared to be annoyed; and, as I set her down gently on the bank, said:

"Bernard, I must request you never to play such a prank again."

"That is all very well," I said; "you would not be angry if it were the other fellow."

"He would not think of doing such a thing," she replied.

"I quite believe it," I answered; "he would take very good care of that. Just look at the chap. . . . And I—I did not ruffle a hair of your head. He is very good at picking violets; but, take my word for it, in a case of danger, don't make him your first choice."

M. de la Marche paid me great compliments on this exploit. I had hoped that he would be jealous; he did not even appear to dream of it, but rather made merry over the pitiable state of his toilet. The day was excessively hot, and we were quite dry before the end of the walk. Edmee, however, remained sad and pensive. It seemed to me that she was making an effort to show me as much friendship as at luncheon. This affected me considerably; for I was not only enamoured of her—I loved her. I could not make the distinction then, but both feelings were in me—passion and tenderness.

The chevalier and the abbe returned in time for dinner. They conversed in a low voice with M. de la Marche about the settlement of my affairs, and, from the few words which I could not help overhearing, I gathered that they had just secured my future on the bright lines they had laid before me in the morning. I was too shy and proud to express my simple thanks. This generosity perplexed me; I could not understand it, and I almost suspected that it was a trap they were preparing to separate me from my cousin. I did not realize the advantage of a fortune. Mine were not the wants of a civilized being; and the prejudices of rank were with me a point of honour, and by no means a social vanity. Seeing that they did not speak to me openly, I played the somewhat ungracious part of feigning complete ignorance.

Edmee grew more and more melancholy. I noticed that her eyes rested now on M. de la Marche, now on her father, with a vague uneasiness. Whenever I spoke to her, or even raised my voice in addressing others, she would start and then knit her brows slightly, as if my voice had caused her physical pain. She retired immediately after dinner. Her father followed her with evident anxiety.

"Have you not noticed," said the abbe, turning to M. de la Marche, as soon as they had left the room, "that Mademoiselle de Mauprat has very much changed of late?"

"She has grown thinner," answered the lieutenant-general; "but in my opinion she is only the more beautiful for that."

"Yes; but I fear she may be more seriously ill than she owns," replied the abbe. "Her temperament seems no less changed than her face; she has grown quite sad."

"Sad? Why, I don't think I ever saw her so gay as she was this morning; don't you agree with me, Monsieur Bernard? It was only after our walk that she complained of a slight headache."

"I assure you that she is really sad," rejoined the abbe. "Nowadays, when she is gay, her gaiety is excessive; at such a time there seems to be something strange and forced about her which is quite foreign to her usual manner. Then the next minute she relapses into a state of melancholy, which I never noticed before the famous night in the forest. You may be certain that night was a terrible experience."

"True, she was obliged to witness a frightful scene at Gazeau Tower," said M. de la Marche; "and then she must have been very much exhausted and frightened when her horse bolted from the field and galloped right through the forest. Yet her pluck is so remarkable that . . . What do you think, my dear Monsieur Bernard? When you met her in the forest, did she seem very frightened?"

"In the forest?" I said. "I did not meet her in the forest at all."

"No; it was in Varenne that you met her, wasn't it?"

The abbe hastened to intervene. . . . "By-the-bye, Monsieur Bernard, can you spare me a minute to talk over a little matter connected with your property at . . ."

Hereupon he drew me out of the drawing-room, and said in a low voice:

"There is no question of business; I only want to beg of you not to let a single soul, not even M. de la Marche, suspect that Mademoiselle de Mauprat was at Roche-Mauprat for the fraction of a second."

"And why?" I asked. "Was she not under my protection there? Did she not leave it pure, thanks to me? Must it not be well known to the neighbourhood that she passed two hours there?"

"At present no one knows," he answered. "At the very moment she left it, Roche-Mauprat fell before the attack of the police, and not one of its inmates will return from the grave or from exile to proclaim the fact. When you know the world better, you will understand how important it is for the reputation of a young lady that none should have reason to suppose that even a shadow of danger has fallen upon her honour. Meanwhile, I implore you, in the name of her father, in the name of the affection for her which you expressed this morning in so noble and touching a manner . . ."

"You are very clever, Monsieur l'Abbe," I said, interrupting him. "All your words have a hidden meaning which I can grasp perfectly well, clown as I am. Tell my cousin that she may set her mind at ease. I have nothing to say against her virtue, that is very certain; and I trust I am not capable of spoiling the marriage she desires. Tell her that I claim but one thing of her, the fulfilment of that promise of friendship which she made me at Roche-Mauprat."

"In your eyes, then, that promise has a peculiar solemnity?" said the abbe. "If so, what grounds for distrusting it have you?"

I looked at him fixedly, and as he appeared very much agitated, I took a pleasure in keeping him on the rack, hoping that he would repeat my words to Edmee.

"None," I answered. "Only I observe that you are afraid that M. de la Marche may break off the marriage, if he happens to hear of the adventure at Roche-Mauprat. If the gentleman is capable of suspecting Edmee, and of grossly insulting her on the eve of his wedding, it seems to me that there is one very simple means of mending matters."

"What would you suggest?"

"Why, to challenge him and kill him."

"I trust you will do all you can to spare the venerable M. Hubert the necessity of facing such a hideous danger."

"I will spare him this and many others by taking upon myself to avenge my cousin. In truth, this is my right, Monsieur l'Abbe. I know the duties of a gentleman quite as well as if I had learnt Latin. You may tell her this from me. Let her sleep in peace. I will keep silence, and if that is useless I will fight."

"But, Bernard," replied the abbe in a gentle, insinuating tone, "have you thought of your cousin's affection for M. de la Marche?"

"All the more reason that I should fight him," I cried, in a fit of anger.

And I turned my back on him abruptly.

The abbe retailed the whole of our conversation to the penitent. The part that the worthy priest had to play was very embarrassing. Under the seal of confession he had been intrusted with a secret to which in his conversations with me he could make only indirect allusions, to bring me to understand that my pertinacity was a crime, and that the only honourable course was to yield. He hoped too much of me. Virtue such as this was beyond my power, and equally beyond my understanding.

X

A few days passed in apparent calm. Edmee said she was unwell, and rarely quitted her room. M. de la Marche called nearly every day, his chateau being only a short distance off. My dislike for him grew stronger and stronger in spite of all the politeness he showed me. I understood nothing whatever of his dabblings in philosophy, and I opposed all his opinions with the grossest prejudices and expressions at my command. What consoled me in a measure for my secret sufferings was to see that he was no more admitted than myself to Edmee's rooms.

For a week the sole event of note was that Patience took up his abode in a hut near the chateau. Ever since the Abbe Aubert had found a refuge from ecclesiastical persecution under the chevalier's roof, he had no longer been obliged to arrange secret meetings with the hermit. He had, therefore, strongly urged him to give up his dwelling in the forest and to come nearer to himself. Patience had needed a great deal of persuasion. Long years of solitude had so attached him to his Gazeau Tower that he hesitated to desert it for the society of his friend. Besides, he declared that the abbe would assuredly be corrupted with commerce with the great; that soon, unknown to himself, he would come under the influence of the old ideas, and that his zeal for the sacred cause would grow cold. It is true that Edmee had won Patience's heart, and that, in offering him a little cottage belonging to her father situated in a picturesque ravine near the park gate, she had gone to work with such grace and delicacy that not even his techy pride could feel wounded. In fact, it was to conclude these important negotiations that the abbe had betaken himself to Gazeau Tower with Marcasse on that very evening when Edmee and myself sought shelter there. The terrible scene which followed our arrival put an end to any irresolution still left in Patience. Inclined to the Pythagorean doctrines, he had a horror of all bloodshed. The death of a deer drew tears from him, as from Shakespeare's Jacques; still less could he bear to contemplate the murder of a human being, and the instant that Gazeau Tower had served as the scene of two tragic deaths, it stood defiled in his eyes, and nothing could have induced him to pass another night there. He followed us to Sainte-Severe, and soon allowed his philosophical scruples to be overcome by Edmee's persuasive powers. The little cottage which he was prevailed on to accept was humble enough not to make him blush with shame at a too palpable compromise with civilization; and, though the solitude he found there was less perfect than at Gazeau Tower, the frequent visits of the abbe and of Edmee could hardly have given him a right to complain.

Here the narrator interrupted his story again to expatiate on the development of Mademoiselle de Mauprat's character.

Edmee, hidden away in her modest obscurity, was—and, believe me, I do not speak from bias—one of the most perfect women to be found in France. Had she desired or been compelled to make herself known to the world, she would assuredly have been famous and extolled beyond all her sex. But she found her happiness in her own family, and the sweetest simplicity crowned her mental powers and lofty virtues. She was ignorant of her worth, as I myself was at that time, when, brutelike, I saw only with the eyes of the body, and believed I loved her only because she was beautiful. It should be said, too, that her *fiance*, M. de la Marche, understood her but little better. He had developed the weakly mind with which he was endowed in the frigid school of Voltaire and Helvetius. Edmee had fired her vast intellect with the burning declamations of Jean Jacques. A day came when I could understand her—the day when M. de la Marche could have understood her would never have come.

Edmee, deprived of her mother from the very cradle, and left to her young devices by a father full of confidence and careless good nature, had shaped her character almost alone. The Abbe Aubert, who had confirmed her, had by no means forbidden her to read the philosophers by whom he himself had been lured from the paths of orthodoxy. Finding no one to oppose her ideas or even to discuss them—for her father, who idolized her, allowed himself to be led wherever she wished—Edmee had drawn support from two sources apparently very antagonistic: the philosophy which was preparing the downfall of Christianity, and Christianity which was proscribing the spirit of inquiry. To account for this contradiction, you must recall what I told you about the effect produced on the Abbe Aubert by the *Profession de Foi du Vicaire Savoyard.* Moreover, you must be aware that, in poetic souls, mysticism and doubt often reign side by side. Jean Jacques himself furnishes a striking example of this, and you know what sympathies he stirred among priests and nobles, even when he was chastising them so unmercifully. What miracles may not conviction work when helped by sublime eloquence! Edmee had drunk of this living fount with all the eagerness of an ardent soul. In her rare visits to Paris she had sought for spirits in sympathy with her own. There, however, she had found so many shades of opinion, so little harmony, and—despite the prevailing fashion—so many ineradicable prejudices, that she had returned with a yet deeper love to her solitude and her poetic reveries under the old oaks in the park. She would even then speak of her illusions, and—with a good sense beyond her years, perhaps, too, beyond her sex—she refused all opportunities of direct intercourse with the philosophers whose writings made up her intellectual life.

"I am somewhat of a Sybarite," she would say with a smile. "I would rather have a bouquet of roses arranged for me in a vase in the early morning, than go and gather them myself from out their thorns in the heat of the sun."

As a fact, this remark about her sybaritism was only a jest. Brought up in the country, she was strong, active, brave, and full of life. To all her charms of delicate beauty she united the energy of physical and moral health. She was the proud-spirited and fearless girl, no less than the sweet and affable mistress of the house. I often found her haughty and disdainful. Patience and the poor of the district never found her anything but modest and good-natured.

Edmee loved the poets almost as much as the transcendental philosophers. In her walks she always carried a book in her hand. One day when she had taken Tasso with her she met Patience, who, as was his wont, inquired minutely into both author and subject. Edmee thereupon had to give him an account of the Crusades. This was not the most difficult part of her task. Thanks to the stores of information derived from the abbe and to his prodigious memory for facts, Patience had a passable knowledge of the outlines of universal history. But what he had great trouble in grasping was the connection and difference between epic poetry and history. At first he was indignant at the inventions of the poets, and declared that such impostures ought never to have been allowed. Then, when he had realized that epic poetry, far from leading generations into error, only raised heroic deeds to vaster proportions and a more enduring glory, he asked how it was that all important events had not been sung by the bards, and why the history of man had not been embodied in a popular form capable of impressing itself on every mind without the help of letters. He begged Edmee to explain to him a stanza of *Jerusalem Delivered*. As he took a fancy to it, she read him a canto in French. A few days later she read him another, and soon Patience knew the whole poem. He rejoiced to hear that the heroic tale was popular in Italy; and, bringing together his recollections of it, endeavoured to give them an abridged form in rude prose, but he had no memory for words. Roused by his vivid impressions, he would call up a thousand mighty images before his eyes. He would give utterance to them in improvisations wherein his genius triumphed over the uncouthness of his language, but he could never repeat what he had once said. One would have had to take it down from his dictation, and even that would have been of no use to him; for, supposing he had managed to read it, his memory, accustomed to occupy itself solely with thoughts, had never been able to retain any fragment whatever in its precise words. And yet he was fond of quoting, and at times his language was almost biblical. Beyond, however, certain expressions that he loved, and a number of short sentences that he found means to make his own, he remembered nothing of the pages which had been read to him so often, and he always listened to them again with the same emotion as at first. It was a veritable pleasure to watch the effect of beautiful poetry on this powerful intellect. Little by little the abbe, Edmee, and subsequently I myself, managed to familiarize him with Homer and Dante. He was so struck by the various incidents in the *Divine Comedy* that he could give an analysis of the poem from beginning to end, without forgetting or misplacing the slightest detail in the journey, the encounters, and the emotions of the poet. There, however, his power ended. If he essayed to repeat some of the phrases which had so charmed him when they were read, he flung forth a mass of metaphors and images which savoured of delirium. This initiation into the wonders of poetry marked an epoch in the life of Patience. In the realm of fancy it supplied the action wanting to his real life. In his magic mirror he beheld gigantic combats between heroes ten cubits high; he understood love, which he himself had never known; he fought, he loved, he conquered; he enlightened nations, gave peace to the world, redressed the wrongs of mankind, and raised up temples to the mighty spirit of the universe. He saw in the starry firmament all the gods of Olympus, the fathers of primitive humanity. In the constellations he read the story of the golden age, and of the ages of brass; in the winter wind he heard the songs of Morven, and in the storm-clouds he bowed to the ghosts of Fingal and Comala.

"Before I knew the poets," he said towards the end of his life, "I was a man lacking in one of the senses. I could see plainly that this sense was necessary, since there were so many things calling for its operation. In my solitary walks at night I used to feel a strange uneasiness; I used to wonder why I could not sleep; why I should find such pleasure in gazing upon the stars that I could not tear myself from their presence; why my heart should suddenly beat with joy on seeing certain colours, or grow sad even to tears on hearing certain sounds. At times I was so alarmed on comparing my continual agitation with the indifference of other men of my class that I even began to imagine that I was mad. But I soon consoled myself with the reflection that such madness was sweet, and I would rather have ceased to exist than be cured of it. Now that I know these things have been thought beautiful in all times and by all intelligent beings, I understand what they are, and how they are useful to man. I find joy in the thought that there is not a flower, not a colour, not a breath of air, which has not absorbed the minds and stirred the hearts of other men till it has received a name sacred among all peoples. Since I have learnt that it is allowed to man, without degrading his reason, to people the universe and interpret it by his dreams, I live wholly in the contemplation of the universe; and when the sight of the misery and crime in the world bruises my heart and shakes my reason, I fall back upon my dreams. I say to myself that, since all men are united in their love of the works of God, some day they will also be united in their love of one another. I imagine that education grows more and more perfect from father to son. It may be that I am the first untutored man who has divined truths of which no glimpse was given him from without. It may be, too, that many others before myself have been perplexed by the workings of their hearts and brains and have died without ever finding an answer to the riddle." "Ah, we poor folk," added Patience, "we are never forbidden excess in labour, or in wine, or in any of the debauches which may destroy our minds. There are some people who pay dearly for the work of our arms, so that the poor, in their eagerness to satisfy the wants of their families, may work beyond their strength. There are taverns and other places more dangerous still, from which, so it is said, the government draws a good profit; and there are priests, too, who get up in their pulpits to tell us what we owe to the lord of our village, but never what the lord owes to us. Nowhere is there a school where they teach us our real rights; where they show us how to distinguish our true and decent wants from the shameful and fatal ones; where, in short, they tell us what we can and ought to think about when we have borne the burden and heat of the day for the profit of others, and are sitting in the evening at the door of our huts, gazing on the red stars as they come out on the horizon."

Thus would Patience reason; and, believe me, in translating his words into our conventional language, I am robbing them of all their grace, all their fire, and all their vigour. But who could repeat the exact words of Patience? His was a language used by none but himself; it was a mixture of the limited, though forcible, vocabulary of the peasants and of the boldest metaphors of the poets, whose poetic turns he would often make bolder still. To this mixed idiom his sympathetic mind gave order and logic. An incredible wealth of thought made up for the brevity of the phrases that clothed it. You should have seen how desperately his will and convictions strove to overcome the impotence of his language; any other than he would have failed to come out of the struggle with honour. And I assure you that any one capable of something more serious than laughing at his solecisms and audacities of phrase, would have found in this man material for the most important studies on the development of the human mind, and an incentive to the most tender admiration for primitive moral beauty.

When, subsequently, I came to understand Patience thoroughly, I found a bond of sympathy with him in my own exceptional destiny. Like him, I had been without education; like him, I had sought outside myself for an explanation of my being—just as one seeks the answer to a riddle. Thanks to the accidents of my birth and fortune, I had arrived at complete development, while Patience, to the hour of his death, remained groping in the darkness of an ignorance from which he neither would nor could emerge. To me, however, this was only an additional reason for recognising the superiority of that powerful nature which held its course more boldly by the feeble light of instinct, than I myself by all the brilliant lights of knowledge; and which, moreover, had not had a single evil inclination to subdue, while I had had all that a man may have.

At the time, however, at which I must take up my story, Patience was still, in my eyes, merely a grotesque character, an object of amusement for Edmee, and of kindly compassion for the Abbe Aubert. When they spoke to me about him in a serious tone, I no longer understood them, and I imagined they took this subject as a sort of text whereon to build a parable proving to me the advantages of education, the necessity of devoting myself to study early in life, and the futility of regrets in after years.

Yet this did not prevent me from prowling about the copses about his new abode, for I had seen Edmee crossing the park in that direction, and I hoped that if I took her by surprise as she was returning, I should get a conversation with her. But she was always accompanied by the abbe, and sometimes even by her father, and if she remained alone with the old peasant, he would escort her to the chateau afterwards. Frequently I have concealed myself in the foliage of a giant yew-tree, which spread out its monstrous shoots and drooping branches to within a few yards of the cottage, and have seen Edmee sitting at the door with a book in her hand while Patience was listening with his arms folded and his head sunk on his breast, as though he were overwhelmed by the effort of attention. At that time I imagined that Edmee was trying to teach him to read, and thought her mad to persist in attempting an impossible education. But how beautiful she seemed in the light of the setting sun, beneath the yellowing vine leaves that overhung the cottage door! I used to gaze on her and tell myself that she belonged to me, and vow never to yield to any force or persuasion which should endeavour to make me renounce my claim.

For some days my agony of mind had been intense. My only method of escaping from it had been to drink heavily at supper, so that I might be almost stupefied at the hour, for me so painful and so galling, when she would leave the drawing-room after kissing her father, giving her hand to M. de la Marche, and saying as she passed by me, "Good-night, Bernard," in a tone which seemed to say, "To-day has ended like yesterday, and to-morrow will end like to-day."

In vain would I go and sit in the arm-chair nearest her door, so that she could not pass without at least her dress brushing against me; this was all I ever got from her. I would not put out my hand to beg her own, for she might have given it with an air of unconcern, and I verily believe I should have crushed it in my anger.

Thanks to my large libations at supper, I generally succeeded in besotting myself, silently and sadly. I then used to sink into my favourite arm-chair and remain there, sullen and drowsy, until the fumes of the wine had passed away, and I could go and air my wild dreams and sinister plans in the park.

None seemed to notice this gross habit of mine. They showed me such kindness and indulgence in the family that they seemed afraid to express disapproval, however much I deserved it. Nevertheless, they were well aware of my shameful passion for wine, and the abbe informed Edmee of it. One evening at supper she looked at me fixedly several times and with a strange expression. I stared at her in return, hoping that she would say something to provoke me, but we got no further than an exchange of malevolent glances. On leaving the table she whispered to me very quickly, and in an imperious tone:

"Break yourself of this drinking, and pay attention to what the abbe has to say to you."

This order and tone of authority, so far from filling me with hope, seemed to me so revolting that all my timidity vanished in a moment. I waited for the hour when she usually went up to her room and, going out a little before her, took up my position on the stairs.

"Do you think," I said to her when she appeared, "that I am the dupe of your lies, and that I have not seen perfectly, during the month I have been here, without your speaking a word to me, that you are merely fooling me, as if I were a booby? You lied to me and now you despise me because I was honest enough to believe your word."

"Bernard," she said, in a cold tone, "this is neither the time nor the place for an explanation."

"Oh, I know well enough," I replied, "that, according to you, it will never be the time or the place. But I shall manage to find both, do not fear. You said that you loved me. You threw your arms about my neck and said, as you kissed me—yes, here, I can still feel your lips on my cheeks: 'Save me, and I swear on the gospel, on my honour, by the memory of my mother and your own, that I will be yours.' I can see through it; you said that because you were afraid that I should use my strength, and now you avoid me because you are afraid I shall claim my right. But you will gain nothing by it. I swear that you shall not trifle with me long."

"I will never be yours," she replied, with a coldness which was becoming more and more icy, "if you do not make some change in your language, and manners, and feelings. In your present state I certainly do not fear you. When you appeared to me good and generous, I might have yielded to you, half from fear and half from affection. But from the moment I cease to care for you, I also cease to be afraid of you. Improve your manners, improve your mind, and we will see."

"Very good," I said, "that is a promise I can understand. I will act on it, and if I cannot be happy, I will have my revenge."

"Take your revenge as much as you please," she said. "That will only make me despise you."

So saying, she drew from her bosom a piece of paper, and burnt it in the flame of her candle.

"What are you doing?" I exclaimed.

"I am burning a letter I had written to you," she answered. "I wanted to make you listen to reason, but it is quite useless; one cannot reason with brutes."

"Give me that letter at once," I cried, rushing at her to seize the burning paper.

But she withdrew it quickly and, fearlessly extinguishing it in her hand, threw the candle at my feet and fled in the darkness. I ran after her, but in vain. She was in her room before I could get there, and had slammed the door and drawn the bolts. I could hear the voice of Mademoiselle Leblanc asking her young mistress the cause of her fright.

"It is nothing," replied Edmee's trembling voice, "nothing but a joke."

I went into the garden, and strode up and down the walks at a furious rate. My anger gave place to the most profound melancholy. Edmee, proud and daring, seemed to me more desirable than ever. It is the nature of all desire to be excited and nourished by opposition. I felt that I had offended her, and that she did not love me, that perhaps she would never love me; and, without abandoning my criminal resolution to make her mine by force, I gave way to grief at the thought of her hatred of me. I went and leaned upon a gloomy old wall which happened to be near, and, burying my face in my hands, I broke into heart-rending sobs. My sturdy breast heaved convulsively, but tears would not bring the relief I longed for. I could have roared in my anguish, and I had to bite my handkerchief to prevent myself from yielding to the temptation. The weird noise of my stifled sobs attracted the attention of some one who was praying in the little chapel on the other side of the wall which I had chanced to lean against. A Gothic window, with its stone mullions surmounted by a trefoil, was exactly on a level with my head.

"Who is there?" asked some one, and I could distinguish a pale face in the slanting rays of the moon which was just rising.

It was Edmee. On recognising her I was about to move away, but she passed her beautiful arm between the mullions, and held me back by the collar of my jacket, saying:

"Why are you crying, Bernard?"

I yielded to her gentle violence, half ashamed at having betrayed my weakness, and half enchanted at finding that Edmee was not unmoved by it.

"What are you grieved at?" she continued. "What can draw such bitter tears from you?"

"You despise me; you hate me; and you ask why I am in pain, why I am angry!"

"It is anger, then, that makes you weep?" she said, drawing back her arm.

"Yes; anger or something else," I replied.

"But what else?" she asked.

"I can't say; probably grief, as you suggest. The truth is my life here is unbearable; my heart is breaking. I must leave you, Edmee, and go and live in the middle of the woods. I cannot stay here any longer."

"Why is life unbearable? Explain yourself, Bernard. Now is our opportunity for an explanation."

"Yes, with a wall between us. I can understand that you are not afraid of me now."

"And yet it seems to me that I am only showing an interest in you; and was I not as affectionate an hour ago when there was no wall between us?"

"I begin to see why you are fearless, Edmee; you always find some means of avoiding people, or of winning them over with pretty words. Ah, they were right when they told me that all women are false, and that I must love none of them."

"And who told you that? Your Uncle John, I suppose, or your Uncle Walter; or was it your grandfather, Tristan?"

"You can jeer—jeer at me as much as you like. It is not my fault that I was brought up by them. There were times, however, when they spoke the truth."

"Bernard, would you like me to tell you why they thought women false?"

"Yes, tell me."

"Because they were brutes and tyrants to creatures weaker than themselves. Whenever one makes one's self feared one runs the risk of being deceived. In your childhood, when John used to beat you, did you never try to escape his brutal punishment by disguising your little faults?"

"I did; that was my only resource."

"You can understand, then, that deception is, if not the right, at least the resource of the oppressed."

"I understand that I love you, and in that at any rate there can be no excuse for your deceiving me."

"And who says that I have deceived you?"

"But you have; you said you loved me; you did not love me."

"I loved you, because at a time when you were wavering between detestable principles and the impulses of a generous heart I saw that you were inclining towards justice and honesty. And I love you now, because I see that you are triumphing over these vile principles, and that your evil inspirations are followed by tears of honest regret. This I say before God, with my hand on my heart, at a time when I can see your real self. There are other times when you appear to me so below yourself that I no longer recognise you and I think I no longer love you. It rests with you, Bernard, to free me from all doubts, either about you or myself."

"And what must I do?"

"You must amend your bad habits, open your ears to good counsel and your heart to the precepts of morality. You are a savage, Bernard; and, believe me, it is neither your awkwardness in making a bow, nor your inability to turn a compliment that shocks me. On the contrary, this roughness of manner would be a very great charm in my eyes, if only there were some great ideas and noble feelings beneath it. But your ideas and your feelings are like your manners, that is what I cannot endure. I know it is not your fault, and if I only saw you resolute to improve I should love you as much for your defects as for your qualities. Compassion brings affection in its train. But I do not love evil, I never loved it; and, if you cultivate it in yourself instead of uprooting it, I can never love you. Do you understand me?"

"No."

"What, no!"

"No, I say. I am not aware that there is any evil in me. If you are not displeased at the lack of grace in my legs, or the lack of whiteness in my hands, or the lack of elegance in my words, I fail to see what you find to hate in me. From my childhood I have had to listen to evil precepts, but I have not accepted them. I have never considered it permissible to do a bad deed; or, at least, I have never found it pleasurable. If I have done wrong, it is because I have been forced to do it. I have always detested my uncles and their ways. I do not like to see others suffer; I do not rob a fellow-creature; I despise money, of which they made a god at Roche-Mauprat; I know how to keep sober, and, though I am fond of wine, I would drink water all my life if, like my uncles, I had to shed blood to get a good supper. Yet I fought for them; yet I drank with them. How could I do otherwise? But now, when I am my own master, what harm am I doing? Does your abbe, who is always prating of virtue, take me for a murderer or a thief? Come, Edmee, confess now; you know well enough that I am an honest man; you do not really think me wicked; but I am displeasing to you because I am not clever, and you like M. de la Marche because he has a knack of making unmeaning speeches which I should blush to utter."

"And if, to be pleasing to me," she said with a smile, after listening most attentively, and without withdrawing her hand which I had taken through the bars, "if, in order to be preferred to M. de la Marche, it were necessary to acquire more wit, as you say, would you not try?"

"I don't know," I replied, after hesitating a moment; "perhaps I should be fool enough; for the power you have over me is more than I can understand; but it would be a sorry piece of cowardice and a great folly."

"Why, Bernard?"

"Because a woman who could love a man, not for his honest heart, but for his pretty wit, would be hardly worth the pains I should have to take; at least so it seems to me."

She remained silent in her turn, and then said to me as she pressed my hand:

"You have much more sense and wit than one might think. And since you force me to be quite frank with you, I will own that, as you now are and even should you never change, I have an esteem and an affection for you which will last as long as my life. Rest assured of that, Bernard, whatever I may say in a moment of anger. You know I have a quick temper—that runs in the family. The blood of the Mauprats will never flow as smoothly as other people's. Have a care for my pride, then, you know so well what pride is, and do not ever presume upon rights you have acquired. Affection cannot be commanded; it must be implored or inspired. Act so that I may always love you; never tell me that I am forced to love you."

"That is reasonable enough," I answered; "but why do you sometimes speak to me as if I were forced to obey you? Why, for instance, this evening did you *forbid* me to drink and *order* me to study?"

"Because if one cannot command affection which does not exist, one can at least command affection which does exist; and it is because I am sure yours exists that I commanded it."

"Good!" I cried, in a transport of joy; "I have a right then to order yours also, since you have told me that it certainly exists. . . . Edmee, I order you to kiss me."

"Let go, Bernard!" she cried; "you are breaking my arm. Look, you have scraped it against the bars."

"Why have you intrenched yourself against me?" I said, putting my lips to the little scratch I had made on her arm. "Ah, woe is me! Confound the bars! Edmee, if you would only bend your head down I should be able to kiss you . . . kiss you as my sister. Edmee, what are you afraid of?"

"My good Bernard," she replied, "in the world in which I live one does not kiss even a sister, and nowhere does one kiss in secret. I will kiss you every day before my father, if you like; but never here."

"You will never kiss me!" I cried, relapsing into my usual passion. "What of your promise? What of my rights?"

"If we marry," she said, in an embarrassed tone, "when you have received the education I implore you to receive, . . ."

"Death of my life! Is this a jest? Is there any question of marriage between us? None at all. I don't want your fortune, as I have told you."

"My fortune and yours are one," she replied. "Bernard, between near relations as we are, mine and thine are words without meaning. I should never suspect you of being mercenary. I know that you love me, that you will work to give me proof of this, and that a day will come when your love will no longer make me fear, because I shall be able to accept it in the face of heaven and earth."

"If that is your idea," I replied, completely drawn away from my wild passion by the new turn she was giving to my thoughts, "my position is very different; but, to tell you the truth, I must reflect on this; I had not realized that this was your meaning."

"And how should I have meant otherwise?" she answered. "Is not a woman dishonoured by giving herself to a man who is not her husband? I do not wish to dishonour myself; and, since you love me, you would not wish it either. You would not do me an irreparable wrong. If such were your intention you would be my deadliest enemy."

"Stay, Edmee, stay!" I answered. "I can tell you nothing about my intentions in regard to you, for I have never had any very definite. I have felt nothing but wild desires, nor have I ever thought of you without going mad. You wish me to marry you? But why—why?"

"Because a girl who respects herself cannot be any man's except with the thought, with the intention, with the certainty of being his forever. Do you not know that?"

"There are so many things I do not know or have never thought of."

"Education will teach you, Bernard, what you ought to think about the things which must concern you—about your position, your duties, your feelings. At present you see but dimly into your heart and conscience. And I, who am accustomed to question myself on all subjects and to discipline my life, how can I take for master a man governed by instinct and guided by chance?"

"For master! For husband! Yes, I understand that you cannot surrender your whole life to an animal such as myself . . . but that is what I have never asked of you. No, I tremble to think of it."

"And yet, Bernard, you must think of it. Think of it frequently, and when you have done so you will realize the necessity of following my advice, and of bringing your mind into harmony with the new life upon which you have entered since quitting Roche-Mauprat. When you have perceived this necessity you must tell me, and then we will make several necessary resolutions."

She withdrew her hand from mine quickly, and I fancy she bade me good-night; but this I did not hear. I stood buried in my thoughts, and when I raised my head to speak to her she was no longer there. I went into the chapel, but she had returned to her room by an upper gallery which communicated with her apartments.

I went back into the garden, walked far into the park, and remained there all night. This conversation with Edmee had opened a new world to me. Hitherto I had not ceased to be the Roche-Mauprat man, nor had I ever contemplated that it was possible or desirable to cease to be so. Except for some habits which had changed with circumstances, I had never moved out of the narrow circle of my old thoughts. I felt annoyed that these new surroundings of mine should have any real power over me, and I secretly braced my will so that I should not be humbled. Such was my perseverance and strength of character that I believed nothing would ever have driven me from my intrenchment of obstinacy, had not Edmee's influence been brought to bear upon me. The vulgar comforts of life, the satisfactions of luxury, had no attraction for me beyond their novelty. Bodily repose was a burden to me, and the calm that reigned in this house, so full of order and silence, would have been unbearable, had not Edmee's presence and the tumult of my own desires communicated to it some of my disorder, and peopled it with some of my visions. Never for a single moment had I desired to become the head of this house, the possessor of this property; and it was with genuine pleasure that I had just heard Edmee do justice to my disinterestedness. The thought of coupling two ends so entirely distinct as my passion and my interests was still more repugnant to me. I roamed about the park a prey to a thousand doubts, and then wandered into the open country unconsciously. It was a glorious night. The full moon was pouring down floods of soft light upon the ploughed lands, all parched by the heat of the sun. Thirsty plants were straightening their bowed stems—each leaf seemed to be drinking in through all its pores all the dewy freshness of the night. I, too, began to feel a soothing influence at work. My heart was still beating violently, but regularly. I was filled with a vague hope; the image of Edmee floated before me on the paths through the meadows, and no longer stirred the wild agonies and frenzied desires which had been devouring me since the night I first beheld her.

I was crossing a spot where the green stretches of pasture were here and there broken by clumps of young trees. Huge oxen with almost white skins were lying in the short grass, motionless, as if plunged in peaceful thought. Hills sloped gently up to the horizon, and their velvety contours seemed to ripple in the bright rays of the moon. For the first time in my life I realized something of the voluptuous beauty and divine effluence of the night. I felt the magic touch of some unknown bliss. It seemed that for the first time in my life I was looking on moon and meadows and hills. I remembered hearing Edmee say that nothing our eyes can behold is more lovely than Nature; and I was astonished that I had never felt this before. Now and them I was on the point of throwing myself on my knees and praying to God: but I feared that I should not know how to speak to Him, and that I might offend Him by praying badly. Shall I confess to you a singular fancy that came upon me, a childish revelation, as it were, of poetic love from out of the chaos of my ignorance? The moon was lighting up everything so plainly that I could distinguish the tiniest flowers in the grass. A little meadow daisy seemed to me so beautiful with its golden calyx full of diamonds of dew and its white collaret fringed with purple, that I plucked it, and covered it with kisses, and cried in a sort of delirious intoxication:

"It is you, Edmee! Yes, it is you! Ah, you no longer shun me!"

But what was my confusion when, on rising, I found there had been a witness of my folly. Patience was standing before me.

I was so angry at having been surprised in such a fit of extravagance that, from a remnant of the Hamstringer instinct, I immediately felt for a knife in my belt; but neither belt nor knife was there. My silk waistcoat with its pocket reminded me that I was doomed to cut no more throats. Patience smiled.

"Well, well! What is the matter?" said the anchorite, in a calm and kindly tone. "Do you imagine that I don't know perfectly well how things stand? I am not so simple but that I can reason; I am not so old but that I can see. Who is it that makes the branches of my yew shake whenever the holy maiden is sitting at my door? Who is it that follows us like a young wolf with measured steps through the copse when I take the lovely child to her father? And what harm is there in it? You are both young; you are both handsome; you are of the same family; and, if you chose, you might become a noble and honest man as she is a noble and honest girl."

All my wrath had vanished as I listened to Patience speaking of Edmee. I had such a vast longing to talk about her that I would even have been willing to have heard evil spoken of her, for the sole pleasure of hearing her name pronounced. I continued my walk by the side of Patience. The old man was tramping through the dew with bare feet. It should be mentioned, however, that his feet had long been unacquainted with any covering and had attained a degree of callosity that rendered them proof against anything. His only garments were a pair of blue canvas breeches which, in the absence of braces, hung loosely from his hips, and a coarse shirt. He could not endure any constraint in his clothes; and his skin, hardened by exposure, was sensitive to neither heat nor cold. Even when over eighty he was accustomed to go bareheaded in the broiling sun and with half-open shirt in the winter blasts. Since Edmee had seen to his wants he had attained a certain cleanliness. Nevertheless, in the disorder of his toilet and his hatred of everything that passed the bounds of the strictest necessity (though he could not have been charged with immodesty, which had always been odious to him), the cynic of the old days was still apparent. His beard was shining like silver. His bald skull was so polished that the moon was reflected in it as in water. He walked slowly, with his hands behind his back and his head raised, like a man who is surveying his empire. But most frequently his glances were thrown skywards, and he interrupted his conversation to point to the starry vault and exclaim:

"Look at that; look how beautiful it is!"

He is the only peasant I have ever known to admire the sky; or, at least, he is the only one I have ever seen who was conscious of his admiration.

"Why, Master Patience," I said to him, "do you think I might be an honest man if I chose? Do you think that I am not one already?"

"Oh, do not be angry," he answered. "Patience is privileged to say anything. Is he not the fool of the chateau?"

"On the contrary, Edmee maintains that you are its sage."

"Does the holy child of God say that? Well, if she believes so, I will try to act as a wise man, and give you some good advice, Master Bernard Mauprat. Will you accept it?"

"It seems to me that in this place every one takes upon himself to give advice. Never mind, I am listening."

"You are in love with your cousin, are you not?"

"You are very bold to ask such a question."

"It is not a question, it is a fact. Well, my advice is this: make your cousin love you, and become her husband."

"And why do you take this interest in me, Master Patience?"

"Because I know you deserve it."

"Who told you so? The abbe?"

"No."

"Edmee?"

"Partly. And yet she is certainly not very much in love with you. But it is your own fault."

"How so, Patience?"

"Because she wants you to become clever; and you—you would rather not. Oh, if I were only your age; yes, I, poor Patience; and if I were able, without feeling stifled, to shut myself up in a room for only two hours a day; and if all those I met were anxious to teach me; if they said to me, 'Patience, this is what was done yesterday; Patience, this is what will be done to-morrow.' But, enough! I have to find out everything myself, and there is so much that I shall die of old age before finding out a tenth part of what I should like to know. But, listen: I have yet another reason for wishing you to marry Edmee."

"What is that, good Monsieur Patience?"

"This La Marche is not the right man for her. I have told her so—yes, I have; and himself too, and the abbe, and everybody. He is not a man, that thing. He smells as sweet as a whole flower-garden; but I prefer the tiniest sprig of wild thyme."

"Faith! I have but little love for him myself. But if my cousin likes him, what then, Patience?"

"Your cousin does not like him. She thinks he is a good man; she thinks him genuine. She is mistaken; he deceives her, as he deceives everybody. Yes, I know: he is a man who has not any of this (and Patience put his hand to his heart). He is a man who is always proclaiming: 'In me behold the champion of virtue, the champion of the unfortunate, the champion of all the wise men and friends of the human race, etc., etc.' While I—Patience—I know that he lets poor folk die of hunger at the gates of his chateau. I know that if any one said to him, 'Give up your castle and eat black bread, give up your lands and become a soldier, and then there will be no more misery in the world, the human race—as you call it—will be saved,' his real self would answer, 'Thanks, I am lord of my lands, and I am not yet tired of my castle.' Oh! I know them so well, these sham paragons. How different with Edmee! You do not know that. You love her because she is as beautiful as the daisy in the meadows, while I—I love her because she is good as the moon that sheds light on all. She is a girl who gives away everything that she has; who would not wear a jewel, because with the gold in a ring a man could be kept alive for a year. And if she finds a foot-sore child by the road-side, she takes off her shoes and gives them to him, and goes on her way bare-footed. Then, look you, hers is a heart that never swerves. If to-morrow the village of Saint-Severe were to go to her in a body and say: 'Young lady, you have lived long enough in the lap of wealth, give us what you have, and take your turn at work'— 'That is but fair, my good friends,' she would reply, and with a glad heart she would go and tend the flocks in the fields. Her mother was the same. I knew her mother when she was quite young, young as yourself; and I knew yours too. Oh, yes. She was a lady with a noble mind, charitable and just to all. And you take after her, they say."

"Alas, no," I answered, deeply touched by these words of Patience. "I know neither charity nor justice."

"You have not been able to practise them yet, but they are written in your heart. I can read them there. People call me a sorcerer, and so I am in a measure. I know a man directly I see him. Do you remember what you said to me one day on the heath at Valide? You were with Sylvain and I with Marcasse. You told me that an honest man avenges his wrongs himself. And, by-the-bye, Monsieur Mauprat, if you are not satisfied with the apologies I made you at Gazeau Tower, you may say so. See, there is no one near; and, old as I am, I have still a fist as good as yours. We can exchange a few healthy blows—that is Nature's way. And, though I do not approve of it, I never refuse satisfaction to any one who demands it. There are some men, I know, who would die of mortification if they did not have their revenge: and it has taken me—yes, the man you see before you—more than fifty years to forget an insult I once received . . . and even now, whenever I think of it, my hatred of the nobles springs up again, and I hold it as a crime to have let my heart forgive some of them."

"I am fully satisfied, Master Patience; and in truth I now feel nothing but affection for you."

"Ah, that comes of my scratching your back. Youth is ever generous. Come, Mauprat, take courage. Follow the abbe's advice; he is a good man. Try to please your cousin; she is a star in the firmament. Find out truth; love the people; hate those who hate them; be ready to sacrifice yourself for them. . . . Yes, one word more—listen. I know what I am saying—become the people's friend."

"Is the people, then, better than the nobility, Patience? Come now, honestly, since you are a wise man, tell me the truth."

"Ay, we are worth more than the nobles, because they trample us under foot, and we let them. But we shall not always bear this, perhaps. No; you will have to know it sooner or later, and I may as well tell you now. You see yonder stars? They will never change. Ten thousand years hence they will be in the same place and be giving forth as much light as to-day; but within the next hundred years, maybe within less, there will be many a change on this earth. Take the word of a man who has an eye for the truth of things, and does not let himself be led astray by the fine airs of the great. The poor have suffered enough; they will turn upon the rich, and their castles will fail and their lands be carved up. I shall not see it; but you will. There will be ten cottages in the place of this park, and ten families will live on its revenue. There will no longer be servants or masters, or villein or lord. Some nobles will cry aloud and yield only to force, as your uncles would do if they were alive, and as M. de la Marche will do in spite of all his fine talk. Others will sacrifice themselves generously, like Edmee, and like yourself, if you listen to wisdom. And in that hour it will be well for Edmee that her husband is a man and not a mere fop. It will be well for Bernard Mauprat that he knows how to drive a plough or kill the game which the good God has sent to feed his family; for old Patience will then be lying under the grass in the churchyard, unable to return the services which Edmee has done him. Do not laugh at what I say, young man; it is the voice of God that is speaking. Look at the heavens. The stars live in peace, and nothing disturbs their eternal order. The great do not devour the small, and none fling themselves upon their neighbours. Now, a day will come when the same order will reign among men. The wicked will be swept away by the breath of the Lord. Strengthen your legs, Seigneur Mauprat, that you may stand firm to support Edmee. It is Patience that warns you; Patience who wishes you naught but good. But there will come others who wish you ill, and the good must make themselves strong."

We had reached Patience's cottage. He had stopped at the gate of his little inclosure, resting one hand on the cross-bar and waving the other as he spoke. His voice was full of passion, his eyes flashed fire, and his brow was bathed in sweat. There seemed to be some weird power in his words as in those of the prophets of old. The more than plebeian simplicity of his dress still further increased the pride of his gestures and the impressiveness of his voice. The French Revolution has shown since that in the ranks of the people there was no lack of eloquence or of pitiless logic; but what I saw at that moment was so novel, and made such an impression on me, that my unruly and unbridled imagination was carried away by the superstitious terrors of childhood. He held out his hand, and I responded with more of terror than affection. The sorcerer of Gazeau Tower hanging the bleeding owl above my head had just risen before my eyes again.

XI

When I awoke on the morrow in a state of exhaustion, all the incidents of the previous night appeared to me as a dream. I began to think that Edmee's suggestion of becoming my wife had been a perfidious trick to put off my hopes indefinitely; and, as to the sorcerer's words, I could not recall them without a feeling of profound humiliation. Still, they had produced their effect. My emotions had left traces which could never be effaced. I was no longer the man of the day before, and never again was I to be quite the man of Roche-Mauprat.

It was late, for not until morning had I attempted to make good my sleepless night. I was still in bed when I heard the hoofs of M. de la Marche's horse on the stones of the courtyard. Every day he used to come at this hour; every day he used to see Edmee at the same time as myself; and now, on this very day, this day when she had tried to persuade me to reckon on her hand, he was going to see her before me, and to give his soulless kiss to this hand that had been promised to myself. The thought of it stirred up all my doubts again. How could Edmee endure his attentions if she really meant to marry another man? Perhaps she dared not send him away; perhaps it was my duty to do so. I was ignorant of the ways of the world into which I was entering. Instinct counselled me to yield to my hasty impulses; and instinct spoke loudly.

I hastily dressed myself. I entered the drawing-room pale and agitated. Edmee was pale too. It was a cold, rainy morning. A fire was burning in the great fire-place. Lying back in an easy chair, she was warming her little feet and dozing. It was the same listless, almost lifeless, attitude of the days of her illness. M. de la Marche was reading the paper at the other end of the room. On seeing that Edmee was more affected than myself by the emotions of the previous night, I felt my anger cool, and, approaching her noiselessly, I sat down and gazed on her tenderly.

"Is that you, Bernard?" she asked without moving a limb, and with eyes still closed.

Her elbows were resting on the arms of her chair and her hands were gracefully crossed under her chin. At that period it was the fashion for women to have their arms half bare at all times. On one of Edmee's I noticed a little strip of court-plaster that made my heart beat. It was the slight scratch I had caused against the bars of the chapel window. I gently lifted the lace which fell over her elbow, and, emboldened by her drowsiness, pressed my lips to the darling wound. M. de la Marche could see me, and, in fact, did see me, as I intended he should. I was burning to have a quarrel with him. Edmee started and turned red; but immediately assuming an air of indolent playfulness, she said:

"Really, Bernard, you are as gallant this morning as a court abbe. Do you happen to have been composing a madrigal last night?"

I was peculiarly mortified at this jesting. However, paying her back in her own coin, I answered:

"Yes; I composed one yesterday evening at the chapel window; and if it is a poor thing, cousin, it is your fault."

"Say, rather, that it is the fault of your education," she replied, kindling.

And she was never more beautiful than when her natural pride and spirit were roused.

"My own opinion is that I am being very much over-educated," I answered; "and that if I gave more heed to my natural good sense you would not jeer at me so much."

"Really, it seems to me that you are indulging in a veritable war of wits with Bernard," said M. de la Marche, folding his paper carelessly and approaching us.

"I cry quits with her," I answered, annoyed at this impertinence. "Let her keep her wit for such as you."

I had risen to insult him, but he did not seem to notice it; and standing with his back to the fire he bent down towards Edmee and said, in a gentle and almost affectionate voice:

"What is the matter with him?" as if he were inquiring after the health of her little dog.

"How should I know?" she replied, in the same tone.

Then she rose and added:

"My head aches too much to remain here. Give me your arm and take me up to my room."

She went out, leaning upon his arm. I was left there stupefied.

I remained in the drawing-room, resolved to insult him as soon as he should return. But the abbe now entered, and soon afterward my Uncle Hubert. They began to talk on subjects which were quite strange to me (the subjects of their conversation were nearly always so). I did not know what to do to obtain revenge. I dared not betray myself in my uncle's presence. I was sensible to the respect I owed to him and to his hospitality. Never had I done such violence to myself at Roche-Mauprat. Yet, in spite of all efforts, my anger showed itself. I almost died at being obliged to wait for revenge. Several times the chevalier noticed the change in my features and asked in a kind tone if I were ill. M. de la Marche seemed neither to observe nor to guess anything. The abbe alone examined me attentively. More than once I caught his blue eyes anxiously fixed on me, those eyes in which natural penetration was always veiled by habitual shyness. The abbe did not like me. I could easily see that his kindly, cheerful manners grew cold in spite of himself as soon as he spoke to me; and I noticed, too, that his face would invariably assume a sad expression at my approach.

The constraint that I was enduring was so alien to my habits and so beyond my strength that I came nigh to fainting. To obtain relief I went and threw myself on the grass in the park. This was a refuge to me in all my troubles. These mighty oaks, this moss which had clung to their branches through the centuries, these pale, sweet-scented wild flowers, emblems of secret sorrow, these were the friends of my childhood, and these alone I had found the same in social as in savage life. I buried my face in my hands; and I never remember having suffered more in any of the calamities of my life, though some that I had to bear afterward were very real. On the whole I ought to have accounted myself lucky, on giving up the rough and perilous trade of a cut-throat, to find so many unexpected blessings—affection, devotion, riches, liberty, education, good precepts and good examples. But it is certain that, in order to pass from a given state to its opposite, though it be from evil to good, from grief to joy, from fatigue to repose, the soul of a man must suffer; in this hour of birth of a new destiny all the springs of his being are strained almost to breaking— even as at the approach of summer the sky is covered with dark clouds, and the earth, all a-tremble, seems about to be annihilated by the tempest.

At this moment my only thought was to devise some means of appeasing my hatred of M. de la Marche without betraying and without even arousing a suspicion of the mysterious bond which held Edmee in my power. Though nothing was less respected at Roche-Mauprat than the sanctity of an oath, yet the little reading I had had there—those ballads of chivalry of which I have already spoken—had filled me with an almost romantic love of good faith; and this was about the only virtue I had acquired there. My promise of secrecy to Edmee was therefore inviolable in my eyes.

"However," I said to myself, "I dare say I shall find some plausible pretext for throwing myself upon my enemy and strangling him."

To confess the truth, this was far from easy with a man who seemed bent on being all politeness and kindness.

Distracted by these thoughts, I forgot the dinner hour; and when I saw the sun sinking behind the turrets of the castle I realized too late that my absence must have been noticed, and that I could not appear without submitting to Edmee's searching questions, and to the abbe's cold, piercing gaze, which, though it always seemed to avoid mine, I would suddenly surprise in the act of sounding the very depths of my conscience.

I resolved not to return to the house till nightfall, and I threw myself upon the grass and tried to find rest for my aching head in sleep. I did fall asleep in fact. When I awoke the moon was rising in the heavens, which were still red with the glow of sunset. The noise which had aroused me was very slight; but there are some sounds which strike the heart before reaching the ear; and the subtlest emanations of love will at times pierce through the coarsest organization. Edmee's voice had just pronounced my name a short distance away, behind some foliage. At first I thought I had been dreaming; I remained where I was, held my breath and listened. It was she, on her way to the hermit's, in company with the abbe. They had stopped in a covered walk five or six yards from me, and they were talking in low voices, but in those clear tones which, in an exchange of confidence, compels attention with peculiar solemnity.

"I fear," Edmee was saying, "that there will be trouble between him and M. de la Marche; perhaps something very serious—who knows? You do not understand Bernard."

"He must be got away from here, at all costs," answered the abbe. "You cannot live in this way, continually exposed to the brutality of a brigand."

"It cannot be called living. Since he set foot in the house I have not had a moment's peace of mind. Imprisoned in my room, or forced to seek the protection of my friends, I am almost afraid to move. It is as much as I dare to do to creep downstairs, and I never cross the corridor without sending Leblanc ahead as a scout. The poor woman, who has always found me so brave, now thinks I am mad. The suspense is horrible. I cannot sleep unless I first bolt the door. And look, abbe, I never walk about without a dagger, like the heroine of a Spanish ballad, neither more nor less."

"And if this wretch meets you and frightens you, you will plunge it into your bosom? Oh! that must not be. Edmee, we must find some means of changing a position which is no longer tenable. I take it that you do not wish to deprive him of your father's friendship by confessing to the latter the monstrous bargain you were forced to make with this bandit at Roche-Mauprat. But whatever may happen—ah! my poor little Edmee, I am not a bloodthirsty man, but twenty times a day I find myself deploring that my character of priest prevents me from challenging this creature, and ridding you of him forever."

This charitable regret, expressed so artlessly in my very ear, made me itch to reveal myself to them at once, were it only to put the abbe's warlike humour to the proof; but I was restrained by the hope that I should at last discover Edmee's real feelings and real intentions in regard to myself.

"Have no fear," she said, in a careless tone. "If he tries my patience too much, I shall not have the slightest hesitation in planting this blade in his cheek. I am quite sure that a little blood-letting will cool his ardour."

Then they drew a few steps nearer.

"Listen to me, Edmee," said the abbe, stopping again. "We cannot discuss this matter with Patience. Let us come to some decision before we put it aside. Your relations with Bernard are now drawing to a crisis. It seems to me, my child, that you are not doing all you ought to ward off the evils that may strike us; for everything that is painful to you will be painful to all of us, and will touch us to the bottom of our hearts."

"I am all attention, excellent friend," answered Edmee; "scold me, advise me, as you will."

So saying she leant back against the tree at the foot of which I was lying among the brushwood and long grass. I fancy she might have seen me, for I could see her distinctly. However, she little thought that I was gazing on her divine face, over which the night breeze was throwing, now the shadows of the rustling leaves, and now the pale diamonds that the moon showers down through the trees of the forest.

"My opinion, Edmee," answered the abbe, crossing his arms on his breast and striking his brow at intervals, "is that you do not take the right view of your situation. At times it distresses you to such an extent that you lose all hope and long to die—yes, my dear child, to such an extent that your health plainly suffers. At other times, and I must speak candidly at the risk of offending you a little, you view your perils with a levity and cheerfulness that astound me."

"That last reproach is delicately put, dear friend," she replied; "but allow me to justify myself. Your astonishment arises from the fact that you do not know the Mauprat race. It is a tameless, incorrigible race, from

which naught but Headbreakers and Hamstringers may issue. Even in
those who have been most polished by education there remains many a
stubborn knot—a sovereign pride, a will of iron, a profound contempt for
life. Look at my father. In spite of his adorable goodness, you see that he
is sometimes so quick-tempered that he will smash his snuff-box on the
table, when you get the better of him in some political argument, or when
you win a game of chess. For myself, I am conscious that my veins are as
full-blooded as if I had been born in the noble ranks of the people; and I
do not believe that any Mauprat has ever shone at court for the charm of
his manners. Since I was born brave, how would you have me set much
store by life? And yet there are weak moments in which I get discouraged
more than enough, and bemoan my fate like the true woman that I am.
But, let some one offend me, or threaten me, and the blood of the strong
surges through me again; and then, as I cannot crush my enemy, I fold
my arms and smile with compassion at the idea that he should ever have
hoped to frighten me. And do not look upon this as mere bombast, abbe.
To-morrow, this evening perhaps, my words may turn to deeds. This
little pearl-handled knife does not look like deeds of blood; still, it will
be able to do its work, and ever since Don Marcasse (who knows what he
is about) sharpened it, I have had it by me night and day, and my mind
is made up. I have not a very strong fist, but it will no doubt manage to
give myself a good stab with this knife, even as it manages to give my
horse a cut with the whip. Well, that being so, my honour is safe; it is
only my life, which hangs by a thread, which is at the mercy of a glass of
wine, more or less, that M. Bernard may happen to drink one of these
evenings; of some change meeting, or some exchange of looks between
De la Marche and myself that he may fancy he has detected; a breath of
air perhaps! What is to be done? Were I to grieve, would my tears wash
away the past? We cannot tear out a single page of our lives; but we can
throw the book into the fire. Though I should weep from night till morn,
would that prevent Destiny from having, in a fit of ill-humour, taken me
out hunting, sent me astray in the woods, and made me stumble across a
Mauprat, who led me to his den, where I escaped dishonour and perhaps
death only by binding my life forever to that of a savage who had none
of my principles, and who probably (and who undoubtedly, I should say)
never will have them? All this is a misfortune. I was in the full sunlight
of a happy destiny; I was the pride and joy of my old father; I was about
to marry a man I esteem and like; no sorrows, no fears had come near my
path; I knew neither days fraught with danger nor nights bereft of sleep.
Well, God did not wish such a beautiful life to continue; His will be done.
There are days when the ruin of all my hopes seems to me so inevitable

that I look upon myself as dead and my *fiance* as a widower. If it were not for my poor father, I should really laugh at it all; for I am so ill built for vexation and fears that during the short time I have known them they have already tired me of life."

"This courage is heroic, but it is also terrible," cried the abbe, in a broken voice. "It is almost a resolve to commit suicide, Edmee."

"Oh, I shall fight for my life," she answered, with warmth; "but I shall not stand haggling with it a moment if my honour does not come forth safe and sound from all these risks. No; I am not pious enough ever to accept a soiled life by way of penance for sins of which I never had a thought. If God deals so harshly with me that I have to choose between shame and death . . ."

"There can never be any shame for you, Edmee; a soul so chaste, so pure in intention . . ."

"Oh, don't talk of that, dear abbe! Perhaps I am not as good as you think; I am not very orthodox in religion—nor are you, abbe! I give little heed to the world; I have no love for it. I neither fear nor despise public opinion; it will never enter into my life. I am not very sure what principle of virtue would be strong enough to prevent me from falling, if the spirit of evil took me in hand. I have read *La Nouvelle Heloise*, and I shed many tears over it. But, because I am a Mauprat and have an unbending pride, I will never endure the tyranny of any man—the violence of a lover no more than a husband's blow; only a servile soul and a craven character may yield to force that which it refuses to entreaty. Sainte Solange, the beautiful shepherdess, let her head be cut off rather than submit to the seigneur's rights. And you know that from mother to daughter the Mauprats have been consecrated in baptism to the protection of the patron saint of Berry."

"Yes; I know that you are proud and resolute," said the abbe, "and because I respect you more than any woman in the world I want you to live, and be free, and make a marriage worthy of you, so that in the human family you may fill the part which beautiful souls still know how to make noble. Besides, you are necessary to your father; your death would hurry him to his grave, hearty and robust as the Mauprat still is. Put away these gloomy thoughts, then, and these violent resolutions. It is impossible. This adventure of Roche-Mauprat must be looked upon only as an evil dream. We both had a nightmare in those hours of horror; but it is time for us to awake; we cannot remain paralyzed with fear like children. You have only one course open to you, and that I have already pointed out."

"But, abbe, it is the one which I hold the most impossible of all. I have sworn by everything that is most sacred in the universe and the human heart."

117

"An oath extorted by threats and violence is binding on none; even human laws decree this. Divine laws, especially in a case of this nature, absolve the human conscience beyond a doubt. If you were orthodox, I would go to Rome—yes, I would go on foot—to get you absolved from so rash a vow; but you are not a submissive child of the Pope, Edmee—nor am I."

"You wish me, then, to perjure myself?"

"Your soul would not be perjured."

"My soul would! I took an oath with a full knowledge of what I was doing and at a time when I might have killed myself on the spot; for in my hand I had a knife three times as large as this. But I wanted to live; above all, I wanted to see my father again and kiss him. To put an end to the agony which my disappearance must have caused him, I would have bartered more than my life, I would have bartered my immortal soul. Since then, too, as I told you last night, I have renewed my vow, and of my own free-will, moreover; for there was a wall between my amiable *fiance* and myself."

"How could you have been so imprudent, Edmee? Here again I fail to understand you."

"That I can quite believe, for I do not understand myself," said Edmee, with a peculiar expression.

"My dear child, you must open your hear to me freely. I am the only person here who can advise you, since I am the only one to whom you can tell everything under the seal of a friendship as sacred as the secrecy of Catholic confession can be. Answer me, then. You do not really look upon a marriage between yourself and Bernard Mauprat as possible?"

"How should that which is inevitable be impossible?" said Edmee. "There is nothing more possible than throwing one's self into the river; nothing more possible than surrendering one's self to misery and despair; nothing more possible, consequently, than marrying Bernard Mauprat."

"In any case I will not be the one to celebrate such an absurd and deplorable union," cried the abbe. "You, the wife and the slave of this Hamstringer! Edmee, you said just now that you would no more endure the violence of a lover than a husband's blow."

"You think the he would beat me?"

"If he did not kill you."

"Oh, no," she replied, in a resolute tone, with a wave of the knife, "I would kill him first. When Mauprat meets Mauprat . . .!"

"You can laugh, Edmee? O my God! you can laugh at the thought of such a match! But, even if this man had some affection and esteem for you, think how impossible it would be for you to have anything in common; think of the coarseness of his ideas, the vulgarity of his speech. The heart rises in disgust at the idea of such a union. Good God! In what language would you speak to him?"

Once more I was on the point of rising and falling on my panegyrist; but I overcame my rage. Edmee began to speak, and I was all ears again.

"I know very well that at the end of three or four days I should have nothing better to do than cut my own throat; but since sooner or later it must come to that, why should I not go forward to the inevitable hour? I confess that I shall be sorry to leave life. Not all those who have been to Roche-Mauprat have returned. I went there not to meet death, but to betroth myself to it. Well, then, I will go on to my wedding-day, and if Bernard is too odious, I will kill myself after the ball."

"Edmee, your head seems full of romantic notions at present," said the abbe, losing patience. "Thank God, your father will never consent to the marriage. He has given his word to M. de la March, and you too have given yours. This is the only promise that is valid."

"My father would consent—yes, with joy—to an arrangement which perpetuated his name and line directly. As to M. de la March, he will release me from any promise without my taking the trouble to ask him; as soon as he hears that I passed two hours at Roche-Mauprat there will be no need of any other explanation."

"He would be very unworthy of the esteem I feel for him, if he considered your good name tarnished by an unfortunate adventure from which you came out pure."

"Thanks to Bernard," said Edmee; "for after all I ought to be grateful to him; in spite of his reservations and conditions, he performed a great and inconceivable action, for a Hamstringer."

"God forbid that I should deny the good qualities which education may have developed in this young man; and it may still be possible, by approaching him on this better side of his, to make him listen to reason."

"And make him consent to be taught? Never. Even if he should show himself willing, he would no more be able than Patience. When the body is made for an animal life, the spirit can no longer submit to the laws of the intellect."

"I think so too; but that is not the point. I suggest that you should have an explanation with him, and make him understand that he is bound in honour to release you from your promise and resign himself to your marriage with M. de la Marche. Either he is a brute unworthy of the slightest esteem and consideration, or he will realize his crime and folly and yield honestly and with a good grace. Free me from the vow of secrecy to which I am bound; authorize me to deal plainly with him and I will guarantee success."

"And I—I will guarantee the contrary," said Edmee. "Besides, I could not consent to this. Whatever Bernard may be, I am anxious to come out of our duel with honour; and if I acted as you suggest, he would have cause to believe that up to the present I have been unworthily trifling with him."

"Well, there is only one means left, and that is to trust to the honour and discretion of M. de la Marche. Set before him the details of your position, and then let him give the verdict. You have a perfect right to intrust him with your secret, and you are quite sure of his honour. If he is coward enough to desert you in such a position, your remaining resource is to take shelter from Bernard's violence behind the iron bars of a convent. You can remain there a few years; you can make a show of taking the veil. The young man will forget you, and they will set you free again."

"Indeed, that is the only reasonable course to take, and I had already thought of it; but it is not yet time to make the move."

"Very true; you must first see the result of your confession to M. de la Marche. If, as I make no doubt, he is a man of mettle, he will take you under his protection, and then procure the removal of this Bernard, whether by persuasion or authority."

"What authority, abbe, if you please?"

"The authority which our customs allow one gentleman to exercise over his equal—honour and the sword."

"Oh, abbe! You too, then are a man with a thirst for blood. Well, that is precisely what I have hitherto tried to avoid, and what I will avoid, though it cost me my life and honour. I do not wish that there should be any fight between these two men."

"I understand: one of the two is very rightly dear to you. But evidently in this duel it is not M. de la Marche who would be in danger."

"Then it would be Bernard," cried Edmee. "Well, I should hate M. de la Marche, if he insisted on a duel with this poor boy, who only knows how to handle a stick or a sling. How can such ideas occur to you, abbe? You must really loathe this unfortunate Bernard. And fancy me getting my husband to cut his throat as a return for having saved my life at the risk of his own. No, no; I will not suffer any one either to challenge him, or humiliate him, or persecute him. He is my cousin; he is a Mauprat; he is almost a brother. I will not let him be driven out of this home. Rather I will go myself."

"These are very generous sentiments, Edmee," answered the abbe. "But with what warmth you express them! I stand confounded; and, if I were not afraid of offending you, I should confess that this solicitude for young Mauprat suggests to me a strange thought."

"Well, what is it, then?" said Edmee, with a certain brusqueness.

"If you insist, of course I will tell you: you seem to take a deeper interest in this young man than in M. de la Marche, and I could have wished to think otherwise."

"Which has the greater need of this interest, you bad Christian?" said Edmee with a smile. "Is it not the hardened sinner whose eyes have never looked upon the light?"

"But, come, Edmee! You love M. de la Marche, do you not? For Heaven's sake do not jest."

"If by love," she replied in a serious tone, "you mean a feeling of trust and friendship, I love M. de la Marche; but if you mean a feeling of compassion and solicitude, I love Bernard. It remains to be seen which of these two affections is the deeper. That is your concern, abbe. For my part, it troubles me but little; for I feel that there is only one being whom I love with passion, and that is my father; and only one thing that I love with enthusiasm, and that is my duty. Probably I shall regret the attentions and devotion of the lieutenant-general, and I shall share in the grief that I must soon cause him when I announce that I can never be his wife. This necessity, however, will by no means drive me to desperation, because I know that M. de la Marche will quickly recover. . . . I am not joking, abbe; M. de la Marche is a man of no depth, and somewhat cold."

"If your love for him is no greater than this, so much the better. It makes one trial less among your many trials. Still, this indifference robs me of my last hope of seeing you rescued from Bernard Mauprat."

"Do not let this grieve you. Either Bernard will yield to friendship and loyalty and improve, or I shall escape him."

"But how?"

"By the gate of the convent—or of the graveyard."

As she uttered these words in a calm tone, Edmee shook back her long black hair, which had fallen over her shoulders and partly over her pale face.

"Come," she said, "God will help us. It is folly and impiety to doubt him in the hour of danger. Are we atheists, that we let ourselves be discouraged in this way? Let us go and see Patience. . . . He will bring forth some wise saw to ease our minds; he is the old oracle who solves all problems without understanding any."

They moved away, while I remained in a state of consternation.

Oh, how different was this night from the last! How vast a step I had just taken in life, no longer on the path of flowers but on the arid rocks! Now I understood all the odious reality of the part I had been playing. In the bottom of Edmee's heart I had just read the fear and disgust I inspired in her. Nothing could assuage my grief; for nothing now could arouse my anger. She had no affection for M. de la Marche; she was trifling neither with him nor with me; she had no affection for either of us. How could I have believed that her generous sympathy for me and her sublime devotion to her word were signs of love? How, in the hours when this presumptuous fancy left me, could I have believed that in order to resist my passion she must needs feel love for another? It had come to pass, then, that I had no longer any object on which to vent my rage; now it could result only in Edmee's flight or death? Her death! At the mere thought of it the blood ran cold in my veins, a weight fell on my heart, and I felt all the stings of remorse piercing it. This night of agony was for me the clearest call of Providence. At last I understood those laws of modesty and sacred liberty which my ignorance had hitherto outraged and blasphemed. They astonished me more than ever; but I could see them; their sanction was their own existence. Edmee's strong, sincere soul appeared before me like the stone of Sinai on which the finger of God has traced the immutable truth. Her virtue was not feigned; her knife was sharpened, ready to cut out the stain of my love. I was so terrified at having been in danger of seeing her die in my arms; I was so horrified at the gross insult I had offered her while seeking to overcome her resistance, that I began to devise all manner of impossible plans for righting the wrongs I had done, and restoring her peace of mind.

The only one which seemed beyond my powers was to tear myself away from her; for while these feelings of esteem and respect were springing up in me, my love was changing its nature, so to speak, and growing vaster and taking possession of all my being. Edmee appeared to me in a new light. She was no longer the lovely girl whose presence stirred a tumult in my senses; she was a young man of my own age, beautiful as a seraph, proud, courageous, inflexible in honour, generous, capable of that sublime friendship which once bound together brothers in arms, but with no passionate love except for Deity, like the paladins of old, who, braving a thousand dangers, marched to the Holy Land under their golden armour.

From this hour I felt my love descending from the wild storms of the brain into the healthy regions of the heart. Devotion seemed no longer an enigma to me. I resolved that on the very next morning I would give proof of my submission and affection. It was quite late when I returned to the chateau, tired out, dying of hunger, and exhausted by the emotions I had experienced. I entered the pantry, found a piece of bread, and began eating it, all moist with my tears. I was leaning against the stove in the dime light of a lamp that was almost out, when I suddenly saw Edmee enter. She took a few cherries from a chest and slowly approached the stove, pale and deep in thought. On seeing me she uttered a cry and let the cherries fall.

"Edmee," I said, "I implore you never to be afraid of me again. That is all I can say now; for I do not know how to explain myself; and yet I had resolved to say many things."

"You must tell me them some other time, cousin," she answered, trying to smile.

But she was unable to disguise the fear she felt at finding herself alone with me.

I did not try to detain her. I felt deeply pained and humiliated at her distrust of me, and I knew I had no right to complain. Yet never had any man stood in greater need of a word of encouragement.

Just as she was going out of the room I broke down altogether, and burst into tears, as on the previous night at the chapel window. Edmee stopped on the threshold and hesitated a moment. Then, yielding to the kindly impulses of her heart, she overcame her fears and returned towards me. Pausing a few yards from my chair, she said:

"Bernard, you are unhappy. Tell me; is it my fault?"

I was unable to reply; I was ashamed of my tears, but the more I tried to restrain them the more my breast heaved with sobs. With men as physically strong as I was, tears are generally convulsions; mine were like the pangs of death.

"Come now! Just tell me what is wrong," cried Edmee, with some of the bluntness of sisterly affection.

And she ventured to put her hand on my shoulder. She was looking at me with an expression of wistfulness, and a big tear was trickling down her cheek. I threw myself on my knees and tried to speak, but that was still impossible. I could do no more than mutter the word *to-morrow* several times.

"'To-morrow?' What of tomorrow?" said Edmee. "Do you not like being here? Do you want to go away?"

"I will go, if it will please you," I replied. "Tell me; do you wish never to see me again?"

"I do not wish that at all," she rejoined. "You will stop here, won't you."

"It is for you to decide," I answered.

She looked at me in astonishment. I was still on my knees. She leant over the back of my chair.

"Yes; I am quite sure that you are good at heart," she said, as if she were answering some inner objection. "A Mauprat can be nothing by halves; and as soon as you have once known a good quarter of an hour, it is certain you ought to have a noble life before you."

"I will make it so," I answered.

"You mean it?" she said with unaffected joy.

"On my honour, Edmee, and on yours. Dare you give me your hand?"

"Certainly," she said.

She held out her hand to me; but she was still trembling.

"You have been forming good resolutions, then?" she said.

"I have been forming such resolutions," I replied, "that you will never have to reproach me again. And now, Edmee, when you return to your room, please do not bolt your door any more. You need no longer be afraid of me. Henceforth I shall only wish what you wish."

She again fixed on me a look of amazement. Then, after pressing my hand, she moved away, but turned round several times to look at me again, as if unable to believe in such a sudden conversion. At last, stopping in the doorway, she said to me in an affectionate tone:

"You, too, must go and get some rest. You look tired; and for the last two days you have seemed sad and very much altered. If you do not wish to make me anxious, you will take care of yourself, Bernard."

She gave me a sweet little nod. In her big eyes, already hollowed by suffering, there was an indefinable expression, in which distrust and hope, affection and wonder, were depicted alternately or at times all together.

"I will take care of myself; I will get some sleep; and I will not be sad any longer," I answered.

"And you will work?"

"And I will work—but, you, Edmee, will you forgive me for all the pain I have caused you? and will you try to like me a little?"

"I shall like you very much," she replied, "if you are always as you are this evening."

On the morrow, at daybreak, I went to the abbe's room. He was already up and reading.

"Monsieur Aubert," I said to him, "you have several times offered to give me lessons. I now come to request you to carry out your kind offer."

I had spent part of the night in preparing this opening speech and in deciding how I had best comport myself in the abbe's presence. Without really hating him, for I could quite see that he meant well and that he bore me ill-will only because of my faults, I felt very bitter towards him. Inwardly I recognised that I deserved all the bad things he had said about me to Edmee; but it seemed to me that he might have insisted somewhat more on the good side of mine to which he had given a merely passing word, and which could not have escaped the notice of a man so observant as himself. I had determined, therefore, to be very cold and very proud in my bearing towards him. To this end I judged with a certain show of logic, that I ought to display great docility as long as the lesson lasted, and that immediately afterwards I ought to leave him with a very curt expression of thanks. In a word, I wished to humiliate him in his post of tutor; for I was not unaware that he depended for his livelihood on my uncle, and that, unless he renounced this livelihood or showed himself ungrateful, he could not well refuse to undertake my education. My reasoning here was very good; but the spirit which prompted it was very bad; and subsequently I felt so much regret for my behaviour that I made him a sort of friendly confession with a request for absolution.

However, not to anticipate events, I will simply say that the first few days after my conversation afforded me an ample revenge for the prejudices, too well founded in many respects, which this man had against me. He would have deserved the title of "the just," assigned him by Patience, had not a habit of distrust interfered with his first impulses. The persecutions of which he had so long been the object had developed in him this instinctive feeling of fear, which remained with him all his life, and made trust in others always very difficult to him, though all the more flattering and touching perhaps when he accorded it. Since then I have observed this characteristic in many worthy priests. They generally have the spirit of charity, but not the feeling of friendship.

I wished to make him suffer, and I succeeded. Spite inspired me. I behaved as a nobleman might to an inferior. I preserved an excellent bearing, displayed great attention, much politeness, and an icy stiffness. I determined to give him no chance to make me blush at my ignorance, and, to this end, I acted so as to anticipate all his observations by accusing myself at once of knowing nothing, and by requesting him to teach me the very rudiments of things. When I had finished my first lesson I saw in his penetrating eyes, into which I had managed to penetrate myself, a desire to pass from this coldness to some sort of intimacy; but I carefully avoided making any response. He thought to disarm me by praising my attention and intelligence.

"You are troubling yourself unnecessarily, monsieur," I replied. "I stand in no need of encouragement. I have not the least faith in my intelligence, but of my attention I certainly am very sure; but since it is solely for my own good that I am doing my best to apply myself to this work, there is no reason why you should compliment me on it."

With these words I bowed to him and withdrew to my room, where I immediately did the French exercise that he had set me.

When I went down to luncheon, I saw that Edmee was already aware of the execution of the promise I had made the previous evening. She at once greeted me with outstretched hand, and frequently during luncheon called me her "dear cousin," till at last M. de la Marche's face, which was usually expressionless, expressed surprise or something very near it. I was hoping that he would take the opportunity to demand an explanation of my insulting words of the previous day; and although I had resolved to discuss the matter in a spirit of great moderation, I felt very much hurt at the care which he took to avoid it. This indifference to an insult that I had offered implied a sort of contempt, which annoyed me very much; but the fear of displeasing Edmee gave me strength to restrain myself.

Incredible as it may seem, my resolve to supplant him was not for one moment shaken by this humiliating apprenticeship which I had now to serve before I could manage to obtain the most elementary notions of things in general. Any other than I, filled like myself with remorse for wrongs committed, would have found no surer method of repairing them than by going away, and restoring to Edmee her perfect independence and absolute peace of mind. This was the only method which did not occur to me; or if it did, it was rejected with scorn, as a sign of apostasy. Stubbornness, allied to temerity, ran through my veins with the blood of the Mauprats. No sooner had I imagined a means of winning her whom I loved than I embraced it with audacity; and I think it would not have been otherwise even had her confidences to the abbe in the park shown me that her love was given to my rival. Such assurance on the part of a young man who, at the age of seventeen, was taking his first lesson in French grammar, and who, moreover, had a very exaggerated notion of the length and difficulty of the studies necessary to put him on a level with M. de la March, showed, you must allow, a certain moral force.

I do not know if I was happily endowed in the matter of intelligence. The abbe assured me that I was; but, for my own part, I think that my rapid progress was due to nothing but my courage. This was such as to make me presume too much on my physical powers. The abbe had told me that, with a strong will, any one of my age could master all the rules of the language within a month. At the end of the month I expressed myself with facility and wrote correctly. Edmee had a sort of occult influence over my studies; at her wish I was not taught Latin; for she declared that I was too old to devote several years to a fancy branch of learning, and that the essential thing was to shape my heart and understanding with ideas, rather than to adorn my mind with words.

Of an evening, under pretext of wishing to read some favourite book again, she read aloud, alternately with the abbe, passages from Condillac, Fenelon, Bernardin de Saint-Pierre, Jean Jacques, and even from Montaigne and Montesquieu. These passages, it is true, were chosen beforehand and adapted to my powers. I understood them fairly well, and I secretly wondered at this; for if during the day I opened these same books at random, I found myself brought to a standstill at every line. With the superstition natural to young lovers, I willingly imagined that in passing through Edmee's mouth the authors acquired a magic clearness, and that by some miracle my mind expanded at the sound of her voice. However, Edmee was careful to disguise the interest she took in teaching me herself. There is no doubt that she was mistaken in thinking that she ought not to betray her solicitude: it would only have roused me to still greater efforts in my work. But in this, imbued as she was with the teachings of *Emile*, she was merely putting into practice the theories of her favourite philosopher.

As it was, I spared myself but little; for my courage would not admit of any forethought. Consequently I was soon obliged to stop. The change of air, of diet, and of habits, my lucubrations, the want of vigorous exercise, my intense application, in a word, the terrible revolution which my nature had to stir up against itself in order to pass from the state of a man of the woods to that of an intelligent being, brought on a kind of brain fever which made me almost mad for some weeks, then an idiot for some days, and finally disappeared, leaving me a mere wreck physically, with a mind completely severed from the past, but sternly braced to meet the future.

One night, when I was at the most critical stage of my illness, during a lucid interval, I caught sight of Edmee in my room. At first I thought I was dreaming. The night-light was casting an unsteady glimmer over the room. Near me was a pale form lying motionless on an easy chair. I could distinguish some long black tresses falling loosely over a white dress. I sat up, weak though I was and scarcely able to move, and tried to get out of bed. Patience, however, suddenly appeared by the bedside and gently stopped me. Saint-Jean was sleeping in another arm-chair. Every night there used to be two men watching me thus, ready to hold me down by force whenever I became violent during my delirium. Frequently the abbe was one; sometimes the worthy Marcasse, who, before leaving Berry to go on his annual round through the neighbouring province, had returned to have a farewell hunt in the outhouses of the chateau, and who kindly offered to relieve the servants in their painful task of keeping watch over me.

As I was wholly unconscious of my illness, it was but natural that the unexpected presence of the hermit in my room should cause me considerable astonishment, and throw me into a state of great agitation. My attacks had been so violent that evening that I had no strength left. I abandoned myself, therefore, to my melancholy ravings, and, taking the good man's hand, I asked him if it was really Edmee's corpse that he had placed in the arm-chair by my bedside.

"It is Edmee's living self," he answered, in a low voice; "but she is still asleep, my dear monsieur, and we must not wake her. If there is anything you would like, I am here to attend to you, and right gladly I do it."

"My good Patience, you are deceiving me," I said; "she is dead, and so am I, and you have come to bury us. But you must put us in the same coffin, do you hear? for we are betrothed. Where is her ring? Take it off and put it on my finger; our wedding-night has come."

He tried in vain to dispel this hallucination. I held to my belief that Edmee was dead, and declared that I should never be quiet in my shroud until I had been given my wife's ring. Edmee, who had sat up with me for several nights, was so exhausted that our voices did not awaken her. Besides, I was speaking in a whisper, like Patience, with that instinctive tendency to imitate which is met with only in children or idiots. I persisted in my fancy, and Patience, who was afraid that it might turn into madness, went and very carefully removed a cornelian ring from one of Edmee's fingers and put it on mine. As soon as I felt it there, I carried it to my lips; and then with my arms crossed on my breast, in the manner of a corpse in a coffin, I fell into a deep sleep.

On the morrow when they tried to take the ring from me I resisted violently, and they abandoned the attempt. I fell asleep again and the abbe removed it during my sleep. But when I opened my eyes I noticed the theft, and once more began to rave. Edmee, who was in the room, ran to me at once and pressed the ring over my finger, at the same time rebuking the abbe. I immediately grew calm, and gazing, on her with lack-lustre eyes, said:

"Is it not true that you are my wife in death as in life?"

"Certainly," she replied. "Set your mind at rest."

"Eternity is long," I said, "and I should like to spend it in recalling your caresses. But I send my thoughts back in vain; they bring me no remembrance of your love."

She leant over and gave me a kiss.

"Edmee, that is very wrong," said the abbe; "such remedies turn to poison."

"Let me do as I like, abbe," she replied, with evident impatience, sitting down near my bed; "I must ask you to let me do as I please."

I fell asleep with one of my hands in hers, repeating at intervals:

"How sweet it is in the grave! Are we not fortunate to be dead?"

During my convalescence Edmee was much more reserved, but no less attentive. I told her my dreams and learnt from her how far my recollections were of real events. Without her testimony I should always have believed that I had dreamt everything. I implored her to let me keep the ring, and she consented. I ought to have added, to show my gratitude for all her goodness, that I should keep it as a pledge of friendship, and not as a sign of our engagement; but such a renunciation was beyond me.

One day I asked for news of M. de la Marche. It was only to Patience that I dared to put this question.

"Gone," he answered.

"What! Gone?" I replied. "For long?"

"Forever, please God! I don't know anything about it, for I ask no questions; but I happened to be in the garden when he took leave of her, and it was all as cold as a December night. Still, *au revoir* was said on both sides, but though Edmee's manner was kind and honest as it always is, the other had the face of a farmer when he sees frosts in April. Mauprat, Mauprat, they tell me that you have become a great student and a genuine good fellow. Remember what I told you; when you are old there will probably no longer be any titles or estate. Perhaps you will be called 'Father' Mauprat, as I am called 'Father' Patience, though I have never been either a priest or a father of a family."

"Well, what are you driving at?"

"Remember what I once told you," he repeated. "There are many ways of being a sorcerer, and one may read the future without being a servant of the devil. For my part, I give my consent to your marriage with your cousin. Continue to behave decently. You are a wise man now, and can read fluently from any book set before you. What more do you want? There are so many books here that the sweat runs from my brow at the very sight of them; it seems as if I were again starting the old torment of not being able to learn to read. But you have soon cured yourself. If M. Hubert were willing to take my advice, he would fix the wedding for the next Martinmas."

"That is enough, Patience!" I said. "This is a painful subject with me; my cousin does not love me."

"I tell you she does. You lie in your throat, as the nobles say. I know well enough how she nursed you; and Marcasse from the housetop happened to look through her window and saw her on her knees in the middle of the room at five o'clock in the morning the day that you were so ill."

These imprudent assertions of Patience, Edmee's tender cares, the departure of M. de la Marche, and, more than anything else, the weakness of my brain, enabled me to believe what I wished; but in proportion as I regained my strength Edmee withdrew further and further within the bounds of calm and discreet friendship. Never did man recover his health with less pleasure than I mine; for each day made Edmee's visits shorter; and when I was able to leave my room I had merely a few hours a day near her, as before my illness. With marvellous skill she had given me proof of the tenderest affection without ever allowing herself to be drawn into a fresh explanation concerning our mysterious betrothal. If I had not yet sufficient greatness of soul to renounce my rights, I had at least developed enough honour not to refer to them; and I found myself on exactly the same terms with her as at the time when I had fallen ill. M. de la Marche was in Paris; but according to her he had been summoned thither by his military duties and ought to return at the end of the winter on which we were entering. Nothing that the chevalier or the abbe said tended to show that there had been a quarrel between Edmee and him. They rarely spoke of the lieutenant-general, but when they had to speak of him they did so naturally and without any signs of repugnance. I was again filled with my old doubts, and could find no remedy for them except in the kingdom of my own will. "I will force her to prefer me," I would say to myself as I raised my eyes from my book and watched Edmee's great, inscrutable eyes calmly fixed on the letters which her father occasionally received from M. de la Marche, and which he would hand to her as soon as he had read them. I buried myself in my work again. For a long time I suffered from frightful pains in the head, but I overcame them stoically. Edmee again began the course of studies which she had indirectly laid down for my winter evenings. Once more I astonished the abbe by my aptitude and the rapidity of my conquests. The kindness he had shown me during my illness had disarmed me; and although I was still unable to feel any genuine affection for him, knowing well that he was of little service to me with my cousin, I gave him proof of much more confidence and respect than in the past. His talks were as useful to me as my reading. I was allowed to accompany him in his walks in the park and in his philosophical visits to Patience's snow-covered hut. This gave me an opportunity of seeing Edmee more frequently and for longer periods. My behaviour was such that all her mistrust vanished, and she no longer feared to be alone with me. On such occasions, however, I had but little scope for displaying my heroism; for the abbe, whose vigilance nothing could lull to sleep, was always at our heels. This supervision no longer annoyed me; on the contrary, I was pleased at it; for, in spite of all my resolutions, the storms of passion would still sweep my senses into a mysterious disorder; and once or twice when I found myself alone with Edmee I left her abruptly and went away, so that she might not perceive my agitation.

Our life, then, was apparently calm and peaceful, and for some time it was so in reality; but soon I disturbed it more than ever by a vice which education developed in me, and which had hitherto been hidden under coarser but less fatal vices. This vice, the bane of my new period of life, was vanity.

In spite of their theories, the abbe and my cousin made the mistake of showing too much pleasure at my rapid progress. They had so little expected perseverance from me that they gave all the credit to my

exceptional abilities. Perhaps, too, in the marked success of the philosophical ideas they had applied to my education they saw something of
a triumph for themselves. Certain it is, I was not loath to let myself be
persuaded that I had great intellectual powers, and that I was a man very
much above the average. My dear instructors were soon to gather the sad
fruit of their imprudence, and it was already too late to check the flight
of my immoderate conceit.

Perhaps, too, this abominable trait in my character, kept under by the
bad treatment I had endured in childhood, was now merely revealing its
existence. There is reason to believe that we carry within us from our earliest years the seeds of those virtues and vices which are in time made to
bear fruit by the action of our environment. As for myself, I had not yet
found anything whereon my vanity could feed; for on what could I have
prided myself at the beginning of my acquaintance with Edmee? But no
sooner was food forthcoming than suffering vanity rose up in triumph,
and filled me with as much presumption as previously it had inspired me
with bashfulness and boorish reserve. I was, moreover, as delighted at being able at last to express my thoughts with ease as a young falcon fresh
from the nest trying its wings for the first time. Consequently, I became as
talkative as I had been silent. The others were too indulgent to my prattle.
I had not sense enough to see that they were merely listening to me as
they would to a spoilt child. I thought myself a man, and what is more, a
remarkable man. I grew arrogant and superlatively ridiculous.

My uncle, the chevalier, who had not taken any part in my education,
and who only smiled with fatherly good-nature at the first steps I took in
my new career, was the first to notice the false direction in which I was
advancing. He found it unbecoming that I should raise my voice as loudly
as his own, and mentioned the matter to Edmee. With great sweetness
she warned me of this, and, lest I should feel annoyed at her speaking of
it, told me that I was quite right in my argument, but that her father was
now too old to be converted to new ideas, and that I ought to sacrifice
my enthusiastic affirmations to his patriarchal dignity. I promised not to
repeat the offence; and I did not keep my word.

The fact is, the chevalier was imbued with many prejudices. Considering the days in which he lived, he had received a very good education
for a country nobleman; but the century had moved more rapidly than he.
Edmee, ardent and romantic; the abbe, full of sentiment and systems, had
moved even more rapidly than the century; and if the vast gulf which lay
between them and the patriarch was scarcely perceptible, this was owing
to the respect which they rightly felt for him, and to the love he had for his
daughter. I rushed forward at full speed, as you may imagine, into Edmee's

ideas, but I had not, like herself, sufficient delicacy of feeling to maintain a becoming reticence. The violence of my character found an outlet in politics and philosophy, and I tasted unspeakable pleasure in those heated disputes which at that time in France, not only at all public meetings but also in the bosoms of families, were preluding the tempests of the Revolution. I doubt if there was a single house, from palace to hovel, which had not its orator—rugged, fiery, absolute, and ready to descend into the parliamentary arena. I was the orator of the chateau of Sainte-Severe, and my worthy uncle, accustomed to a resemblance of authority over those about him, which prevented him from seeing the real revolt of their minds, could ill endure such candid opposition as mine. He was proud and hot-tempered, and, moreover, had a difficulty in expressing himself which increased his natural impatience, and made him feel annoyed with himself. He would give a furious kick to the burning logs on the hearth; he would smash his eye-glasses into a thousand pieces; scatter clouds of snuff about the floor, and shout so violently as to make the lofty ceilings of his mansion ring with his resonant voice. All this, I regret to say, amused me immensely; and with some sentence but newly spelt out from my books I loved to destroy the frail scaffolding of ideas which had served him all his life. This was great folly and very foolish pride on my part; but my love of opposition and my desire to display intellectually the energy which was wanting in my physical life were continually carrying me away. In vain would Edmee cough, as a hint that I should say no more, and make an effort to save her father's *amour propre* by bringing forward some argument in his favour, though against her own judgement; the lukewarmness of her help, and my apparent submission to her only irritated my adversary more and more.

"Let him have his say," he would cry; "Edmee, you must not interfere; I want to beat him on all points. If you continually interrupt us, I shall never be able to make him see his absurdity."

And then the squall would blow stronger from both sides, until at last the chevalier, seriously offended, would walk out of the room, and go and vent his ill-humour on his huntsman or his hounds.

What most contributed to the recurrence of these unseemly wrangles and to the growth of my ridiculous obstinacy was my uncle's extreme goodness and the rapidity of his recovery. At the end of an hour he had entirely forgotten my rudeness and his own irritation. He would speak to me as usual and inquire into all my wishes and all my wants with that fatherly solicitude which always kept him in a benevolent mood. This incomparable man could never had slept had he not, before going to bed, embraced all his family, and atoned, either by a word or a kindly glance, for any ebullitions of temper which the meanest of his servants might have had to bear during the day. Such goodness ought to have disarmed me and closed my mouth forever. Each evening I vowed that it should; but each morning I returned, as the Scriptures say, to my vomit again.

Edmee suffered more and more every day from this development of my character. She cast about for means to cure it. If there was never *fiancee* stronger-minded and more reserved than she, never was there mother more tender. After many discussions with the abbe she resolved to persuade her father to change the routine of our life somewhat, and to remove our establishment to Paris for the last weeks of the carnival. Our long stay in the country; the isolation which the position of Sainte-Severe and the bad state of the roads had left us since the beginning of winter; the monotony of our daily life—all tended to foster our wearisome quibbling. My character was being more and more spoilt by it; and though it afforded my uncle even greater pleasure than myself, his health suffered as a result, and the childish passions daily aroused were no doubt hastening his decay. The abbe was suffering from *ennui;* Edmee was depressed. Whether in consequence of our mode of life or owing to causes unknown to the rest, it was her wish to go, and we went; for her father was uneasy about her melancholy, and sought only to do as she desired. I jumped for joy at the thought of seeing Paris; and while Edmee was flattering herself that intercourse with the world would refine the grossness of my pedantry, I was dreaming of a triumphal progress through the world which had been held up to such scorn by our philosophers. We started on our journey one fine morning in March; the chevalier with his daughter and Mademoiselle Leblanc in one post-chaise; myself in another with the abbe, who could ill conceal his delight at the thought of seeing the capital for the first time in him life; and my valet Saint-Jean, who, lest he should forget his customary politeness, made profound bows to every individual we passed.

XII

Old Bernard, tired from talking so long, had promised to resume his story on the morrow. At the appointed hour we called upon him to keep his word; and he continued thus:

This visit marked a new phase in my life. At Sainte-Severe I had been absorbed in my love and my work. I had concentrated all my energies upon these two points. No sooner had I arrived at Paris than a thick curtain seemed to fall before my eyes, and, for several days, as I could not understand anything, I felt astonished at nothing. I formed a very exaggerated estimate of the passing actors who appeared upon the scene; but I formed no less exaggerated an estimate of the ease with which I should soon rival these imaginary powers. My enterprising and presumptuous nature saw challenges everywhere and obstacles nowhere.

Though I was in the same house as my uncle and cousin, my room was on a separate floor, and henceforth I spent the greater part of my time with the abbe. I was far from being dazed by the material advantages of my position; but in proportion as I realized how precarious or painful were the positions of many others, the more conscious I became of the comfort of my own. I appreciated the excellent character of my tutor, and the respect my lackey showed me no longer seemed objectionable. With the freedom that I enjoyed, and the unlimited money at my command, and the restless energy of youth, it is astonishing that I did not fall into some excess, were it only gambling, which might well have appealed to my combative instincts. It was my own ignorance of everything that prevented this; it made me extremely suspicious, and the abbe, who was very observant, and held himself responsible for my actions, managed most cleverly to work upon my haughty reserve. He increased it in regard to such things as might have done me harm, and dispelled it in contrary cases. Moreover, he was careful to provide me with sufficient reasonable distractions, which while they could not take the place of the joys of love, served at least to lessen the smart of its wounds. As to temptations to debauchery, I felt none. I had too much pride to yearn for any woman in which I had not seen, as in Edmee, the first of her sex.

We used all to meet at dinner, and as a rule we paid visits in the evening. By observing the world from a corner of a drawing-room, I learnt more of it in a few days than I should have done in a whole year from guesses and inquiries. I doubt whether I should ever have understood society, if I had always been obliged to view it from a certain distance. My brain refused to form a clear image of the ideas which occupied the brains of others. But as soon as I found myself in the midst of this chaos, the confused mass was compelled to fall into some sort of order and reveal a large part of its elements. This path which led me into life was not without charms for me, I remember, at its beginning. Amid all the conflicting interests of the surrounding world I had nothing to ask for, aim at, or argue about. Fortune had taken me by the hand. One fine morning she had lifted me out of an abyss and put me down on a bed of roses and made me a young gentleman. The eagerness of others was for me but an amusing spectacle. My heart was interested in the future only on one mysterious point, the love which I felt for Edmee.

My illness, far from robbing me of my physical vigour, had but increased it. I was no longer the heavy, sleepy animal, fatigued by digestion and stupefied by weariness. I felt the vibrations of all my fibres filling my soul with unknown harmonies; and I was astonished to discover within myself faculties of which I had never suspected the use. My good kinfolk were delighted at this, though apparently not surprised. They had allowed themselves to augur so well of me from the beginning that it seemed as if they had been accustomed all their lives to the trade of civilizing barbarians.

The nervous system which had just been developed in me, and which made me pay for the pleasures and advantages it brought by keen and constant sufferings during the rest of my life, had rendered me specially sensitive to impressions from without; and this quickness to feel the effect of external things was helped by an organic vigour such as is only found among animals or savages. I was astounded at the decay of the faculties in other people. These men in spectacles, these women with their sense of smell deadened by snuff, these premature graybeards, deaf and gouty before their time, were painful to behold. To me society seemed like a vast hospital; and when with my robust constitution I found myself in the midst of these weaklings, it seemed to me that with a puff of my breath I could have blown them into the air as if they had been so much thistle-down.

This unfortunately led me into the error of yielding to that rather stupid kind of pride which makes a man presume upon his natural gifts. For a long time it induced me to neglect their real improvement, as if this were a work of supererogation. The idea that gradually grew up in me of the worthlessness of my fellows prevented me from rising above those whom I henceforth looked upon as my inferiors. I did not realize that society is made up of so many elements of little value in themselves, but so skilfully and solidly put together that before adding the least extraneous particle a man must be a qualified artificer. I did not know that in this society there is no resting-place between the role of the great artist and that of the good workman. Now, I was neither one nor the other, and, if the truth must be told, all my ideas have never succeeded in lifting me out of the ordinary ruck; all my strength has only enabled me with much difficulty to do as others do.

In a few weeks, then, I passed from an excess of admiration to an excess of contempt for society. As soon as I understood the workings of its springs they seemed to me so miserably regulated by a feeble generation that the hopes of my mentors, unknown to themselves, were doomed to disappointment. Instead of realizing my own inferiority and endeavouring to efface myself in the crowd, I imagined that I could give proof of my superiority whenever I wished; and I fed on fancies which I blush to recall. If I did not show myself egregiously ridiculous, it was thanks to the very excess of this vanity which feared to stultify itself before others.

At that time Paris presented a spectacle which I shall not attempt to set before you, because no doubt you have often eagerly studied it in the excellent pictures which have been painted by eye-witnesses in the form of general history or private memoirs. Besides, such a picture would exceed the limits of my story, for I promised to tell you only the cardinal events in my moral and philosophical development. In order to give you some idea of the workings of my mind at this period it will suffice to mention that the War of Independence was breaking out in America; that Voltaire was receiving his apotheosis in Paris; that Franklin, the prophet of a new political religion, was sowing the seed of liberty in the very heart of the Court of France; while Lafayette was secretly preparing his romantic expedition. The majority of young patricians were being carried away either by fashion, or the love of change, or the pleasure inherent in all opposition which is not dangerous.

Opposition took a graver form and called for more serious work in the case of the old nobles, and among the members of the parliaments. The spirit of the League was alive again in the ranks of these ancient patricians and these haughty magistrates, who for form's sake were still supporting the tottering monarchy with one arm, while with the other they gave considerable help to the invasions of philosophy. The privileged classes of society were zealously lending a hand to the imminent destruction of their privileges by complaining that these had been curtailed by the kings. They were bringing up their children in constitutional principles, because they imagined they were going to found a new monarchy in which the people would help them to regain their old position above the throne; and it is for this reason that the greatest admiration for Voltaire and the most ardent sympathies with Franklin were openly expressed in the most famous salons in Paris.

So unusual and, if it must be said, so unnatural a movement of the human mind had infused fresh life into the vestiges of the Court of Louis XIV, and replaced the customary coldness and stiffness by a sort of quarrelsome vivacity. It had also introduced certain serious forms into the frivolous manners of the regency, and lent them an appearance of depth. The pure but colourless life of Louis XVI counted for nothing, and influenced nobody. Never had there been such serious chatter, so many flimsy maxims, such an affectation of wisdom, so much inconsistency between words and deeds as might have been found at this period among the so-called enlightened classes.

It was necessary to remind you of this in order that you might understand the admiration which I had at first for a world apparently so disinterested, so courageous, so eager in the pursuit of truth, and likewise the disgust which I was soon to feel for so much affectation and levity, for such an abuse of the most hallowed words and the most sacred convictions. For my own part, I was perfectly sincere; and I founded my philosophic fervour (that recently discovered sentiment of liberty which was then called the cult of reason) on the broad base of an inflexible logic. I was young and of a good constitution, the first condition perhaps of a healthy mind; my reading, though not extensive, was solid, for I had been fed on food easy of digestion. The little I knew served to show me, therefore, that others either knew nothing at all, or were giving themselves the lie.

At the commencement of our stay in Paris the chevalier had but few visitors. The friend and contemporary of Turgot and several other distinguished men, he had not mixed with the gilded youth of his day, but had lived soberly in the country after loyally serving in the wars. His circle of friends, therefore, was composed of a few grave gentlemen of the long robe, several old soldiers, and a few nobles from his own province, both old and young, who, thanks to a respectable fortune, were able, like himself, to come and spend the winter in Paris. He had, moreover, kept up a slight intercourse with a more brilliant set, among whom Edmee's beauty and refined manners were noticed as soon as she appeared. Being an only daughter, and passably rich, she was sought after by various important matrons, those procuresses of quality who have always a few young proteges whom they wish to clear from debt at the expense of some family in the provinces. And then, when it became known that she was engaged to M. de la Marche, the almost ruined scion of a very illustrious family, she was still more kindly received, until by degrees the little salon which she had chosen for her father's old friends became too small for the wits by quality and profession, and the grand ladies with a turn for philosophy who wished to know the young Quakeress, the Rose of Berry (such were the names given her by a certain fashionable woman).

This rapid success in a world in which she had hitherto been unknown by no mean dazzled Edmee; and the control which she possessed over herself was so great that, in spite of all the anxiety with which I watched her slightest movement, I could never discover if she felt flattered at causing such a stir. But what I could perceive was the admirable good sense manifested in everything she did and everything she said. Her manner, at once ingenuous and reserved, and a certain blending of unconstraint with modest pride, made her shine even among the women who were the most admired and the most skilled in attracting attention. And this is the place to mention that at first I was extremely shocked at the tone and bearing of these women, whom everybody extolled; to me they seemed ridiculous in their studied posings, and their grand society manners looked very much like insufferable effrontery. Yes, I, so intrepid at heart, and but lately so coarse in my manners, felt ill at ease and abashed in their presence; and it needed all Edmee's reproaches and remonstrances to prevent me from displaying a profound contempt for this meretriciousness of glances, of toilets, and allurements which was known in society as allowable coquetry, as the charming desire to please, as amiability, and as grace. The abbe was of my opinion. When the guests had gone we members of the family used to gather round the fireside for a short while before separating. It is at such a time that one feels an impulse to bring together one's scattered impressions and communicate them to some sympathetic being. The abbe, then, would break the same lances as myself with my uncle and cousin. The chevalier, who was an ardent admirer of the fair sex, of which he had had but little experience, used to take upon himself, like a true French knight, to defend all the beauties that we were attacking so unmercifully. He would laughingly accuse the abbe of arguing about women as the fox in the fable argued about the grapes. For myself, I used to improve under the abbe's criticisms; this was an emphatic way of letting Edmee know how much I preferred her to all others. She, however, appeared to be more scandalized than flattered, and seriously reproved me for the tendency to malevolence which had its origin, she said, in my inordinate pride.

It is true that after generously undertaking the defence of the persons in question, she would come over to our opinion as soon as, Rousseau in hand, we told her that the women in Paris society had cavalier manners and a way of looking a man in the face which must needs be intolerable in the eyes of a sage. When once Rousseau had delivered judgment, Edmee would object no further; she was ready to admit with him that the greatest charm of a woman is the intelligent and modest attention she gives to serious discussions, and I always used to remind her of the comparison of a superior woman to a beautiful child with its great eyes full of feeling and sweetness and delicacy, with its shy questionings and its objections full of sense. I hoped that she would recognise herself in this portrait upon the text, and, enlarging the portrait:

"A really superior woman," I said, looking at her earnestly, "is one who knows enough to prevent her from asking a ridiculous or unseasonable question, or from ever measuring swords with men of merit. Such a woman knows when to be silent, especially with the fools whom she could laugh at, or the ignorant whom she could humiliate. She is indulgent towards absurdities because she does not yearn to display her knowledge, and she is observant of whatsoever is good, because she desires to improve herself. Her great object is to understand, not to instruct. The great art (since it is recognised that art is required even in the commerce of words) is not to pit against one another two arrogant opponents, eager to parade their learning and to amuse the company by discussing questions the solution of which no one troubles about, but to illumine every unprofitable disputation by bringing in the help of all who can throw a little light on the points at issue. This is a talent of which I can see no signs among the hostesses who are so cried up. In their houses I always find two fashionable barristers, and a thunderstruck audience, in which no one dares to be judge. The only art these ladies have is to make the man of genius ridiculous, and the ordinary man dumb and inert. One comes away from such houses saying, 'Those were fine speeches,' and nothing more."

I really think that I was in the right here; but I cannot forget that my chief cause of anger against these women arose from the fact that they paid no attention to people, however able they might think themselves, unless they happened to be famous—the *people* being myself, as you may easily imagine. On the other hand, now that I look back on those days without prejudice and without any sense of wounded vanity, I am certain that these women had a way of fawning on public favourites which was much more like childish conceit than sincere admiration or candid sympathy. They became editors, as it were, of the conversation, listening with all their might and making peremptory signals to the audience to listen to every triviality issuing from an illustrious mouth; while they would suppress a yawn and drum with their fans at all remarks, however excellent, as soon as they were unsigned by a fashionable name. I am ignorant of the airs of the intellectual women of the nineteenth century; nay, I do not know if the race still exists. Thirty years have passed since I mixed in society; but, as to the past, you may believe what I tell you. There were five or six of these women who were absolutely odious to me. One of them had some wit, and scattered her epigrams right and left. These were at once hawked about in all drawing-rooms, and I had to listen to them twenty times in a single day. Another had read Montesquieu, and gave lessons in law to the oldest magistrates. A third used to play the harp execrably, but it was agreed that her arms were the most beautiful in France, and we had to endure the harsh scraping of her nails over the strings so that she might have an opportunity of removing her gloves like a coy little girl. What can I say of the others, except that they vied with one another in all those affectations and fatuous insincerities, by which all the men childishly allowed themselves to be duped. One alone was really pretty, said nothing, and gave pleasure by her very lack of artificiality. To her I might have been favourably inclined because of her ignorance, had she not gloried in this, and tried to emphasize her difference from the others by a piquant ingenuousness. One day I discovered that she had plenty of wit, and straightway I abhorred her.

Edmee alone preserved all the freshness of sincerity and all the distinction of natural grace. Sitting on a sofa by the side of M. de Malesherbes, she was for me the same being that I had gazed on so many times in the light of the setting sun, as she sat on the stone seat at the door of Patience's cottage.

XIII

You will readily believe that all the homage paid to my cousin fanned into fresh flames the jealousy which had been smouldering in my breast. Since the day when, in obedience to her command, I began to devote myself to work, I could hardly say whether I had dared to count on her promise that she would become my wife as soon as I was able to understand her ideas and feelings. To me, indeed, it seemed that the time for this had already arrived; for it is certain that I understood Edmee, better perhaps than any of the men who were paying their addresses to her in prose and verse. I had firmly resolved not to presume upon the oath extorted from her at Roche-Mauprat; yet, when I remembered her last promise, freely given at the chapel window, and the inferences which I could have drawn from her conversation with the abbe which I had overheard in the parlour at Sainte-Severe; when I remembered her earnestness in preventing me from going away and in directing my education; the motherly attentions she had lavished on me during my illness—did not all these things give me, if not some right, at least some reason to hope? It is true that her friendship would become icy as soon as my passion betrayed itself in words or looks; it is true that since the first day I saw her I had not advanced a single step towards close affection; it is also true that M. de la Marche frequently came to the house, and that she always showed him as much friendship as myself, though with less familiarity and more respect in it, a distinction which was naturally due to the difference in our characters and our ages, and did not indicate any preference for one or the other. It was possible, therefore, to attribute her promise to the prompting of her conscience; the interest which she took in my studies to her worship of human dignity as it stood rehabilitated by philosophy; her quiet and continued affection for M. de la March to a profound regret, kept in subjection by the strength and wisdom of her mind. These perplexities I felt very acutely. The hope of compelling her love by submission and devotion had sustained me; but this hope was beginning to grow weak; for though, as all allowed, I had made prodigious efforts and extraordinary progress, Edmee's regard for me had been very far from increasing in the same proportion. She had not shown any astonishment at what she called my lofty intellect; she had always believed in it; she had praised it unreasonably. But she was not blind to the faults in my character, to the vices of my soul. She had reproached me with these with an inexorable sweetness, with a patience calculated to drive me to despair; for she seemed to have made up her mind that, whatever the future might bring, she would never love me more and never less.

Meanwhile all were paying court to her and none were accepted. It had, indeed, been given out that she was engaged to M. de la Marche, but no one understood any better than myself the indefinite postponement of the marriage. People came to the conclusion that she was seeking a pretext to get rid of him, and they could find no ground for her repugnance except by supposing that she had conceived a great passion for myself. My strange history had caused some stir; the women examined me with curiosity; the men seemed interested in me and showed me a sort of respect which I affected to despise, but to which, however, I was far from insensible. And, since nothing finds credence in the world until it is embellished with some fiction, people strangely exaggerated my wit, my capabilities and my learning; but, as soon as they had seen M. de la Marche and myself in Edmee's company, all their inferences were annihilated by the composure and ease of our manners. To both of us Edmee was the same in public as in private; M. de la Marche, a soulless puppet, was perfectly drilled in conventional manners; and myself, a prey to divers passions, but inscrutable by reason of my pride and also, I must confess, of my pretensions to the sublimity of the *American manner.* I should tell you that I had been fortunate enough to be introduced to Franklin as a sincere devotee of liberty. Sir Arthur Lee had honoured me with a certain kindness and some excellent advice; consequently my head was somewhat turned, even as the heads of those whom I railed at so bitterly were turned, and to such an extent that this little vainglory brought sorely needed relief to my agonies of mind. Perhaps you will shrug your shoulders when I own that I took the greatest pleasure in the world in leaving my hair unpowdered, in wearing big shoes, and appearing everywhere in a dark-coloured coat, of aggressively simple cut and stiffly neat—in a word, in aping, as far as was then permissible without being mistaken for a regular plebeian, the dress and ways of the Bonhomme Richard! I was nineteen, and I was living in an age when every one affected a part—that is my only excuse.

I might plead also that my too indulgent and too simple tutor openly approved of my conduct; that my Uncle Hubert, though he occasionally laughed at me, let me do as I wished, and that Edmee said absolutely nothing about this ridiculous affectation, and appeared never to notice it.

Meanwhile spring had returned; we were going back to the country; the salons were being gradually deserted. For myself, I was still in the same state of uncertainty. I noticed one day that M. de la Marche seemed anxious to find an opportunity of speaking to Edmee in private. At first I found pleasure in making him suffer, and did not stir from my chair. However, I thought I detected on Edmee's brow that slight frown which I knew so well, and after a silent dialogue with myself I went out of the room, resolving to observe the results of this *tete-a-tete*, and to learn my fate, whatever it might be.

At the end of an hour I returned to the drawing-room. My uncle was there; M. de la Marche was staying to dinner; Edmee seemed meditative but not melancholy; the abbe's eyes were putting questions to her which she did not understand, or did not wish to understand.

M. de la Marche accompanied my uncle to the Comedie Francaise. Edmee said that she had some letters to write and requested permission to remain at home. I followed the count and the chevalier, but after the first act I made my escape and returned to the house. Edmee had given orders that she was not to be disturbed; but I did not consider that this applied to myself; the servants thought it quite natural that I should behave as the son of the house. I entered the drawing-room, fearful lest Edmee should have retired to her bed-room; for there I could not have followed her. She was sitting near the fire and amusing herself by pulling out the petals of the blue and white asters which I had gathered during a walk to the tomb of Jean Jacques Rousseau. These flowers brought back to me a night of ecstasy, under the clear moonlight, the only hours of happiness, perhaps, that I could mention in all my life.

"Back already?" she said, without any change of attitude.

"Already is an unkind word," I replied. "Would you like me to retire to my room, Edmee?"

"By no means; you are not disturbing me at all; but you would have derived more profit from seeing *Merope* than from listening to my conversation this evening; for I warn you that I feel a complete idiot."

"So much the better, cousin; I shall not feel humiliated this evening, since for the first time we shall be upon a footing of equality. But, might I ask you why you so despise my asters? I thought that you would probably keep them as a souvenir."

"Of Rousseau?" she asked with a malicious little smile, and without raising her eyes to mine.

"Naturally that was my meaning," I answered.

"I am playing a most interesting game," she said; "do not interrupt me."

"I know it," I said. "All the children in Varenne play it, and there is not a lass but believes in the decree of fate that it revels. Would you like me to read your thoughts as you pull out these petals four by four?"

"Come, then, O mighty magician!"

"A little, that is how some one loves you; much, that is how you love him; passionately, that is how another loves you; not at all, thus do you love this other."

"And might I inquire, Sir Oracle," replied Edmee, whose face became more serious, "who some one and another may be? I suspect that you are like the Pythonesses of old; you do not know the meaning of your auguries yourself."

"Could you not guess mine, Edmee?"

"I will try to interpret the riddle, if you will promise that afterward you will do what the Sphinx did when vanquished by OEdipus."

"Oh, Edmee," I cried; "think how long I have been running my head against walls on account of you and your interpretations. And yet you have not guessed right a single time."

"Oh, good heavens! I have," she said, throwing the bouquet on to the mantel-piece. "You shall see. I love M. de la Marche a little, and I love you much. He loves me passionately, and you love me not at all. That is the truth."

"I forgive you this malicious interpretation with all my heart for the sake of the word 'much,'" I replied.

I tried to take her hands. She drew them away quickly, though, in fact, she had no need to fear; for had she given me them, I merely intended to press them in brotherly fashion; but this appearance of distrust aroused memories which were dangerous for me. I fancy she showed a great deal of coquetry that evening in her expression and manners; and, until then, I had never seen the least inclination toward it. I felt my courage rising, though I could not explain why; and I ventured on some pointed remarks about her interview with M. de la Marche. She made no effort to deny my interpretations, and began to laugh when I told her that she ought to thank me for my exquisite politeness in retiring as soon as I saw her knit her brow.

Her supercilious levity was beginning to irritate me a little, when a servant entered and handed her a letter, saying that some one was waiting for an answer.

"Go to my writing-table and cut a pen for me, please," she said to me.

With an air of unconcern she broke the seal and ran through the letter, while I, quite ignorant of the contents, began preparing her writing materials.

For some time the crow-quill had been cut ready for use; for some time the paper with its coloured vignette had been waiting by the side of the amber writing-case; yet Edmee paid no attention to them and made no attempt to use them. The letter lay open in her lap; her feet were on the fire-dogs, her elbows on the arm of her chair in her favourite attitude of meditation. She was completely absorbed. I spoke to her softly; she did not hear me. I thought that she had forgotten the letter and had fallen asleep. After a quarter of an hour the servant came back and said that the messenger wished to know if there was any answer.

"Certainly," she replied; "ask him to wait."

She read the letter again with the closest attention, and began to write slowly; then she threw her reply into the fire, pushed away the arm-chair with her foot, walked round the room a few times, and suddenly stopped in front of me and looked at me in a cold, hard manner.

"Edmee," I cried, springing to me feet, "what is the matter, and how does that letter which is worrying you so much concern myself?"

"What is that to you?" she replied.

"What is that to me?" I cried. "And what is the air I breathe to me? and what is the blood that flows in my veins? Ask me that, if you like, but do not ask how one of your words or one of your glances can concern me; for you know very well that my life depends on them."

"Do not talk nonsense now, Bernard," she answered, returning to her arm-chair in a distracted manner. "There is a time for everything."

"Edmee, Edmee! do not play with the sleeping lion, do not stir up the fire which is smouldering in the ashes."

She shrugged her shoulders, and began to write with great rapidity. Her face was flushed, and from time to time she passed her fingers through the long hair which fell in ringlets over her shoulders. She was dangerously beautiful in her agitation; she looked as if in love—but with whom? Doubtless with him to whom she was writing. I began to feel the fires of jealousy. I walked out of the room abruptly and crossed the hall. I looked at the man who had brought the letter; he was in M. de la Marche's livery. I had no further doubts; this, however, only increased my rage. I returned to the drawing-room and threw open the door violently. Edmee did not even turn her head; she continued writing. I sat down opposite her, and stared at her with flashing eyes. She did not deign to raise her own to mine. I even fancied that I noticed on her ruby lips the dawn of a smile which seemed an insult to my agony. At last she finished her letter and sealed it. I rose and walked towards her, feeling strongly tempted to snatch it from her hands. I had learnt to control myself somewhat better than of old; but I realized how, with passionate souls, a single instant may destroy the labours of many days.

"Edmee," I said to her, in a bitter tone, and with a frightful grimace that was intended to be a sarcastic smile, "would you like me to hand this letter to M. de la Marche's lackey, and at the same time tell him in a whisper at what time his master may come to the tryst?"

"It seems to me," she replied, with a calmness that exasperated me, "that it was possible to mention the time in my letter, and that there is no need to inform a servant of it."

"Edmee, you ought to be a little more considerate of me," I cried.

"That doesn't trouble me the least in the world," she replied.

And throwing me the letter she had received across the table she went out to give the answer to the messenger herself. I do not know whether she had told me to read this letter; but I do know that the impulse which urged me to do so was irresistible. It ran somewhat as follows:

"Edmee, I have at last discovered the fatal secret which, according to you, sets an impassable barrier in the way of our union. Bernard loves you; his agitation this morning betrayed him. But you do not love him, I am sure . . . that would be impossible! You would have told me frankly. The obstacle, then, must be elsewhere. Forgive me! It has come to my knowledge that you spent two hours in the brigand's den. Unhappy girl! your misfortune, your prudence, your sublime delicacy make you still nobler in my eyes. And why did you not confide to me at once the misfortune of which you were a victim? I could have eased your sorrow and my own by a word. I could have helped you to hide your secret. I could have wept with you; or, rather, I could have wiped out the odious recollection by displaying an attachment proof against anything. But there is no need to despair; there is still time to say this word, and I do so now: Edmee, I love you more than ever; more than ever I am resolved to offer you my name; will you deign to accept it?"

This note was signed Adhemar de la Marche.

I had scarcely finished reading it when Edmee returned, and came towards the fire-place with an anxious look, as if she had forgotten some precious object. I handed her the letter that I had just read; but she took it absently, and, stooping over the hearth with an air of relief, eagerly seized a crumpled piece of paper which the flames had merely scorched. This was the first answer she had written to M. de la Marche's note, the one she had not judged fit to send.

"Edmee," I said, throwing myself on my knees, "let me see that letter. Whatever if may be, I will submit to the decree dictated by your first impulse."

"You really would?" she asked, with an indefinable expression. "Supposing I loved M. de la Marche, and that I was making a great sacrifice for your sake in refusing him, would you be generous enough to release me from my word?"

I hesitated for a moment. A cold sweat broke out all over me. I looked her full in the face; but her eyes were inscrutable and betrayed no hint of her thoughts. If I had fancied that she really loved me and that she was putting my virtue to the test, I should perhaps have played the hero; but I was afraid of some trap. My passion overmastered me. I felt that I had not the strength to renounce my claim with a good grace; and hypocrisy was repugnant to me. I rose to my feet, trembling with rage.

"You love him!" I cried. "Confess that you love him!"

"And if I did," she answered, putting the letter in her pocket, "where would be the crime?"

"The crime would be that hitherto you have lied in telling me that you did not love him."

"Hitherto is saying a good deal," she rejoined, looking at me fixedly; "we have not discussed the matter since last year. At that time it was possible that I did not love Adhemar very much, and at present it might be possible that I loved him more than you. If I compare the conduct of both to-day I see on the one hand a man without proper pride and without delicacy, presuming upon a promise which my heart perhaps has never ratified; on the other I see an admirable friend whose sublime devotion is ready to brave all prejudices; who—believing that I bear the smirch of an indelible shame—is none the less prepared to cover the blot with his protection."

"What! this wretch believes that I have done violence to you, and yet does not challenge me to a duel?"

"That is not what he believes, Bernard. He knows that you rescued me from Roche-Mauprat; but he thinks that you helped me too late, and that I was the victim of the other brigands."

"And he wants to marry you, Edmee? Either the man's devotion is sublime, as you say, or he is deeper in debt than you think."

146

"How dare you say that?" said Edmee angrily. "Such an odious explanation of generous conduct can proceed only from an unfeeling soul or a perverse mind. Be silent, unless you wish me to hate you."

"Say that you hate me, Edmee; say so without fear; I know it."

"Without fear! You should know likewise that I have not yet done you the honour to fear you. However, tell me this: without inquiring into what I intend to do, can you understand that you ought to give me my liberty, and abandon your barbarous rights?"

"I understand nothing except that I love you madly, and that these nails of mine shall tear out the heart of any man who tries to win you from me. I know that I shall force you to love me, and that, if I do not succeed, I will at any rate not let you belong to another while I am alive. The man will have to walk over my body riddled with wounds and bleeding from every pore, ere he can put the wedding-ring on your finger; with my last breath, too, I will dishonour you by proclaiming that you are my mistress, and thus cloud the joy of any man who may triumph over me; and if I can stab you as I die, I will, so that in the tomb, at least, you may be my wife. That is what I purpose doing, Edmee. And now, practise all your arts on me; lead me on from trap to trap; rule me with your admirable diplomacy. I may be duped a hundred times because of my ignorance, but have I not sworn by the name of Mauprat?"

"Mauprat the Hamstringer!" she added with freezing irony.

And she turned to go out.

I was about to seize her arm when the bell rang; it was the abbe who had returned. As soon as he appeared Edmee shook hands with him, and retired to her room without saying a single word to me.

The good abbe, noticing my agitation, questioned me with that assurance which his claims on my affections were henceforth to give him. The present matter, however, was the only one on which we had never had an explanation. In vain had he sought to introduce it. He had not given me a single lesson in history without leading up to some famous love affairs and drawing from them an example or a precept of moderation or generosity; but he had not succeeded in making me breathe a word on this subject. I could not bring myself to forgive him altogether for having done me an ill turn with Edmee. I even had a suspicion that he was still injuring my cause; and I therefore put myself on guard against all the arguments of his philosophy and all the seductions of his friendship. On this special evening I was more unassailable than ever. I left him ill at ease and depressed, and went and threw myself on my bed, where I buried my head in the clothes so as to stifle the customary sobs, those pitiless conquerors of my pride and my rage.

XIV

The next day I was in a state of gloomy despair; Edmee was icily cold; M. de la Marche did not come. I fancied I had seen the abbe going to call on him, and subsequently telling Edmee the result of their interview. However, they betrayed no signs of agitation, and I had to endure my suspense in silence. I could not get a minute with Edmee alone. In the morning I went on foot to M. de la Marche's house. What I intended saying to him I do not know; my state of exasperation was such that it drove me to act without either object or plan. Having learnt that he had left Paris, I returned. I found my uncle very depressed. On seeing me he frowned, and, after forcing himself to exchange a few meaningless words with me, left me to the abbe, who tried to draw me on to speak, but succeeded no better than the night before. For several days I sought an opportunity of speaking with Edmee, but she always managed to avoid it. Preparations were being made for the return to Sainte-Severe; she seemed neither sorry nor pleased at the prospect. I determined to slip a note between the page of her book asking for an interview. Within five minutes I received the following reply:

"An interview would lead to nothing. You are persisting in your boorish behaviour; I shall persevere in what I believe to be the path of integrity. An upright conscience cannot go from its word. I had sworn never to be any man's but yours. I shall not marry, for I did not swear that I would be yours whatever might happen. If you continue to be unworthy of my esteem I shall take steps to remain free. My poor father is sinking into the grave; a convent shall be my refuge when the only tie which binds me to the world is broken."

I had fulfilled all the conditions imposed by Edmee, and now, it seemed, her only return was an order that I should break them. I thus found myself in the same position as on the day of her conversation with the abbe.

I passed the remainder of the day shut up in my room. All through the night I walked up and down in violent agitation. I made no effort to sleep. I will not tell you the thoughts that passed through my mind; they were not unworthy of an honest man. At daybreak I was at Lafayette's house. He procured me the necessary papers for leaving France. He told me to go and await him in Spain, whence he was going to sail for the United States. I returned to our house to get the clothes and money indispensable to the humblest of travellers. I left a note for my uncle, so that he might not feel uneasy at my absence; this I promised to explain very soon in a long letter. I begged him to refrain from passing sentence on me until it arrived, and assured him that I should never forget all his goodness.

I left before any one in the house was up; for I was afraid that my resolution might be shaken at the least sign of friendship, and I felt that I could no longer impose upon a too generous affection. I could not, how-ever, pass Edmee's door without pressing my lips to the lock. Then, hiding my head in my hands, I rushed away like a madman, and scarcely stopped until I had reached the other side of the Pyrenees. There I took a short rest, and wrote to Edmee that, as far as concerned myself, she was free; that I would not thwart a single wish of hers; but that it was impossible for me to be a witness of my rival's triumph. I felt firmly convinced that she loved him; and I resolved to crush out my own love. I was promising more than I could perform; but these first manifestations of wounded pride gave me confidence in myself. I also wrote to my uncle to tell him I should not hold myself worthy of the boundless affection he had bestowed on me until I had won my spurs as a knight. I confided to him my hopes of a soldier's fame and fortune with all the candour of conceit; and since I felt sure that Edmee would read this letter I feigned unclouded delight and an ardour that knew no regrets; I did not know whether my uncle was aware of the real cause of my departure; but my pride could not bring itself to confess. It was the same with the abbe, to whom I likewise wrote a letter full of gratitude and affection. I ended by begging my uncle to put himself to no expense on my account over the gloomy keep at Roche-Mauprat, assuring him that I could never bring myself to live there. I urged him to consider the fief as his daughter's property, and only asked that he would be good enough to advance me my share of the income for two or three years, so that I might pay the expenses of my own outfit, and thus prevent my de-votion to the American cause from being a burden to the noble Lafayette.

My conduct and my letters apparently gave satisfaction. Soon after I reached the coast of Spain I received from my uncle a letter full of kindly exhortations, and of mild censure for my abrupt departure. He gave me a father's blessing, and declared on his honour that the fief of Roche-Mauprat would never be accepted by Edmee, and sent me a considerable sum of money exclusive of the income due me in the future. The abbe expressed the same mild censure, together with still warmer exhortations. It was easy to see that he preferred Edmee's tranquility to my happiness, and that he was full of genuine joy at my departure. Nevertheless he had a liking for me, and his friendship showed itself touchingly through the cruel satisfaction that was mingled with it. He expressed envy of my lot; proclaimed his enthusiasm for the cause of independence; and declared that he himself had more than once felt tempted to throw off the cassock and take up the musket. All this, however, was mere boyish affectation; his timid, gentle nature always kept him the priest under the mask of the philosopher.

Between these two letters I found a little note without any address, which seemed as if it had been slipped in as an after-thought. I was not slow to see that it was from the one person in the world who was of real interest to me. Yet I had not the courage to open it. I walked up and down the sandy beach, turning over this little piece of paper in my hands, fearful that by reading it I might destroy the kind of desperate calm my resolution had given me. Above all, I dreaded lest it might contain expressions of thanks and enthusiastic joy, behind which I should have divined the rapture of contented love for another.

"What can she be writing to me about?" I said to myself. "Why does she write at all? I do not want her pity, still less her gratitude."

I felt tempted to throw this fateful little note into the sea. Once, indeed I held it out over the waves, but I immediately pressed it to my bosom, and kept it hidden there a few moments as if I had been a believer in that second sight preached by the advocates of magnetism, who assert that they can read with the organs of feeling and thought as well as with their eyes.

At last I resolved to break the seal. The words I read were these:

"You have done well, Bernard; but I give you no thanks, as your absence will cause me more suffering than I can tell. Still, go wherever honour and love of truth call you; you will always be followed by my good wishes and prayers. Return when your mission is accomplished; you will find me neither married nor in a convent."

In this note she had inclosed the cornelian ring she had given me during my illness and which I had returned on leaving Paris. I had a little gold box made to hold this ring and note, and I wore it near my heart as a talisman. Lafayette, who had been arrested in France by order of the Government, which was opposed to his expedition, soon came and joined us after escaping from prison. I had had time to make my preparations, and I sailed full of melancholy, ambition, and hope.

You will not expect me to give an account of the American war. Once again I will separate my existence from the events of history as I relate my own adventures. Here, however, I shall suppress even my personal adventures; in my memory these form a special chapter in which Edmee plays the part of a Madonna, constantly invoked but invisible. I cannot think that you would be the least interested in listening to a portion of my narrative from which this angelic figure, the only one worthy of your attention, firstly by reason of her own worth, and then from her influence on myself, was entirely absent. I will only state that from the humble position which I gladly accepted in the beginning in Washington's army, I rose regularly but rapidly to the rank of officer. My military education did not take long. Into this, as into everything that I have undertaken during my life, I put my whole soul, and through the pertinacity of my will I overcame all obstacles.

I won the confidence of my illustrious chiefs. My excellent constitution fitted me well for the hardships of war; my old brigand habits too were of immense service to me; I endured reverses with a calmness beyond the reach of most of the young Frenchmen who had embarked with me, however brilliant their courage might otherwise have been. My own was cool and tenacious, to the great surprise of our allies, who more than once doubted my origin, on seeing how quickly I made myself at home in the forests, and how often my cunning and suspiciousness made me a match for the savages who sometimes harassed our manoeuvres.

In the midst of my labours and frequent changes of place I was fortunate enough to be able to cultivate my mind through my intimacy with a young man of merit whom Providence sent me as a companion and friend. Love of the natural sciences had decided him to join our expedition, and he never failed to show himself a good soldier; but it was easy to see that political sympathy had played only a secondary part in his decision. He had no desire for promotion, no aptitude for strategic studies. His herbarium and his zoological occupations engaged his thoughts much more than the successes of the war and the triumph of liberty. He fought too well, when occasion arose, to ever deserve the reproach of lukewarmness; but up to the eve of a fight and from the morrow he seemed to have forgotten that he was engaged in anything beyond a scientific expedition into the wilds of the New World. His trunk was always full, not of money and valuables, but of natural history specimens; and while we were lying on the grass on the alert for the least noise which might reveal the approach of the enemy, he would be absorbed in the analysis of some plant or insect. He was an admirable young man, as pure as an angel, as unselfish as a stoic, as patient as a savant, and withal cheerful and affectionate. When we were in danger of being surprised, he could think and talk of nothing but the precious pebbles and the invaluable bits of grass that he had collected and classified; and yet were one of us wounded, he would nurse him with a kindness and zeal that none could surpass.

One day he noticed my gold box as I was putting it in my bosom, and he immediately begged me to let him have it, to keep a few flies' legs and grasshoppers' wings which he would have defended with the last drop of his blood. It needed all the reverence I had for the relics of my love to resist the demands of friendship. All he could obtain from me was permission to hide away a very pretty little plant in my precious box. This plant, which he declared he was the first to discover, was allowed a home by the side of my *fiancee's* ring and note only on condition that it should be called Edmunda sylvestris; to this he consented. He had given the name of Samuel Adams to a beautiful wild apple-tree; he had christened some industrous bee or other Franklin; and nothing pleased him more than to associate some honoured name with his ingenious observations.

The attachment I felt for him was all the more genuine from its being my first friendship with a man of my own age. The pleasure which I derived from this intimacy gave me a new insight into life, and revealed capacities and needs of the soul of which I had hitherto been ignorant. As I could never wholly break away from that love of chivalry which had been implanted in me in early childhood, it pleased me to look upon him as my "brother in arms," and I expressed a wish that he would give me this special title too, to the exclusion of every other intimate friend. He caught at the idea with a gladness of heart that showed me how lively was the sympathy between us. He declared that I was a born naturalist, because I was so fitted for a roving life and rough expeditions. Sometimes he would reproach me with absent-mindedness, and scold me seriously for carelessly stepping upon interesting plants, but he would assert that I was endowed with a sense of method, and that some day I might invent, not a theory of nature, but an excellent system of classification. His prophecy was never fulfilled, but his encouragement aroused a taste for study in me, and prevented my mind from being wholly paralyzed by camp life. To me he was as a messenger from heaven; without him I should perhaps have become, if not the Hamstringer of Roche-Mauprat, at all events the savage of Varenne again. His teachings revived in me the consciousness of intellectual life. He enlarged my ideas and also ennobled my instincts; for, though his marvellous integrity and his modest disposition prevented him from throwing himself into philosophical discussions, he had an innate love of justice, and he judged all questions of sentiment and morality with unerring wisdom. He acquired an ascendency over me which the abbe had never been able to acquire, owing to the attitude of mutual distrust in which we had been placed from the beginning. He revealed to me the wonders of a large part of the physical world, but what he taught me of chiefest value was to learn to know myself, and to ponder over my own impressions. I succeeded in controlling my impulses up to a certain point. I could never subdue my pride and violent temper. A man cannot change the essence of his nature, but he can guide his divers faculties towards a right path; he can almost succeed in turning his faults to account—and this, indeed, is the great secret and the great problem of education.

The conversations with my friend Arthur led me into such a train of thought that from my recollections of Edmee's conduct I came to deduce logically the motives which must have inspired it. I found her noble and generous, especially in those matters which, owing to my distorted vision and false judgment, had caused me most pain. I did not love her the more for this—that would have been impossible—but I succeeded in understanding why I loved her with an unconquerable love in spite of all she had made me suffer. This sacred fire burned in my soul without growing dim for one instant during the whole six years of our separation. In spite of the rich vitality which pulsed through my veins; in spite of the promptings of an external nature full of voluptuousness; in spite of the bad examples and numerous opportunities which tempted mortal weakness in the freedom of a roving, military life, I call God to witness that I preserved my robe of innocence undefiled, and that I never felt the kiss of a woman. Arthur, whose calmer organization was less susceptible to temptation, and who, moreover, was almost entirely engrossed in intellectual labour, did not always practise the same austerity; nay, he frequently advised me not to run the risk of an exceptional life, contrary to the demands of Nature. When I confided to him that a master-passion removed all weaknesses from my path and made a fall impossible, he ceased to reason against what he called my fanaticism (this was a word very much in vogue and applied indiscriminately to almost everything). I observed, indeed, that he had a more profound esteem for me, I may even say a sort of respect which did not express itself in words, but which was revealed by a thousand little signs of compliance and deference.

One day, when he was speaking of the great power exercised by gentleness of manners in alliance with a resolute will, citing both good and bad examples from the history of men, especially the gentleness of the apostles and the hypocrisy of the priests of all religions, it came into my mind to ask him if, with my headstrong nature and hasty temper, I should ever be able to exercise any influence on my fellows. When I used this last word I was, of course, thinking only of Edmee. Arthur replied that the influence which I exercised would be other than that of studied gentleness.

"Your influence," he said, "will be due to your natural goodness of heart. Warmth of soul, ardour and perseverance in affection, these are what are needed in family life, and these qualities make our defects loved even by those who have to suffer from them most. We should endeavour, therefore, to master ourselves out of love for those who love us; but to propose to one's self a system of moderation in the most intimate concerns of love and friendship would, in my opinion, be a childish task, a work of egotism which would kill all affection, in ourselves first, and soon afterwards in the others. I was speaking of studied moderation only in the exercise of authority over the masses. Now, should your ambition ever . . ."

"You believe, then," I said, without listening to the last part of his speech, "that, such as I am, I might make a woman happy and force her to love me, in spite of all my faults and the harm they cause?"

"O lovelorn brain!" he exclaimed. "How difficult it is to distract your thoughts! . . . Well, if you wish to know, Bernard, I will tell you what I think of your love-affair. The person you love so ardently loves you, unless she is incapable of love or quite bereft of judgment."

I assured him that she was as much above all other women as the lion is above the squirrel, the cedar above the hyssop, and with the help of metaphors I succeeded in convincing him. Then he persuaded me to tell him a few details, in order, as he said, that he might judge of my position with regard to Edmee. I opened my heart without reserve, and told him my history from beginning to end. At this time we were on the outskirts of a beautiful forest in the last rays of the setting sun. The park at Sainte-Severe, with its fine lordly oaks which had never known the insult of an axe, came into my thoughts as I gazed on these trees of the wilds, exempt from all human care, towering out above our heads in their might and primitive grace. The glowing horizon reminded me of the evening visits to Patience's hut, and Edmee sitting under the golden vine-leaves, and the notes of the merry parrots brought back to me the warbling of the beautiful exotic birds she used to keep in her room. I wept as I thought of the land of my birth so far away, of the broad ocean between us which had swallowed so many pilgrims in the hour of their return to their native shores. I also thought of the prospects of fortune, of the dangers of war, and for the first time I felt the fear of death; for Arthur, pressing my hand in his, assured me that I was loved, and that in each act of harshness or distrust he found but a new proof of affection.

"My boy," he said, "cannot you see that if she did not want to marry you, she would have found a hundred ways of ridding herself of your pretensions forever? And if she had not felt an inexhaustible affection for you, would she have taken so much trouble, and imposed so many sacrifices upon herself to raise you from the abject condition in which she found you, and make you worthy of her? Well, you are always dreaming of the mighty deeds of the knight-errants of old: cannot you see that you are a noble knight condemned by your lady to rude trials for having failed in the laws of gallantry, for having demanded in an imperious tone the love which ought to be sued for on bended knee?"

He then entered into a detailed examination of my misdeeds, and found that the chastisement was severe but just. Afterwards he discussed the probabilities of the future, and very sensibly advised me to submit until she thought right to pardon me.

"But," I said, "is there no shame in a man ripened, as I am now, by reflection, and roughly tried by war, submitting like a child to the caprices of a woman?"

"No," replied Arthur, "there is no shame in that; and the conduct of this woman is not dictated by caprice. One can win nothing but honour in repairing any evil one has done; and how few men are capable of it! It is only just that offended modesty should claim its rights and its natural independence. You have behaved like Albion; do not be astonished that Edmee behaves like Philadelphia. She will not yield, except on condition of a glorious peace, and she is right."

He wished to know how she had treated me during the two years we had been in America. I showed him the few short letters I had received from her. He was struck by the good sense and perfect integrity which seemed manifested in their lofty tone and manly precision. In them Edmee had made me no promise, nor had she even encouraged me by holding out any direct hopes; but she had displayed a lively desire for my return, and had spoken of the happiness we should all enjoy when, as we sat around the fire, I should while away the evenings at the chateau with accounts of my wonderful adventures; and she had not hesitated to tell me that, together with her father, I was the one object of her solicitude in life. Yet, in spite of this never-failing tenderness, a terrible suspicion harassed me. In these short letters from my cousin, as in those from her father and in the long, florid and affectionate epistles from the Abbe Aubert, they never gave me any news of the events which might be, and ought to be, taking place in the family. Each spoke of his or her own self and never mentioned the others; or at most they only spoke of the chevalier's attacks of the gout. It was as though an agreement had been made between the three that none should talk about the occupations and state of mind of the other two.

"Shed light and ease my mind on this matter if you can," I said to Arthur. "There are moments when I fancy that Edmee must be married, and that they have agreed not to inform me until I return, and what is to prevent this, in fact? Is it probable that she likes me enough to live a life of solitude out of love for me, when this very love, in obedience to the dictation of a cold reason and an austere conscience, can resign itself to seeing my absence indefinitely prolonged with the war? I have duties to perform here, no doubt; honour demands that I should defend my flag until the day of the triumph or the irreparable defeat of the cause I serve; but I feel that Edmee is dearer to me than these empty honours, and that to see her but one hour sooner I would leave my name to the ridicule or the curses of the world."

"This last thought," replied Arthur, with a smile, "is suggested to you by the violence of your passion; but you would not act as you say, even if the opportunity occurred. When we are grappling with a single one of our faculties we fancy the others annihilated; but let some extraneous shock arouse them, and we realize that our soul draws its life from several sources at the same time. You are not insensible to fame, Bernard; and if Edmee invited you to abandon it you would perceive that it was dearer to you than you thought. You have ardent republican convictions, and Edmee herself was the first to inspire you with them. What, then, would you think of her, and, indeed, what sort of woman would she be, if she said to you to-day, 'There is something more important than the religion I preached to you and the gods I revealed; something more august and more sacred, and that is my own good pleasure'? Bernard, your love is full of contradictory desires. Inconsistency, moreover, is the mark of all human loves. Men imagine that a woman can have no separate existence of her own, and that she must always be wrapped up in them; and yet the only woman they love deeply is she whose character seems to raise her above the weakness and indolence of her sex. You see how all the settlers in this country dispose of the beauty of their slaves, but they have no love for them, however beautiful they may be; and if by chance they become genuinely attached to one of them, their first care is to set her free. Until then they do not think that they are dealing with a human being. A spirit of independence, the conception of virtue, a love of duty, all these privileges of lofty souls are essential, therefore, in the woman who is to be one's companion through life; and the more your mistress gives proof of strength and patience, the more you cherish her, in spite of what you may have to suffer. You must learn, then, to distinguish love from desire; desire wishes to break through the very impediments by which it is attracted, and it dies amid the ruins of the virtue it has vanquished; love wishes to live, and in order to do that, it would fain see the object of its worship long defended by that wall of adamant whose strength and splendour mean true worth and true beauty."

In this way would Arthur explain to me the mysterious springs of my passion, and throw the light of his wisdom upon the stormy abyss of my soul. Sometimes he used to add:

"If Heaven had granted me the woman I have now and then dreamed of, I think I should have succeeded in making a noble and generous passion of my love; but science has asked for too much of my time. I have not had leisure to look for my ideal; and if perchance it has crossed my path, I have not been able either to study it or recognise it. You have been fortunate, Bernard, but then, you do not sound the deeps of natural history; one man cannot have everything."

As to my suspicions about Edmee's marriage, he rejected them with contempt as morbid fancies. To him, indeed, Edmee's silence showed an admirable delicacy of feeling and conduct.

"A vain person," he said, "would take care to let you know all the sacrifices she had made on your account, and would enumerate the titles and qualities of the suitors she had refused. Edmee, however, has too noble a soul, too serious a mind, to enter into these futile details. She looks upon your covenant as inviolable, and does not imitate those weak consciences which are always talking of their victories, and making a merit of doing that in which true strength finds no difficulty. She is so faithful by nature that she never imagines that any one can suspect her of being otherwise."

These talks poured healing balm on my wounds. When at last France openly declared herself an ally of America, I received a piece of news from the abbe that entirely set my mind at ease on one point. He wrote to me that I should probably meet an old friend again in the New World; the Count de la Marche had been given command of a regiment, and was setting out for the United States.

"And between ourselves," added the abbe, "it is quite time that he made a position for himself. This young man, though modest and steady, has always been weak enough to yield to the prejudices of noble birth. He has been ashamed of his poverty, and has tried to hide it as one hides a leprosy. The result is that his efforts to prevent others from seeing the progress of his ruin, have now ruined him completely. Society attributes the rupture between Edmee and him to these reverses of fortune; and people even go so far as to say that he was but little in love with her person, and very much with her dowry. I cannot bring myself to credit him with contemptible views; and I can only think that he is suffering those mortifications which arise from a false estimate of the value of the good things of this world. If you happen to meet him, Edmee wishes you to show him some friendship, and to let him know how great an interest she has always taken in him. Your excellent cousin's conduct in this matter, as in all others, has been full of kindness and dignity."

XV

One the eve of M. de la Marche's departure, and after the abbe's letter had been sent, a little incident had happened in Varenne which, when I heard of it in America, caused me considerable surprise and pleasure. Moreover, it is linked in a remarkable manner with the most important events of my life, as you will see later.

Although rather seriously wounded in the unfortunate affair of Savannah, I was actively engaged in Virginia, under General Greene, in collecting the remains of the army commanded by Gates, whom I considered a much greater hero than his more fortunate rival, Washington. We had just learnt of the landing of M. de Ternay's squadron, and the depression which had fallen on us at this period of reverses and distress was beginning to vanish before the prospect of re-enforcements. These, as a fact, were less considerable than we had expected. I was strolling through the woods with Arthur, a short distance from the camp, and we were taking advantage of this short respite to have a talk about other matters than Cornwallis and the infamous Arnold. Long saddened by the sight of the woes of the American nation, by the fear of seeing injustice and cupidity triumphing over the cause of the people, we were seeking relief in a measure of gaiety. When I had an hour's leisure I used to escape from my stern toils to the oasis of my own thoughts in the family at Sainte-Severe. At such a time I was wont to tell my kind friend Arthur some of the comic incidents of my entry into life after leaving Roche-Mauprat. At one time I would give him a description of the costume in which I first appeared; at another I would describe Mademoiselle Leblanc's contempt and loathing for my person, and her recommendation to her friend Saint-Jean never to approach within arms' length of me. As I thought of these amusing individuals, the face of the solemn hidalgo, Marcasse, somehow arose in my memory, and I began to give a faithful and detailed picture of the dress, and bearing, and conversation of this enigmatic personage. Not that Marcasse was actually as comic as he appeared to be in my imagination; but at twenty a man is only a boy, especially when he is a soldier and has just escaped great dangers, and so is filled with careless pride at the conquest of his own life. Arthur would laugh right heartily as he listened to me, declaring that he would give his whole collection of specimens for such a curious animal as I had just described. The pleasure he derived from my childish chatter increased my vivacity, and I do not know whether I should have been able to resist the temptation to exaggerate my uncle's peculiarities, when suddenly at a turn in our path we found ourselves in the presence of a tall man, poorly dressed, and terribly haggard, who was walking towards us with a serious pensive expression, and carrying in his hand a long naked sword, the point of which was peacefully lowered to the ground. This individual bore such a strong resemblance to the one I had just described to Arthur, struck by the parallel, burst into uncontrollable laughter, and moving aside to make way for Marcasse's double, threw himself upon the grass in a convulsive fit of coughing.

For myself, I was far from laughing; for nothing that has a supernatural air about it fails to produce a vivid impression even on the man most accustomed to dangers. With staring eyes and outstretched arms we drew near to each other, myself and he, not the shade of Marcasse, but the venerable person himself, in flesh and blood, of the hidalgo mole-catcher.

Petrified with astonishment when I saw what I had taken for his ghost slowly carry his hand to the corner of his hat and raise it without bending the fraction of an inch, I started back a yard or two; and this movement, which Arthur thought was a joke on my part, only increased his merriment. The weasel-hunter was by no means disconcerted; perhaps in his judicial gravity he was thinking that this was the usual way to greet people on the other side of the ocean.

But Arthur's laughter almost proved infectious when Marcasse said to me with incomparable gravity:

"Monsieur Bernard, I have had the honour of searching for you for a long time."

"For a long time, in truth, my good Marcasse," I replied, as I shook my old friend's hand with delight. "But, tell me by what strange power I have been lucky enough to draw you hither. In the old days you passed for a sorcerer; is it possible that I have become one too without knowing it?"

"I will explain all that, my dear general," answered Marcasse, who was apparently dazzled by my captain's uniform. "If you will allow me to accompany you I will tell you many things—many things!"

On hearing Marcasse repeat his words in a low voice, as if furnishing an echo for himself, a habit which only a minute before I was in the act of imitating, Arthur burst out laughing again. Marcasse turned toward him and after surveying him intently bowed with imperturbable gravity. Arthur, suddenly recovering his serious mood, rose and, with comic dignity, bowed in return almost to the ground.

We returned to the camp together. On the way Marcasse told me his story in that brief style of his, which, as it forced his hearer to ask a thousand wearisome questions, far from simplifying his narrative, made it extraordinarily complicated. It afforded Arthur great amusement; but

as you would not derive the same pleasure from listening to an exact re-
production of this interminable dialogue, I will limit myself to telling you
how Marcasse had come to leave his country and his friends, in order to
give the American cause the help of his sword.

M. de la Marche happened to be setting out for America at the very
time when Marcasse came to his castle in Berry for a week, to make his
annual round among the beams and joists in the barns. The inmates of the
chateau, in their excitement at the count's departure, indulged in wonderful commentaries on that far country, so full of dangers and marvels, from
which, according to the village wiseacres, no man ever returned without a
vast fortune, and so many gold and silver ingots that he needed ten ships
to carry them all. Now, under his icy exterior, Don Marcasse, like some
hyperborean volcano, concealed a glowing imagination, a passionate love
of the marvellous. Accustomed to live in a state of equilibrium on narrow
beams in evidently loftier regions than other men, and not insensible to
the glory of astounding the bystanders every day by the calm daring of
his acrobatic movements, he let himself be fired by these pictures of El-
dorado; and his dreams were the more extravagant because, as usual, he
unbosomed himself to no one. M. de la Marche, therefore, was very much
surprised when, on the eve of his departure, Marcasse presented himself,
and proposed to accompany him to America as his valet. In vain did M.
de la Marche remind him that he was very old to abandon his calling and
run the risks of a new kind of life. Marcasse displayed so much firmness
that in the end he gained his point. Various reasons led M. de la Marche
to consent to the strange request. He had resolved to take with him a servant older still than the weasel-hunter, a man who was accompanying him
only with great reluctance. But this man enjoyed his entire confidence, a
favour which M. de la Marche was very slow to grant, since he was only
able to keep up the outward show of a man of quality, and wished to be
served faithfully, and with economy and prudence. He knew, however,
that Marcasse was scrupulously honest, and even singularly unselfish; for
there was something of Don Quixote in the man's soul as well as in his
appearance. He had found in some ruins a sort of treasure-trove, that is to
say, an earthenware jar containing a sum of about ten thousand francs in
old gold and silver coins; and not only had he handed it over to the owner
of the ruins, whom he might easily have deceived, but further he had
refused to accept any reward, declaring emphatically in his abbreviated
jargon, "honesty would die selling itself."

Marcasse's economy, his discretion, his punctuality, seemed likely to
make him a valuable man, if he could be trained to put these qualities at
the service of others. The one thing to be feared was that he might not

be able to accustom himself to his loss of independence. However, M. de la Marche thought that, before M. de Ternay's squadron sailed, he would have time to test his new squire sufficiently.

On his side, Marcasse felt many regrets at taking leave of his friends and home; for if he had "friends everywhere and everywhere a native place," as he said, in allusion to his wandering life, he still had a very marked preference for Varenne; and of all his castles (for he was accustomed to call every place he stopped at "his"), the chateau of Sainte-Severe was the only one which he arrived at with pleasure and left with regret. One day, when he had missed his footing on the roof and had rather a serious fall, Edmee, then still a child, had won his heart by the tears she had shed over this accident, and the artless attentions she had shown him. And ever since Patience had come to dwell on the edge of the park, Marcasse had felt still more attracted toward Sainte-Severe; for in Patience Marcasse had found his Orestes. Marcasse did not always understand Patience; but Patience was the only man who thoroughly understood Marcasse, and who knew how much chivalrous honesty and noble courage lay hidden beneath that odd exterior. Humbly bowing to the hermit's intellectual superiority, the weasel-hunter would stop respectfully whenever the poetic frenzy took possession of Patience and made his words unintelligible. At such a time Marcasse would refrain from questions and ill-timed remarks with touching gentleness; would lower his eyes, and nodding his head from time to time as if he understood and approved, would, at least, afford his friend the innocent pleasure of being listened to without contradiction.

Marcasse, however, had understood enough to make him embrace republican ideas and share in those romantic hopes of universal levelling and a return to the golden age, which had been so ardently fostered by old Patience. Having frequently heard his friend say that these doctrines were to be cultivated with prudence (a precept, however, to which Patience gave but little heed himself), the hidalgo, inclined to reticence both by habit and inclination, never spoke of his philosophy; but he proved himself a more efficacious propagandist by carrying about from castle to cottage, and from house to farm, those little cheap editions of *La Science du Bonhomme Richard,* and other small treatises on popular patriotism, which, according to the Jesuits, a secret society of Voltairian philosophers, devoted to the diabolical practice of freemasonry, circulated gratis among the lower classes.

Thus in Marcasse's sudden resolution there was as much revolutionary enthusiasm as love of adventure. For a long time the dormouse and polecat had seemed to him overfeeble enemies for his restless valour, even as the granary floor seemed to afford too narrow a field. Every day he read the papers of the previous day in the servants' hall of the houses he visited;

and it appeared to him that this war in America, which was hailed as the awakening of the spirit of justice and liberty in the New World, ought to produce a revolution in France. It is true he had a very literal notion of the way in which ideas were to cross the seas and take possession of the minds of our continent. In his dreams he used to see an army of victorious Americans disembarking from numberless ships, and bringing the olive branch of peace and the horn of plenty to the French nation. In these same dreams he beheld himself at the head of a legion of heroes returning to Varenne as a warrior, a legislator, a rival of Washington, suppressing abuses, cutting down enormous fortunes, assigning to each proletarian a suitable share, and, in the midst of his far-reaching and vigorous measures, protecting the good and fair-dealing nobles, and assuring an honourable existence to them. Needless to say, the distress inseparable from all great political crises never entered into Marcasse's mind, and not a single drop of blood sullied the romantic picture which Patience had unrolled before his eyes.

From these sublime hopes to the role of valet to M. de la Marche was a far cry; but Marcasse could reach his goal by no other way. The ranks of the army corps destined for America had long been filled, and it was only in the character of a passenger attached to the expedition that he could take his place on one of the merchant ships that followed the expedition. He had questioned the abbe on these points without revealing his plans. His departure quite staggered all the inhabitants of Varenne.

No sooner had he set foot on the shores of the States than he felt an irresistible inclination to take his big hat and his big sword and go off all alone through the woods, as he had been accustomed to do in his own country. His conscience, however, prevented him from quitting his master after having pledged himself to serve him. He had calculated that fortune would help him, and fortune did. The war proved much more bloody and vigorous than had been expected, and M. de la Marche feared, though wrongly, that he might be impeded by the poor health of his gaunt squire. Having a suspicion, too, of the man's desire for liberty, he offered him a sum of money and some letters of recommendation, to enable him to join the American troops as a volunteer. Marcasse, knowing the state of his master's fortune, refused the money, and only accepted the letters; and then set off with as light a step as the nimblest weasels that he had ever killed.

His intention was to make for Philadelphia; but, through a chance occurrence which I need not relate, he learnt that I was in the South, and, rightly calculating that he would obtain both advice and help from me, he had set out to find me, alone, on foot, through unknown countries almost uninhabited and often full of danger of all kinds. His clothes alone had suffered; his yellow face had not changed its tint, and he was no more surprised at his latest exploit than if he had merely covered the distance from Sainte-Severe to Gazeau Tower.

The only fresh habit that I noticed in him, was that he would turn round from time to time, and look behind him, as if he had felt inclined to call some one; then immediately after he would smile and sigh almost at the same instant. I could not resist a desire to ask him the cause of his uneasiness.

"Alas!" he replied, "habit can't get rid of; a poor dog! good dog! Always saying, 'Here Blaireau! Blaireau, here!'"

"I understand," I said, "Blaireau is dead, and you cannot accustom yourself to the idea that you will never see him at your heels again."

"Dead!" he exclaimed, with an expression of horror. "No, thank God! Friend Patience, great friend! Blaireau quite well off, but sad like his master; his master alone!"

"If Blaireau is with Patience," said Arthur, "he is well off, as you say; for Patience wants nothing. Patience will love him because he loves his master, and you are certain to see your good friend and faithful dog again."

Marcasse turned his eyes upon the individual who seemed to be so well acquainted with his life; but, feeling sure that he had never seen him before, he acted as he was wont to do when he did not understand; he raised his hat and bowed respectfully.

On my immediate recommendation Marcasse was enrolled in my company and, a little while afterward, was made a sergeant. The worthy man went through the whole campaign with me, and went through it bravely; and in 1782, when I rejoined Rochambeau's army to fight under the French flag, he followed me, as he was anxious to share my lot until the end. In the early days I looked upon him rather as an amusement than a companion; but his excellent conduct and calm fearlessness soon won for him the esteem of all, and I had reason to be proud of my *protege*. Arthur also conceived a great friendship for him; and, when off duty, he accompanied us in all our walks, carrying the naturalist's box and running the snakes through with his sword.

But when I tried to make him speak of my cousin, he by no means satisfied me. Whether he did not understand how eager I felt to learn all the details of the life she was leading far away from me, or whether in this matter he was obeying one of those inviolable laws which governed his conscience, I could never obtain from him any clear solution of the doubts which harassed me. Quite early he told me that there was no question of her marriage with any one; but, accustomed though I was to his vague manner of expressing himself, I imagined he seemed embarrassed in making this assertion and had the air of a man who had sworn to keep a secret.

Honour forbade me to insist to such an extent as to let him see my hopes, and so there always remained between us a painful point which I tried to avoid touching upon, but to which, in spite of myself, I was continually returning. As long as Arthur was near me, I retained my reason, and interpreted Edmee's letters in the most loyal way; but when I was unfortunate enough to be separated from him, my sufferings revived, and my stay in America became more irksome to me every day.

Our separation took place when I left the American army to fight under the command of the French general. Arthur was an American; and, moreover, he was only waiting for the end of the war to retire from the service, and settle in Boston with Dr. Cooper, who loved him as his son, and who had undertaken to get him appointed principal librarian to the library of the Philadelphia Society. This was all the reward Arthur desired for his labours.

The events which filled my last years in America belong to history. It was with a truly personal delight that I hailed the peace which proclaimed the United States a free nation. I had begun to chafe at my long absence from France; my passion had been growing ever greater, and left no room for the intoxication of military glory. Before my departure I went to take leave of Arthur. Then I sailed with the worthy Marcasse, divided between sorrow at parting from my only friend, and joy at the prospect of once more seeing my only love. The squadron to which my ship belonged experienced many vicissitudes during the passage, and several times I gave up all hope of ever kneeling before Edmee under the great oaks of Sainte-Severe. At last, after a final storm off the coast of France, I set foot on the shores of Brittany, and fell into the arms of my poor sergeant, who had borne our common misfortunes, if not with greater physical courage, at least with a calmer spirit, and we mingled our tears.

XVI

We set out from Brest without sending any letter to announce our coming.

When we arrived near Varenne we alighted from the post-chaise and, ordering the driver to proceed by the longest road to Saint-Severe, took a short cut through the woods. As soon as I saw the trees in the park raising their venerable heads above the copses like a solemn phalanx of druids in the middle of a prostrate multitude, my heart began to beat so violently that I was forced to stop.

"Well," said Marcasse, turning round with an almost stern expression, as if he would have reproached me for my weakness.

But a moment later I saw that his own face, too, was betraying unexpected emotion. A plaintive whining and a bushy tail brushing against his legs had made him start. He uttered a loud cry on seeing Blaireau. The poor animal had scented his master from afar, and had rushed forward with all the speed of his first youth to roll at his feet. For a moment we thought he was going to die there, for he remained motionless and convulsed, as it were, under Marcasse's caressing hand; then suddenly he sprang up, as if struck with an idea worthy of a man, and set off with the speed of lightning in the direction of Patience's hut.

"Yes, go and tell my friend, good dog!" exclaimed Marcasse; "a better friend than you would be more than man."

He turned towards me, and I saw two big tears trickling down the cheeks of the impassive hidalgo.

We hastened our steps till we reached the hut. It had undergone striking improvements; a pretty rustic garden, inclosed by a quickset hedge with a bank of stones behind, extended round the little house. The approach to this was no longer a rough little path, but a handsome walk, on either side of which splendid vegetables stretched out in regular rows, like an army in marching order. The van was composed of a battalion of cabbages; carrots and lettuces formed the main body; and along the hedge some modest sorrel brought up the rear. Beautiful apple-trees, already well grown, spread their verdant shade above these plants; while pear-trees, alternately standards and espaliers, with borders of thyme and sage kissing the feet of sunflowers and gilliflowers, convicted Patience of a strange return to ideas of social order, and even to a taste for luxuries.

The change was so remarkable that I thought I should no longer find Patience in the cottage. A strange feeling of uneasiness began to come over me; my fear almost turned into certainty when I saw two young men from the village occupied in trimming the espaliers. Our passage had lasted more than four months, and it must have been quite six months since we had had any news of the hermit. Marcasse, however, seemed to feel no fear; Blaireau had told him plainly that Patience was alive, and the footmarks of the little dog, freshly printed in the sand of the walk, showed the direction in which he had gone. Notwithstanding, I was so afraid of seeing a cloud come over the joy of this day, that I did not dare to question the gardeners about Patience. Silently I followed the hidalgo, whose eyes grew full of tears as they gazed upon this new Eden, and whose prudent mouth let no sound escape save the word "change," which he repeated several times.

At last I grew impatient; the walk seemed interminable, though very short in reality, and I began to run, my heart beating wildly.

"Perhaps Edmee," I said to myself, "is here!"

However, she was not there, and I could only hear the voice of the hermit saying:

"Now, then! What is the matter? Has the poor dog gone mad? Down, Blaireau! You would never have worried your master in this way. This is what comes of being too kind!"

"Blaireau is not mad!" I exclaimed, as I entered. "Have you grown deaf to the approach of a friend, Master Patience?"

Patience, who was in the act of counting a pile of money, let it fall on the table and came towards me with the old cordiality. I embraced him heartily; he was surprised and touched at my joy. Then he examined me from head to foot, and seemed to be wondering at the change in my appearance, when Marcasse arrived at the door.

Then a sublime expression came over Patience's face, and lifting his strong arms to heaven, he exclaimed:

"The words of the canticle! Now let me depart in peace; for mine eyes have seen him I yearned for."

The hidalgo said nothing; he raised his hat as usual; then sitting down he turned pale and shut his eyes. His dog jumped up on his knees and displayed his affection by attempts at little cries which changed into a series of sneezes (you remember that he was born dumb). Trembling with old age and delight, he stretched out his pointed nose towards the long nose of his master; but his master did not respond with the customary "Down, Blaireau!"

Marcasse had fainted.

This loving soul, no more able than Blaireau to express itself in words, had sunk beneath the weight of his own happiness. Patience ran and fetched him a large mug of wine of the district, in its second year—that is to say, the oldest and best possible. He made him swallow a few drops; its strength revived him. The hidalgo excused his weakness on the score of fatigue and the heat. He would not or could not assign it to its real sense. There are souls who die out, after burning with unsurpassable moral beauty and grandeur, without ever having found a way, and even without ever having felt the need, of revealing themselves to others.

When Patience, who was as demonstrative as his friend was the contrary, had recovered from his first transports, he turned to me and said:

"Now, my young officer, I see that you have no wish to remain here long. Let us make haste, then, to the place you are burning to reach. There is some one who will be much surprised and much delighted, you may take my word."

We entered the park, and while crossing it, Patience explained the change which had come over his habitation and his life.

"For myself," he said to me, "you see that I have not changed. The same appearance, the same ways; and if I offered you some wine just now, that does not prevent me from drinking water myself. But I have money, and land, and workmen—yes, I have. Well, all this is in spite of myself, as you will see. Some three years ago Mademoiselle Edmee spoke of the difficulty she had in bestowing alms so as to do real good. The abbe was as unskilful as herself. People would impose on them every day and use their money for bad ends; whereas proud and hard-working day-labourers might be in a state of real distress without any one being able to discover the fact. She was afraid that if she inquired into their wants they might take it as an insult; and when worthless fellows appealed to her she preferred being their dupe to erring against charity. In this manner she used to give away a great deal of money and do very little good. I then made her understand how money was the thing that was the least necessary to the necessitous. I explained that men were really unfortunate, not when they were unable to dress better than their fellows, or go to the tavern on Sundays, or display at high-mass a spotlessly white stocking with a red garter above the knee, or talk about 'My mare, my cow, my vine, my barn, etc.,' but rather when they were afflicted with poor health and a bad season, when they could not protect themselves against the cold, and heat and sickness, against the pangs of hunger and thirst. I told her, then, not to judge of the strength and health of peasants by myself, but to go in person and inquire into their illnesses and their wants.

"These folk are not philosophers," I said; "they have their little vanities, they are fond of finery, spend the little they earn on cutting a figure, and have not foresight enough to deprive themselves of a passing pleasure in order to lay by something against a day of real need. In short, they do not know how to use their money; they tell you they are in debt, and, though that may be true, it is not true that they will use the money you give them to pay what they owe. They take no thought of the morrow; they will agree to as high a rate of interest as may be asked, and with your money they will buy a hemp-field or a set of furniture so as to astonish their neighbours and make them jealous. Meanwhile their debts go on increasing year by year, and in the end they have to sell their hemp-field and their furniture, because the creditor, who is always one of themselves, calls for repayment or for more interest than they can furnish. Everything goes; the principal takes all their capital, just as the interest has taken all their income. Then you grow old and can work no longer; your children abandon you, because you have brought them up badly, and because they

have the same passions and the same vanities as yourself. All you can do is
to take a wallet and go from door to door to beg your bread, because you
are used to bread and would die if you had to live on roots like the sorcerer
Patience, that outcast of Nature, whom everybody hates and despises because he has not become a beggar.

"The beggar, moreover, is hardly worse off than the day-labourer;
probably he is better off. He is no longer troubled with pride, whether
estimable or foolish; he has no longer to suffer. The folks in his part of the
country are good to him; there is not a beggar that wants for a bed or supper as he goes his round. The peasants load him with bits of bread, to such
an extent that he has enough to feed both poultry and pigs in the little
hovel where he has left a child and an old mother to look after his animals.
Every week he returns there and spends two or three days, doing nothing
except counting the pennies that have been given him. These poor coins
often serve to satisfy the superfluous wants which idleness breeds. A peasant rarely takes snuff; many beggars cannot do without it; they ask for it
more eagerly than for bread. So the beggar is no more to be pitied than the
labourer; but he is corrupt and debauched, when he is not a scoundrel and
a brute, which, in truth, is seldom enough.

"'This, then, is what ought to be done,' I said to Edmee; 'and the abbe
tells me that this is also the idea of your philosophers. You who are always
ready to help the unfortunate, should give without consulting the special
fancies of the man who asks, but only after ascertaining his real wants.'

"Edmee objected that it would be impossible for her to obtain the necessary information; that she would have to give her whole time to it, and
neglect the chevalier, who is growing old and can no longer read anything
without his daughter's eyes and head. The abbe was too fond of improving
his mind from the writings of the wise to have time for anything else.

"'That is what comes of all this study of virtue!' I said to her; 'it makes
a man forget to be virtuous.'

"'You are quite right,' answered Edmee; 'but what is to be done?'

"I promised to think it over; and this is how I went to work. Instead of
taking my walks as usual in the direction of the woods, I paid a visit every
day to the small holdings. It cost me a great effort; I like to be alone; and
everywhere I had shunned my fellow-men for so many years that I had
lost touch with them. However, this was a duty and I did it. I went to various houses, and by way of conversation, first of all over hedges, and then
inside the houses themselves, I made inquiries as to those points which I
wanted to learn. At first they gave me a welcome such as they would give
to a lost dog in time of drought; and with a vexation I could scarce conceal
I noticed the hatred and distrust on all their faces. Though I had not cared

to live among other men, I still had an affection for them; I knew that they were unfortunate rather than vicious; I had spent all my time in lamenting their woes and railing against those that caused them; and when for the first time I saw a possibility of doing something for some of them, these very men shut their doors the very moment they caught sight of me in the distance, and their children (those pretty children that I love so much!) would hide themselves in ditches so as to escape the fever which, it was said, I could give with a glance. However, as Edmee's friendship for me was well known, they did not dare to repulse me openly, and I succeeded in getting the information we wanted. Whenever I told her of any distress she at once supplied a remedy. One house was full of cracks; and while the daughter was wearing an apron of cotton-cloth at four francs an ell, the rain was falling on the grandmother's bed and the little children's cradles. The roof and walls were repaired; we supplied the materials and paid the workmen; but no more money for gaudy aprons. In another case, an old woman had been reduced to beggary because she had listened too well to her heart, and given all she had to her children, who had turned her out of doors, or made her life so unbearable that she preferred to be a tramp. We took up the old woman's cause, and threatened that we would bring the matter before the courts at our own expense. Thus we obtained for her a pension, to which we added when it was not sufficient. We induced several old persons who were in a similar position to combine and live together under the same roof. We chose one as head, and gave him a little capital, and as he was an industrious and methodical man, he turned it to such profit that his children came and made their peace with him, and asked to be allowed to help in his establishment.

"We did many other things besides; I need not give you details, as you will see them yourself. I say 'we,' because, though I did not wish to be concerned in anything beyond what I had already done, I was gradually drawn on and obliged to do more and more, to concern myself with many things, and finally with everything. In short, it is I who make the investigations, superintend the works, and conduct all negotiations. Mademoiselle Edmee wished me to keep a sum of money by me, so that I might dispose of it without consulting her first. This I have never allowed myself to do; and, moreover, she has never once opposed any of my ideas. But all this, you know, has meant much work and many worries. Ever since the people realized that I was a little Turgot they have grovelled before me, and that has pained me not a little. And so I have various friends that I don't care for, and various enemies that I could well do without. The sham poor owe me a grudge because I do not let myself be duped by them; and there are perverse and worthless people who think one is always doing too much for others, and never enough for them. With all this bustle and all these bickerings, I can no longer take my walk during the night, and my sleep during the day. I am now Monsieur Patience, and no longer the sorcerer of Gazeau Tower; but alas! I am a hermit no more; and, believe me, I would wish with all my heart that I could have been born selfish, so that I might throw off my harness, and return to my savage life and my liberty."

When Patience had given us this account of his work we complimented him on it; but we ventured to express a doubt about his pretended self-sacrifice; this magnificent garden seemed to indicate a compromise with "those superfluous necessities," the use of which by others he had always deplored.

"That?" he said, waving his arm in the direction of his inclosure. "That does not concern me; they made it against my wishes; but, as they were worthy folk and my refusal would have grieved them, I was obliged to allow it. You must know that, if I have stirred ingratitude in many hearts, I have also made a few happy ones grateful. So, two or three families to whom I had done some service, tried all possible means to give me pleasure in return; and, as I refused everything, they thought they would give me a surprise. Once I had to pay a visit to Berthenoux for several days, on some confidential business which had been entrusted to me; for people have come to imagine me a very clever man, so easy is it to pass from one extreme to another. On my return I found this garden, marked out, planted and inclosed as you see it. In vain did I get angry, and explain that I did not want to work, that I was too old, and that the pleasure of eating a little more fruit was not worth the trouble that this garden was going to cost me; they finished it without heeding what I said, and declared that I need not trouble in the least, because they would undertake to cultivate it for me. And, indeed, for the last two years the good folk have not failed to come, now one and now another, and give such time in each season as was necessary to keep it in perfect order. Besides, though I have altered nothing in my own ways of living, the produce of this garden has been very useful; during the winter I was able to feed several poor people with my vegetables; while my fruit has served to win the affection of the little children, who no longer cry out 'wolf' when they see me, but have grown bold enough to come and kiss the sorcerer. Other people have forced me to accept presents of wine, and now and then of white bread, and cheeses of cow's milk. All these things, however, only enable me to be polite to the village elders when they come and report the deserving cases of the place, so that I may make them known at the castle. These honours have not turned my head, as you see; nay, more, I may say that when I have done about all that I have to do, I shall leave the cares of greatness behind me, and return to my philosopher's life, perhaps to Gazeau Tower—who knows?"

We were now at the end of our walk. As I set foot on the steps of the chateau, I was suddenly filled with a feeling of devoutness; I clasped my hands and called upon Heaven in a sort of terror. A vague, indefinable fear arose in me; I imagined all manner of things that might hinder my happiness. I hesitated to cross the threshold of the house; then I rushed forward. A mist came over my eyes, a buzzing filled my ears. I met Saint-Jean, who, not recognising me, gave a loud cry and threw himself in my path to prevent me from entering without being announced. I pushed him aside, and he sank down astounded on one of the hall chairs while I hastened to the door of the drawing-room. But, just as I was about to throw it open, I was seized with a new fear and checked myself; then I opened it so timidly that Edmee, who was occupied at some embroidery on a frame, did not raise her eyes, thinking that in this slight noise she recognised the respectful Saint-Jean. The chevalier was asleep and did not wake. This old man, tall and thin like all the Mauprats, was sitting with his head sunk on his breast; and his pale, wrinkled face, which seemed already wrapped in the torpor of the grave, resembled one of those angular heads in carved oak which adorned the back of his big arm-chair. His feet were stretched out in front of a fire of dried vine-branches, although the sun was warm and a bright ray was falling on his white head and making it shine like silver. And how could I describe to you my feelings on beholding Edmee? She was bending over her tapestry and glancing from time to time at her father to notice his slightest movements. But what patience and resignation were revealed in her whole attitude! Edmee was not fond of needlework; her mind was too vigorous to attach much importance to the effect of one shade by the side of another shade, and to the regularity of one stitch laid against another stitch. Besides, the blood flowed swiftly in her veins, and when her mind was not absorbed in intellectual work she needed exercise in the open air. But ever since her father, a prey to the infirmities of old age, had been almost unable to leave his arm-chair, she had refused to leave him for a single moment; and, since she could not always be reading and working her mind, she had felt the necessity of taking up some of those feminine occupations which, as she said, "are the amusements of captivity." She had conquered her nature then in truly heroic fashion. In one of those secret struggles which often take place under our eyes without our suspecting the issue involved, she had done more than subdue her nature, she had even changed the circulation of her blood. I found her thinner; and her complexion had lost that first freshness of youth which, like the bloom that the breath of morning spreads over fruit, disappears at the slightest shock from without, although it may have been respected by the heat of the sun. Yet in this premature paleness and in this somewhat unhealthy thinness there seemed to be an indefinable charm; her eyes, more sunken, but inscrutable as ever, showed less pride and more melancholy than of old; her mouth had become more mobile, and her smile was more delicate and less contemptuous. When she spoke to me, I seemed to behold two persons in her, the old and the new; and I found that, so far from having lost her beauty, she had attained ideal perfection. Still, I remember several persons at that time used to declare that she had "changed very much," which with them meant that she had greatly deteriorated. Beauty, however, is like a temple in which the profane see naught but the external magnificence. The divine mystery of the artist's thought reveals itself only to profound sympathy, and the inspiration in each detail of the sublime work remains unseen by the eyes of the vulgar. One of your modern authors, I fancy, has said this in other words and much better. As for myself, at no moment in her life did I find Edmee less beautiful than at any other. Even in the hours of suffering, when beauty in its material sense seems obliterated, hers but assumed a divine form in my eyes, and in her face I beheld the splendour of a new moral beauty. However, I am but indifferently endowed with artistic feeling, and had I been a painter, I could not have created more than a single type, that which filled my whole soul; for in the course of my long life only one woman has seemed to me really beautiful; and that woman was Edmee.

For a few seconds I stood looking at her, so touchingly pale, sad yet calm, a living image of filial piety, of power in thrall to affection. Then I rushed forward and fell at her feet without being able to say a word. She uttered no cry, no exclamation of surprise, but took my head in her two arms and held it for some time pressed to her bosom. In this strong pressure, in this silent joy I recognised the blood of my race, I felt the touch of a sister. The good chevalier, who had waked with a start, stared at us in astonishment, his body bent forward and his elbow resting on his knee; then he said:

"Well, well! What is the meaning of this?"

He could not see my face, hidden as it was in Edmee's breast. She pushed me towards him; and the old man clasped me in his feeble arms with a burst of generous affection that gave him back for a moment the vigour of youth.

I leave you to imagine the questions with which I was overwhelmed, and the attentions that were lavished on me. Edmee was a veritable mother to me. Her unaffected kindness and confidence savoured so much of heaven that throughout the day I could not think of her otherwise than if I had really been her son.

I was very much touched at the pleasure they took in preparing a big surprise for the abbe; I saw in this a sure proof of the delight he would feel at my return. They made me hide under Edmee's frame, and covered me with the large green cloth that was generally thrown over her work. The abbe sat down quite close to me, and I gave a shout and seized him by the legs. This was a little practical joke that I used to play on him in the old days. When, throwing aside the frame, and sending the balls of wool rolling over the floor, I came out from my hiding-place, the expression of terror and delight on his face was most quaint.

But I will spare you all these family scenes to which my memory goes back too readily.

XVII

An immense change had taken place in me during the course of six years. I had become a man very much like other men; my instincts had managed to bring themselves into harmony with my affections, my intuitions with my reason. This social education had been carried on quite naturally; all I had to do was to accept the lessons of experience and the counsels of friendship. I was far from being a learned man; but I had developed a power of acquiring solid learning very rapidly. My notions of things in general were as clear as could be obtained at that time. Since then I know that real progress has been made in human knowledge; I have watched it from afar and have never thought of denying it. And as I notice that not all men of my age show themselves as reasonable, it pleases me to think that I was put on a fairly right road early in life, since I have never stopped in the blind alley of errors and prejudices.

The progress I had made intellectually seemed to satisfy Edmee.

"I am not astonished at it," she said. "I could see it in your letters; but I rejoice at it with a mother's pride."

My good uncle was no longer strong enough to engage in the old stormy discussions; and I really think that if he had retained his strength he would have been somewhat grieved to find that I was no longer the indefatigable opponent who had formerly irritated him so persistently. He even made a few attempts at contradiction to test me; but at this time I should have considered it a crime to have gratified him. He showed a little temper at this, and seemed to think that I treated him too much as an old man. To console him I turned the conversation to the history of the past, to the years through which he himself had lived, and questioned him on many points wherein his experience served him better than my knowledge. In this way I obtained many healthy notions for the guidance of my own conduct, and at the same time I fully satisfied his legitimate *amour propre*. He now conceived a friendship for me from genuine sympathy, just as formerly he had adopted me from natural generosity and family pride. He did not disguise from me that his great desire, before falling into the sleep that knows no waking, was to see me married to Edmee; and when I told him that this was the one thought of my life, the one wish of my soul, he said:

"I know, I know. Everything depends on her, and I think she can no longer have any reasons for hesitation. . . . At all events," he added, after a moment's silence and with a touch of peevishness, "I cannot see any that she could allege at present."

From these words, the first he had ever uttered on the subject which most interested me, I concluded that he himself had long been favourable to my suit, and that the obstacle, if one still existed, lay with Edmee. My uncle's last remark implied a doubt which I dared not try to clear up, and which caused me great uneasiness. Edmee's sensitive pride inspired me with such awe, her unspeakable goodness filled me with such respect that I dared not ask her point-blank to decide my fate. I made up my mind to act as if I entertained no other hope than that she would always let me be her brother and friend.

An event which long remained inexplicable afforded some distraction to my thoughts for a few days. At first I had refused to go and take possession of Roche-Mauprat.

"You really must," my uncle had said, "go and see the improvements I have made in your property, the lands which have been brought under cultivation, the cattle that I have put on each of your metayer-farms. Now is the time for you to see how your affairs stand, and show your tenants that you take an interest in their work. Otherwise, on my death, everything will go from bad to worse and you will be obliged to let it, which may bring you in a larger income, perhaps, but will diminish the value of the property. I am too old now to go and manage your estate. For the last two years I have been unable to leave off this miserable dressing-gown; the abbe does not understand anything about it; Edmee has an excellent head; but she cannot bring herself to go to that place; she says she would be too much afraid, which is mere childishness."

"I know that I ought to display more courage," I replied; "and yet, uncle, what you are asking me to do is for me the most difficult thing in the world. I have not set foot on that accursed soil since the day I left it, bearing Edmee away from her captors. It is as if you were driving me out of heaven to send me on a visit to hell."

The chevalier shrugged his shoulders; the abbe implored me to bring myself to do as he wished, as the reluctance I showed was a veritable disappointment to my uncle. I consented, and with a determination to conquer myself, I took leave of Edmee for two days. The abbe wanted to accompany me, to drive away the gloomy thoughts which would no doubt besiege me; but I had scruples about taking him from Edmee even for this short time; I knew how necessary he was to her. Tied as she was to the chevalier's arm-chair, her life was so serious, so retired, that the least change was acutely felt. Each year had increased her isolation, and it had become almost complete since the chevalier's failing health had driven from his table those happy children of wine, songs, and witticisms. He had been a great sportsman; and Saint Hubert's Day, which fell on his birthday, had formerly brought all the nobility of the province to his house. Year after year the courtyards had resounded with the howls of the pack; year after year the stables had held their two long rows of spirited horses in their glistening stalls; year after year the sound of the horn had echoed through the great woods around, or sent out its blast under the windows of the big hall at each toast of the brilliant company. But those glorious days had long disappeared; the chevalier had given up hunting; and the hope of obtaining his daughter's hand no longer brought round his arm-chair young men, who were bored by his old age, his attacks of gout, and the stories which he would repeat in the evening without remembering that he had already told them in the morning. Edmee's obstinate refusals and the dismissal of M. de la Marche had caused great astonishment, and given rise to many conjectures among the curious. One young man who was in love with her, and had been rejected like the rest, was impelled by a stupid and cowardly conceit to avenge himself on the only woman of his own class who, according to him, had dared to repulse him. Having discovered that Edmee had been carried off by the Hamstringers, he spread a report that she had spent a night of wild debauch at Roche-Mauprat. At best, he only deigned to concede that she had yielded only to violence. Edmee commanded too much respect and esteem to be accused of having shown complaisance to the brigands; but she soon passed for having been a victim of their brutality. Marked with an indelible stain, she was no longer sought in marriage by any one. My absence only served to confirm this opinion. I had saved her from death, it was said, but not from shame, and it was impossible for me to make her my wife; I was in love with her, and had fled lest I should yield to the temptation to marry her. All this seemed so probable that it would have been difficult to make the public accept the true version. They were the less ready to accept it from the fact that Edmee had been unwilling to put an end to the evil reports by giving her hand to a man she could not love. Such, then, were the causes of her isolation; it was not until later that I fully understood them. But I could see the austerity of the chevalier's home and Edmee's melancholy calm, and I was afraid to drop even a dry leaf in the sleeping waters. Thus I begged the abbe to remain with them until my return. I took no one with me except my faithful sergeant Marcasse. Edmee had declared that he must not leave me, and had arranged that henceforth he was to share Patience's elegant hut and administrative life.

I arrived at Roche-Mauprat one foggy evening in the early days of autumn; the sun was hidden, and all Nature was wrapped in silence and mist. The plains were deserted; the air alone seemed alive with the noise of great flocks of birds of passage; cranes were drawing their gigantic triangles across the sky, and storks at an immeasurable height were filling the clouds with mournful cries, which fell upon the saddened country like the dirge of parting summer. For the first time in the year I felt a chilliness in the air. I think that all men are filled with an involuntary sadness at the approach of the inclement season. In the first hoar-frosts there is something which bids man remember the approaching dissolution of his own being.

My companion and I had traversed woods and heaths without saying a single word; we had made a long *detour* to avoid Gazeau Tower, which I felt I could not bear to look upon again. The sun was sinking in shrouds of gray when we passed the portcullis at Roche-Mauprat. This portcullis was broken; the drawbridge was never raised, and the only things that crossed it now were peaceful flocks and their careless shepherds. The fosses were half-filled, and the bluish osiers were already spreading out their flexible branches over the shallow waters; nettles were growing at the foot of the crumbling towers, and the traces of the fire seemed still fresh upon the walls. The farm buildings had all been repaired; and the court, full of cattle and poultry and sheep-dogs and agricultural implements, contrasted strangely with the gloomy inclosure in which I still seemed to see the red flames of the besiegers shooting up, and the black blood of the Mauprats flowing.

I was received with the quiet and somewhat chilly hospitality of the peasants of Berry. They did not lay themselves out to please me, but they let me want for nothing. Quarters were found for me in the only one of the old wings which had not been damaged in the siege, or subsequently abandoned to the ravages of time. The massive architecture of the body of the building dated from the tenth century; the door was smaller than the windows, and the windows themselves gave so little light that we had to take candles to find our way, although the sun had hardly set. The building had been restored provisionally to serve as an occasional lodging for the new seigneur or his stewards. My Uncle Hubert had often been there to see to my interests so long as his strength had allowed him; and they showed me to the room which he had reserved for himself, and which had therefore been known as the master's room. The best things that had been saved from the old furniture had been placed there; and, as it was cold and damp, in spite of all the trouble they had taken to make it habitable, the tenant's servant preceded me with a firebrand in one hand and a fagot in the other.

Blinded by the smoke which she scattered round me in clouds, and deceived by the new entrance which they had made in another part of the courtyard, and by certain corridors which they had walled up to save the trouble of looking after them, I reached the room without recognising anything; indeed, I could not have said in what part of the old buildings I was, to such an extent had the new appearance of the courtyard upset my recollections, and so little had my mind in its gloom and agitation been impressed by surrounding objects.

While the servant was lighting the fire, I threw myself into a chair, and, burying my head in my hands, fell into a melancholy train of thought. My position, however, was not without a certain charm; for the past naturally appears in an embellished or softened form to the minds of young men, those presumptuous masters of the future. When, by dint of blowing the brand, the servant had filled the room with dense smoke, she went off to fetch some embers and left me alone. Marcasse had remained in the stable to attend to our horses. Blaireau had followed me; lying down by the hearth, he glanced at me from time to time with a dissatisfied air, as if to ask me the reason of such wretched lodging and such a poor fire.

Suddenly, as I cast my eyes round the room, old memories seemed to awaken in me. The fire, after making the green wood hiss, sent a flame up the chimney, and the whole room was illumined with a bright though unsteady light, which gave all the objects a weird, ambiguous appearance. Blaireau rose, turned his back to the fire and sat down between my legs, as if he thought that something strange and unexpected was going to happen.

I then realized that this place was none other than my grandfather Tristan's bed-room, afterward occupied for several years by his eldest son, the detestable John, my cruelest oppressor, the most crafty and cowardly of the Hamstringers. I was filled with a sense of terror and disgust on recognising the furniture, even the very bed with twisted posts on which my grandfather had given up his blackened soul to God, amid all the torments of a lingering death agony. The arm-chair which I was sitting in was the one in which John the Crooked (as he was pleased to call himself in his facetious days) used to sit and think out his villainies or issue his odious orders. At this moment I thought I saw the ghosts of all the Mauprats passing before me, with their bloody hands and their eyes dulled with wine. I got up and was about to yield to the horror I felt by taking to flight, when suddenly I saw a figure rise up in front of me, so distinct, so recognisable, so different in its vivid reality from the chimeras that had just besieged me, that I fell back in my chair, all bathed in a cold sweat. Standing by the bed was John Mauprat. He had just got out, for he was holding the half-opened curtain in his hand. He seemed to me the same as formerly, only he was still thinner, and paler and more hideous. His head was shaved, and his body wrapped in a dark winding-sheet. He gave me a hellish glance; a smile full of hate and contempt played on his thin, shrivelled lips. He stood motionless with his gleaming eyes fixed on me, and seemed as if about to speak. In that instant I was convinced that what I was looking on was a living being, a man of flesh and blood; it seems incredible, therefore, that I should have felt paralyzed by such childish fear. But it would be idle for me to deny it, nor have I ever yet been able to find an explanation; I was riveted to the ground with fear. The man's glance petrified me; I could not utter a sound. Blaireau rushed at him; then he waved the folds of his funeral garment, like a shroud all foul with the dampness of the tomb, and I fainted.

When I recovered consciousness Marcasse was by my side, anxiously endeavouring to lift me. I was lying on the ground rigid as a corpse. It was with a great difficulty that I collected my thoughts; but, as soon as I could stand upright, I seized Marcasse and hurriedly dragged him out of the accursed room. I had several narrow escapes of falling as I hastened down the winding stairs, and it was only on breathing the evening air in the courtyard, and smelling the healthy odour of the stables, that I recovered the use of my reason.

I did not hesitate to look upon what had just happened as an hallucination. I had given proof of my courage in war in the presence of my worthy sergeant; I did not blush, therefore, to confess the truth to him. I answered his questions frankly, and I described my horrible vision with such minute details that he, too, was impressed with the reality of it, and, as he walked about with me in the courtyard, kept repeating with a thoughtful air:

"Singular, singular! Astonishing!"

"No, it is not astonishing," I said, when I felt that I had quite recovered. "I experienced a most painful sensation on my way here; for several days I had struggled to overcome my aversion to seeing Roche-Mauprat again.

Last night I had a nightmare, and I felt so exhausted and depressed this morning that, if I had not been afraid of offending my uncle, I should have postponed this disagreeable visit. As we entered the place, I felt a chill come over me; there seemed to be a weight on my chest, and I could not breathe. Probably, too, the pungent smoke that filled the room disturbed my brain. Again, after all the hardships and dangers of our terrible voyage, from which we have hardly recovered, either of us, is it astonishing that my nerves gave way at the first painful emotion?"

"Tell me," replied Marcasse, who was still pondering the matter, "did you notice Blaireau at the moment? What did Blaireau do?"

"I thought I saw Blaireau rush at the phantom at the moment when it disappeared; but I suppose I dreamt that like the rest."

"Hum!" said the sergeant. "When I entered, Blaireau was wildly excited. He kept coming to you, sniffing, whining in his way, running to the bed, scratching the wall, coming to me, running to you. Strange, that! Astonishing, captain, astonishing, that!"

After a silence of a few moments:

"Devil don't return!" he exclaimed, shaking his head. "Dead never return; besides, why dead, John? Not dead! Still two Mauprats! Who knows? Where the devil? Dead don't return; and my master—mad? Never. Ill? No."

After this colloquy the sergeant went and fetched a light, drew his faithful sword from the scabbard, whistled Blaireau, and bravely seized the rope which served as a balustrade for the staircase, requesting me to remain below. Great as was my repugnance to entering the room again, I did not hesitate to follow Marcasse, in spite of his recommendation. Our first care was to examine the bed; but while we had been talking in the courtyard the servant had brought clean sheets, had made the bed, and was now smoothing the blankets.

"Who has been sleeping there?" asked Marcasse, with his usual caution.

"Nobody," she replied, "except M. le Chevalier or M. l'Abbe Aubert, in the days when they used to come."

"But yesterday, or to-day, I mean?" said Marcasse.

"Oh! yesterday and to-day, nobody, sir; for it is quite two years since M. le Chevalier came here; and as for M. l'Abbe, he never sleeps here, now that he comes alone. He arrives in the morning, has lunch with us, and goes back in the evening."

"But the bed was disarranged," said Marcasse, looking at her attentively.

"Oh, well! that may be, sir," she replied. "I do not know how they left it the last time some one slept here; I did not pay any attention to that as I put on the sheets; all I know is that M. Bernard's cloak was lying on the top."

"My cloak?" I exclaimed. "It was left in the stable."

"And mine, too," said Marcasse. "I have just folded both together and put them on the corn-bin."

"You must have had two, then," replied the servant; "for I am sure I took one off the bed. It was a black cloak, not new."

Mine, as a fact, was lined with red and trimmed with gold lace. Marcasse's was light gray. It could not, therefore, have been one of our cloaks brought up for a moment by the man and then taken back to the stable.

"But, what did you do with it?" said the sergeant.

"My word, sir," replied the fat girl, "I put it there, over the arm-chair. You must have taken it while I went to get a candle. I can't see it now."

We searched the room thoroughly; the cloak was not to be found. We pretended that we needed it, not denying that it was ours. The servant unmade the bed in our presence, and then went and asked the man what he had done with it. Nothing could be found either in the bed or in the room; the man had not been upstairs. All the farm-folk were in a state of excitement, fearing that some one might be accused of theft. We inquired if a stranger had not come to Roche-Mauprat, and if he was not still there. When we ascertained that these good people had neither housed or seen any one, we reassured them about the lost cloak by saying that Marcasse had accidentally folded it with the two others. Then we shut ourselves in the room, in order to explore it at our ease; for it was now almost evident that what I had seen was by no means a ghost, but John Mauprat himself, or a man very like him, whom I had mistaken for John.

Marcasse having aroused Blaireau by voice and gesture, watched all his movements.

"Set your mind at rest," he said with pride; "the old dog has not forgotten his old trade. If there is a hole, a hole as big as your hand, have no fear. Now, old dog! Have no fear."

Blaireau, indeed, after sniffing everywhere, persisted in scratching the wall where I had seen the apparition; he would start back every time his pointed nose came to a certain spot in the wainscotting; then, wagging his bushy tail with a satisfied air, he would return to his master as if to tell him to concentrate his attention on this spot. The sergeant then began to examine the wall and the woodwork; he tried to insinuate his sword into some crack; there was no sign of an opening. Still, a door might have been there, for the flowers carved on the woodwork would hide a skilfully constructed sliding panel. The essential thing was to find the spring that made this panel work; but that was impossible in spite of all the efforts we made for two long hours. In vain did we try to shake the panel; it gave forth the same sound as the others. They were all sonorous, showing that the wainscot was not in immediate contact with the masonry. Still, there might be a gap of only a few inches between them. At last Marcasse, perspiring profusely, stopped, and said to me:

"This is very stupid; if we searched all night we should not find a spring if there is none; and however hard we hammered, we could not break in the door if there happened to be big iron bars behind it, as I have sometimes seen in other old country-houses."

"The axe might help us to find a passage," I said, "if there is one; but why, simply because your dog scratches the wall, persist in believing that John Mauprat, or the man who resembles him, could not have come in and gone out by the door?"

"Come in, if you like," replied Marcasse, "but gone out—no, on my honour! For, as the servant came down I was on the staircase brushing my boots. As soon as I heard something fall here, I rushed up quickly three stairs at a time, and found that it was you—like a corpse, stretched out on the floor, very ill; no one inside nor outside, on my honour!

"In that case, then, I must have dreamt of my fiend of an uncle, and the servant must have dreamt of the black cloak; for it is pretty certain that there is no secret door here; and even if there were one, and all the Mauprats, living and dead, knew the secret of it, what were that to us? Do we belong to the police that we should hunt out these wretched creatures? And if by chance we found them hidden somewhere, should we not help them to escape, rather than hand them over to justice? We are armed; we need not be afraid that they will assassinate us to-night; and if they amuse themselves by frightening us, my word, woe betide them! I have no eye for either relatives or friends when I am startled in my sleep. So come, let us attack the omelette that these good people my tenants are preparing for us; for if we continue knocking and scratching the walls they will think we are mad."

Marcasse yielded from a sense of duty rather than from conviction. He seemed to attach great importance to the discovery of this mystery, and to be far from easy in his mind. He was unwilling to let me remain alone in the haunted room, and pretended that I might fall ill again and have a fit.

"Oh, this time," I said, "I shall not play the coward. The cloak has cured me of my fear of ghosts; and I should not advise any one to meddle with me."

The hildago was obliged to leave me alone. I loaded my pistols and put them on the table within reach of my hand; but these precautions were a pure waste of time; nothing disturbed the silence of the room, and the heavy red silk curtains, with their coat of arms at the corners in tarnished silver, were not stirred by the slightest breath. Marcasse returned and, delighted at finding me as cheerful as he had left me, began preparing our supper with as much care as if we had come to Roche-Mauprat for the sole purpose of making a good meal. He made jokes about the capon which was still singing on the spit, and about the wine which was so like a brush in the throat. His good humour increased when the tenant appeared, bringing a few bottles of excellent Madeira, which had been left with him by the chevalier, who liked to drink a glass or two before setting foot in the stirrup. In return we invited the worthy man to sup with us, as the least tedious way of discussing business matters.

"Good," he said; "it will be like old times when the peasants used to eat at the table of the seigneurs of Roche-Mauprat. You are doing the same, Monsieur Bernard, you are quite right."

"Yes, sir," I replied very coldly; "only I behave thus with those who owe me money, not those to whom I owe it."

This reply, and the word "sir," frightened him so much that he was at great pains to excuse himself from sitting down to table. However, I insisted, as I wished to give him the measure of my character at once. I treated him as a man I was raising to my own level, not as one to whom I wished to descend. I forced him to be cleanly in his jokes, but allowed him to be free and facetious within the limits of decent mirth. He was a frank, jovial man. I questioned him minutely to discover if he was not in league with the phantom who was in the habit of leaving his cloak upon the bed. This, however, seemed far from probable; the man evidently had such an aversion for the Hamstringers, that, had not a regard for my relationship held him back, he would have been only too glad to have given them such a dressing in my presence as they deserved. But I could not allow him any license on this point; so I requested him to give me an account of my property, which he did with intelligence, accuracy, and honesty.

As he withdrew I noticed that the Madeira had had considerable effect on him; he seemed to have no control over his legs, which kept catching in the furniture; and yet he had been in sufficient possession of his faculties to reason correctly. I have always observed that wine acts much more powerfully on the muscles of peasants than on their nerves; that they rarely lose their heads, and that, on the contrary, stimulants produce in them a bliss unknown to us; the pleasure they derive from drunkenness is quite different from ours and very superior to our febrile exaltation.

When Marcasse and I found ourselves alone, though we were not drunk, we realized that the wine had filled us with gaiety and light-heartedness which we should not have felt at Roche-Mauprat, even without the adventure of the ghost. Accustomed as we were to speak our thoughts freely, we confessed mutually, and agreed that we were much better prepared than before supper to receive all the bogies of Varenne.

This word "bogey" reminded me of the adventure which had brought me into far from friendly contact with Patience at the age of thirteen. Marcasse knew about it already, but he knew very little of my character at that time, and I amused myself by telling him of my wild rush across the fields after being thrashed by the sorcerer.

"This makes me think," I concluded by saying, "that I have an imagination which easily gets overexcited, and that I am not above fear of the supernatural. Thus the apparition just now . . ."

"No matter, no matter," said Marcasse, looking at the priming of my pistols, and putting them on the table by my bed. "Do not forget that all the Hamstringers are not dead; that, if John is in this world, he will do harm until he is under the ground, and trebly locked in hell."

The wine was loosening the hidalgo's tongue; on those rare occasions when he allowed himself to depart from his usual sobriety, he was not wanting in wit. He was unwilling to leave me, and made a bed for himself by the side of mine. My nerves were excited by the incidents of the day, and I allowed myself, therefore, to speak of Edmee, not in such a way as to deserve the shadow of a reproach from her if she had heard my words, but more freely than I might have spoken with a man who was as yet my inferior and not my friend, as he became later. I could not say exactly how much I confessed to him of my sorrows and hopes and anxieties; but those confidences had a disastrous effect, as you will soon see.

We fell asleep while we were talking, with Blaireau at his master's feet, the hidalgo's sword across his knees near the dog, the light between us, my pistols ready to hand, my hunting-knife under my pillow, and the bolts shot. Nothing disturbed our repose. When the sun awakened us the cocks were crowing merrily in the courtyard, and the labourers were cracking their rustic jokes as they yoked the oxen under our windows.

"All the same there is something at the bottom of it."

Such was Marcasse's first remark as he opened his eyes, and took up the conversation where he had dropped it the night before.

"Did you see or hear anything during the night?" I asked.

"Nothing at all," he replied. "All the same, Blaireau has been disturbed in his sleep; for my sword has fallen down; and then, we found no explanation of what happened here."

"Let who will explain it," I answered. "I shall certainly not trouble myself."

"Wrong, wrong; you are wrong!"

"That may be, my good sergeant; but I do not like this room at all, and it seems to me so ugly by daylight, that I feel that I must get far away from it, and breathe some pure air."

"Well, I will go with you; but I shall return. I do not want to leave this to chance. I know what John Mauprat is capable of; you don't."

"I do not wish to know; and if there is any danger here for myself or my friends, I do not wish you to return."

Marcasse shook his head and said nothing. We went round the farm once more before departing. Marcasse was very much struck with a certain incident to which I should have paid but little attention. The farmer wished to introduce me to his wife, but she could not be persuaded to see me, and went and hid herself in the hemp-field. I attributed this to the shyness of youth.

"Fine youth, my word!" said Marcasse; "youth like mine fifty years old and more! There is something beneath it, something beneath, I tell you."

"What the devil can there be?"

"Hum! She was very friendly with John Mauprat in her day. She found his crooked legs to her liking. I know about it; yes, I know many other things, too; many things—you may take my word!"

"You shall tell me them the next time we come; and that will not be so soon; for my affairs are going on much better than if I interfered with them; and I should not like to get into the habit of drinking Madeira to prevent myself from being frightened at my own shadow. And now, Marcasse, I must ask you as a favour not to tell any one what has happened. Everybody has not your respect for your captain."

"The man who does not respect my captain is an idiot," answered the hidalgo, in a tone of authority; "but, if you order me, I will say nothing."

He kept his word. I would not on any account have had Edmee's mind disturbed by this stupid tale. However, I could not prevent Marcasse from carrying out his design; early the following morning he disappeared, and I learnt from Patience that he had returned to Roche-Mauprat under the pretence of having forgotten something.

XVIII

While Marcasse was devoting himself to serious investigations, I was spending days of delight and agony in Edmee's presence. Her behaviour, so constant and devoted, and yet in many respects so reserved, threw me into continual alternations of joy and grief. One day while I was taking a walk the chevalier had a long conversation with her. I happened to return when their discussion had reached its most animated stage. As soon as I appeared, my uncle said to me:

"Here, Bernard; come and tell Edmee that you love her; that you will make her happy; that you have got rid of your old faults. Do something to get yourself accepted; for things cannot go on as they are. Our position with our neighbours is unbearable; and before I go down to the grave I should like to see my daughter's honour cleared from stain, and to feel sure that some stupid caprice of hers will not cast her into a convent, when she ought to be filling that position in society to which she is entitled, and which I have worked all my life to win for her. Come, Bernard, at her feet, lad! Have the wit to say something that will persuade her! Otherwise I shall think—God forgive me!—that it is you that do not love her and do not honestly wish to marry her."

"I! Great heavens!" I exclaimed. "Not wish to marry her—when for seven years I have had no other thought; when that is the one wish of my heart, and the only happiness my mind can conceive!"

Then I poured forth all the thoughts that the sincerest passion could suggest. She listened to me in silence, and without withdrawing her hands, which I covered with kisses. But there was a serious expression in her eyes, and the tone of her voice made me tremble when, after reflecting a few moments, she said:

"Father, you should not doubt my word; I have promised to marry Bernard; I promised him, and I promised you; it is certain, therefore, that I shall marry him."

Then she added, after a fresh pause, and in a still severe tone:

"But if, father, you believe that you are on the brink of the grave, what sort of heart do you suppose I can have, that you bid me think only of myself, and put on my wedding-dress in the hour of mourning for you? If, on the contrary, you are, as I believe, still full of vigour, in spite of your sufferings, and destined to enjoy the love of your family for many a long year yet, why do you urge me so imperiously to cut short the time I have requested? Is not the question important enough to demand my most serious reflection? A contract which is to bind me for the rest of my life, and on which depends, I do not say my happiness, for that I would gladly sacrifice to your least wish, but the peace of my conscience and the dignity of my conduct (since no woman can be sufficiently sure of herself to answer for a future which has been fettered against her will), does not such a contract bid me weigh all its risks and all its advantages for several years at least?"

"Good God!" said the chevalier. "Have you not been weighing all this for the last seven years? You ought to have arrived at some conclusion about your cousin by now. If you are willing to marry him, marry him; but if not, for God's sake say so, and let another man come forward."

"Father," replied Edmee, somewhat coldly, "I shall marry none but him."

"'None but him' is all very well," said the chevalier, tapping the logs with the tongs; "but that does not necessarily mean that you will marry him."

"Yes, I will marry him, father," answered Edmee. "I could have wished to be free a few months more; but since you are displeased at all these delays, I am ready to obey your orders, as you know."

"Parbleu! that is a pretty way of consenting," exclaimed my uncle, "and no doubt most gratifying to your cousin! By Jove! Bernard, I have lived many years in this world, but I must own that I can't understand these women yet, and it is very probable that I shall die without ever having understood them."

"Uncle," I said, "I can quite understand my cousin's aversion for me; it is only what I deserve. I have done all I could to atone for my errors. But, is it altogether in her power to forget a past which has doubtless caused her too much pain? However, if she does not forgive me, I will imitate her severity: I will not forgive myself. Abandoning all hope in this world, I will tear myself away from her and you, and chasten myself with a punishment worse than death."

"That's it! Go on! There's an end of everything!" said the chevalier, throwing the tongs into the fire. "That is just what you have been aiming at, I suppose, Edmee?"

I had moved a few steps towards the door; I was suffering intensely. Edmee ran after me, took me by the arm, and brought me back towards her father.

"It is cruel and most ungrateful of you to say that," she said. "Does it show a modest spirit and generous heart, to forget a friendship, a devotion, I may even venture to say, a fidelity of seven years, because I ask to prove you for a few months more? And even if my affection for you should never be as deep as yours for me, is what I have hitherto shown you of so little account that you despise it and reject it, because you are vexed at not inspiring me with precisely as much as you think you are entitled to? You know at this rate a woman would have no right to feel affection. However, tell me, is it your wish to punish me for having been a mother to you by leaving me altogether, or to make some return only on condition that I become your slave?"

"No, Edmee, no," I replied, with my heart breaking and my eyes full of tears, as I raised her hand to my lips; "I feel that you have done far more for me than I deserved; I feel that it would be idle to think of tearing myself from your presence; but can you account it a crime in me to suffer by your side? In any case it is so involuntary, so inevitable a crime, that it must needs escape all your reproaches and all my own remorse. But let us talk of this no more. It is all I can do. Grant me your friendship still; I shall hope to show myself always worthy of you in the future."

"Come, kiss each other," said the chevalier, much affected, "and never separate. Bernard, however capricious Edmee may seem, never abandon her, if you would deserve the blessing of your foster-father. Though you should never be her husband, always be a brother to her. Remember, my lad, that she will soon be alone in the world, and that I shall die in sorrow if I do not carry with me to the grave a conviction that a support and a defender still remains to her. Remember, too, that it is on your account, on account of a vow, which her inclination, perhaps, would reject, but which her conscience respects, that she is thus forsaken and slandered . . ."

The chevalier burst into tears, and in a moment all the sorrows of the unfortunate family were revealed to me.

"Enough, enough!" I cried, falling at their feet. "All this is too cruel. I should be the meanest wretch on earth if I had need to be reminded of my misdeeds and my duties. Let me weep at your knees; let me atone for the wrong I have done you by eternal grief, by eternal renunciation. Why not have driven me away when I did the wrong? Why not, uncle, have blown out my brains with your pistol, as if I had been a wild beast? What have I done to be spared, I who repaid your kindness with the ruin of your honour? No, no; I can see that Edmee ought not to marry me; that would be accepting the shame of the insult I have drawn upon her. All I ask is to be allowed to remain here; I will never see her face, if she makes this a condition; but I will lie at her door like a faithful dog and tear to pieces the first man who dares to present himself otherwise than on his knees; and if some day an honest man, more fortunate than myself, shows himself worthy of her love, far from opposing him, I will intrust to him the dear and sacred task of protecting and vindicating her. I will be but a friend, a brother to her, and when I see that they are happy together, I will go far away from them and die in peace."

My sobs choked me; the chevalier pressed his daughter and myself to his heart, and we mingled our tears, swearing to him that we would never leave each other, either during his life or after his death.

"Still, do not give up all hope of marrying her," whispered the chevalier to me a few moments later, when we were somewhat calmer. "She has strange whims; but nothing will persuade me to believe that she does not love you. She does not want to explain matters yet. Woman's will is God's will."

"And Edmee's will is my will," I replied.

A few days after this scene, which brought the calmness of death into my soul in place of the tumult of life, I was strolling in the park with the abbe.

"I must tell you," he said, "of an adventure which befell me yesterday. There is a touch of romance in it. I had been for a walk in the woods of Briantes, and had made my way down to the spring of Fougeres. It was as warm, you remember, as in the middle of summer; and our beautiful plants, in their autumn red, seemed more beautiful than ever as they stretched their delicate tracery over the stream. The trees have very little foliage left; but the carpet of dried leaves one walks upon gives forth a sound which to me is full of charm. The satiny trunks of the birches and young oaks are covered with moss and creepers of all shades of brown, and tender green, and red and fawn, which spread out into delicate stars and rosettes, and maps of all countries, wherein the imagination can behold new worlds in miniature. I kept gazing lovingly on these marvels of grace and delicacy, these arabesques in which infinite variety is combined with unfailing regularity, and as I remembered with pleasure that you are not, like the vulgar, blind to these adorable coquetries of nature, I gathered a few with the greatest care, even bringing away the bark of the tree on which they had taken root, in order not to destroy the perfection of their designs. I made a little collection, which I left at Patience's as I passed; we will go and see them, if you like. But, on our way, I must tell you what happened to me as I approached the spring. I was walking upon the wet stones with my head down, guided by the slight noise of the clear little jet of water which bursts from the heart of the mossy rock. I was about to sit down on the stone which forms a natural seat at the side of it, when I saw that the place was already occupied by a good friar whose pale, haggard face was half-hidden by his cowl of coarse cloth. He seemed much frightened at my arrival; I did my best to reassure him by declaring that my intention was not to disturb him, but merely to put my lips to the little bark channel which the woodcutters have fixed to the rock to enable one to drink more easily.

"'Oh, holy priest,' he said to me in the humblest tone, 'why are you not the prophet whose rod could smite the founts of grace? and why cannot my soul, like this rock, give forth a stream of tears?'

"Struck by the manner in which this monk expressed himself, by his sad air, by his thoughtful attitude in this poetic spot, which has often made me dream of the meeting of the Saviour and the woman of Samaria, I allowed myself to be drawn into a more intimate conversation. I learnt from the monk that he was a Trappist, and that he was making a penitential tour.

"'Ask neither my name nor whence I come,' he said. 'I belong to an illustrious family who would blush to know that I am still alive. Besides, on entering the Trappist order, we abjure all pride in the past; we make ourselves like new-born children; we become dead to the world that we may live again in Jesus Christ. But of this be sure: you behold in me one of the most striking examples of the miraculous power of grace; and if I could make known to you the tale of my religious life, of my terrors, my remorse, and my expiations, you would certainly be touched by it. But of what avail the indulgence and compassion of man, if the pity of God will not deign to absolve me?'

"You know," continued the abbe, "that I do not like monks, that I distrust their humility and abhor their lives of inaction. But this man spoke in so sad and kindly a manner; he was so filled with a sense of his duty; he seemed so ill, so emaciated by asceticism, so truly penitent, that he won my heart. In his looks and in his talk were bright flashes which betrayed a powerful intellect, indefatigable energy, and indomitable perseverance. We spent two whole hours together, and I was so moved by what he said that on leaving him I expressed a wish to see him again before he left this neighbourhood. He had found a lodging for the night at the Goulets farm, and I tried in vain to persuade him to accompany me to the chateau. He told me that he had a companion he could not leave.

"'But, since you are so sympathetic,' he said, 'I shall esteem it a pleasure to meet you here to-morrow towards sunset; perhaps I may even venture to ask a favour of you; you can be of service to me in an important matter which I have to arrange in this neighbourhood; more than this I cannot tell you at the present moment.'

"I assured him that he could reckon on me, and that I should only be too happy to oblige a man such as himself."

"And the result is, I suppose, that you are waiting impatiently for the hour of your appointment?" I said to the abbe.

"I am," he replied; "and my new acquaintance has so many attractions for me that, if I were not afraid of abusing the confidence he has placed in me, I should take Edmee to the spring of Fougeres."

"I fancy," I replied, "that Edmee has something better to do than to listen to the declamations of your monk, who perhaps, after all, is only a knave, like so many others to whom you have given money blindly. You will forgive me, I know, abbe; but you are not a good physiognomist, and you are rather apt to form a good or bad opinion of people for no reason except that your own romantic nature happens to feel kindly or timidly disposed towards them."

The abbe smiled and pretended that I said this because I bore him a grudge; he again asserted his belief in the Trappist's piety, and then went back to botany. We passed some time at Patience's, examining the collection of plants; and as my one desire was to escape from my own thoughts, I left the hut with the abbe and accompanied him as far as the wood where he was to meet the monk. In proportion as we drew near to the place the abbe seemed to lose more and more of his eagerness of the previous evening, and even expressed a fear that he had gone too far. This hesitation, following so quickly upon enthusiasm, was very characteristic of the abbe's mobile, loving, timid nature, with its strange union of the most contrary impulses, and I again began to rally him with all the freedom of friendship.

"Come, then," he said, "I should like to be satisfied about this; you must see him. You can study his face for a few minutes, and then leave us together, since I have promised to listen to his secrets."

As I had nothing better to do I followed the abbe; but as soon as we reached a spot overlooking the shady rocks whence the water issues, I stopped and examined the monk through the branches of a clump of ash-trees. Seated immediately beneath us by the side of the spring, he had his eyes turned inquiringly on the angle of the path by which he expected the abbe to arrive; but he did not think of looking at the place where we were, and we could examine him at our ease without being seen by him.

No sooner had I caught sight of him than, with a bitter laugh, I took the abbe by the arm, drew him back a short distance, and, not without considerable agitation, said to him:

"My dear abbe, in bygone years did you never catch sight of the face of my uncle, John de Mauprat?"

"Never, as far as I know," replied the abbe, quite amazed. "But what are you driving at?"

"Only this, my friend; you have made a pretty find here; this good and venerable Trappist, in whom you see so much grace and candour, and contrition, and intelligence, is none other than John de Mauprat, the Hamstringer."

"You must be mad!" cried the abbe, starting back. "John de Mauprat died a long time ago."

"John Mauprat is not dead, nor perhaps Antony Mauprat either; and my surprise is less than yours only because I have already met one of these two ghosts. That he has become a monk, and is repenting for his sins, is very possible; but alas! it is by no means impossible that he has disguised himself in order to carry out some evil design, and I advise you to be on your guard."

The abbe was so frightened that he no longer wanted to keep his appointment. I suggested that it would be well to learn what the old sinner was aiming at. But, as I knew the abbe's weak character, and feared that my Uncle John would manage to win his heart by his lying confessions and wheedle him into some false step, I made up my mind to hide in a thicket whence I could see and hear everything.

But things did not happen as I had expected. The Trappist, instead of playing the politician, immediately made known his real name to the abbe. He declared that he was full of contrition, and that, as his conscience would not allow him to make the monk's habit a refuge from punishment (he had really been a Trappist for several years), he was about to put himself into the hands of justice, that he might atone in a striking way for the crimes with which he was polluted. This man, endowed as he was with conspicuous abilities, had acquired a mystic eloquence in the cloister. He spoke with so much grace and persuasiveness that I was fascinated no less than the abbe. It was in vain that the latter attempted to combat a resolution which appeared to him insane; John Mauprat showed the most unflinching devotion to his religious ideas. He declared that, having committed the crimes of the old barbarous paganism, he could not ransom his soul save by a public expiation worthy of the early Christians.

"It is possible," he said, "to be a coward with God as well as with man, and in the silence of my vigils I hear a terrible voice answering to my tears: 'Miserable craven, it is the fear of man that has thrown you upon the bosom of God, and if you had not feared temporal death, you would never have thought of life eternal!'

"Then I realize that what I most dread is not God's wrath, but the rope and the hangman that await me among my fellows. Well, it is time to end this sense of secret shame; not until the day when men crush me beneath their abuse and punishment shall I fell absolved and restored in the sight of Heaven; then only shall I account myself worthy to say to Jesus my Saviour: 'Give ear to me, innocent victim, Thou who heardest the penitent thief; give ear to a sullied but contrite victim, who has shared in the glory of Thy martyrdom and been ransomed by Thy blood!'"

"If you persist in your enthusiastic design," said the abbe, after unsuccessfully bringing forward all possible objections, "you must at least let me know in what way you thought I could be of service to you."

"I cannot act in this matter," replied the Trappist, "without the consent of a young man who will soon be the last of the Mauprats; for the chevalier has not many days to wait before he will receive the heavenly reward due to his virtues; and as for myself, I cannot avoid the punishment I am about to seek, except by falling back into the endless night of the cloister. I speak of Bernard Mauprat; I will not call him my nephew, for if he heard me he would blush to think that he bore this shameful title. I heard of his return from America, and this news decided me to undertake the journey at the painful end of which you now behold me."

It seemed to me that while he was saying this he kept casting sideglances towards the clump of trees where I was, as if he had guessed my presence there. Perhaps the movement of some branches had betrayed me.

"May I ask," said the abbe, "what you now have in common with this young man? Are you not afraid that, embittered by the harsh treatment formerly lavished on him at Roche-Mauprat, he may refuse to see you?"

"I am certain that he will refuse; for I know the hatred that he still has for me," said the Trappist, once more looking towards the spot where I was. "But I hope that you will persuade him to grant me an interview; for you are a good and generous man, Monsieur l'Abbe. You promised to oblige me; and, besides, you are young Mauprat's friend, and you will be able to make him understand that his interests are at stake and the honour of his name."

"How so?" answered the abbe. "No doubt he will be far from pleased to see you appear before the courts to answer for crimes which have since been effaced in the gloom of the cloister. He will certainly wish you to forego this public expiation. How can you hope that he will consent?"

"I have hope, because God is good and great; because His grace is mighty; because it will touch the heart of him who shall deign to hear the prayer of a soul which is truly penitent and deeply convinced; because my eternal salvation is in the hands of this young man, and he cannot wish to avenge himself on me beyond the grave. Moreover, I must die at peace with those I have injured; I must fall at the feet of Bernard Mauprat and obtain his forgiveness of my sins. My tears will move him, or, if his unrelenting soul despises them, I shall at least have fulfilled an imperious duty."

Seeing that he was speaking with a firm conviction that he was being heard by me, I was filled with disgust; I thought I could detect the deceit and cowardice that lay beneath this vile hypocrisy. I moved away and waited for the abbe some distance off. He soon rejoined me; the interview had ended by a mutual promise to meet again soon. The abbe had undertaken to convey the Trappist's words to me, while the latter had threatened in the most honeyed tone in the world to come and see me if I refused his request. The abbe and I agreed to consult together, without informing the chevalier or Edmee, that we might not disquiet them unnecessarily. The Trappist had gone to stay at La Chatre, at the Carmelite convent; this had thoroughly aroused the abbe's suspicions, in spite of his first enthusiasm at the penitence of the sinner. The Carmelites had persecuted him in his youth, and in the end the prior had driven him to secularize himself. The prior was still alive, old but implacable; infirm, and withdrawn from the world, but strong in his hatred, and his passion for intrigue. The abbe could not hear his name without shuddering, and he begged me to act prudently in this affair.

"Although John Mauprat," he said, "is under the bane of the law, and you are at the summit of honour and prosperity, do not despise the weakness of your enemy. Who knows what cunning and hatred may do? They can usurp the place of the just and cast him out on the dung-heap; they can fasten their crimes on others and sully the robe of innocence with their vileness. Maybe you have not yet finished with the Mauprats."

The poor abbe did not know that there was so much truth in his words.

XIX

After thoroughly reflecting on the Trappist's probable intentions, I decided that I ought to grant him the interview he had requested. In any case, John Mauprat could not hope to impose upon me, and I wished to do all in my power to prevent him from pestering my great-uncle's last days with his intrigues. Accordingly, the very next day I betook myself to the town, where I arrived towards the end of Vespers. I rang, not without emotion, at the door of the Carmelites.

The retreat chosen by the Trappist was of those innumerable mendicant societies which France supported at that time. Though its rules were ostensibly most austere, this monastery was rich and devoted to pleasure. In that age of scepticism the small number of the monks was entirely out of proportion to the wealth of the establishment which had been founded for them; and the friars who roamed about the vast monasteries in the most remote parts of the provinces led the easiest and idlest lives they had ever known, in the lap of luxury, and entirely freed from the control of opinion, which always loses its power when man isolates himself. But this isolation, the mother of the "amiable vices," as they used to phrase it, was dear only to the more ignorant. The leaders were a prey to the painful dreams of an ambition which had been nurtured in obscurity and embittered by inaction. To do something, even in the most limited sphere and with the help of the feeblest machinery; to do something at all costs—such was the one fixed idea of the priors and abbes.

The prior of the Carmelites whom I was about to see was the personification of this restless impotence. Bound to his great arm-chair by the gout, he offered a strange contrast to the venerable chevalier, pale and unable to move like himself, but noble and patriarchal in his affliction. The prior was short, stout, and very petulant. The upper part of his body was all activity; he would turn his head rapidly from side to side; he would brandish his arms while giving orders. He was sparing of words, and his muffled voice seemed to lend a mysterious meaning to the most trivial things. In short, one-half of his person seemed to be incessantly striving to drag along the other, like the bewitched man in the Arabian Nights, whose robe hid a body that was marble up to the waist.

He received me with exaggerated attention, got angry because they did not bring me a chair quickly enough, stretched out his fat, flabby hand to draw this chair quite close to his own, and made a sign to a tall, bearded satyr, whom he called the Brother Treasurer, to go out; then, after overwhelming me with questions about my journey, and my return, and my health, and my family, while his keen restless little eyes were darting glances at me from under eyelids swollen and heavy from intemperance, he came to the point.

"I know, my dear child," he said, "what brings you here; you wish to pay your respects to your holy relative, to the Trappist, that model of faith and holiness whom God has sent to us to serve as an example to the world, and reveal to all the miraculous power of grace."

"Prior," I answered, "I am not a good enough Christian to judge of the miracle you mention. Let devout souls give thanks to Heaven for it. For myself, I have come here because M. Jean de Mauprat desires to inform me, as he has said, of plans which concern myself, and to which I am ready to listen. If you will allow me to go and see him—"

"I did not want him to see you before myself, young man," exclaimed the prior, with an affectation of frankness, at the same time seizing my hands in his, at the touch of which I could not repress a feeling of disgust. "I have a favour to ask of you in the name of charity, in the name of the blood which flows in your veins . . ."

I withdrew one of my hands, and the prior, noticing my expression of displeasure, immediately changed his tone with admirable skill.

"You are a man of the world, I know. You have a grudge against him who once was Jean de Mauprat, and who to-day is the humble Brother Jean Nepomucene. But if the precepts of our divine Master, Jesus Christ, cannot persuade you to pity, there are considerations of public propriety and of family pride which must make you share my fears and assist my efforts. You know the pious but rash resolution which Brother John has formed; you ought to assist me in dissuading him from it, and you will do so, I make no doubt."

"Possibly, sir," I replied very coldly; "but might I ask to what my family is indebted for the interest you are good enough to take in its affairs?"

"To that spirit of charity which animates all the followers of Christ," answered the monk, with very well assumed dignity.

Fortified with this pretext, on the strength of which the clergy have always taken upon themselves to meddle in all family secrets, it was not difficult for him to put an end to my questions; and, though he could not destroy the suspicions which I felt at heart, he succeeded in proving to my ears that I ought to be grateful to him for the care which he had taken of the honour of my name. I wanted to find out what he was driving at; it was as I had foreseen. My Uncle John claimed from me his share in the fief of Roche-Mauprat; and the prior was deputed to make me understand that I had to choose between paying a considerable sum of money (for he spoke of the interest accruing through the seven years of possession, besides a seventh part of the whole estate) and the insane step he intended taking, the scandal of which could not fail to hasten the chevalier's death and cause me, perhaps, "strange personal embarrassments." All this was hinted with consummate skill under the cover of the most Christian solicitude for my own welfare, the most fervent admiration for the Trappist's zeal, and the most sincere anxiety about the results of this "firm resolve." Finally, it was made evident that John Mauprat was not coming to ask me for the means of existence, but that I should have to humbly beseech him to accept the half of my possessions, if I wished to prevent him from dragging my name and probably my person to the felon's dock.

I tried a final objection.

"If," I said, "this resolve of Brother Nepomucene, as you call him, is as fixed as you say; if the only one care he has in the world is for his own salvation, will you explain to me how the attractions of temporal wealth can possibly turn him from it? There seems to be a contradiction in this which I fail to understand."

The prior was somewhat embarrassed by the piercing glance I turned on him, but he immediately started on one of those exhibitions of simplicity which are the supreme resource of rogues:

"Mon Dieu! my dear son," he exclaimed, "you do not know, then, the immense consolation a pious soul can derive from the possession of worldly wealth? Just as perishable riches must be despised when they represent vain pleasures, even so must they be resolutely defended by the upright man when they afford him the means of doing good. I will not hide from you that if I were the holy Trappist I would not yield my rights to any one; I would found a religious society for the propagation of the faith and the distribution of alms with the wealth which, in the hands of a brilliant young nobleman like yourself, is only squandered on horses and dogs. The Church teaches us that by great sacrifices and rich offerings we may cleanse our souls of the blackest sins. Brother Nepomucene, a prey to holy fear, believes that a public expiation is necessary for his salvation. Like a devout martyr, he wishes to satisfy the implacable justice of men with blood. But how much sweeter for you (and safer, at the same time) to see him raise some holy altar to the glory of God, and hide in the blessed peace of the cloister the baleful lustre of the name he has already abjured! He is so much swayed by the spirit of his order, he has conceived such a love for self-denial, for humility and poverty, that it will need all my efforts and much help from on high to make him agree to this change of expiations."

"It is you, then, prior, who from sheer goodness of heart are undertaking to alter this fatal resolution? I admire your zeal, and I thank you for it; but I do not think there will be any need of all these negotiations. M. Jean de Mauprat claims his share of the inheritance; nothing can be more just. Even should the law refuse all civil rights to a man who owed his safety only to flight (a point which I will pass over), my relative may rest assured that there would never be the least dispute between us on this ground, if I were the absolute possessor of any fortune whatever. But you are doubtless aware that I owe the enjoyment of this fortune only to the kindness of my great-uncle, the Chevalier Hubert de Mauprat; that he had enough to do to pay the debts of the family, which amounted to more than the total value of the estate; that I can alienate nothing without his permission, and that, in reality, I am merely the depositary of a fortune which I have not yet accepted."

The prior stared at me in astonishment, as if dazed by an unexpected blow. Then he smiled with a crafty expression, and said:

"Very good! It appears that I have been mistaken, and that I must apply to M. Hubert de Mauprat. I will do so; for I make no doubt that he will be very grateful to me for saving his family from a scandal which may have very good results for one of his relatives in the next world, but which, for a certainty, will have very bad ones for another relation in the present world."

"I understand, sir," I replied. "This is a threat. I will answer in the same strain: If M. Jean de Mauprat ventures to importune my uncle and cousin, it is with me that he will have to deal; and it will not be before the courts that I shall summon him to answer for certain outrages which I have by no means forgotten. Tell him that I shall grant no pardon to the Trappist penitent unless he remains faithful to the role he has adopted. If M. Jean de Mauprat is without resources, and he asks my help, I may, out of the income I receive, furnish him with the means of living humbly and decently, according to the spirit of the vows he has taken; but if ecclesiastical ambition has taken possession of his mind, and he thinks, by stupid, childish threats, to intimidate my uncle to such an extent that he will be able to extort from him the wherewithal to satisfy his new tastes, let him undeceive himself—tell him so from me. The old man's peace of mind and his daughter's future have only myself as guardian, and I shall manage to guard them, though it be at the risk of my life and my honour."

"And yet honour and life are of some importance at your age," replied the abbe, visibly irritated, but feigning a suaver manner than ever. "Who knows into what folly religious fervour may lead the Trappist? For, between ourselves be it said, my child—you see, I am a man of moderation—I knew the world in my youth, and I do not approve of these violent resolves, which are more often dictated by pride than piety. For instance, I have consented to temper the austerity of our rules; my friars look well-fed, and they wear shirts. Rest assured, my good sir, I am far from approving of your uncle's design, and I shall do all that is possible to hinder it. Yet, if he still persists, how will my efforts profit you? He has obtained his superior's permission, and may, after all, yield to his fatal inspiration. You may be seriously compromised by an affair of this kind; for, although reports say that you are a worthy young gentleman, though you have abjured the errors of the past, and though, perhaps, your soul has always hated iniquity, you have certainly been involved in many misdeeds which human laws condemn and punish. Who can tell into what involuntary revelations Brother Nepomucene may find himself drawn if he sets in motion the machinery of criminal proceedings? Can he set it in motion against himself without at the same time setting it in motion against you? Believe me, I wish for peace—I am a kindly man."

"Yes, a very kindly man, father," I answered, in a tone of irony. "I see that perfectly. But do not let this matter cause you needless anxiety; for there is one very clear argument which must reassure both of us. If a veritable religious impulse urges Brother John the Trappist to make a public reparation, it will be easy to make him understand that he ought to hesitate before he drags another than himself into the abyss; the spirit of Christ forbids him to do this. But, if the truth is, as I presume, that M. Jean de Mauprat has not the least wish to hand himself over to justice, his threats are but little calculated to terrify me, and I shall take steps to prevent them from making more stir than is desirable."

"So that is the only answer I am to give him?" asked the prior, darting a vindictive glance at me.

"Yes, sir," I replied; "unless he would prefer to come here and receive the answer from my own mouth. I came with a determination to conquer the disgust which his presence arouses in me; and I am astonished that, after expressing so much eagerness to see me, he should remain in the background when I arrive."

"Sir," answered the prior, with ridiculous majesty, "my duty is to see that the peace of our Lord reigns in this holy place. I must, therefore, set myself against any interview which might lead to violent explanations . . ."

"You are much too easily frightened, sir," I replied. "There is nothing to arouse passion in this matter. However, as it was not I who called for these explanations, and as I came here out of pure compliance, I most willingly refrain from pushing them further, and I thank you for having been good enough to act as intermediary."

With that, I made a profound bow and retired.

XX

I gave an account of this interview to the abbe, who was waiting for me at Patience's. He was entirely of my own opinion; he thought, like myself, that the prior, so far from endeavouring to turn the Trappist from his pretended designs, was trying with all his power to frighten me, in the hope that I should be brought to make considerable sacrifices of money. In his eyes it was clear that this old man, faithful to the monkish spirit, wished to put into the hands of a clerical Mauprat the fruit of the labours and thrift of a lay Mauprat.

"That is the indelible mark of the Catholic clergy," he said. "They cannot live without waging war on the families around them, and being ever on the watch for opportunities to spoil them. They look upon this wealth as their property, and upon all ways of recovering it as lawful. It is not as easy as you think to protect one's self against this smooth-faced brigandage. Monks have stubborn appetites and ingenious minds. Act with caution and be prepared for anything. You can never induce a Trappist to show fight. Under the shelter of his hood, with head bowed and hands crossed, he will accept the cruelest outrages; and, knowing quite well that you will not assassinate him, he will hardly fear you. Again, you do not know what justice can become in man's hands, and how a criminal trial is conducted and decided when one of the parties will not stick at any kind of bribery and intimidation. The Church is powerful, the law grandiloquent. The words 'honesty' and 'integrity' have for centuries been ringing against the hardened walls of courts of justice; but that has not prevented judges from being false or verdicts from being iniquitous. Have a care; have a care! The Trappist may start the cowled pack on his own track and throw them off by disappearing at the right point and leading them on yours. Remember that you have wounded many an *amour propre* by disappointing the pretensions of the dowry-hunters. One of the most incensed of them, and at the same time one of the most malicious, is a near relative of a magistrate who is all-powerful in the province. De la Marche has given up the gown for the sword; but among his old colleagues he may have left some one who would like to do you an ill-turn. I am sorry you were not able to join him in America, and get on good terms with him. Do not shrug your shoulders; you may kill a dozen of them, and things will go from bad to worse. They will avenge themselves; not on your life, perhaps, for they know that you hold that cheap, but on your honour; and your great-uncle will die of grief. In short—"

"My dear abbe," I said, interrupting him, "you have a habit of seeing everything black at the first glance, when you do not happen to see the sun in the middle of the night. Now let me tell you some things which ought to drive out these gloomy presentiments. I know John Mauprat of old; he is a signal impostor, and, moreover, the rankest of cowards. He will sink into the earth at the sight of me, and as soon as I speak I will make him confess that he is neither Trappist, nor monk, nor saint. All this is a mere sharper's trick. In the old days I have heard him making plans which prevent me from being astonished at his impudence now; so I have but little fear of him."

"There you are wrong," replied the abbe. "You should always fear a coward, because he strikes from behind while you are expecting him in front. If John Mauprat were not a Trappist, if the papers he showed me were lies, the prior of the Carmelites is too shrewd and cautious to have let himself be deceived. Never would he have espoused the cause of a layman, and never would he mistake a layman for one of his own cloth. However, we must make inquiries; I will write to the superior of the Trappist monastery at once, but I am certain he will confirm what I know already. It is even possible that John Mauprat is a genuine devotee. Nothing becomes such a character better than certain shades of the Catholic spirit. The inquisition is the soul of the Church, and the inquisition should smile on John Mauprat. I firmly believe that he would give himself up to the sword of justice solely for the pleasure of compassing your ruin with his own, and that the desire to found a monastery with your money is a sudden inspiration, the honour of which belongs entirely to the prior of the Carmelites . . ."

"That is hardly probable, my dear abbe," I said. "Besides, where can these discussions lead us? Let us act. Let us keep the chevalier in sight, so that the unclean beast may not come and poison the calm of his last days.

Write to the Trappist superior; I will offer the creature a pension, and when he comes, let us carefully watch his slightest movements. My sergeant, Marcasse, is an admirable bloodhound. Let us put him on the track, and if he can manage to tell us in vulgar speech what he has seen and heard, we shall soon know everything that is happening in the province."

Chatting thus, we arrived at the chateau towards the close of day. As I entered the silent building, I was seized with a fond, childish uneasiness, such as may come upon a mother when she leaves her babe a moment. The eternal security which nothing had ever disturbed within the bounds of the old sacred walls, the decrepitude of the servants, the way in which the doors always stood open, so that beggars would sometimes enter the drawing-room without meeting any one and without giving umbrage— the whole atmosphere of peace and trust and isolation—formed a strange contrast to the thoughts of strife, and the cares with which John's return and the prior's threats had filled my mind for some hours. I quickened my pace, and, seized with an involuntary trembling, I crossed the billiard-room. At that moment I thought I saw a dark shadow pass under the windows of the ground floor, glide through the jasmines, and disappear in the twilight. I threw open the door of the drawing-room and stood still. There was not a sound, not a movement. I was going to look for Edmee in her father's room, when I thought I saw something white moving near the chimney-corner where the chevalier always sat.

"Edmee! Is that you?" I exclaimed.

No one answered. My brow was covered with a cold sweat and my knees were trembling. Ashamed of this strange weakness, I rushed towards the hearth, repeating Edmee's name in agonized tones.

"Have you come at last, Bernard?" she replied, in a trembling voice.

I seized her in my arms. She was kneeling beside her father's armchair and pressing to her lips the old man's icy hands.

"Great God!" I cried, when by the dim light in the room I could distinguish the chevalier's livid face. "Is our father dead?"

"Perhaps," she said, in a stifled voice; "perhaps he has only fainted, please God! But, a light, for Heaven's sake! Ring the bell! He has only been in this state for a moment."

I rang in all haste. The abbe now came in, and fortunately we succeeded in bringing my uncle back to life.

But when he opened his eyes, his mind seemed to be struggling against the impressions of a fearful dream.

"Has he gone? Has the vile phantom gone?" he repeated several times. "Ho, there, Saint-Jean! My pistols! Now, my men! Throw the fellow out of the window!"

I began to suspect the truth.

"What has happened?" I said the Edmee, in a low tone. "Who has been here in my absence?"

"If I told you," answered Edmee, "you would hardly believe it. You would think my father and I were mad. But I will tell you everything presently; let us attend to him."

With her soft words and loving attentions she succeeded in calming the old man. We carried him to his room, and he fell into a quiet sleep. When Edmee had gently withdrawn her hand from his and lowered the wadded curtain over his head, she joined the abbe and myself, and told us that a quarter of an hour before we returned a mendicant friar had entered the drawing-room, where, as usual, she was embroidering near her father, who had fallen asleep. Feeling no surprise at an incident which frequently happened, she had risen to get her purse from the mantel-piece, at the same time addressing a few words to the monk. But just as she was turning round to offer him an alms the chevalier had awakened with a start, and eyeing the monk from head to foot, had cried in a tone half of anger and half of fear:

"What the devil are you doing here in that garb?"

Thereupon Edmee had looked at the monk's face and had recognised

. . .

"A man you would never dream of," she said; "the frightful John Mauprat. I had only seen him a single hour in my life, but that repulsive face has never left my memory, and I have never had the slightest attack of fever without seeing it again. I could not repress a cry.

"'Do not be afraid,' he said, with a hideous smile. 'I come here not as an enemy, but as a supplicant.'

"And he went down on his knees so near my father, that, not knowing what he might do, I rushed between them, and hastily pushed back the arm-chair to the wall. Then the monk, speaking in a mournful tone, which was rendered still more terrifying by the approach of night, began to pour out some lamentable rigmarole of a confession, and ended by asking pardon for his crimes, and declaring that he was already covered by the black veil which parricides wear when they go to the scaffold.

"'This wretched creature has gone mad,' said my father, pulling the bell-rope.

"But Saint-Jean is deaf, and he did not come. So we had to sit in unspeakable agony and listen to the strange talk of the man who calls himself a Trappist and declares that he had come to give himself up to justice in expiation of his transgressions. Before doing so, he wished to implore my father's forgiveness and his last blessing. While saying this he was moving forward on his knees, and speaking with an intense passion. In the sound of this voice, uttering words of extravagant humility, there seemed to be insult and a menace. As he continued moving nearer to my father, and as the idea of the foul caresses which he apparently wished to lavish on him filled me with disgust, I ordered him in a somewhat imperious tone to rise and speak becomingly. My father angrily ordered him to say no more and depart; and as at this moment he cried, 'No, you must let me clasp your knees!' I pushed him back to prevent him from touching my father. I shudder to think that my glove has touched that unclean gown. He turned towards me, and, though he still feigned penitence and humility, I could see rage gleaming in his eyes. My father made a violent effort to get up, and in fact he got up, as if by a miracle; but the next instant he fell back fainting in his chair. Then steps were heard in the billiard-room, and the monk rushed out by the glass door with the speed of lightning. It was then that you found me half-dead and frozen with terror at the feet of my prostate father."

"The abominable coward has lost no time, you see, abbe," I cried. "His aim was to frighten the chevalier and Edmee, and he has succeeded; but he reckoned without me, and I swear that—though he should have to be treated in the Roche-Mauprat fashion—if he ever dares to come here again—"

"That is enough, Bernard," said Edmee. "You make me shudder. Speak seriously, and tell me what all this means."

When I had informed her of what had happened to the abbe and myself, she blamed us for not warning her.

"Had I known," she said, "what to expect I should not have been frightened, and I could have taken care never to be left alone in the house with my father, and Saint-Jean, who is hardly more active. Now, however, I am no longer afraid; I shall be on my guard. But the best thing, Bernard dear, is to avoid all contact with this loathsome man, and to make him as liberal an allowance as possible to get rid of him. The abbe is right; he may prove formidable. He knows that our kinship with him must always prevent us from summoning the law to protect us against his persecutions; and though he cannot injure us as seriously as he flatters himself, he can at least cause us a thousand annoyances, which I am reluctant to face. Throw him gold and let him take himself off. But do not leave me again, Bernard; you see you have become absolutely necessary to me; brood no more over the wrong you pretend to have done me."

I pressed her hand in mine, and vowed never to leave her, though she herself should order me, until this Trappist had freed the country from his presence.

The abbe undertook the negotiations with the monastery. He went into the town the following day, carrying from me a special message to the Trappist that I would throw him out of the window if he ever took it into his head to appear at Sainte-Severe again. At the same time I proposed to supply him with money, even liberally, on condition that he would immediately withdraw to his convent or to any other secular or religious retreat he might choose, and that he would never again set foot in Berry.

The prior received the abbe with all the signs of profound contempt and holy aversion for his state of heresy. Far from attempting to wheedle him like myself, he told him that he wished to have nothing to do with this business, that he washed his hands of it, and that he would confine himself to conveying the decisions on both sides, and affording a refuge to Brother Nepomucene, partly out of Christian charity, and partly to edify his monks by the example of a truly devout man. According to him, Brother Nepomucene would be the second of that name placed in the front rank of the heavenly host by virtue of the canons of the Church.

The next day the abbe was summoned to the convent by a special messenger, and had an interview with the Trappist. To his great surprise, he found that the enemy had changed his tactics. He indignantly refused help of any sort, declaring that his vow of poverty and humility would not allow it; and he strongly blamed his dear host, the prior, for daring to suggest, without his consent, an exchange of things eternal for things temporal. On other matters he refused to explain his views, and took refuge in ambiguous and bombastic replies. God would inspire him, he said, and at the approaching festival of the Virgin, at the august and sublime hour of holy communion, he expected to hear the voice of Jesus speaking to his heart and announcing the line of conduct he ought to follow. The abbe was afraid of betraying uneasiness, if he insisted on probing this "Christian mystery," so he returned with this answer, which was least of all calculated to reassure me. He did not appear again either at the castle or in the neighbourhood, and kept himself so closely shut up in the convent that few people ever saw his face. However, it soon became known, and the prior was most active in spreading the news, that John Mauprat had been converted to the most zealous and exemplary piety, and was now staying at the Carmelite convent for a term, as a penitent from La Trappe. Every day they reported some fresh virtuous trait, some new act of austerity of this holy personage. Devotees, with a thirst for the marvellous, came to see him, and brought him a thousand little presents, which he obstinately refused. At times he would hide so well that people said he had returned to his monastery; but just as we were congratulating ourselves on getting rid of him, we would hear that he had recently inflicted some terrible mortifications on himself in sackcloth and ashes; or else that he had gone barefooted on a pilgrimage into some of the wildest and most desolate parts of Varenne. People went so far as to say that he could work miracles. If the prior had not been cured of his gout, that was because, in a spirit of true penitence, he did not wish to be cured.

This state of uncertainty lasted almost two months.

XXI

These days, passed in Edmee's presence, were for me days of delight, yet of suffering. To see her at all hours, without fear of being indiscreet, since she herself would summon me to her side, to read to her, talk with her on all subjects, share the loving attentions she bestowed on her father, enter into half her life exactly as if we had been brother and sister—this was great happiness, no doubt, but it was a dangerous happiness, and again the volcano kindled in my breast. A few confused words, a few troubled glances betrayed me. Edmee was by no means blind, but she was impenetrable; her dark and searching eyes, fixed on me as on her father, with the solicitude of an absorbing affection, would at times suddenly grow cold, just as the violence of my passion was ready to break out. Her countenance would then express nothing but patient curiosity and an unswerving resolve to read to the bottom of my soul without letting me see even the surface of her own.

My sufferings, though acute, were dear to me at first; it pleased me to think that I was secretly offering them to Edmee as an expiation of my past faults. I hoped that she would perceive this and be satisfied with me. She saw it, and said nothing. My agony grew more intense; but still some days passed before I lost all power to hide it. I say days, because whoever has loved a woman, and has been much alone with her, yet always kept in check by her severity, must have found days like centuries. How full life seemed and yet how consuming! What languor and unrest! What tenderness and rage! It was as though the hours were years; and at this very day, if I did not bring in dates to rectify the error of my memory, I could easily persuade myself that these two months filled half my life.

Perhaps, too, I should like to persuade myself of this, in order to find some excuse for the foolish and culpable conduct into which I fell in spite of all the good resolutions which I had but lately formed. The relapse was so sudden and complete that I should still blush at the thought, if I had not cruelly atoned for it, as you will soon see.

After a night of agony, I wrote her an insane letter which came nigh to producing terrible consequences for me; it was somewhat as follows:

"You do not love me, Edmee; you will never love me. I know this; I ask for nothing, I hope for nothing. I would only remain near you and consecrate my life to your service and defence. To be useful to you I will do all that my strength will allow; but I shall suffer, and, however I try to hide it, you will see it; and perhaps you will attribute to wrong causes the sadness I may not be able to suppress with uniform heroism. You pained me deeply yesterday, when you advised me to go out a little 'to distract my thoughts.' To distract my thoughts from you, Edmee! What bitter mockery! Do not be cruel, sister; for then you become my haughty betrothed of evil days again . . . and, in spite of myself, I again become the brigand whom you used to hate. . . . Ah, if you knew how unhappy I am! In me there are two men who are incessantly waging a war to the death. It is to be hoped that the brigand will fall; but he defends himself step by step, and he cries aloud because he feels himself covered with wounds and mortally stricken. If you knew, Edmee, if you only knew what struggles, what conflicts, rend my bosom; what tears of blood my heart distils; and what passions often rage in that part of my nature which the rebel angels rule! There are nights when I suffer so much that in the delirium of my dreams I seem to be plunging a dagger into your heart, and thus, by some sombre magic, to be forcing you to love me as I love you. When I awake, in a cold sweat, bewildered, beside myself, I feel tempted to go and kill you, so as to destroy the cause of my anguish. If I refrain from this, it is because I fear that I should love you dead with as much passion and tenacity as if you were alive. I am afraid of being restrained, governed, swayed by your image as I am by your person. Then, again, a man cannot destroy the being he loves and fears; for when she has ceased to exist on earth she still exists in himself. It is the lover's soul which serves as a coffin for his mistress and which forever preserves her burning remains, that it may feed on them without ever consuming them. But, great Heaven! what is this tumult in my thoughts? You see, Edmee, to what an extent my mind is sick; take pity on me, then. Bear with me, let me be sad, never doubt my devotion. I am often mad, but I worship you always. A word, a look from you, will always recall me to a sense of duty, and this duty will be sweet when you deign to remind me of it. As I write to you, Edmee, the sky is full of clouds that are darker and heavier than lead; the thunder is rumbling, and doleful ghosts of purgatory seem to be floating in the glare of the lightning. The weight of the storm lies on my soul; my bewildered mind quivers like the flashes which leap from the firmament. It seems as if my whole being were about to burst like the tempest. Ah, could I but lift up to you a voice like unto its voice! Had I the power to lay bare the agonies and passions which rend me within! Often, when a storm has been sweeping over the great oaks above, you have told me that you enjoy gazing upon the fury of the one and the resistance of the other. This, you say, is a battle of mighty forces; and in the din in the air you fancy you can detect the curses of the north wind and the mournful cries of the venerable branches. Which suffers the more, Edmee, the tree which resists, or the wind which exhausts itself in the attack? Is it not always the wind that yields and falls? And then the sky, grieved at the defeat of her noble son, sheds a flood of tears upon the earth. You love these wild images, Edmee; and whenever you behold strength vanquished by resistance you smile cruelly, and there is a look in your inscrutable eyes that seems to insult my misery. Well, you have cast me to the ground, and, though shattered, I still suffer; yes, learn this, since you wish to know it, since you are merciless enough to question me and to feign compassion. I suffer, and I no longer try to remove the foot which the proud conqueror has placed on my broken heart."

The rest of this letter, which was very long, very rambling and absurd from beginning to end, was in the same strain. It was not the first time that I had written to Edmee, though I lived under the same roof, and never left her except during the hours of rest. My passion possessed me to such a degree that I was irresistibly drawn to encroach upon my sleep in order to write to her, I could never feel that I had talked enough about her, that I had sufficiently renewed my promises of submission—a submission in which I was constantly failing. The present letter, however, was more daring and more passionate than any of the others. Perhaps, in some mysterious way, it was written under the influence of the storm which was rending the heavens while I, bent over my table, with moist brow and dry, burning hand, drew this frenzied picture of my sufferings. A great calm, akin to despair, seemed to come over me as I threw myself upon my bed after going down to the drawing-room and slipping my letter into Edmee's work-basket. Day was breaking, and the horizon showed heavy with the dark wings of the storm, which was flying to other regions. The trees, laden with rain, were tossing under the breeze, which was still blowing freshly. Profoundly sad, but blindly resigned to my suffering, I fell asleep with a sense of relief, as if I had made a sacrifice of my life and hopes. Apparently Edmee did not find my letter, for she gave me no answer. She generally replied verbally, and these letters of mine were a means of drawing from her those professions of sisterly friendship with which I had perforce to be satisfied, and which, at least, poured soothing balm into my wound. I ought to have known that this time my letter must either lead to a decisive explanation, or be passed over in silence. I suspected the abbe of having taken it and thrown it into the fire; I accused Edmee of scorn and cruelty; nevertheless, I held my tongue.

The next day the weather was quite settled again. My uncle went for a drive, and during the course of it told us that he should not like to die without having had one last great fox-hunt. He was passionately devoted to this sport, and his health had so far improved that he again began to show a slight inclination for pleasure and exercise. Seated in a very light, narrow *berline,* drawn by strong mules, so that he might move rapidly over the sandy paths in our woods, he had already followed one or two little hunts which we had arranged for his amusement. Since the Trappist's visit, the chevalier had entered, as it were, upon a fresh term of life. Endowed with strength and pertinacity, like all his race, it seemed as if he had been decaying for want of excitement, for the slightest demand on his energy immediately set his stagnant blood in motion. As he was very much pleased with this idea of a hunt, Edmee undertook to organize, with my help, a general battue and to join in the sport herself. One of the greatest delights of the good old man was to see her on horseback, as she boldly pranced around his carriage and offered him all the flowering sprigs which she plucked from the bushes she passed. It was arranged that I should ride with her, and that the abbe should accompany the chevalier in the carriage. All the gamekeepers, foresters, huntsmen, and even poachers of Varenne were invited to this family function. A splendid meal was prepared with many goose-pies and much local wine. Marcasse, whom I had made my manager at Roche-Mauprat, and who had a considerable knowledge of the art of fox-hunting, spent two whole days in stopping up the earths. A few young farmers in the neighbourhood, interested in the battue and able to give useful advice, graciously offered to join the party; and, last of all, Patience, in spite of his aversion for the destruction of innocent animals, consented to follow the hunt as a spectator. On the appointed day, which opened warm and cloudless on our happy plans and my own implacable destiny, some fifty individuals met with horns, horses, and hounds. At the end we were to play havoc with the rabbits, of which there were too many on the estate. It would be easy to destroy them wholesale by falling back upon that part of the forest which had not been beaten during the hunt. Each man therefore armed himself with a carbine, and my uncle also took one, to shoot from his carriage, which he could still do with much skill.

Edmee was mounted on a very spirited Limousin mare, which she amused herself by exciting and quieting with a touching coquetry to please her old father. For the first two hours she hardly left the carriage at all, and the chevalier, now full of new life, gazed on her with smiles and tears of love. Just as in the daily rotation of our globe, ere passing into night, we take leave of the radiant orb which is going to reign over another hemisphere, even so did the old man find some consolation for his death in the thought that the youth and vigour and beauty of his daughter were surviving him for another generation.

When the hunt was in full swing, Edmee, who certainly inherited some of the martial spirit of the family, and the calmness of whose soul could not always restrain the impetuosity of her blood, yielded to her father's repeated signs—for his great desire now was to see her gallop—and went after the field, which was already a little distance ahead.

"Follow her! follow her!" cried the chevalier, who had no sooner seen her galloping off than his fond paternal vanity had given place to uneasiness.

I did not need to be told twice; and digging my spurs into my horse's flanks, I rejoined Edmee in a cross-path which she had taken to come up with the hunt. I shuddered as I saw her bending like a reed under the branches, while her horse, which she was still urging on, carried her between the trees with the rapidity of lightning.

"For God's sake, Edmee," I cried, "do not ride so fast! You will be killed!"

"Let me have a gallop," she said gaily. "My father has allowed me. You must not interfere; I shall rap you on the knuckles if you try to stop my horse."

"At least let me follow you, then," I said, keeping close to her. "Your father wished it; and I shall at least be there to kill myself if anything happens to you."

Why I was filled with these gloomy forebodings I do not know, for I had often seen Edmee galloping through the woods. I was in a peculiar state; the heat of noon seemed mounting to my brain, and my nerves were strangely excited. I had eaten no breakfast, as I had felt somewhat out of sorts in the morning, and, to sustain myself, had swallowed several cups of coffee mixed with rum. At first I experienced a horrible sense of fear; then, after a few minutes, the fear gave way to an inexpressible feeling of love and delight. The excitement of the gallop became so intense that I imagined my only object was to pursue Edmee. To see her flying before me, as light as her own black mare, whose feet were speeding noiselessly over the moss, one might have taken her for a fairy who had suddenly appeared in this lonely spot to disturb the mind of man and lure him away to her treacherous haunts. I forgot the hunt and everything else. I saw nothing but Edmee; then a mist fell upon my eyes, and I could see her no more. Still, I galloped on; I was in a state of silent frenzy, when she suddenly stopped.

"What are we doing?" she said. "I cannot hear the hunt any longer, and here is the river in front. We have come too far to the left."

"No, no, Edmee," I answered, without knowing in the least what I was saying. "Another gallop and we shall be there."

"How red you are!" she said. "But how shall we cross the river?"

"Since there is a road, there must be a ford," I replied. "Come on! come on!"

I was filled with an insane desire to go on galloping, I believe my idea was to plunge deeper and deeper into the forest with her; but this idea was wrapped in a haze, and when I tried to pierce it, I was conscious of nothing but a wild throbbing of my breast and temples.

Edmee made a gesture of impatience.

"These woods are accursed!" she said. "I am always losing my way in them."

No doubt she was thinking of the fatal day when she had been carried far from another hunt and brought to Roche-Mauprat. I thought of it too, and the ideas that came into my mind produced a sort of dizziness. I followed her mechanically towards the river. Suddenly I realized that she was on the other bank. I was filled with rage on seeing that her horse was cleverer and braver than my own. Before I could get the animal to take the ford, which was rather a nasty one, Edmee was a long way ahead of me again. I dug my spurs into its sides till the blood streamed from them. At last, after being nearly thrown several times, I reached the other bank, and, blind with rage, started in pursuit of Edmee. I overtook her, and seizing the mare's bridle, I exclaimed:

"Stop, Edmee, I say! You shall not go any farther."

At the same time I shook the reins so violently that her horse reared. She lost her balance, and, to avoid falling, jumped lightly to the ground between our two animals, at the risk of being hurt. I was on the ground almost as soon as herself. I at once pushed the horses away. Edmee's, which was very quiet, stopped and began to browse. Mine bolted out of sight. All this was the affair of an instant.

I had caught Edmee in my arms; she freed herself and said, in a sharp tone:

"You are very brutal, Bernard; and I hate these ways of yours. What is the matter with you?"

Perplexed and confused, I told her that I thought her mare was bolting, and that I was afraid some accident might happen to her if she allowed herself to be carried away by the excitement of the ride.

"And to save me," she replied, "you make me fall, at the risk of killing me! Really, that was most considerate of you."

"Let me help you to mount again," I said.

And without waiting for her permission, I took her in my arms and lifted her off the ground.

"You know very well that I do not mount in this way!" she exclaimed, now quite irritated. "Leave me alone; I don't want your help."

But I was no longer in a state to obey her. I was losing my head; my arms were tightening around her waist, and it was in vain that I endeavoured to take them away. My lips touched her bosom in spite of myself. She grew pale with anger.

"Oh, how unfortunate I am!" I said, with my eyes full of tears; "how unfortunate I am to be always offending you, and to be hated more and more in proportion as my love for you grows greater!"

Edmee was of an imperious and violent nature. Her character, hardened by trials, had every year developed greater strength. She was no longer the trembling girl making a parade of courage, but in reality more ingenuous than bold, whom I had clasped in my arms at Roche-Mauprat. She was now a proud, fearless woman, who would have let herself be killed rather than give the slightest countenance to an audacious hope. Besides, she was now the woman who knows that she is passionately loved and is conscious of her power. She repulsed me, therefore, with scorn; and as I followed her distractedly, she raised her whip and threatened to leave a mark of ignominy on my face if I dared to touch even her stirrup.

I fell on my knees and begged her not to leave me thus without forgiving me. She was already in her saddle, and, as she looked round for the way back, she exclaimed:

"That was the one thing wanting—to behold this hateful spot again! Do you see where we are?"

I looked in my turn, and saw that we were on the edge of the forest, quite close to the shady little pond at Gazeau. A few yards from us, through the trees which had grown denser since Patience left, I perceived the door of the tower, opening like a big black mouth behind the green foliage.

I was seized with a fresh dizziness. A terrible struggle was taking place between two instincts. Who shall explain the mysterious workings of man's brain when his soul is grappling with the senses, and one part of his being is striving to strangle the other? In an organization like mine, such a conflict, believe me, was bound to be terrible; and do not imagine that the will makes but a feeble resistance in natures carried away by passion; it is idiotic to say to a man who lies spent with such struggles, "You ought to have conquered yourself."

XXII

How shall I describe to you what I felt at the unexpected sight of Gazeau Tower? I had seen it but twice in my life; each time I had taken part in a painfully stirring scene there. Yet these scenes were as naught beside the one awaiting me on this third encounter; there must be a curse on certain places.

I fancied I could still see the blood of the two Mauprats sprinkled on the shattered door. Their life of crime and their tragic end made me shudder at the violent instincts which I felt in myself. I was filled with a horror of my own feelings, and I understood why Edmee did not love me. But, as if yonder deplorable blood had power to stir a fatal sympathy, I felt the wild strength of my passion increasing in proportion as my will made greater efforts to subdue it. I had trampled down all other passions; scarcely a trace of them remained in me. I was sober; if not gentle and patient, I was at least capable of affection and sympathy; I had a profound sense of the laws of honour, and the highest respect for the dignity of others. Love, however, was still the most formidable of my enemies; for it was inseparably connected with all that I had acquired of morality and delicacy; it was the tie that bound the old man to the new, an indissoluble tie, which made it almost impossible for me to find the golden mean between reason and passion.

Standing before Edmee, who was about to leave me behind and on foot; furious at seeing her escape me for the last time (since after the insult I had just offered her she would doubtless never run the risk of being alone with me again), I gazed on her with a terrible expression. I was livid; my fists were clinched. I had but to resolve, and the slightest exertion of my strength would have snatched her from her horse, thrown her to the ground and left her at the mercy of my desires. I had but to let my old savage instincts reign for a second and I could have slaked, extinguished the fires which had been consuming me for seven years. Never did Edmee know the danger her honour ran in that minute of agony, and never have I ceased to feel remorse for it; but God alone shall be my Judge, for I triumphed, and this was the last evil thought of my life. In this thought, moreover, lay the whole of my crime; the rest was the work of fate.

Filled with fear, I suddenly turned my back on her and, wringing my hands in despair, hastened away by the path which had brought me thither. I cared little where I went; I only knew that I had to tear myself away from perilous temptations. It was a broiling day; the odour of the woods seemed intoxicating; the mere sight of them was stirring up the instincts of my old savage life; I had to flee or fall. With an imperious gesture, Edmee ordered me to depart from her presence. The idea that any danger could possibly threaten her except from myself naturally did not come into my head or her own. I plunged into the forest. I had not gone more than thirty paces when I heard the report of a gun from the spot where I had left Edmee. I stopped, petrified with horror; why, I know not; for in the middle of a battue the report of a gun was by no means extraordinary; but my soul was so sorrowful that it seemed ready to find fresh woe in everything. I was about to retrace my steps and rejoin Edmee at the risk of offending her still more when I thought I heard the moaning of a human being in the direction of Gazeau Tower. I rushed forward, and then fell upon my knees, as if stunned by emotion. It took me some minutes to recover; my brain seemed full of doleful sights and sounds; I could no longer distinguish between illusion and reality; though the sun was shining brightly I began to grope my way among the trees. All of a sudden I found myself face to face with the abbe; he was anxiously looking for Edmee. The chevalier had driven to a certain spot to watch the field pass, and not seeing his daughter, had been filled with apprehension. The abbe had plunged into the forest at once, and, soon finding the tracks of our horses, had come to see what had happened to us. He had heard the gun, but had thought nothing of it. Seeing me pale and apparently dazed, with my hair disarranged, and without either horse or gun (I had let mine fall on the spot where I had half fainted, and had not thought of picking it up), he was as terrified as myself; nor did he know any more than I for what reason.

"Edmee!" he said to me, "where is Edmee?"

I made a rambling reply. He was so alarmed at seeing me in such a state that he felt secretly convinced I had committed some crime, as he subsequently confessed to me.

"Wretched boy!" he said, shaking me vigorously by the arm to bring me to my senses. "Be calm; collect your thoughts, I implore you! . . ."

I did not understand a word, but I led him towards the fatal spot; and there—a sight never to be forgotten—Edmee was lying on the ground rigid and bathed in blood. Her mare was quietly grazing a few yards away. Patience was standing by her side with his arms crossed on his breast, his face livid, and his heart so full that he was unable to answer a word to the abbe's cries and sobs. For myself, I could not understand what was taking place. I fancy that my brain, already bewildered by my previous emotions, must have been completely paralyzed. I sat down on the ground by Edmee's side. She had been shot in the breast in two places. I gazed on her lifeless eyes in a state of absolute stupor.

"Take away that creature," said Patience to the abbe, casting a look of contempt on me. "His perverse nature is what it always was."

"Edmee, Edmee!" cried the abbe, throwing himself upon the grass and endeavouring to stanch the blood with his handkerchief.

"Dead, dead!" said Patience. "And there is the murderer! She said so as she gave up her pure soul to God; and Patience will avenge her! It is very hard; but it must be so! It is God's will, since I alone was here to learn the truth."

"Horrible, horrible!" exclaimed the abbe.

I heard the sound of this last word, and with a smile I repeated it like an echo.

Some huntsmen now appeared. Edmee was carried away. I believe that I caught sight of her father walking without help. However, I should not dare to affirm that this was not a mere extravagant vision (for I had no definite consciousness of anything, and these awful moments have left in my mind nothing but vague memories, as of a dream), had I not been assured that the chevalier got out of the carriage without any help, walked about, and acted with as much presence of mind as a young man. On the following day he fell into a state of absolute dotage and insensibility, and never rose from his arm-chair again.

But what happened to myself? I do not know. When I recovered my reason, I found that I was in another part of the forest near a little waterfall, to the murmur of which I was listening mechanically with a sort of vague delight. Blaireau was asleep at my feet, while his master, leaning against a tree, was watching me attentively. The setting sun was sending shafts of ruddy gold between the slender stems of the young ash-trees; the wild flowers seemed to be smiling at me; and birds were warbling sweet melodies. It was one of the most beautiful days of the year.

"What a gorgeous evening!" I said to Marcasse. "This spot is as beautiful as an American forest. Well, old friend, what are you doing there? You ought to have awakened me sooner. I have had such hideous dreams."

Marcasse came and knelt down beside me; two streams of tears were running down his withered, sallow cheeks. On his face, usually so impassive, there was an ineffable expression of pity and sorrow and affection.

"Poor master!" he said, "delirium, head bad, that's all. Great misfortune! But fidelity not changed. Always with you; if need be, ready to die with you."

His tears and words filled me with sadness; but this was owing to an instinctive sympathy enhanced by the weak state of my nerves, for I did not remember a thing. I threw myself into his arms and wept like himself; he pressed me to his bosom, as a father might his son. I was fully conscious that some frightful misfortune had overtaken me, but I was afraid to learn what it was, and nothing in the world would have induced me to ask him.

He took me by the arm and led me through the forest. I let myself be taken like a child. Then a fresh sense of weariness came over me, and he was obliged to let me sit down again for half an hour. At last he lifted me up and succeeded in leading me to Roche-Mauprat, where we arrived very late. I do not know what happened to me during the night. Marcasse told me subsequently that I had been very delirious. He took upon himself to send to the nearest village for a barber, who bled me early in the morning, and a few minutes later I recovered my reason.

But what a frightful service they seemed to have done me. Dead! Dead! Dead! This was the only word I could utter. I did nothing but groan and toss about on my bed. I wanted to get up and run to Sainte-Severe. My poor sergeant would throw himself at my feet, or plant himself in front of the door to prevent me. To keep me back, he would tell me various things which I did not in the least understand. However, his manifest solicitude for me and my own feeling of exhaustion made me yield, though I could not explain his conduct. In one of these struggles my vein opened again, and I returned to bed before Marcasse noticed it. Gradually I sank into a deep swoon, and I was almost dead when, seeing my blue lips and purple cheeks, he took it into his head to lift up the bed-clothes, and found me lying in a pool of blood.

However, this was the most fortunate thing that could have happened to me. For several days I remained in a state of prostration in which there was but little difference between my waking and sleeping hours. Thanks to this, I understood nothing, and therefore did not suffer.

One morning, having managed to make me take a little nourishment, and noticing that with my strength my melancholy and anxiety were re-turning, Marcasse announced, with a simple, genuine delight, that Edmee was not dead, and that they did not despair of saving her. These words fell upon me like a thunderbolt; for I was still under the impression that this frightful adventure was a delusion of my delirium. I began to shout and to brandish my arms in a terrible manner. Marcasse fell on his knees by my bed and implored me to be calm, and a score of times he repeated the following words, which to me were like the meaningless words one hears in dreams:

"You did not do it on purpose; I know well enough. No, you did not do it on purpose. It was an accident; a gun going off in your hand by chance."

"Come, now, what do you mean?" I exclaimed impatiently. "What gun? What accident? What have I to do with it?"

"Don't you know, then, sir, how she was hit?"

I passed my hands over my brow as if to bring back to my mind the energy of life, and as I had no clear recollection of the mysterious event which had unhinged it, I thought that I was mad, and remained silent and dismayed, fearful lest any word should escape to betray the loss of my faculties.

At last, little by little, I collected my thoughts. I asked for some wine, as I felt weak; and no sooner had I drunk a few drops than all the scenes of the fatal day unrolled themselves before me as if by magic. I even remembered the words that I had heard Patience utter immediately after the event. It was as if they had been graven in that part of the memory which preserves the sound of words, even when the other part which treasures up their sense is asleep. For one more moment I was uncertain; I wondered if my gun could have gone off in my hands just as I was leaving Edmee. I distinctly remembered firing it at a pewit an hour before, for Edmee had wanted to examine the bird's plumage. Further, when I heard the shot which had hit her, my gun was in my hands, and I had not thrown it down until a few seconds later, so it could not have been this weapon which had gone off on falling. Besides, even granting a fatality which was incredible, I was much too far from Edmee at that moment to have shot her. Finally, I had not a single bullet on me throughout the day; and it was impossible for my gun to have been loaded, unknown to myself, since I had not unslung it after killing the pewit.

Quite convinced, therefore, that I was not the cause of the hideous accident, it remained to me to find an explanation of this crushing catastrophe. To me it was perfectly simple; some booby with a gun, I thought, must have caught sight of Edmee's horse through the branches and mistaken it for a wild beast; and I did not dream of accusing any one of a deliberate attempt at murder. I discovered, however, that I was accused myself. I drew the truth from Marcasse. He informed me that the chevalier and all the people who took part in the hunt had attributed the misfortune to a pure accident, their opinion being that, to my great sorrow, my gun had gone off when my horse threw me, for it was believed that I had been thrown. This was practically the view they all took. In the few words that Edmee had been able to utter she seemed to confirm the supposition. Only one person accused me, and that was Patience; but he had accused me before none but his two friends, Marcasse and the Abbe Aubert, and then only after pledging them to secrecy.

"There is no need," added Marcasse, "for me to tell you that the abbe maintains an absolute silence, and refuses to believe that you are guilty. As for myself, I swear to you that I shall never—"

"Stop! stop!" I said. "Do not tell me even that; it would imply that some one in the world might actually believe it. But Edmee said something extraordinary to Patience just as she was dying; for she is dead; it is useless for you to try to deceive me. She is dead, and I shall never see her again."

"She is not dead!" cried Marcasse.

And his solemn oaths convinced me, for I knew that he would have tried in vain to lie; his simple soul would have risen in revolt against his charitable intentions. As for Edmee's words, he frankly refused to repeat them; from which I gathered that their testimony seemed overwhelming. Thereupon I dragged myself out of bed, and stubbornly resisted all Marcasse's efforts to keep me back; I had the farmer's horse saddled and started off at a gallop. I staggered into the drawing-room without meeting any one except Saint-Jean, who uttered a cry of terror on seeing me, and rushed off without answering my questions.

The drawing-room was empty. Edmee's embroidery frame, buried under the green cloth, which her hand, perchance, would never lift again, seemed to me like a bier under its pall. My uncle's big arm-chair was no longer in the chimney-corner. My portrait, which I had had painted in Philadelphia and had sent over during the American war, had been taken down from the wall. These were signs of death and malediction.

I left this room with all haste and went upstairs with the courage of innocence, but with despair in my soul. I waled straight to Edmee's room, knocked, and entered at once. Mademoiselle Leblanc was coming towards the door; she gave a loud scream and ran away, hiding her face in her hands as if she had seen a wild beast. Who, then, could have been spreading hideous reports about me? Had the abbe been disloyal enough to do so? I learnt later that Edmee, though generous and unshaken in her lucid moments, had openly accused me in her delirium.

I approached her bed and, half delirious myself, forgetting that my sudden appearance might be a deathblow to her, I pulled the curtains aside with an eager hand and gazed on her. Never have I seen more marvellous beauty. Her big dark eyes had grown half as large again; they were shining with an extraordinary brilliancy, though without any expression, like diamonds. Her drawn, colourless cheeks, and her lips, as white as her cheeks, gave her the appearance of a beautiful marble head. She looked at me fixedly, with as little emotion as if she had been looking at a picture or a piece of furniture; then, turning her face slightly towards the wall, she said, with a mysterious smile:

"This is the flower they call *Edmea sylvestris.*"

I fell upon my knees; I took her hand; I covered it with kisses; I broke into sobs. But she gave no heed; her hand remained in mine icy and still, like a piece of alabaster.

XXIII

The abbe came in and greeted me in a cold and sombre manner. Then he made a sign to me, and drawing me away from the bed, said:

"You must be mad! Return at once; and if you are wise, you will remain away. It is the only thing left for you to do."

"And since when," I cried, flying into a passion, "have you had the right to drive me out of the bosom of my family?"

"Alas! you have no longer a family," he answered, with an accent of sorrow that somewhat disarmed me. "What were once father and daughter are now naught but two phantoms, whose souls are already dead and whose bodies soon will be. Show some respect for the last days of those who loved you."

"And how can I show my respect and grief by quitting them?" I replied, quite crushed.

"On this point," said the abbe, "I neither wish nor ought to say anything; for you know that your presence here is an act of rashness and a profanation. Go away. When they are no more (and the day cannot be far distant), if you have any claims to this house, you may return, and you will certainly not find me here to contest them or affirm them. Meanwhile, as I have no knowledge of these claims, I believe I may take upon myself to see that some respect is paid to the last hours of these two holy people."

"Wretched man!" I said, "I do not know what prevents me from tearing you to pieces! What abominable impulse urges you to be everlastingly turning the dagger in my breast? Are you afraid that I may survive this blow? Cannot you see that three coffins will be taken out together from this house? do you imagine that I have come here for aught but a farewell look and a farewell blessing?"

"You might say a farewell pardon," replied the abbe, in a bitter tone, and with a gesture of merciless condemnation.

"What I say is that you are mad!" I cried, "and that if you were not a priest, this hand of mine should crush the life out of you for daring to speak to me in this way."

"I have but little fear of you, sir," he rejoined. "To take my life would be doing me a great service; but I am sorry that your threats and anger should lend weight to the charges under which you lie. If I saw that you were moved to penitence, I would weep with you; but your assurance fills me with loathing. Hitherto, I had seen in you nothing worse than a raging lunatic; to-day I seem to see a scoundrel. Begone, sir!"

I fell into an arm-chair, choking with rage and anguish. For a moment I hoped that I was about to die. Edmee was dying by my side, and before me was a judge so firmly convinced of my guilt that his usual gentle, timid nature had become harsh and pitiless. The imminent loss of her I loved was hurrying me into a longing for death. Yet the horrible charge hanging over me began to rouse my energies. I did not believe that such an accusation could stand for a single instant against the voice of truth. I imagined that one word from me, one look, would be sufficient to make it fall to the ground; but I felt so dazed, so deeply wounded, that this means of defence was denied me. The more grievously the disgrace of such a suspicion weighed upon my mind, the more clearly I realized that it is almost impossible for a man to defend himself successfully when his only weapon is the pride of slandered innocence.

I sat there overwhelmed, unable to utter a word. It seemed as if a dome of lead were weighing on my skull. Suddenly the door opened and Mademoiselle Leblanc approached me stiffly; in a tone full of hatred she informed me that some one outside wished to speak to me. I went out mechanically, and found Patience waiting with his arms folded, in his most dignified attitude, and with an expression on his face which would have compelled both respect and fear if I had been guilty.

"Monsieur de Mauprat," he said, "I must request you to grant me a private interview. Will you kindly follow me to my cottage?"

"Yes, I will," I replied. "I am ready to endure any humiliation, if only I can learn what is wanted of me and why you are all pleased to insult the most unfortunate of men. Lead the way, Patience, and go quickly; I am eager to return here."

Patience walked in front of me with an impassive air. When we arrived at his little dwelling, we found my poor sergeant, who had just arrived likewise. Not finding any horse on which he could follow me, and not wishing to quit me, he had come on foot, and so quickly that he was bathed in perspiration. Nevertheless, the moment he saw us he sprang up full of life from the bench on which he had thrown himself under the bower of vine-branches, and came to meet us.

"Patience!" he cried, in a dramatic style which would have made me smile had it been possible for me to display a glimmer of mirth at such a moment. "Old fool! . . . Slanderer at your age? . . . Fie, sir! . . . Ruined by good fortune . . . you are . . . yes."

Patience, impassive as ever, shrugged his shoulders and said to his friend:

"Marcasse, you do not know what you are saying. Go and rest awhile at the bottom of the orchard. This matter does not concern you. I want to speak to your master alone. I wish you to go," he added, taking him by the arm; and there was a touch of authority in his manner to which the sergeant, in spite of his ticklish prided, yielded from instinct and habit.

As soon as we were alone Patience proceeded to the point; he began by a series of questions to which I resolved to submit, so that I might the more quickly obtain some light on the state of affairs around me.

"Will you kindly inform me, monsieur," he said, "what you purpose doing now?"

"I purpose remaining with my family," I answered, "as long as I have a family; and when this family is no more, what I shall do concerns no one."

"But, sir," replied Patience, "if you were told that you could not remain under the same roof with them without causing the death of one or the other, would you persist in staying?"

"If I were convinced that this was so," I rejoined, "I would not appear in their presence. I would remain at their door and await the last day of their life, or the first day of their renewed health, and again implore a love I have not yet ceased to deserve."

"Ah, we have come to this!" said Patience, with a smile of contempt. "I should not have believed it. However, I am very glad; it makes matters clearer."

"What do you mean?" I cried. "Speak, you wretch! Explain yourself!"

"You are the only wretch here," he answered coldly, at the same time sitting down on the one stool in the cottage, while I remained standing before him.

I wanted to draw an explanation from him, at all costs. I restrained my feelings; I even humbled myself so far as to say that I should be ready to accept advice, if he would consent to tell me the words that Edmee had uttered immediately after the event, and those which she had repeated in her hours of delirium.

"That I will not," replied Patience sternly; "you are not worthy to hear any words from that mouth, and I shall certainly never repeat them to you. Why do you want to know them? Do you hope to hide anything from men hereafter? God saw you; for Him there are no secrets. Leave this place; stay at Roche-Mauprat; keep quiet there; and when your uncle is dead and your affairs are settled, leave this part of the country. If you take my advice, you will leave it this very day. I do not want to put the law on your track, unless your actions force me. But others besides myself, if they are not certain of the truth, have at least a suspicion of it. Before two days have passed a chance word said in public, the indiscretion of some servant, may awaken the attention of justice, and from that point to the scaffold, when a man is guilty, is but a single step. I used not to hate you; I even had a liking for you; take this advice, then, which you say you are ready to follow. Go away at once, or remain in hiding and ready for flight. I do not desire your ruin; Edmee would not desire it either—so—do you understand?"

"You must be insane to think that I could listen to such advice. I, hide myself! or flee like a murderer! You can't dream of that! Come on! come on! I defy the whole of you! I know not what fury and hatred are fretting you and uniting you all against me; I know not why you want to keep me from seeing my uncle and cousin; but I despise your follies. My place is here; I shall not quit it except by order of my cousin or uncle; and this order, too, I must take from their own lips; I cannot allow sentence to be brought me by any outsider. So, thanks for your wisdom, Monsieur Patience; in this case my own will suffice. I am your humble servant, sir."

I was preparing to leave the cottage when he rushed in front of me, and for a moment I saw that he was ready to use force to detain me. In spite of his advanced age, in spite of my height and strength, he might still have been a match, perhaps more than a match, for me in a struggle of this kind. Short, bent, broad-shouldered, he was a Hercules.

He stopped, however, just as he was about to lay hands on me, and, seized with one of those fits of deep tenderness to which he was subject in his moments of greatest passion, he gazed at me with eyes of pity, and said, in a gentle tone:

"My poor boy! you whom I loved as a son (for I looked upon you as Edmee's brother), do not hasten to your ruin. I beseech you in the name of her whom you have murdered, and whom you still love—I can see it—but whom you may never behold again. Believe me, but yesterday your family was a proud vessel, whose helm was in your hands; to-day it is a drifting wreck, without either sail or pilot—left to be handled by cabinboys, as friend Marcasse says. Well, my poor mariner, do not persist in drowning yourself; I am throwing you a rope; take it—a day more, and it may be too late. Remember that if the law gets hold of you, the man who is trying to save you to-day, to-morrow will be obliged to appear against you and condemn you. Do not compel me to do a thing the very thought of which brings tears to my eyes. Bernard, you have been loved, my lad; even to-day you may live on the past."

I burst into tears, and the sergeant, who returned at this moment, began to weep also; he implored me to go back to Roche-Mauprat; but I soon recovered and, thrusting them both away, said:

"I know that both of you are excellent men, and both most generous; you must have some love for me too, since, though you believe me blackened with a hideous crime, you can still think of saving my life. But have no fears on my account, good friends; I am innocent of this crime, and my one wish is that the matter may be fully investigated, so that I may be acquitted—yes, this is inevitable, I owe it to my family to live until my honour has been freed from stain. Then, if I am condemned to see my cousin die, as I have no one in the world to love but her, I will blow my brains out. Why, then, should I be downcast? I set little store by my life. May God make the last hours of her whom I shall certainly not survive painless and peaceful—that is all I ask of Him."

Patience shook his head with a gloomy, dissatisfied expression. He was so convinced of my crime that all my denials only served to alienate his pity. Marcasse still loved me, though he thought I was guilty. I had no one in the world to answer for my innocence, except myself.

"If you persist on returning to the chateau," exclaimed Patience, "you must swear before you leave that you will not enter your cousin's room, or your uncle's, without the abbe's permission."

"What I swear is that I am innocent," I replied, "and that I will allow no man to saddle me with a crime. Back, both of you! Let me pass! Patience, if you consider it your duty to denounce me, go and do so. All that I ask is that I may not be condemned without a hearing; I prefer the bar of justice to that of mere opinion."

I rushed out of the cottage and returned to the chateau. However, not wishing to make a scandal before the servants, and knowing quite well that they could not hide Edmee's real condition from me, I went and shut myself up in the room I usually occupied.

But in the evening, just as I was leaving it to get news of the two patients, Mademoiselle Leblanc again told me that some one wished to speak with me outside. I noticed that her face betrayed a sense of joy as well as fear. I concluded that they had come to arrest me, and I suspected (rightly, as it transpired) that Mademoiselle Leblanc had denounced me. I went to the window, and saw some of the mounted police in the courtyard.

"Good," I said; "let my destiny take its course."

But, before quitting, perhaps forever, this house in which I was leaving my soul, I wished to see Edmee again for the last time. I walked straight to her room. Mademoiselle Leblanc tried to throw herself in front of the door; I pushed her aside so roughly that she fell, and, I believe, hurt herself slightly. She immediately filled the house with her cries; and later, in the trial, made a great pother about what she was pleased to call an attempt to murder her. I at once entered Edmee's room; there I found the abbe and the doctor. I listened in silence to what the latter was saying. I learnt that the wounds in themselves were not mortal, that they would not even be very serious, had not a violent disturbance in the brain complicated the evil and made him fear tetanus. This frightful word fell upon me like a death sentence. In America I had seen many men die of this terrible malady, the result of wounds received in the war. I approached the bed. The abbe was so alarmed that he did not think of preventing me. I took Edmee's hand, cold and lifeless, as ever. I kissed it a last time, and, without saying a single word to the others, went and gave myself up to the police.

XXIV

I was immediately thrown into prison at La Chatre. The public prosecutor for the district of Issoudun took in hand this case of the attempted murder of Mademoiselle de Mauprat, and obtained permission to have a monitory published on the morrow. He went to the village of Sainte-Severe, and then to the farms in the neighbourhood of the Curat woods, where the event had happened, and took the depositions of more than thirty witnesses. Then, eight days after I had been arrested, the writ of arrest was issued. If my mind had been less distracted, or if some one had interested himself in me, this breach of the law and many others that occurred during the trial might have been adduced as powerful arguments in my favour. They would at least have shown that the proceedings were inspired by some secret hatred. In the whole course of the affair an invisible hand directed everything with pitiless haste and severity.

The first examination had produced but a single indictment against me; this came from Mademoiselle Leblanc. The men who had taken part in the hunt declared that they knew nothing, and had no reason to regard the occurrence as a deliberate attempt at murder. Mademoiselle Leblanc, however, who had an old grudge against me for certain jokes I had ventured to make at her expense, and who, moreover, had been suborned, as I learned afterward, declared that Edmee, on recovering from her first swoon, at a time when she was quite calm and in full possession of her reason, had confided to her, under a pledge of secrecy, that she had been insulted, threatened, dragged from her horse, and finally shot by me. This wicked old maid, putting together the various revelations that Edmee had made in her delirium, had, cleverly enough, composed a connected narrative, and added to it all the embellishments that hatred could suggest. Distorting the incoherent words and vague impressions of her mistress, she declared upon oath that Edmee had seen me point the barrel of my carbine at her, with the words, "As I swore, you shall die by my hand."

Saint-Jean, who was examined the same day, declared that he knew nothing beyond what Mademoiselle Leblanc had told him that evening, and his deposition was very similar to hers. He was honest enough, but dull and narrow-minded. From love of exactness, he omitted no trifling detail which might be interpreted against me. He asserted that I had always been subject to pains in the head, during which I lost my senses; that several times previously, when my nerves were disordered, I had spoken of blood and murder to some individual whom I always fancied I could see; and, finally, that my temper was so violent that I was "capable of throwing the first thing that came to hand at any one's head, though as a fact I had never, to his knowledge, committed any excess of this kind." Such are the depositions that frequently decide life and death in criminal cases.

Patience could not be found on the day of this inquiry. The abbe declared that his ideas on the occurrence were so vague that he would undergo all the penalties inflicted on recalcitrant witnesses rather than express his opinion before fuller investigations had been made. He requested the public prosecutor to give him time, promising on his honour that he would not resist the demands of justice, and representing that at the end of a few days, by inquiring into certain things, he would probably arrive at a conviction of some sort; in this event he undertook to speak plainly, either for or against me. This delay was granted.

Marcasse simply said that if I had inflicted the wounds on Mademoiselle de Mauprat, about which he was beginning to feel very doubtful, I had at least inflicted them unintentionally; on this he was prepared to stake his honour and his life.

Such was the result of the first inquiry. It was resumed at various times during the following days, and several false witnesses swore that they had seen me shoot Mademoiselle de Mauprat, after vainly endeavouring to make her yield to my wishes.

One of the most baneful instruments of ancient criminal procedure was what was known as the monitory; this was a notice from the pulpit, given out by the bishop and repeated by all vicars to their parishioners, ordering them to make inquiries about the crime in question, and to reveal all the facts which might come to their knowledge. This was merely a modified form of the inquisitorial principle which reigned more openly in other countries. In the majority of cases, the monitory, which had, as a fact, been instituted in order to encourage informers in the name of religion, was a marvel of ridiculous atrocity; it frequently set forth the crime and all the imaginary circumstances the plaintiffs were eager to prove; it was, in short, the publication of a ready-made case, which gave the first knave that came a chance of earning some money by making a lying depo-sition in favour of the highest bidder. The inevitable effect of the monitory, when it was drawn up with a bias, was to arouse public hatred against the accused. The devout especially, receiving their opinions ready-made from the clergy, pursued the victim without mercy. This is what happened in my own case; but here the clergy of the province were playing a further secret part which almost decided my fate.

The case was taken to the assizes at the court of Bourges, and pro-ceedings began in a very few days.

You can imagine the gloomy despair with which I was filled. Edmee's condition was growing more and more serious; her mind was completely unhinged. I felt no anxiety as to the result of the trial; I never imagined it was possible to convict me of a crime I had not committed; but what were honour and life to me, if Edmee were never to regain the power of recog-nising my innocence? I looked upon her as already dead, and as having cursed me dying! So I was inflexibly resolved to kill myself immediately after receiving my sentence, whatever it might be. Until then I felt that it was my duty to live, and to do what might be necessary for the triumph of truth; but I was plunged in such a state of stupor that I did not even think of ascertaining what was to be done. Had it not been for the cleverness and zeal of my counsel, and the sublime devotion of Marcasse, my listlessness would have left me to the most terrible fate.

Marcasse spent all his time in expeditions on my behalf. In the eve-ning he would come and throw himself on a bundle of straw at the foot of my trunkle bed, and, after giving me news of Edmee and the chevalier, whom he went to see every day, he would tell me the results of his pro-ceedings. I used to grasp his hand affectionately; but I was generally so absorbed by the news he had just given me of Edmee, that I never heard anything further.

This prison of La Chatre had formerly been the stronghold of the Elevains of Lombaud, the seigneurs of the province. Nothing was left of it but a formidable square tower at the top of a ravine where the Indre forms a narrow, winding valley, rich with the most beautiful vegetation. The weather was magnificent. My room, situated at the top of the tower, received the rays of the rising sun, which cast the long, thin shadows of a triple row of poplars as far as the eye could see. Never did landscape more smiling, fresh, and pastoral offer itself to the eyes of a prisoner. But how could I find pleasure in it? Words of death and contumely came to me in every breeze that blew through the wall-flowers growing in the crannies. Every rustic sound, every tune on the pipe that rose to my room, seemed to contain an insult or to proclaim profound contempt for my sorrow. There was nothing, even to the bleating of the flocks, which did not appear to me an expression of neglect or indifference.

For some time Marcasse had had one fixed idea, namely, that Edmee had been shot by John Mauprat. It was possible; but as there was no evidence to support the conjecture, I at once ordered him not to make known his suspicions. It was not for me to clear myself at the expense of others. Although John Mauprat was capable of anything, it was possible that he had never thought of committing this crime; and as I had not heard him spoken of for more than six weeks, it seemed to me that it would have been cowardly to accuse him. I clung to the belief that one of the men in the battue had fired at Edmee by mistake, and that a feeling of fear and shame prevented him from confessing his misadventure. Marcasse had the courage to go and see all those who had taken part in the hunt, and, with such eloquence as Heaven had granted him, implored them not to fear the penalty for unintentional murder, and not to allow an innocent man to be accused in their stead. All these efforts were fruitless; from none of the huntsmen did my poor friend obtain a reply which left him any nearer a solution of the mystery that surrounded us.

On being transferred to Bourges, I was thrown into the castle which had belonged to the old dukes of Berry; this was henceforth to be my prison. It was a great grief to me to be separated from my faithful sergeant. He would have been allowed to follow me, but he had a presentiment that he would soon be arrested at the suggestion of my enemies (for he persisted in believing that I was the victim of a plot), and thus be unable to serve me any more. He wished, therefore, to lose no time, and to continue his investigations as long as they "should not have seized his person."

Two days after my removal to Bourges, Marcasse produced a document which had been drawn up at his instance by two notaries of La Chatre. It contained the depositions of ten witnesses to the effect that for some days before the attempted assassination, a mendicant friar had been prowling about Varenne; that he had appeared in different places very close together; and, notably, that he had slept at Notre-Dame de Poligny the night before the event. Marcasse maintained that this monk was John Mauprat. Two women declared that they had thought they recognised him either as John or Walter Mauprat, who closely resembled him. But Walter had been found drowned the day after the capture of the keep; and the whole town of La Chatre, on the day when Edmee was shot, had seen the Trappist engaged with the Carmelite prior from morning till night in conducting the procession and services for the pilgrimage of Vaudevant. These depositions, therefore, so far from being favourable to me, produced a very bad effect, and threw odium on my defence. The

Trappist conclusively proved his alibi, and the prior of the Carmelites helped him to spread a report that I was a worthless villain. This was a time of triumph for John Mauprat; he proclaimed aloud that he had come to deliver himself up to his natural judges to suffer punishment for his crimes in the past; but no one could think of prosecuting such a holy man. The fanaticism that he inspired in our eminently devout province was such that no magistrate would have dared to brave public opinion by proceeding against him. In his own depositions, Marcasse gave an account of the mysterious and inexplicable appearance of the Trappist at Roche-Mauprat, the steps he had taken to obtain an interview with M. Hubert and his daughter, his insolence in entering and terrifying them in their drawing-room, and the efforts the Carmelite prior had made to obtain considerable sums of money from me on behalf of this individual. All these depositions were treated as fairy tales, for Marcasse admitted that he had not seen the Trappist in any of the places mentioned, and neither the chevalier nor his daughter was able to give evidence. It is true that my answers to the various questions put to me confirmed Marcasse's statements; but as I declared in all sincerity that for some two months the Trappist had given me no cause for uneasiness or displeasure, and as I refused to attribute the murder to him, it seemed for some days as if he would be forever reinstated in public opinion. My lack of animosity against him did not, however, diminish that which my judges showed against me. They made use of the arbitrary powers which magistrates had in bygone days, especially in remote parts of the provinces, and they paralyzed all my lawyer's efforts by a fierce haste. Several legal personages, whose names I will not menton, indulged, even publicly, in a strain of invective against me which ought to have excluded them from any court dealing with questions of human dignity and morality. They intrigued to induce me to confess, and almost went so far as to promise me a favourable verdict if I at least acknowledged that I had wounded Mademoiselle de Mauprat accidently. The scorn with which I met these overtures alienated them altogether. A stranger to all intrigue, at a time when justice and truth could not triumph except by intrigue, I was a victim of two redoubtable enemies, the Church and the Law; the former I had offended in the person of the Carmelite prior; and the latter hated me because, of the suitors whom Edmee had repulsed, the most spiteful was a man closely related to the chief magistrate.

Nevertheless, a few honest men to whom I was almost unknown, took an interest in my case on account of the efforts of others to make my name odious. One of them, a Monsieur E—, who was not without influence, for he was the brother of the sheriff of the province and acquainted with all the deputies, rendered me a service by the excellent suggestions he made for throwing light on this complicated affair.

Patience, convinced as he was of my guilt, might have served my enemies without wishing to do so; but he would not. He had resumed his roaming life in the woods, and, though he did not hide, could never be found. Marcasse was very uneasy about his intentions and could not understand his conduct at all. The police were furious to find that an old man was making a fool of them, and that without going beyond a radius of a few leagues. I fancy that the old fellow, with his habits and constitution, could have lived for years in Varenne without falling into their hands, and, moreover, without feeling that longing to surrender which a sense of *ennui* and the horror of solitude so frequently arouse, even in great criminals.

XXV

The day of the public trial came. I went to face it quite calmly; but the sight of the crowd filled me with a profound melancholy. No support, no sympathy for me there! It seemed to me that on such an occasion I might at least have looked for that show of respect to which the unfortunate and friendless are entitled. Yet, on all the faces around I saw nothing but a brutal and insolent curiosity. Girls of the lower classes talked loudly of my looks and my youth. A large number of women belonging to the nobility or moneyed classes displayed their brilliant dresses in the galleries, as if they had come to some *fete*. A great many monks showed their shaven crowns in the middle of the populace, which they were inciting against me; from their crowded ranks I could frequently catch the words "brigand," "ungodly," and "wild beast." The men of fashion in the district were lolling on the seats of honour, and discussing my passion in the language of the gutter. I saw and heard everything with that tranquility which springs from a profound disgust of life; even as a traveller who has come to the end of his journey, may look with indifference and weariness on the eager bustle of those who are setting off for a more distant goal.

The trial began with that emphatic solemnity which at all times has been associated with the exercise of judicial power. My examination was short, in spite of the innumerable questions that were asked me about my whole life. My answers singularly disappointed the expectations of public curiosity, and shortened the trial considerably. I confined myself to three principal replies, the substance of which I never changed. Firstly, to all questions concerning my childhood and education, I replied that I had not come into the defendant's dock to accuse others. Secondly, to those bearing on Edmee, the nature of my feeling for her, and my relations with her, I replied that Mademoiselle de Mauprat's worth and reputation could not permit even the simplest question as to the nature of her relations with any man whatever; and that, as to my feelings for her, I was accountable for them to no one. Thirdly, to those which were designed to make me confess my pretended crime, I replied that I was not even the unwilling author of the accident. In brief answers I gave some details of the events immediately preceding it; but, feeling that I owed it to Edmee as much as to myself to be silent about the tumultuous impulses that had stirred me, I explained the scene which had resulted in my quitting her, as being due to a fall from my horse; and that I had been found some distance from her body was, I said, because I had deemed it advisable to run after my horse, so that I might again escort her. Unfortunately all this was not very clear, and, naturally, could not be. My horse had gone off in the direction opposite to that which I said; and the bewildered state in which I had been found before I knew of the accident, was not sufficiently explained by a fall from my horse. They questioned me especially about the gallop I had had with my cousin through the wood, instead of following the hunt as we had intended; they would not believe that we had gone astray, guided altogether by chance. It was impossible, they said, to look upon chance as a reasonable being, armed with a gun, waiting for Edmee at Gazeau Tower at an appointed time, in order to shoot her the moment I turned my back for five minutes. They pretended that I must have taken her to this out-of-the-way spot either by craft or force to outrage her; and that I had tried to kill her either from rage at not succeeding, or from fear of being discovered and punished for my crime.

Then all the witnesses for and against me were heard. It is true that among the former Marcasse was the only one who could really be considered as a witness for the defence. The rest merely affirmed that a "monk bearing a resemblance to the Mauprats" had been roaming about Varenne at the period in question, and that he had even appeared to hide himself on the evening of the event. Since then he had not been seen. These depositions, which I had not solicited, and which I declared had not been taken at my request, caused me considerable astonishment; for among the witnesses who made them I saw some of the most honest folk in the country. However, they had no weight except in the eyes of Monsieur E—, the magistrate, who was really interested in discovering the truth. He interposed, and asked me how it was that M. Jean de Mauprat had not been summoned to confront these witnesses, seeing that he had taken the trouble to put in his affidavit to prove an alibi. This objection was received with a murmur of indignation. There were not a few people, however, who by no means looked upon John Mauprat as a saint; but they took no interest in myself, and had merely come to the trial as to a play.

The enthusiasm of the bigots reached a climax when the Trappist suddenly stood up in the crowd. Throwing back his cowl in a theatrical manner, he boldly approached the bar, declaring that he was a miserable sinner worthy of all scorn, but on this occasion, when it was the duty of every one to strive for truth, he considered it incumbent on him to set an example of simple candour by voluntarily offering himself for any examination which might shed light on the judges' minds. These words were greeted with applause. The Trappist was admitted to the witness-box, and confronted with the witnesses, who all declared, without any hesitation, that the monk they had seen wore the same habit as this man, and that there was a family likeness, a sort of distant resemblance between the two; but that it was not the same person—on this point they had not the least doubt.

The result of this incident was a fresh triumph for the Trappist. No one seemed to notice that, as the witnesses had displayed so much candour, it was difficult to believe that they had not really seen another Trappist. At this moment I remembered that, at the time of the abbe's first interview with John Mauprat at the spring at Fougeres, the latter had let fall a few words about a friar of the same order who was travelling with him, and had passed the night at the Goulets farm. I thought it advisable to mention this fact to my counsel. He discussed it in a low voice with the abbe, who was sitting among the witnesses. The latter remembered the circumstance quite clearly, but was unable to add any further details.

When it came to the abbe's turn to give evidence he looked at me with an expression of agony; his eyes filled with tears, and he answered the formal questions with difficulty, and in an almost inaudible voice. He made a great effort to master himself, and finally he gave his evidence in these words:

"I was driving in the woods when M. le Chevalier Hubert de Mauprat requested me to alight, and see what had become of his daughter, Edmee, who had been missing from the field long enough to cause him uneasiness. I ran for some distance, and when I was about thirty yards from Gazeau Tower I found M. Bernard de Mauprat in a state of great agitation. I had just heard a gun fired. I noticed that he was no longer carrying his carbine; he had thrown it down (discharged, as has been proved), a few yards away. We both hastened to Mademoiselle de Mauprat, whom we found lying on the ground with two bullets in her. Another man had reached her before

229

us and was standing near her at this moment. He alone can make known the words he heard from her lips. She was unconscious when I saw her."

"But you heard the exact words from this individual," said the president; "for rumour has it that there is a close friendship between yourself and the learned peasant known as Patience."

The abbe hesitated, and asked if the laws of conscience were not in this case at variance with the laws of the land; and if the judges had a right to ask a man to reveal a secret intrusted to his honour, and to make him break his word.

"You have taken an oath here in the name of Christ to tell the truth, the whole truth," was the reply. "It is for you to judge whether this oath is not more solemn than any you may have made previously."

"But, if I had received this secret under the seal of the confessional," said the abbe, "you certainly would not urge me to reveal it."

"I believe, Monsieur l'Abbe," said the president, "that it is some time since you confessed any one."

At this unbecoming remark I noticed an expression of mirth on John Mauprat's face—a fiendish mirth, which brought back to me the man as I knew him of old, convulsed with laughter at the sight of suffering and tears.

The annoyance which the abbe felt at this personal attack gave him the courage which might otherwise have been wanting. He remained for a few moments with downcast eyes. They thought that he was humiliated; but, as soon as he raised his head, they saw his eyes flashing with the malicious obstinacy of the priest.

"All things considered," he said, in the most gentle tone, "I think that my conscience bids me keep this secret; I shall keep it."

"Aubert," said the King's advocate, angrily, "you are apparently unaware of the penalties which the law inflicts on witnesses who behave as you are doing."

"I am aware of them," replied the abbe, in a still milder tone.

"Doubtless, then, you do not intend to defy them?"

"I will undergo them if necessary," rejoined the abbe, with an imperceptible smile of pride, and such a dignified bearing that all the women were touched.

Women are excellent judges of things that are delicately beautiful.

"Very good," replied the public prosecutor. "Do you intend to persist in this course of silence?"

"Perhaps," replied the abbe.

"Will you tell us whether, during the days that followed this attempt to murder Mademoiselle de Mauprat, you were in a position to hear the words she uttered, either during her delirium or during her lucid intervals?"

"I can give you no information on that point," answered the abbe. "It would be against my inclinations, and, moreover, in my eyes, an outrage on propriety, to repeat words which, in the case of delirium, could prove absolutely nothing, and, if uttered in a lucid moment, could only have been the outpouring of a genuinely filial affection."

"Very good," said the King's advocate, rising. "We shall call upon the Court to deliberate on your refusal of evidence, taking this incident in connection with the main question."

"And I," said the president, "in virtue of my discretionary power, do order that Aubert be meanwhile arrested and taken to prison."

The abbe allowed himself to be led away with unaffected calmness. The spectators were filled with respect, and a profound silence reigned in court, in spite of the bitter efforts of the monks and cures, who continued to revile the heretic in an undertone.

When the various witnesses had been heard (and I must say that those who had been suborned played their part very feebly in public), to crown all, Mademoiselle Leblanc appeared. I was surprised to find the old maid so bitter against me and able to turn her hatred to such account. In truth, the weapons she could bring against me were only too powerful. In virtue of the right which domestics claim to listen at doors and overhear family secrets, this skilled misinterpreter and prolific liar had learnt and shaped to her own purposes most of the facts in my life which could be utilized for my ruin. She related how, seven years before, I had arrived at the chateau of Sainte-Severe with Mademoiselle de Mauprat, whom I had rescued from the roughness and wickedness of my uncles.

"And let that be said," she added, turning toward John Mauprat with a polite bow, "without any reference to the holy man in this court, who was once a great sinner, and is now a great saint. But at what a price," she continued, facing the judges again, "had this miserable bandit saved my dear mistress! He had dishonoured her, gentlemen; and, throughout the days that followed, the poor young lady had abandoned herself to grief and shame on account of the violence which had been done her, for which nothing could bring consolation. Too proud to breath her misfortune to a single soul, and too honest to deceive any man, she broke off her engagement with M. de la Marche, whom she loved passionately, and who returned her passion. She refused every offer of marriage that was made her, and all from a sense of honour, for in reality she hated M. Bernard. At first she wanted to kill herself; indeed, she had one of her father's little hunting-knives sharpened and (M. Marcasse can tell you the same, if he chooses to remember) she would certainly have killed herself, if I had not thrown this knife into the well belonging to the house. She had to think, too, of defending herself against the night attacks of her persecutor; and, as long as she had this knife, she always used to put it under her pillow; every night she would bolt the door of her room; and frequently I have seen her rush back, pale and ready to faint, quite out of breath, like a person who has just been pursued and had a great fright. When this gentleman began to receive some education, and learn good manners, mademoiselle, seeing that she could never have any other husband, since he was always talking of killing any man who dared to present himself, hoped he would get rid of his fierceness, and was most kind and good to him. She even nursed him during his illness; not that she liked and esteemed him as much as M. Marcasse was pleased to say in his version; but she was always afraid that in his delirium he might reveal, either to the servants or her father, the secret of the injury he had done her. This her modesty and pride made her most anxious to conceal, as all the ladies present will readily understand. When the family went to Paris for the winter of '77, M. Bernard became jealous and tyrannical and threatened so frequently to kill M. de la Marche that mademoiselle was obliged to send the latter away. After that she had some violent scenes with Bernard, and declared that she did not and never would love him. In his rage and grief—for it cannot be denied that he was enamoured of her in his tigerish fashion—he went off to America, and during the six years he spent there his letters seemed to show that he had much improved. By the time he returned, mademoiselle had made up her mind to be an old maid, and had become quite calm again. And M. Bernard, too, seemed to have grown into a fairly good young gentleman. However, through seeing her every day and everlastingly leaning over the back of her arm-chair, or winding her skeins of wool and whispering to her while her father was asleep, he fell so deeply in love again that he lost his head. I do not wish to be too hard on him, poor creature! and I fancy his right place is in the asylum rather than on the scaffold. He used to shout and groan all night long; and the letters he wrote her were so stupid that she used to smile as she read them and then put them in her pocket without answering them. Here is one of these letters that I found upon her when I undressed her after the horrible deed; a bullet has gone through it, and it is stained with blood, but enough may still be read to show that monsieur frequently intended to kill mademoiselle."

So saying, she put down on the table a sheet of paper half burnt and half covered with blood, which sent a shudder through the spectators—genuine with some of them, mere affectation with many others.

Before this letter was read, she finished her deposition, and ended it with some assertions which perplexed me considerably; for I could no longer distinguish the boundary between truth and perfidy.

"Ever since her accident," she said, "mademoiselle has been hovering between life and death. She will certainly never recover, whatever the doctors may declare. I venture to say that these gentlemen, who only see the patient at certain hours, do not understand her illness as well as I, who have never left her for a single night. They pretend that her wounds are going on well and that her head is deranged; whereas I say that her wounds are going on badly, and that her head is better than they say. Mademoiselle very rarely talks irrationally, and if by chance she does, it is in the presence of these gentlemen, who confuse and frighten her. She then makes such efforts not to appear mad that she actually becomes so; but as soon as they leave her alone with me or Saint-Jean or Monsieur l'Abbe, who could quite well have told you how things are, if he had wished, she becomes calm again, and sweet and sensible as usual. She says that she could almost die of pain, although to the doctors she pretends that she is scarcely suffering at all. And then she speaks of her murderer with the generosity that becomes a Christian; a hundred times a day she will say:

"'May God pardon him in the next life as I pardon him in this! After all, a man must be very fond of a woman to kill her! I was wrong not to marry him; perhaps he would have made me happy. I drove him to despair and he has avenged himself on me. Dear Leblanc, take care never to betray the secret I have told you. A single indiscreet word might send him to the scaffold, and that would be the death of my father.'

"The poor young lady is far from imagining that things have come to this pass; that I have been summoned by the law and my religion to make known what I would rather conceal; and that, instead of going out to get an apparatus for her shower-baths, I have come here to confess the truth. The only thing that consoles me is that it will be easy to hide all this from M. le Chevalier, who has no more sense now than a babe just born. For myself, I have done my duty; may God be my judge!"

After speaking thus with perfect self-possession and great volubility, Mademoiselle Leblanc sat down again amid a murmur of approbation, and they proceeded to read the letter which had been found on Edmee.

It was, indeed, the one I had written to her only a few days before the fatal day. They handed it to me; I could not help pressing my lips to the stains of Edmee's blood. Then, after glancing at the writing, I returned the letter, and declared quite calmly that it was written by me.

The reading of this letter was my *coup de grace*. Fate, who seems ingenious in injuring her victims, had obtained (and perhaps some famous hand had contributed to the mutilation) that the passages expressing my obedience and respect should be destroyed. Certain poetic touches which might have furnished an explanation of, and an excuse for, my wild ramblings, were illegible. What showed plain to every eye, and carried conviction to every mind, were the lines that remained intact, the lines that bore witness to the violence of my passion and the vehemence of my frenzy. They were such phrases as these: "Sometimes I feel inclined to rise in the middle of the night and go and kill you! I should have done this a hundred times, if I had been sure that I should love you no more after your death. Be considerate; for there are two men in me, and sometimes the brigand of old lords it over the new man, etc." A smile of triumph played about my enemies' mouths. My supporters were demoralized, and even my poor sergeant looked at me in despair. The public had already condemned me.

This incident afforded the King's advocate a fine chance of thundering forth a pompous address, in which he described me as an incurable blackguard, as an accursed branch of an accursed stock, as an example of the fatality of evil instincts. Then, after exerting himself to hold me up as an object of horror and fear, he endeavoured, in order to give himself an air of impartiality and generosity, to arouse the compassion of the judges in my favour; he proceeded to show that I was not responsible for my actions; that my mind had been perverted in early childhood by foul sights and vile principles, and was not sound, nor ever could have been, whatever the origin and growth of my passions. At last, after going through a course of philosophy and rhetoric, to the great delight of the audience, he demanded that I should be condemned to privation of civil rights and imprisonment for life.

Though my counsel was a man of spirit and intelligence, the letter had so taken him by surprise, the people in court were so unfavourably disposed towards me, and the judges, as they listened to him, so frequently showed signs of incredulity and impatience (an unseemly habit which appears to be the heritage of the magisterial benches of this country), that his defence was tame. All that he seemed justified in demanding with any vigour was a further inquiry. He complained that all the formalities had not been fulfilled; that sufficient light had not been thrown on certain points in the case; that it would be showing too much haste to give a verdict when several circumstances were still wrapped in mystery. He demanded that the doctors should be called to express an opinion as to the possibility of taking Mademoiselle de Mauprat's evidence. He pointed out that the most important, in fact the only important, testimony was that of Patience, and that Patience might appear any day and prove me innocent. Finally, he demanded that they should order a search to be made for the mendicant friar whose resemblance to the Mauprats had not yet been explained, and had been sworn to by trustworthy witnesses. In his opinion it was essential to

discover what had become of Antony Mauprat, and to call upon the Trappist for information on this point. He complained bitterly that they had
deprived him of all means of defence by refusing any delay; and he had
the courage to assert that some evil passions must be responsible for such
blind haste as had marked the conduct of this trial. On this the president
called him to order. Then the King's advocate replied triumphantly that all
formalities had been fulfilled; that the court was sufficiently enlightened;
that a search for the mendicant friar would be a piece of folly and in bad
taste, since John Mauprat had proved his last brother's death, which had
taken place several years before. The court retired to deliberate; at the end
of half an hour they came back with a verdict condemning me to death.

XXVI

Although the haste with which the trial had been conducted and the severity of the sentence were iniquitous, and filled those who were most
bitter against me with amazement, I received the blow with supreme indifference; I no longer felt an interest in anything on earth. I commended
my soul and the vindication of my memory to God. I said to myself that if
Edmee died I should find her again in a better world; that if she survived
me and recovered her reason, she would one day succeed in discovering
the truth, and that then I should live in her heart as a dear and tender
memory. Irritable as I am, and always inclined to violence in the case of
anything that is an obstacle or an offence to me, I am astonished at the
philosophical resignation and the proud calm I have shown on the momentous occasions of life, and above all on this one.

It was two o'clock in the morning. The case had lasted for fourteen
hours. A silence as of death reigned over the court, which was as full and
as attentive as at the beginning, so fond are mortals of anything in the
nature of a show. That offered by the criminal court at this moment was
somewhat dismal. Those men in red robes, as pale and stern and implacable as the Council of Ten at Venice; those ghosts of women decked with
flowers, who, by the dim light of the tapers, looked like mere reflections
of life hovering in the galleries above the priests of death; the muskets
of the guard glittering in the gloom in the back of the court; the heart-
broken attitude of my poor sergeant, who had fallen at my feet; the silent
but vast delight of the Trappist, still standing unwearied near the bar; the

mournful note of some convent bell in the neighbourhood beginning to ring for matins amid the silence of the assembly—was not all this enough to touch the nerves of the wives of the farmers-general and to send a thrill through the brawny breasts of the tanners in the body of the court?

Suddenly, just as the court was about to disperse, a figure like that of the traditional peasant of the Danube—squat, rugged, barefooted, with a long beard, dishevelled hair, a broad, grave brow, and a stern, commanding glance—rose in the midst of the flickering reflections by which the hall was half lighted, and standing erect before the bar, said in a deep, striking voice:

"I, Jean le Houx, known as Patience, oppose this judgment as iniquitous in substance and illegal in form. I demand that it be revised, so that I may give my evidence, which is necessary, may be of sovereign importance, and should have been waited for."

"If you had anything to say," cried the King's advocate, in a passion, "why did you not present yourself when you were summoned. You are imposing on the court by pretending that you have important evidence to give."

"And you," answered Patience, more slowly and in an even deeper tone than before, "you are imposing on the public by pretending that I have not. You know well enough that I must have."

"Remember where you are, witness, and to whom you are speaking."

"I know too well, and I shall not say too much. I hereby declare that I have some important things to say, and that I should have said them at the right time, if you had not done violence to the time. I wish to say them, and I shall; and, believe me, it is better that I should make them known while it is still possible to revise these proceedings. It is even better for the judges than the prisoner; for the one comes to life again in honour, as soon as the others die in infamy."

"Witness," said the irritated magistrate, "the virulence and impertinence of your language will be prejudicial rather than advantageous to the prisoner."

"And who says that I am favourable to the prisoner?" said Patience in a voice of thunder. "What do you know about me? What if it pleases me to change an illegal and worthless verdict into one which is legal and irrevocable?"

"But how can you reconcile this desire to see the laws respected," said the magistrate, genuinely moved by Patience's powerful personality, "with your own breach of them in not appearing when summoned by the public prosecutor?"

"I did not wish to appear."

"Severe penalties may be inflicted on those whose wishes are not in harmony with the laws of the land."

"Possibly."

"Have you come here to-day with the intention of submitting to them?"

"I have come to see that you respect them."

"I warn you that, if you do not change your tone, I shall have you taken off to prison."

"And I warn you that, if you love justice and serve God, you will listen to me and suspend the execution of this sentence. It is not for him who brings truth to humble himself before those who should be seeking it. But you who are listening to me now, you men of the people, whom I will not accuse the great of wishing to dupe, you whose voice is called 'the voice of God,' side with me; embrace the cause of truth, that truth which is in danger of being stifled under false outward shows, or else is about to triumph by unfair means. Go down on your knees, you men of the people, my brothers, my children; pray, implore, require that justice be done and anger repressed. It is your duty, it is your right, and to your own interest; for it is you who are insulted and threatened when laws are violated."

Patience spoke with so much warmth, and his sincerity was so strikingly manifest, that a thrill of sympathy ran through the whole audience. At that time, philosophy was too fashionable with the young men of quality for these not to be among the first to respond to an appeal, though addressed to others than themselves. They rose with chivalrous enthusiasm and turned round to the people, who, carried away by their noble example, rose likewise. There was a wild uproar, and one and all, conscious of their dignity and power, cast away personal prejudices in order to combine for their common rights. Thus, a noble impetuosity and a true word are sometimes sufficient to bring back the masses who have long been led astray by sophism.

A respite was granted, and I was led back to my prison amid the applause of the people. Marcasse followed me. Patience disappeared without giving me a chance to thank him.

The revision of the sentence could not be made without an order from the high court. For my own part, before the verdict was given I had resolved to make no appeal to this court of cassation of the old jurisprudence. But Patience's bearing and words had had as much effect on my mind as on the minds of the spectators. The spirit of resistance and the sense of human dignity, dulled in me and paralyzed, as it were, by grief, suddenly awoke again, and in this hour I realized that man is not made for that selfish concentration of despair which is known as resignation or stoicism. No man can cease to have a regard for his own honour without at the same time ceasing to feel the respect due to the principle of honour. If it is grand to sacrifice personal glory and life to the mysterious decrees of conscience, it is cowardly to abandon both to the fury of an unjust persecution. I felt that I had risen in my own estimation, and I passed the rest of this momentous night in devising means of vindicating myself, with as much persistence as I had previously displayed in abandoning myself to fate. With this feeling of energy I could feel hope springing up anew. Edmee, perhaps, was neither mad nor mortally wounded. She might acquit me; she might recover.

"Who knows?" I said to myself. "Perhaps she has already done me justice. Perhaps it was she who sent Patience to my rescue. Undoubtedly I shall best please her by taking courage again, and not letting myself be crushed by a set of knaves."

But how was I to obtain this order from the high court? It needed a special mandate from the King; who would procure this? Who would cut short those odious delays which the law can introduce at will into the very cases that it has previously hurried on with blind precipitation? Who would prevent my enemies from injuring me and paralyzing all my efforts? In a word, who would fight for me? The abbe alone could have taken up my cause; but he was already in prison on my account. His generous behaviour in the trial had proved that he was still my friend, but his zeal was now fettered. And what could Marcasse do, hampered by his humble birth and enigmatical language? Evening came, and I fell asleep in the hope that help would be sent from on high; for I had prayed to God with my whole soul. A few hours of sleep refreshed me; I was aroused by the noise of bolts being drawn at the other side of my door. O God of goodness! what was my delight on seeing Arthur, my brother in arms, my other self, the man from whom I had had no secret for six long years! I wept like a child on receiving this mark of love from Providence. Arthur did not believe me guilty! Scientific matters connected with the library at Philadelphia had taken him to Paris, where he had heard of this sad affair in which I was implicated. He had broken a lance with all who attacked me, and had not lost a moment in coming to offer help or consolation.

In a transport of joy I poured out my soul to him, and then explained how he could assist me. He wanted to take the coach for Paris that very evening; but I implored him to go to Sainte-Severe first of all to get news of Edmee. Four mortal days had passed since I had received any; and, moreover, Marcasse had never given me such exact details as I could have wished.

"Ease your mind," said Arthur. "I will undertake to bring you the truth. I am a pretty good surgeon; and I have a practised eye. I shall be able to give you some idea of what you have to hope or fear. From Sainte-Severe I shall go straight to Paris."

Two days later I received a long letter from him giving full details about Edmee.

Her condition was extraordinary. She did not speak, nor did she appear to be in pain as long as nothing happened to excite her nerves; but on the first word which stirred up recollections of her troubles she would be seized with convulsions. Her moral isolation formed the greatest obstacle to recovery. Physically she wanted for nothing; she had two good doctors and a most devoted nurse. Mademoiselle Leblanc likewise was very zealous in her attentions, though this dangerous woman often gave her pain by untimely remarks and indiscreet questions. Furthermore, Arthur assured me that, if ever Edmee had thought me guilty and had expressed an opinion on this point, it must have been in some previous phase of her illness; for, during the last fortnight at least, she had been in a state of complete torpor. She would frequently doze, but without quite falling asleep; she could take liquid food and jellies, nor did she ever complain. When her doctors questioned her about her sufferings she answered by careless signs and always negatively; and she would never give any indication that she remembered the affections which had filled her life. Her love for her father, however, that feeling which had always been so deep and powerful in her, was not extinct; she would often shed copious tears; but at such a time she seemed to be deaf to all sounds; in vain would they try to make her understand that her father was not dead, as she appeared to believe. With a gesture of entreaty she would beg them to stop, not the noise (for that did not seem to strike her ear), but the bustle that was going on around her; then, hiding her face in her hands, lying back in her arm-chair and bringing her knees up almost to her breast, she would apparently give way to inconsolable despair. This silent grief, which could no longer control itself and no longer wished to be controlled; this powerful will, which had once been able to quell the most violent storms, and now going adrift on a dead sea and in an unruffled calm—this, said Arthur, was the most painful spectacle he had ever beheld. Edmee seemed to wish to have done with life. Mademoiselle Leblanc, in order to test her and arouse her, had brutally taken upon herself to announce that her father was dead; she had replied by a sign that she knew. A few hours later the doctors had tried to make her understand that he was alive; she had replied by another sign that she did not believe them. They had wheeled the chevalier's arm-chair into her room; they had brought father and daughter face to face and the two had not recognised each other. Only, after a few moments, Edmee, taking her father for a ghost, had uttered piercing cries, and had been seized with convulsions that had opened one of her wounds again, and made the doctors tremble for her life. Since then, they had taken care to keep the two apart, and never to breathe a word about the chevalier in Edmee's presence. She had taken Arthur for one of the doctors of the district and had received him with the same sweetness and the same indifference as the others. He had not dared to speak to her about me; but he extorted me not to despair. There was nothing in Edmee's condition that time and rest could not triumph over; there was but little fever left; none of her vital organs were really affected; her wounds were almost healed; and it did not seem as if her brain were in such an excited condition that it would be permanently deranged. The weak state of her mind, and the prostration of all the other organs could not, according to Arthur, long withstand the vitality of youth and the recuperative power of an admirable constitution. Finally, he advised me to think of myself; I might help towards her recovery, and I might again find happiness in her affection and esteem.

In a fortnight Arthur returned from Paris with an order from the King for the revision of my sentence. Fresh witnesses were heard. Patience did not appear; but I received a note from him containing these words in a shapeless hand, "You are not guilty, so don't despair." The doctors declared that Mademoiselle de Mauprat might be examined without danger, but that her answers would have no meaning. She was now in better health. She had recognised her father, and at present would never leave him; but she could understand nothing that was not connected with him. She seemed to derive great pleasure from tending him like a child, and, on his side, the chevalier would now and then recognise his beloved daughter; but his vital powers were visibly decaying. They questioned him in one of his lucid moments. He replied that his daughter had, indeed, fallen from her horse while hunting, and that she had torn her breast on the stump of a tree, but that not a soul had fired at her, even by mistake, and that only a madman could possibly believe her cousin capable of such a crime. This was all the information they could draw from him. When they asked him what he thought of his nephew's absence, he answered that his nephew was still in the house, and that he saw him every day. Was it that, in his devotion to the good name of a family—alas! so compromised—he thought to defeat the aims of justice by childish lies? This is a point I was never able to ascertain. As for Edmee, it was impossible to examine her. At the first question that was asked her, she shrugged her shoulders and made a sign that she did not wish to be bothered. As the public prosecutor insisted and became more explicit, she stared at him and seemed to be making an effort to understand. He pronounced my name, she gave a loud cry and fainted. He had to abandon all thoughts of taking her evidence. However,

Arthur did not despair. On the contrary, the account of this scene made him think that Edmee's mental faculties might be about to take a favourable turn. He immediately returned to Sainte-Severe, where he remained several days without writing to me, which caused me great anxiety.

When the abbe was questioned again, he persisted in his calm, laconic refusal to give evidence.

My judges, seeing that the information promised by Patience was not forthcoming, hurried on the revision of the trial, and, by another exhibition of haste, gave another proof of their animosity. The appointed day arrived. I was devoured by anxiety. Arthur had written me to keep up my courage, in as laconic a style as Patience. My counsel had been unable to obtain any fresh evidence in my favour. I could see clearly that he was beginning to believe me guilty. All he hoped for was to obtain a further delay.

XXVII

There were even more people present than at the first trial. The guard were forced back to the doors of the court, and the crowd occupied every available space, even to the windows of the mansion of Jacques Coeur, the town-hall of the present day. I was much agitated this time, though I had strength and pride enough not to let it be seen. I was now interested in the success of my case, and, as it seemed as if my hopes were not to be realized, I experienced an indescribable feeling of uneasiness, a sort of suppressed rage, a bitter hatred of these men who would not open their eyes to my innocence, and even of God who seemed to have deserted me.

In this state of agitation I had to make such violent efforts to appear calm that I scarcely noticed what was happening around me. I recovered sufficient presence of mind when my fresh examination took place to answer in the same terms as at the first trial. Then a black veil seemed to fall over my head, an iron ring gripped my brow; the sockets of my eyes went icily cold; I could see nothing but myself, hear nothing but vague, unintelligible sounds. I do not know what actually took place; I do not know if any one announced the apparition which suddenly appeared before me. I only remember that a door opened behind the judges, and that Arthur came forward leading a veiled woman, that he took off her veil after making her sit down in a big arm-chair which the ushers eagerly wheeled toward her, and that a cry of admiration rang through the hall when Edmee's pale, sublime beauty was revealed.

At this moment I forgot the crowd, and the judges, and my cause, and the whole universe. I believe that no human power could have withstood my wild rush. I dashed like a thunderbolt into the middle of the inclosure and, falling at Edmee's feet, I showered kisses on her knees. I have been told that this act won over the public, and that nearly all the ladies burst into tears. The young dandies did not venture to laugh; the judges were affected; and for a moment truth was completely triumphant.

Edmee looked at me for some time. Her face was as expressionless as the face of death. It did not seem as if she could ever recognise me. The spectators were waiting in profound silence for her to show some sign of hatred or affection for me. All at once she burst into tears, threw her arms around my neck, and then lost consciousness. Arthur had her carried out immediately; he had some trouble in making me return to my place. I could not remember where I was or the issues that were at stake; I clung to Edmee's dress, and only wanted to follow her. Arthur addressed the court and requested that the doctors who had examined Edmee in the morning might again pronounce upon the state of her health. He likewise demanded that she should be recalled to give evidence, and to be confronted with me as soon as she recovered from the attack.

"This attack is not serious," he said. "Mademoiselle de Mauprat has had several of the same kind during the last few days and on her way here. After each her mental faculties have taken a more and more favourable turn."

"Go and attend to the invalid," said the president. "She shall be recalled in two hours, if you think she will have recovered from her swoon by then. Meanwhile the court will hear the witness on whose demand the first sentence was not carried out."

Arthur withdrew and Patience was introduced. He was dressed quite neatly; but, after saying a few words, he declared that it would be impossible to continue unless they allowed him to take off his coat. This borrowed finery so embarrassed him and seemed so heavy that he was perspiring profusely. No sooner did the president make a sign of consent, accompanied by a smile of scorn, than he threw to the ground this badge of civilization. Then, after carefully pulling down his shirt-sleeves over his sinewy arms, he spoke almost as follows:

"I will speak the truth, the whole truth. I take the oath for the second time; for I have to speak of things that seem contradictory, things that I cannot explain to myself. I swear before God and man that I will say what I know, and as I know it, without being influenced for or against any one."

He lifted his big hand and turned round towards the people with a simple confidence, as if to say, "You can all see that I am taking an oath, and you know that I am to be trusted." This confidence of his was not ill-founded. Since the incident in the first trial the public mind had been much occupied about this extraordinary man, who had spoken before the court with so much daring, and harangued the people in presence of the judges. His conduct had filled all the democrats and *Philadelphians* with great curiosity and sympathy. The works of Beaumarchais were very fashionable among the upper classes, and this will explain how it was that Patience, though opposed to all the authorities in the province, yet found himself supported and applauded by every man who prided himself on his intelligence. They all thought they saw in him Figaro under a new form. The fame of his private virtues had spread; for you remember that during my stay in America, Patience had made himself known among the people of Varenne and had exchanged his sorcerer's reputation for that of a public benefactor. They had given him the title of the *great judge,* because he was always ready to intervene in disputes, and would always settle to the satisfaction of both sides with admirable good-nature and tact.

This time he spoke in a high, penetrating voice. It was a rich voice of wide compass. His gestures were quiet or animated, according to the circumstances, but always dignified and impressive; the expression on his short, Socratic face was never anything but fine. He had all the qualities of an orator; but there was no vanity in his display of them. He spoke in the plain, concise style that he had been obliged to acquire in his recent intercourse with men, in discussions about their practical interests.

"When Mademoiselle de Mauprat was shot," he said, "I was not more than a dozen paces from her; but the brushwood at that spot is so thick that I could not see more than two paces in front of me. They had persuaded me to take part in the hunt; but it gave me but little pleasure. Finding myself near Gazeau Tower, where I lived for some twenty years, I felt an inclination to see my old cell again, and I was bearing down upon it at a great pace when I heard a shot. That did not frighten me in the least; it seemed but natural that there should be some gun fired during a battue. But when I got through the thicket, that is to day, some two minutes later, I found Edmee—excuse me, I generally call her by this name; I am, so to speak, a sort of foster-father to her—I found Edmee on her knees upon the ground, wounded as you have been told, and still holding the bridle of her horse, which was rearing. She did not know whether she was seriously or slightly wounded, but she had her other hand on her breast, and she was saying:

"'Bernard, this is hideous! I should never have thought that you would kill me. Bernard, where are you? Come and see me die. This will kill father!'

"As she said this she let go the horse's bridle and fell to the ground. I rushed towards her.

"'Ah, you saw it, Patience?' she said. 'Do not speak about it; do not tell my father . . .'

"She threw out her arms, and her body became rigid. I thought that she was dead. She spoke no more until night, after they had extracted the bullets from her breast."

"Did you then see Bernard de Mauprat?"

"I saw him on the spot where the deed was done, just as Edmee lost consciousness and seemed to be giving up her soul; he seemed to be out of his mind. I thought that he was overwhelmed with remorse. I spoke to him sternly, and treated him as a murderer. He made no reply, but sat down on the ground by his cousin's side. He remained there in a dazed condition, even a long time after they had taken her away. No one thought of accusing him. The people thought that he had had a fall, because they saw his horse trotting by the side of the pond; they believed that his carbine had gone off as he fell. The Abbe Aubert was the only one who heard me accuse M. Bernard of having murdered his cousin. During the days that followed, Edmee spoke occasionally, but it was not always in my presence; besides, at this time she was nearly always delirious. I maintain that she told nobody (and least of all Mademoiselle Leblanc) what had passed between herself and M. de Mauprat before the gun was fired. Nor did she confide this to me any more than others. On the rare occasions when she was in possession of her senses she would say in answer to our questions, that Bernard had certainly not done it on purpose, and several times during the first three days she even asked to see him. However, when she was delirious she would sometimes cry, 'Bernard! Bernard! You have committed a great crime. You have killed my father!'

"That was her idea; she used really to think that her father was dead; and she thought so for a long time. Very little, therefore, of what she said is to be taken seriously. The words that Mademoiselle Leblanc has put into her mouth are false. After three days she ceased to talk intelligibly, and at the end of a week she ceased to speak altogether. When she recovered her reason, about a week ago, she sent away Mademoiselle Leblanc, which would clearly show that she had some ground for disliking her maid. That is what I have to say against M. de Mauprat. It rested entirely with myself to keep silent; but having other things to say yet, I wished to make known the whole truth."

Patience paused awhile; the public and the judges themselves, who were beginning to take an interest in me and lose the bitterness of their prejudices, were apparently thunderstruck at hearing evidence so different from what they expected.

Patience continued as follows:

"For several weeks I remained convinced of Bernard's guilt. But I was pondering over the matter the while; I frequently said to myself that a man as good and clever as Bernard, a man for whom Edmee felt so much esteem, and whom M. le Chevalier loved like a son, a man, in short, so deeply imbued with the spirit of justice and truth, could not between one day and the next turn into a scoundrel. Then the idea came into my head that, after all, it might have been some other Mauprat who fired the shot. I do not speak of the one who has become a Trappist," he added, looking among the audience for Jean de Mauprat, who, however was not there; "I speak of the man whose death has never been proved, although the court thought fit to overlook this, and to accept M. Jean de Mauprat's word."

"Witness," said the president, "I must remind you that you are not here to serve as counsel for the prisoner, or to criticise the decisions of this court. You must confine yourself to a statement of facts, and not express your opinion on the question at issue."

"Very well," replied Patience. "I must, however, explain why I did not wish to appear at the first trial, seeing that the only evidence I had was against M. Bernard, and that I could not trust that evidence myself."

"You are not asked to explain this at present. Please keep to your evidence."

"One moment. I have my honour to defend; I have to explain my own conduct, if you please."

"You are not the prisoner; you are not here to plead your own cause. If the court thinks right to prosecute you for contempt you can see to your own defence; but there is no question of that now."

"I beg your pardon. The question is for me to let the court see whether I am an honest man or a false witness. It would seem that this has something to do with the case; the prisoner's life depends on it; the court cannot consider that a matter of indifference."

"Proceed," said the King's advocate, "and try to remember the respect you owe to the court."

"I have no wish to offend the court," replied Patience. "I would merely observe that a man may refuse to submit to the orders of the court from conscientious motives which the court can legally condemn, but which each judge, personally, can understand and excuse. I say, then, that I could not persuade myself of Bernard de Mauprat's guilt; my ears alone knew of it; this was not enough for me. Pardon me, gentlemen, I, too, am a judge. Make inquiries about me; in my village they call me 'the great judge.' When my fellow-villagers ask me to decide some tavern dispute or the boundary of some field, I do not so much listen to their opinions as my own. In judging a man one must take account of more than a single little act. Many previous ones will help to show the truth or falsity of the last that is imputed to him. Thus, being unable to believe that Bernard was a murderer, and having heard more than a dozen people, whom I consider incapable of giving false evidence, testify to the fact that a monk 'bearing a resemblance to the Mauprats' had been prowling about the country, and having myself seen this monk's back and habit as he was passing through Pouligny on the morning of the event, I wished to discover if he was in Varenne; and I learnt that he was still there; that is to say, after leaving it, he had returned about the time of the trial last month. And, what is more, I learnt that he was acquainted with John Mauprat. Who can this monk be? I asked myself; why does the very sight of him frighten all the people in the country? What is he doing in Varenne? If he belongs to the Carmelite convent, why does he not wear their habit? If he is of the same order as John, why is he not staying with him at the Carmelites? If he is collecting money, why, after making a collection in one place, does he not move on to another, instead of returning and bothering people who have given him money only the day before? If he is a Trappist and does not want to stay with the Carmelites like the other, why does he not go back to his own convent? What is this wandering monk? And how does John Mauprat, who has told several people that he does not know him, know him so well that they lunch together from time to time in a tavern at Crevant? I made up my mind, then, to give evidence, though it might, in a measure, do harm to M. Bernard, so as to be able to say what I am now saying, even if it should be of no use. But as you never allow witnesses sufficient time to try to verify what they have reason to believe, I started off immediately for my woods, where I live like the foxes, with a determination not to quit them until I had discovered what this monk was doing in the country. So I put myself on his track and I have discovered who he is; he is the murderer of Edmee de Mauprat; his name is Antony Mauprat."

This revelation caused a great stir on the bench and among the public. Every one looked around for John Mauprat, whose face was nowhere to be seen.

"What proof have you of this?" said the president.

"I am about to tell you," replied Patience. "Having learnt from the landlady at Crevant, to whom I have occasionally been of some assistance, that the two Trappists used to lunch at her tavern from time to time, as I have said, I went and took up my abode about half a league from here, in a hermitage known as Le Trou aux Fades, situated in the middle of the woods and open to the first comer, furniture and all. It is a cave in the rock, containing a seat in the shape of a big stone and nothing else. I lived there for a couple of days on roots and bits of bread that they occasionally brought me from the tavern. It is against my principles to live in a tavern. On the third day the landlady's little boy came and informed me that the two monks were about to sit down to a meal. I hastened back, and hid myself in a cellar which opens into the garden. The door of this cellar is quite close to the apple-tree under which these gentlemen were taking luncheon in the open air. John was sober; the other was eating like a Carmelite and drinking like a Franciscan. I could hear and see everything at my ease.

"'There must be an end of this,' Antony was saying—I easily recognised the man when I saw him drink and heard him swear—'I am tired of playing this game for you. Hide me away with the Carmelites or I shall make a row.'

"'And what row can you make that will not bring you to the gallows, you clumsy fool!' answered John. 'It is very certain that you will not set foot inside the monastery. I don't want to find myself mixed up in a criminal trial; for they would discover what you are in an hour or two.'

"'And why, I should like to know? You make them all believe that you are a saint!'

"'Because I know how to behave like a saint; whereas you—you behave like a fool. Why, you can't stop swearing for an hour, and you would be breaking all the mugs after dinner!'

"'I say, Nepomucene,' rejoined the other, 'do you fancy that you would get off scot-free if I were caught and tried?'

"'Why not?' answered the Trappist. 'I had no hand in your folly, nor did I advise anything of this kind.'

"'Ha! ha! my fine apostle!' cried Antony, throwing himself back in his chair in a fit of laughter. 'You are glad enough about it, now that it is done. You were always a coward; and had it not been for me you would never have thought of anything better than getting yourself made a Trappist, to ape devotion and afterward get absolution for the past, so as to have a right to draw a little money from the "Headbreakers" of Sainte-Severe. By Jove! a mighty fine ambition, to give up the ghost under a monk's cowl after leading a pretty poor life and only tasting half its sweets, let alone hiding like a mole! Come, now; when they have hung my pretty Bernard, and the lovely Edmonde is dead, and when the old neck-breaker has given back his big bones to the earth; when we have inherited all that pretty fortune yonder; you will own that we have done a capital stroke of business—three at a blow! It would cost me rather too much to play the saint, seeing that convent ways are not quite my ways, and that I don't know how to wear the habit; so I shall throw the cowl to the winds, and content myself with building a chapel at Roche-Mauprat and taking the sacrament four times a year.'

"'Everything you have done in this matter is stupid and infamous.'

"'Bless my soul! Don't talk of infamy, my sweet brother, or I shall make you swallow this bottle whole.'

"'I say that it is a piece of folly, and if it succeeds you ought to burn a fine candle to the Virgin. If it does not succeed, I wash my hands of the whole business, do you hear? After I had been in hiding in the secret passage in the keep, and had heard Bernard telling his valet after supper that he was going out of his mind on account of the beautiful Edmee, I happened to throw out a suggestion that there might be a chance here of doing a good stroke of business; and like a fool you took the matter seriously, and, without consulting me or waiting for a favourable moment, you went and did a deed that should have been thought over and properly planned.'

"'A favourable moment, chicken-heart that you are! How the deuce was I to get one? "Opportunity makes the thief." I find myself surprised by the hunt in the middle of the forest; I go and hide in that cursed Gazeau Tower; I see my turtle-doves coming; I overhear a conversation that might make one die of laughing, and see Bernard blubbering and the girl playing the haughty beauty; Bernard goes off like an idiot without showing himself a man; I find on me—God knows how—a rascally pistol already loaded. Bang! . . .'

"'Hold your tongue, you wild brute!' said the other, quite frightened. 'Do you think a tavern is the proper place to talk of these things? Keep that tongue quiet, you wretched creature, or I will never see you again.'

"'And yet you will have to see me, sweet brother mine, when I go and ring the bell at the gate of the Carmelite monastery.'

"'If you come I will denounce you.'

"'You will not denounce me, for I know too much about you.'

"'I am not afraid. I have given proofs of my repentance; I have expiated my sins.'

"'Hypocrite!'

"'Come, now, hold your tongue, you madman!' said the other. 'I must leave you. There is some money.'

"'That all?'

"'What do you expect from a monk? Do you imagine that I am rich?'

"'Your Carmelites are; and you can do what you like with them.'

"'I might give you more, but I would rather not. As soon as you got a couple of louis you would be off for a debauch, and make enough row to betray yourself.'

"'And if you want me to quit this part of the country for some time, what do you suppose I am to travel with?'

"'Three times already I have given you enough to take you away, haven't I? And each time you have come back, after drinking it all in the first place of ill-fame on the frontier of the province! Your impudence sickens me, after the evidence given against you, when the police are on the watch, when Bernard is appealing for a fresh trial. You may be caught at any moment!'

"'That is for you to see to, brother. You can lead the Carmelites by the nose; and the Carmelites can lead the bishop, through some little peccadillo, I suppose, done together on the quiet in the convent after supper . . .'"

Here the president interrupted Patience.

"Witness," he said, "I call you to order. You are outraging a prelate's virtue by daring to retail such a conversation."

"By no means," replied Patience. "I am merely reporting a drunkard's and a murderer's invectives against the prelate. They do not concern me in the least; and every one here knows what value to put upon them; but, if you wish, I will say no more on this point. The discussion lasted for some time longer. The real Trappist wanted to make the sham Trappist leave the country, and the latter persisted in remaining, declaring that, if he were not on the spot, his brother would have him arrested immediately after Bernard's head had been cut off, so that he might have the whole inheritance to himself. John, driven to extremities, seriously threatened to denounce him and hand him over to justice.

"'Enough!' replied Antony. 'You will take good care not to do that, I know; for, if Bernard is acquitted, good-bye to the inheritance!'

"Then they separated. The real Trappist went away looking very anxious; the other fell asleep, with his elbows on the table. I left my hiding-place to take steps for his arrest. It was just then that the police, who had been on my track for some time to force me to come and give evidence, collared me. In vain did I point to the monk as Edmee's murderer; they would not believe me, and said they had no warrant against him. I wanted to arouse the village, but they prevented me from speaking. They brought me here, from station to station, as if I had been a deserter, and for the last week I have been in the cells and no one has deigned to heed my protests. They would not even let me see M. Bernard's lawyer, or inform him that I was in prison; it was only just now that the jailer came, and told me that I must put on my coat and appear in court. I do not know whether all this is according to the law; but one thing is certain, namely, that the murderer might have been arrested and has not been; nor will he be, unless you secure the person of John Mauprat to prevent him from warning, I do not say his accomplice, but his *protege*. I state on oath that, from all I have heard, John Mauprat is above any suspicion of complicity. As to the act of allowing an innocent man to be handed over to the rigour of the law, and of endeavouring to save a guilty man by going so far as to give false evidence, and produce false documents to prove his death . . ."

Patience, noticing that the president was again about to interrupt him, hastened to end his testimony by saying:

"As to that, gentlemen, it is for you, not for me, to judge him."

XXVIII

After this important evidence the trial was suspended for a few minutes. When the judges returned Edmee was brought back into the court. Pale and weak, scarcely able to drag herself to the arm-chair which was reserved for her, she nevertheless displayed considerable mental vigour and presence of mind.

"Do you think you can answer the questions which will be put to you without unduly exciting yourself?" asked the president.

"I hope so, sir," she replied. "It is true that I have recently been seriously ill, and that it is only within the last few days that I have recovered my memory; but I believe I have completely recovered it, and my mind feels quite clear."

"Your name?"

"Solange-Edmonde de Mauprat; *Edmea sylvestris*," she added in an undertone.

I shuddered. As she said these unseasonable words her eyes had assumed a strange expression. I feared that her mind was going to wander still further. My counsel was also alarmed and looked at me inquiringly. No one but myself had understood these two words which Edmee had been in the habit of frequently repeating during the first and last days of her illness. Happily this was the last sign of any disturbance in her faculties. She shook her beautiful head, as if to drive out any troublesome ideas; and, the president having asked her for an explanation of these unintelligible words, she replied with sweetness and dignity:

"It is nothing, sir. Please continue my examination."

"Your age, mademoiselle?"

"Twenty-four."

"Are you related to the prisoner?"

"He is my second cousin, and my father's grand-nephew."

"Do you swear to speak the truth, the whole truth?"

"Yes, sir."

"Raise your hand."

Edmee turned towards Arthur with a sad smile. He took off her glove, and helped to raise her arm, which hung nerveless and powerless by her side. I felt big tears rolling down my cheeks.

With delicacy and simplicity Edmee related how she and I had lost our way in the woods; how I, under the impression that her horse had bolted, had unseated her in my eager anxiety to stop the animal; how a slight altercation had ensued, after which, with a little feminine temper, foolish enough, she had wished to mount her mare again without help; how she had even spoken unkindly to me, not meaning a word of what she said, for she loved me like a brother; how, deeply hurt by her harshness, I had moved away a few yards to obey her; and how, just as she was about to follow me, grieved herself at our childish quarrel, she had felt a violent shock in her breast, and had fallen almost without hearing any report. It was impossible for her to say in which direction she was looking, or from which side the shot had come.

"That is all that happened," she added. "Of all people I am least able to explain this occurrence. In my soul and conscience I can only attribute it to the carelessness of one of the hunting party, who is afraid to confess. Laws are so severe. And it is so difficult to prove the truth."

"So, mademoiselle, you do not think that your cousin was the author of this attempt?"

"No, sir, certainly not! I am no longer delirious, and I should not have let myself be brought before you if I had felt that my mind was at all weak."

"Apparently, then, you consider that a state of mental aberration was responsible for the revelations you made to Patience, to Mademoiselle Leblanc, your companion, and also, perhaps, to Abbe Aubert."

"I made no revelations," she replied emphatically, "either to the worthy Patience, the venerable abbe, or my servant Leblanc. If the meaningless words we utter in a state of delirium are to be called 'revelations,' all the people who frighten us in our dreams would have to be condemned to death. How could I have revealed facts of which I never had any knowledge?"

"But at the time you received the wound, and fell from your horse, you said: 'Bernard, Bernard! I should never have thought that you would kill me!'"

"I do not remember having said so; and, even if I did, I cannot conceive that any one would attach much importance to the impressions of a person who had suddenly been struck to the ground, and whose mind was annihilated, as it were. All that I know is that Bernard de Mauprat would lay down his life for my father or myself; which does not make it very probable that he wanted to murder me. Great God! what would be his object?"

In order to embarrass Edmee, the president now utilized all the arguments which could be drawn from Mademoiselle Leblanc's evidence. As a fact, they were calculated to cause her not a little confusion. Edmee, who was at first somewhat astonished to find that the law was in possession of so many details which she believed were unknown to others, regained her courage and pride, however, when they suggested, in those brutally chaste terms which are used by the law in such a case, that she had been a victim of my violence at Roche-Mauprat. Her spirit thoroughly roused, she proceeded to defend my character and her own honour, and declared that, considering how I had been brought up, I had behaved much more honourably than might have been expected. But she still had to explain all her life from this point onward, the breaking off of her engagement with M. de la Marche, her frequent quarrels with myself, my sudden departure for America, her refusal of all offers of marriage.

"All these questions are abominable," she said, rising suddenly, her physical strength having returned with the exercise of her mental powers. "You ask me to give an account of my inmost feelings; you would sound the mysteries of my soul; you put my modesty on the rack; you would take to yourself rights that belong only to God. I declare to you that, if my own life were now at stake and not another's, you should not extract a word more from me. However, to save the life of the meanest of men I would overcome my repugnance; much more, therefore, will I do for him who is now at the bar. Know then—since you force me to a confession which is painful to the pride and reserve of my sex—that everything which to you seems inexplicable in my conduct, everything which you attribute to Bernard's persecutions and my own resentment, to his threats and my terror, finds its justification in one word: I love him!"

On uttering this word, the red blood in her cheeks, and in the ringing tone of the proudest and most passionate soul that ever existed, Edmee sat down again and buried her face in her hands. At this moment I was so transported that I could not help crying out:

"Let them take me to the scaffold now; I am king of all the earth!"

"To the scaffold! You!" said Edmee, rising again. "Let them rather take me. Is it your fault, poor boy, if for seven years I have hidden from you the secret of my affections; if I did not wish you to know it until you were the first of men in wisdom and intelligence as you are already the first in greatness of heart? You are paying dearly for my ambition, since it has been interpreted as scorn and hatred. You have good reason to hate me, since my pride has brought you to the felon's dock. But I will wash away your shame by a signal reparation; though they send you to the scaffold, you shall go there with the title of my husband."

"Your generosity is carrying you too far, Edmee de Mauprat," said the president. "It would seem that, in order to save your relative, you are accusing yourself of coquetry and unkindness; for, how otherwise do you explain the fact that you exasperated this young man's passion by refusing him for seven years?"

"Perhaps, sir," replied Edmee archly, "the court is not competent to judge this matter. Many women think it no great crime to show a little coquetry with the man they love. Perhaps we have a right to this when we have sacrificed all other men to him. After all, it is a very natural and very innocent ambition to make the man of one's choice feel that one is a soul of some price, that one is worth wooing, and worth a long effort. True, if this coquetry resulted in the condemnation of one's lover to death, one would speedily correct one's self of it. But, naturally, gentlemen, you would not think of atoning for my cruelty by offering the poor young man such a consolation as this."

After saying these words in an animated, ironical tone, Edmee burst into tears. This nervous sensibility which brought to the front all the qualities of her soul and mind, tenderness, courage, delicacy, pride, modesty, gave her face at the same time an expression so varied, so winning in all its moods, that the grave, sombre assembly of judges let fall the brazen cuirass of impassive integrity and the leaden cope of hypocritical virtue. If Edmee had not triumphantly defended me by her confession, she had at least roused the greatest interest in my favour. A man who is loved by a beautiful woman carries with him a talisman that makes him invulnerable; all feel that his life is of greater value than other lives.

Edmee still had to submit to many questions; she set in their proper light the facts which had been misrepresented by Mademoiselle Leblanc. True, she spared me considerably; but with admirable skill she managed to elude certain questions, and so escaped the necessity of either lying or condemning me. She generously took upon herself the blame for all my offences, and pretended that, if we had had various quarrels, it was because she herself took a secret pleasure in them; because they revealed the depth of my love; that she had let me go to America to put my virtue to the proof, thinking that the campaign would not last more than a year, as was then supposed; that afterwards she had considered me in honour bound to submit to the indefinite prolongation, but that she had suffered more than myself from my absence; finally, she quite remembered the letter which had been found upon her, and, taking it up, she gave the mutilated passages with astonishing accuracy, and at the same time called the clerk to follow as she deciphered the words which were half obliterated.

"This letter was so far from being a threatening letter," she said, "and the impression it left on me was so far from filling me with fear or aversion, that it was found on my heart, where I had been carrying it for a week, though I had not even let Bernard know that I had received it."

"But you have not yet explained," said the president, "how it was that seven years ago, when your cousin first came to live in your house, you armed yourself with a knife which you used to put under your pillow every night, after having it sharpened as if to defend yourself in case of need."

"In my family," she answered with a blush, "we have a somewhat romantic temperament and a very proud spirit. It is true that I frequently thought of killing myself, because I felt an unconquerable affection for my cousin springing up in me. Believing myself bound by indissoluble ties to M. de la Marche. I would have died rather than break my word, or marry any other than Bernard. Subsequently M. de la Marche freed me from my promise with much delicacy and loyalty, and I no longer thought of dying."

Edmee now withdrew, followed by all eyes and by a murmur of approbation. No sooner had she passed out of the hall than she fainted again; but this attack was without any grave consequences, and left no traces after a few days.

I was so bewildered, so intoxicated by what she had just said, that henceforth I could scarcely see what was taking place around me. Wholly wrapped up in thoughts of my love, I nevertheless could not cast aside all doubts; for, if Edmee had been silent about some of my actions, it was also possible that she had exaggerated her affection for me in the hope of extenuating my faults. I could not bring myself to think that she had loved me before my departure for America, and, above all, from the very beginning of my stay at Sainte-Severe. This was the one thought that filled my mind; I did not even remember anything further about the case or the object of my trial. It seemed to me that the sole question at issue in this chill Areopagus was this: Is he loved, or is he not? For me, victory or defeat, life or death, hung on that, and that alone.

I was roused from these reveries by the voice of Abbe Aubert. He was thin and wasted, but seemed perfectly calm; he had been kept in solitary confinement and had suffered all the hardships of prison life with the resignation of a martyr. In spite, however, of all precautions, the clever Marcasse, who could work his way anywhere like a ferret, had managed to convey to him a letter from Arthur, to which Edmee had added a few words. Authorized by this letter to say everything, he made a statement similar to that made by Patience, and owned that Edmee's first words after the occurrence had made him believe me guilty; but that subsequently, seeing the patient's mental condition, and remembering my irreproachable behaviour for more than six years, and obtaining a little new light from the preceding trial and the public rumours about the possible existence of Antony Mauprat, he had felt too convinced of my innocence to be willing to give evidence which might injure me. If he gave his evidence now, it was because he thought that further investigations might have enlightened the court, and that his words would not have the serious consequences they might have had a month before.

Questioned as to Edmee's feelings for me, he completely destroyed all Mademoiselle Leblanc's inventions, and declared that not only did Edmee love me ardently, but that she had felt an affection for me from the very first day we met. This he affirmed on oath, though emphasizing my past misdeeds somewhat more than Edmee had done. He owned that at first he had frequently feared that my cousin would be foolish enough to marry me, but that he had never had any fear for her life, since he had always seen her reduce me to submission by a single word or a mere look, even in my most boorish days.

The continuation of the trial was postponed to await the results of the warrants issued for the arrest of the assassin. People compared my trial to that of Calas, and the comparison had no sooner become a general topic of conversation than my judges, finding themselves exposed to a thousand shafts, realized very vividly that hatred and prejudice are bad counsellors and dangerous guides. The sheriff of the province declared himself the champion of my cause and Edmee's knight, and he himself escorted her back to her father. He set all the police agog. They acted with vigour and arrested John Mauprat. When he found himself a prisoner and threatened, he betrayed his brother, and declared that they might find him any night at Roche-Mauprat, hiding in a secret chamber which the tenant's wife helped him to reach, without her husband's knowledge.

They took the Trappist to Roche-Mauprat under a good escort, so that he might show them this secret chamber, which, in spite of his genius for exploring walls and timber-work, the old pole-cat hunter and mole-catcher Marcasse had never managed to reach. They took me there, likewise, so that I might help to find this room or passage leading to it, in case the Trappist should repent of his present sincere intentions. Once again, then, I revisited this abhorred manor with the ancient chief of the brigands transformed into a Trappist. He showed himself so humble and cringing in my presence, he made so light of his brother's life, and expressed such abject submission that I was filled with disgust, and after a few moments begged him not to speak to me any more. Keeping in touch with the mounted police outside, we began our search for the secret chamber. At first John had pretended that he knew of its existence, without knowing its exact location now that three-quarters of the keep had been destroyed. When he saw me, however, he remembered that I had surprised him in my room, and that he had disappeared through the wall. He resigned himself, therefore, to taking us to it, and showing us the secret; this was very curious; but I will not amuse myself by giving you an account of it. The secret chamber was opened; no one was there. Yet the expedition had been made with despatch and secrecy. It did not appear probable that John had had time to warn his brother. The keep was surrounded by the police and all the doors were well guarded. The night was dark, and our invasion had filled all the inmates of the farm with terror. The tenant had no idea what we were looking for, but his wife's agitation and anxiety seemed a sure sign that Antony was still in the keep. She had not sufficient presence of mind to assume a reassured air after we had explored the first room, and that made Marcasse think that there must be a second. Did the Trappist know of this, and was he pretending ignorance? He played his part so well that we were all deceived. We set to work to explore all the nooks and corners of the ruins again. There was one large tower standing apart from the other buildings; it did not seem as if this could offer any one a refuge. The staircase had completely fallen in at the time of the fire, and there could not be found a ladder long enough to reach the top story; even the farmer's ladders tied together with ropes were too short. This top story seemed to be in a state of good preservation and to contain a room lighted by two loopholes. Marcasse, after examining the thickness of the wall, affirmed that there might be a staircase inside, such as might be found in many an old tower. But where was the exit? Perhaps it was connected with some subterranean passage. Would the assassin dare to issue from his retreat as long as we were there? If, in spite of the darkness of the night and the silence of our proceedings, he had got wind of our presence, would he venture into the open as long as we continued on the watch at all points?

"That is not probable," said Marcasse. "We must devise some speedy means of getting up there; and I see one."

He pointed to a beam at a frightful height, all blackened by the fire, and running from the tower over a space of some twenty feet to the garrets of the nearest building. At the end of this beam there was a large gap in the wall of the tower caused by the falling-in of the adjoining parts. In his explorations, indeed, Marcasse had fancied that he could see the steps of a narrow staircase through this gap. The wall, moreover, was quite thick enough to contain one. The mole-catcher had never cared to risk his life on this beam; not that he was afraid of its narrowness or its height; he was accustomed to these perilous "crossings," as he called them; but the beam had been partly consumed by the fire and was so thin in the middle that it was impossible to say whether it would bear the weight of a man, even were he as slender and diaphanous as the worthy sergeant. Up to the present nothing had happened here of sufficient importance for him to risk his life in the experiment. Now, however, the case was different. Marcasse did not hesitate. I was not near him when he formed his plan; I should have dissuaded him from it at all costs. I was not aware of it until he had already reached the middle of the beam, the spot where the burnt wood was perhaps nothing more than charcoal. How shall I describe to you what I felt when I beheld my faithful friend in mid-air, gravely walking toward his goal? Blaireau was trotting in front of him as calmly as in the old days when it was a question of hunting through bundles of hay in search of stoats and dormice. Day was breaking, and the hildalgo's slim outline and his modest yet stately bearing could be clearly seen against the gray sky. I put my hands to my face; I seemed to hear the fatal beam cracking; I stifled a cry of terror lest I should unnerve him at this solemn and critical moment. But I could not suppress this cry, or help raising my head when I heard two shots fired from the tower. Marcasse's hat fell at the first shot; the second grazed his shoulder. He stopped a moment.

"Not touched!" he shouted at us.

And making a rush he was quickly across the aerial bridge. He got into the tower through the gap and darted up the stairs, crying:

"Follow me, my lads! The beam will bear."

Immediately five other bold and active men who had accompanied him got astride upon the beam, and with the help of their hands reached the other end one by one. When the first of them arrived in the garret whither Antony Mauprat had fled, he found him grappling with Marcasse, who, quite carried away by his triumph and forgetting that it was not a question of killing an enemy but of capturing him, set about lunging at him with his long rapier as if he had been a weasel. But the sham Trappist was a formidable enemy. He had snatched the sword from the sergeant's hands, hurled him to the ground, and would have strangled him had not a gendarme thrown himself on him from behind. With his prodigious strength he held his own against the first three assailants; but, with the help of the other two, they succeeded in overcoming him. When he saw that he was caught he made no further resistance and let his hands be bound together. They brought him down the stairs, which were found to lead to the bottom of a dry well in the middle of the tower. Antony was in the habit of leaving and entering by means of a ladder which the farmer's wife held for him and immediately afterwards withdrew. In a transport of delight I threw myself into my sergeant's arms.

"A mere trifle," he said; "enjoyed it. I found that my foot was still sure and my head cool. Ha! ha! old sergeant," he added, looking at his leg, "old hidalgo, old mole-catcher, after this they won't make so many jokes about your calves!"

XXIX

If Anthony Mauprat had been a man of mettle he might have done me a bad turn by declaring that he had been a witness of my attempt to assassinate Edmee. As he had reasons for hiding himself before this last crime, he could have explained why he had kept out of sight, and why he had been silent about the occurrences at Gazeau Tower. I had nothing in my favour except Patience's evidence. Would this have been sufficient to procure my acquittal? The evidence of so many others was against me, even that given by my friends, and by Edmee, who could not deny my violent temper and the possibility of such a crime.

But Antony, in words the most insolent of all the "Hamstringers," was the most cowardly in deeds. He no sooner found himself in the hands of justice than he confessed everything, even before knowing that his brother had thrown him over.

At his trial there were some scandalous scenes, in which the two brothers accused each other in a loathsome way. The Trappist, whose rage was kept in check by his hypocrisy, coldly abandoned the ruffian to his fate, and denied that he had ever advised him to commit the crime. The other, driven to desperation, accused him of the most horrible deeds, including the poisoning of my mother, and Edmee's mother, who had both died of violent inflammation of the intestines within a short time of each other. John Mauprat, he declared, used to be very skilful in the art of preparing poisons and would introduce himself into houses under various disguises to mix them with the food. He affirmed that, on the day that Edmee had been brought to Roche-Mauprat, John had called together all his brothers to discuss plans for making away with this heiress to a considerable fortune, a fortune which he had striven to obtain by crime, since he had tried to destroy the effects of the Chevalier Hubert's marriage. My mother's life, too, had been the price paid for the latter's wish to adopt his brother's child. All the Mauprats had been in favour of making away with Edmee and myself simultaneously, and John was actually preparing the poison when the police happened to turn aside their hideous designs by attacking the castle. John denied the charges with pretended horror, saying humbly that he had committed quite enough mortal sins of debauchery and irreligion without having these added to his list. As it was difficult to take Antony's word for them without further investigation; as this investigation was almost impossible, and as the clergy were too powerful and too much interested in preventing a scandal to allow it, John Mauprat was acquitted on the charge of complicity and merely sent back to the Trappist monastery; the archbishop forbade him ever to set foot in the diocese again, and, moreover, sent a request to his superiors that they would never allow him to leave the convent. He died there a few years later in all the terrors of a fanatic penitence very much akin to insanity.

It is probable that, as a result of feigning remorse in order to find favour among his fellows, he had at last, after the failure of his plans, and under the terrible asceticism of his order, actually experienced the horrors and agonies of a bad conscience and tardy repentance. The fear of hell is the only creed of vile souls.

No sooner was I acquitted and set at liberty, with my character completely cleared, than I hastened to Edmee. I arrived in time to witness my great-uncle's last moments. Towards the end, though his mind remained a blank as to past events, the memory of his heart returned. He recognised me, clasped me to his breast, blessed me at the same time as Edmee, and put my hand into his daughter's. After we had paid the last tribute of affection to our excellent and noble kinsman, whom we were as grieved to lose as if we had not long foreseen and expected his death, we left the province for some time, so as not to witness the execution of Antony, who was condemned to be broken on the wheel. The two false witnesses who had accused me were flogged, branded, and expelled from the jurisdiction of the court. Mademoiselle Leblanc, who could not exactly be accused of giving false evidence, since hers had consisted of mere inferences from facts, avoided the public displeasure by going to another province. Here she lived in sufficient luxury to make us suspect that she had been paid considerable sums to bring about my ruin.

Edmee and I would not consent to be separated, even temporarily, from our good friends, my sole defenders, Marcasse, Patience, Arthur, and the Abbe Aubert. We all travelled in the same carriage; the first two, being accustomed to the open air, were only too glad to sit outside; but we treated them on a footing of perfect equality. From that day forth they never sat at any table but our own. Some persons had the bad taste to express astonishment at this; we let them talk. There are circumstances that obliterate all distinctions, real or imaginary, of rank and education.

We paid a visit to Switzerland. Arthur considered this was essential to the complete restoration of Edmee's health. The delicate, thoughtful attentions of this devoted friend, and the loving efforts we made to minister to her happiness, combined into the beautiful spectacle of the mountains to drive away her melancholy and efface the recollection of the troublous times through which we had just passed. On Patience's poetic nature Switzerland had quite a magic effect. He would frequently fall into such a state of ecstasy that we were entranced and terrified at the same time. He felt strongly tempted to build himself a chalet in the heart of some valley and spend the rest of his life there in contemplation of Nature; but his affection for us made him abandon this project. As for Marcasse, he declared subsequently that, despite all the pleasure he had derived from our society, he looked upon this visit as the most unlucky event of his life. At the inn at Martigny, on our return journey, Blaireau, whose digestion had been impaired by age, fell a victim to the excess of hospitality shown him in the kitchen. The sergeant said not a word, but gazed on him awhile with heavy eye, and then went and buried him under the most beautiful rosetree in the garden; nor did he speak of his loss until more than a year later.

During our journey Edmee was for me a veritable angel of kindness and tender thought; abandoning herself henceforth to all the inspirations of her heart, and no longer feeling any distrust of me, or perhaps thinking that I deserved some compensation for all my sufferings, she repeatedly confirmed the celestial assurances of love which she had given in public, when she lifted up her voice to proclaim my innocence. A few reservations that had struck me in her evidence, and a recollection of the damning words that had fallen from her lips when Patience found her shot, continued, I must confess, to cause me pain for some time longer. I thought, rightly perhaps, that Edmee had made a great effort to believe in my innocence before Patience had given his evidence. But on this point she always spoke most unwillingly and with a certain amount of reserve. However, one day she quite healed my wound by saying with her charming abruptness:

"And if I loved you enough to absolve you in my own heart, and defend you in public at the cost of a lie, what would you say to that?"

A point on which I felt no less concern was to know how far I might believe in the love which she declared she had had for me from the very beginning of our acquaintance. Here she betrayed a little confusion, as if, in her invincible pride, she regretted having revealed a secret she had so jealously guarded. It was the abbe who undertook to confess for her. He assured me that at that time he had frequently scolded Edmee for her affection for "the young savage." As an objection to this, I told him of the conversation between Edmee and himself which I had overheard one evening in the park. This I repeated with that great accuracy of memory I possess. However, he replied:

"That very evening, if you had followed us a little further under the trees, you might have overheard a dispute that would have completely re-assured you, and have explained how, from being repugnant (I may almost say odious) to me, as you then were, you became at first endurable, and gradually very dear."

"You must tell me," I exclaimed, "who worked the miracle."

"One word will explain it," he answered; "Edmee loved you. When she had confessed this to me, she covered her face with her hands and remained for a moment as if overwhelmed with shame and vexation; then suddenly she raised her head and exclaimed:

"'Well, since you wish to know the absolute truth, I love him! Yes, I love him! I am smitten with him, as you say. It is not my fault; why should I blush at it? I cannot help it; it is the work of fate. I have never loved M. de la Marche; I merely feel a friendship for him. For Bernard I have a very different feeling—a feeling so strong, so varied, so full of unrest, of hatred, of fear, of pity, of anger, of tenderness, that I understand nothing about it, and no longer try to understand anything.'"

"'Oh, woman, woman!' I exclaimed, clasping my hands in bewilderment, 'thou art a mystery, an abyss, and he who thinks to know thee is totally mad!'

"'As many times as you like, abbe,' she answered, with a firmness in which there were signs of annoyance and confusion, 'it is all the same to me. On this point I have lectured myself more than you have lectured all your flocks in your whole life. I know that Bernard is a bear, a badger, as Mademoiselle Leblanc calls him, a savage, a boor, and anything else you like. There is nothing more shaggy, more prickly, more cunning, more malicious than Bernard. He is an animal who scarcely knows how to sign his name; he is a coarse brute who thinks he can break me in like one of the jades of Varenne. But he makes a great mistake; I will die rather than ever be his, unless he becomes civilized enough to marry me. But one might as well expect a miracle. I try to improve him, without daring to hope. However, whether he forces me to kill myself or to turn nun, whether he remains as he is or becomes worse, it will be none the less true that I love him. My dear abbe, you know that it must be costing me something to make this confession; and, when my affection for you brings me as a penitent to your feet and to your bosom, you should not humiliate me by your expressions of surprise and your exorcisms! Consider the matter now; examine, discuss, decide! Consider the matter now; examine, discuss, decide! The evil is—I love him. The symptoms are—I think of none but him, I see none but him; and I could eat no dinner this evening because he had not come back. I find him handsomer than any man in the world. When he says that he loves me, I can see, I can feel that it is true; I feel displeased, and at the same time delighted. M. de la Marche seems insipid and prim since I have known Bernard. Bernard alone seems as proud, as passionate, as bold as myself—and as weak as myself; for he cries like a child when I vex him, and here I am crying, too, as I think of him.'"

"Dear abbe," I said, throwing myself on his neck, "let me embrace you till I have crushed your life out for remembering all this."

"The abbe is drawing the long bow," said Edmee archly.

"What!" I exclaimed, pressing her hands as if I would break them. "You have made me suffer for seven years, and now you repent a few words that console me . . ."

"In any case do not regret the past," she said. "Ah, with you such as you were in those days, we should have been ruined if I had not been able to think and decide for both of us. Good God! what would have become of us by now? You would have had far more to suffer from my sternness and pride; for you would have offended me from the very first day of our union, and I should have had to punish you by running away or killing myself, or killing you—for we are given to killing in our family; it is a natural habit. One thing is certain, and that is that you would have been a detestable husband; you would have made me blush for your ignorance; you would have wanted to rule me, and we should have fallen foul of each other; that would have driven my father to despair, and, as you know, my father had to be considered before everything. I might, perhaps, have risked my own fate lightly enough, if I had been alone in the world, for I have a strain of rashness in my nature; but it was essential that my father should remain happy, and tranquil, and respected. He had brought me up in happiness and independence, and I should never have forgiven myself if I had deprived his old age of the blessings he had lavished on my whole life. Do not think that I am full of virtues and noble qualities, as the abbe pretends; I love, that is all; but I love strongly, exclusively, steadfastly. I sacrificed you to my father, my poor Bernard; and Heaven, who would have cursed us if I had sacrificed my father, rewards us to-day by giving us to each other, tried and not found wanting. As you grew greater in my eyes I felt that I could wait, because I knew I had to love you long, and I was not afraid of seeing my passion vanish before it was satisfied, as do the passions of feeble souls. We were two exceptional characters; our loves had to be heroic; the beaten track would have led both of us to ruin."

XXX

We returned to Sainte-Severe at the expiration of Edmee's period of mourning. This was the time that had been fixed for our marriage. When we had quitted the province where we had both experienced so many bitter mortifications and such grievous trials, we had imagined that we should never feel any inclination to return. Yet, so powerful are the recollections of childhood and the ties of family life that, even in the heart of an enchanted land which could not arouse painful memories, we had quickly begun to regret our gloomy, wild Varenne, and sighed for the old oaks in the park. We returned, then, with a sense of profound yet solemn joy. Edmee's first care was to gather the beautiful flowers in the garden and to kneel by her father's grave and arrange them on it. We kissed the hallowed ground, and there made a vow to strive unceasingly to leave a name as worthy of respect and veneration as his. He had frequently carried this ambition to the verge of weakness, but it was a noble weakness, a sacred vanity.

Our marriage was celebrated in the village chapel, and the festivities were confined to the family; none but Arthur, the abbe, Marcasse, and Patience sat down to our modest banquet. What need had we of the outside world to behold our happiness? They might have believed, perhaps, that they were doing us an honour by covering the blots on our escutcheon with their august presence. We were enough to be happy and merry among ourselves. Our hearts were filled with as much affection as they could hold. We were too proud to ask more from any one, too pleased with one another to yearn for greater pleasure. Patience returned to his sober, retired life, resumed the duties of "great judge" and "treasurer" on certain days of the week. Marcasse remained with me until his death, which happened towards the end of the French Revolution. I trust I did my best to repay his fidelity by an unreserved friendship and an intimacy that nothing could disturb.

Arthur, who had sacrificed a year of his life to us, could not bring himself to abjure the love of his country, and his desire to contribute to its progress by offering it the fruits of his learning and the results of his investigations; he returned to Philadelphia, where I paid him a visit after I was left a widower.

I will not describe my years of happiness with my noble wife; such years beggar description. One could not resign one's self to living after losing them, if one did not make strenuous efforts to avoid recalling them too often. She gave me six children; four of these are still alive, and all honourably settled in life. I have lived for them, in obedience to Edmee's dying command. You must forgive me for not speaking further of this loss, which I suffered only ten years ago. I feel it now as keenly as on the first day, and I do not seek to find consolation for it, but to make myself worthy of rejoining the holy comrade of my life in a better world after I have completed my period of probation in this. She was the only woman I ever loved; never did any other win a glance from me or know the pressure of my hand. Such is my nature; what I love I love eternally, in the past, in the present, in the future.

The storms of the Revolution did not destroy our existence, nor did the passions it aroused disturb the harmony of our private life. We gladly gave up a large part of our property to the Republic, looking upon it, indeed, as a just sacrifice. The abbe, terrified by the bloodshed, occasionally abjured this political faith, when the necessities of the hour were too much for the strength of his soul. He was the Girondin of the family.

With no less sensibility, Edmee had greater courage; a woman and compassionate, she sympathized profoundly with the sufferings of all classes. She bewailed the misfortune of her age; but she never failed to appreciate the greatness of its holy fanaticism. She remained faithful to her ideas of absolute equality. At a time when the acts of the Mountain were irritating the abbe, and driving him to despair, she generously sacrificed her own patriotic enthusiasm; and her delicacy would never let her mention in his presence certain names that made him shudder, names for which she herself had a sort of passionate veneration, the like of which I have never seen in any woman.

As for myself, I can truthfully say that it was she who educated me; during the whole course of my life I had the profoundest respect for her judgment and rectitude. When, in my enthusiasm, I was filled with a longing to play a part as a leader of the people, she held me back by showing how my name would destroy any influence I might have; since they would distrust me, and imagine my aim was to use them as an instrument for recovering my rank. When the enemy was at the gates of France, she sent me to serve as a volunteer; when the Republic was overthrown, and a military career came to be merely a means of gratifying ambition, she recalled me, and said:

"You must never leave me again."

Patience played a great part in the Revolution. He was unanimously chosen as judge of his district. His integrity, his impartiality between castle and cottage, his firmness and wisdom will never be forgotten in Varenne.

During the war I was instrumental in saving M. de la Marche's life, and helping him to escape to a foreign country.

Such, I believe, said old Mauprat, are all the events of my life in which Edmee played a part. The rest of it is not worth the telling. If there is anything helpful in my story, try to profit by it, young fellows. Hope to be blessed with a frank counsellor, a severe friend; and love not the man who flatters, but the man who reproves. Do not believe too much in phrenology; for I have the murderer's bump largely developed, and, as Edmee used to say with grim humour, "killing comes natural" to our family. Do not believe in fate, or, at least, never advise any one to tamely submit to it. Such is the moral of my story.

After this old Bernard gave us a good supper, and continued conversing with us for the rest of the evening without showing any signs of discomposure or fatigue. As we begged him to develop what he called the moral of his story a little further, he proceeded to a few general considerations which impressed me with their soundness and good sense.

I spoke of phrenology, he said, not with the object of criticising a system which has its good side, in so far as it tends to complete the series of physiological observations that aim at increasing our knowledge of man; I used the word phrenology because the only fatality that we believe in nowadays is that created by our own instincts. I do not believe that phrenology is more fatalistic than any other system of this kind; and Lavater, who was also accused of fatalism in his time, was the most Christian man the Gospel has ever formed.

Do not believe in any absolute and inevitable fate; and yet acknowledge, in a measure, that we are moulded by instincts, our faculties, the impressions of our infancy, the surroundings of our earliest childhood—in short, by all that outside world which has presided over the development of our soul. Admit that we are not always absolutely free to choose between good and evil, if you would be indulgent towards the guilty—that is to say, just even as Heaven is just; for there is infinite mercy in God's judgments; otherwise His justice would be imperfect.

What I am saying now is not very orthodox, but, take my word for it, it is Christian, because it is true. Man is not born wicked; neither is he born good, as is maintained by Jean Jacques Rousseau, my beloved Edmee's old master. Man is born with more or less of passions, with more or less power to satisfy them, with more or less capacity for turning them to a good or bad account in society. But education can and must find a remedy for everything; that is the great problem to be solved, to discover the education best suited to each individual. If it seems necessary that education should be general and in common, does it follow that it ought to be the same for all? I quite believe that if I had been sent to school when I was ten, I should have become a civilized being earlier; but would any one have thought of correcting my violent passions, and of teaching me how to conquer them as Edmee did? I doubt it. Every man needs to be loved before he can be worth anything; but each in a different way; one with never-failing indulgence, another with unflinching severity. Meanwhile, until some one solves the problem of making education common to all, and yet appropriate to each, try to improve one another.

Do you ask me how? My answer will be brief: by loving one another truly. It is in this way—for the manners of a people mould their laws—that you will succeed in suppressing the most odious and impious of all laws, the *lex talionis,* capital punishment, which is nothing else than the consecration of the principle of fatality, seeing that it supposes the culprit incorrigible and Heaven implacable.

CPSIA information can be obtained at www.ICGtesting.com
Printed in the USA
LVOW08s2040180713

343490LV00001B/35/P